FULL-BODIED
RED.

FULL-BODIED
RED

=BRUCE=
ZIMMERMAN

HarperCollins books may be purchased for educational, business, or sales promotional use. For information please write Special Markets Department, HarperCollins Publishers, Inc., 10 East 53rd Street, New York, NY 10022.

FIRST EDITION

Designed by Claudyne Bianco

Zimmerman, Bruce.
    Full-bodied red: a novel/by Bruce Zimmerman.—1st ed.
        p.   cm.
    ISBN 0-06-017931-7
    I. Title.
    PS3576.I48F85 1993
    813' .54—dc20   92-54758

93 94 95 96 97 ❖/HC 10 9 8 7 6 5 4 3 2 1

THIS BOOK IS FOR THE REAL QUINN,
AND THE REAL CORT.

Once you hear the details of victory, it is hard to distinguish it from a defeat.

—JEAN-PAUL SARTRE

= 1 =

Of all the imposing security gates up and down Glenville Road, the one leading to the R. K. Chesterton estate was easily the most impressive. It was hewn out of huge slabs of granite, with one lane leading in and another lane leading out and a small wooden guard station in between, like something you'd have to go through to enter Yellowstone National Park.

A full moon was shining over the Napa Valley. I pulled my well-worn, twenty-year-old Volkswagen van up to the brightly lit gate and rolled down the window.

"I'm Quinn Parker," I told the uniformed guard working the check station. "I have a ten o'clock appointment with Mr. Matson."

The guard nodded, sort of. He was young enough to have been on temporary loan from the local high school. Pudgy, pimply, with wispy brown hair combed straight back on his head and matted down with a half-tube of Brylcreem. He was completely absorbed in the delicate process of refilling his stapler and only gave me the slightest of side glances. "Hold on a minute," he said.

"Sure thing."

I sat there while he painstakingly bent to the task. His fingers were thick and stumpy, not stapler-loading fingers, and when the kid said a minute he meant a full minute. Five dozen seconds. One-sixtieth of an hour. He picked at the staples and whisked the strays out of the way. Then, satisfied with his work, he turned in my direction. "What was the name again?"

"Quinn Parker."

The kid took a clipboard off a nail on the wall and looked it over. He shook his head. "Nothing here."

"Mr. Matson just called me in San Francisco a couple hours ago," I explained. "It probably hasn't had time to filter down to your clipboard."

I said it with the lighthearted smile I use when an impasse needs clearing, but it didn't work on this kid. He just kept slowly shaking his head and scanned the clipboard. "Nobody told me nothing."

"Trust me."

I sat and waited. Capacity to trust without necessary documentation was not part of his job description. The kid shifted the brunt of his weight from the right butt cheek to the left butt cheek and grimly stared at the clipboard. A doctor examining an X-ray filled with nothing but bad news. My engine idled in the lonely night.

"So what does this mean?" I said at last. "You're not going to let me through?"

"All visitors' names are supposed to be on the list," he said. "That's the rule."

"Then I think you better call the house."

The kid fidgeted. "I don't like to call up there this late unless I have to. Wakes people up."

"This is a case where you have to."

"I don't know ..."

"Look," I said. "When Mr. Matson called me this evening he said our meeting was to take place at ten o'clock sharp. He put particular emphasis on the word 'sharp.' That's about five minutes from now. If I'm late he's going to be very unhappy and I'll be forced to give him reasons, and you'll be at the head of the list ..." I leaned closer and read the kid's nametag. His hand went up instinctively to cover it, like a woman guarding her cleavage. "... Ted Wonciar."

When lighthearted smiles fail, threats usually do the trick. Ted Wonciar put the clipboard back up on its nail, swiveled around in his chair, and punched in a set of numbers on a wall phone directly behind him. He glared at me the entire time, as if committing to memory features and details that might be critically important later when he huddled with a group of FBI men. Someone at the other end answered and Ted turned his back to me and spoke in a hushed tone. I sighed and shook my head. Beware the minimum-wage earner who is authorized to wear gun and holster.

It was a short conversation, then Ted turned around and unsmilingly waved me through. I put the van in gear and started up the long, narrow, gradually ascending mile-long cobblestone road leading to the main house. Rich and powerful people passed through these gates on a regular basis, but Ted had surmised that I was neither. Maybe it was the van. Or the five o'clock shadow. Or perhaps whoever answered on the other end of the phone had clued him in that I'd been summoned to the Chesterton mansion for the sole purpose of having my ass hauled out on the carpet and ground down to a palsied, quivering nub.

The cobblestones were hard on my van's creaky shocks, so I took it slow. To the right and left were rolling vineyards, as far as the eye could see, pale in the moonlight. It was in-between time in the wine country. After the harvest, before the planting. The vines were gnarled and skeletal and ready for the winter's pruning. The road itself was as straight as the barrel of a rifle, with the main estate looming directly ahead, slowly filling the windshield of the approaching visitor. The better to remind you of who's boss, my dear. I took a deep breath to buck up my spirits and kept on driving.

The road widened into a parking apron at the front of the

mansion, and Rogelio the butler was waiting for me at the entrance steps, looking snappy in his starched white uniform. He was somewhere between seventy and eighty, plump, pleasant, with a full head of wavy silver hair and a big reddish nose. He remembered me from my two previous visits, and we shook hands and tried to pretend that it wasn't the least bit unusual that I'd come tooling up to the mansion in the dead of night.

Inside, the house was very silent and very warm. Over the years I'd spent a decent amount of time in the wine country. Had come to know some of the people in the industry, and had, upon occasion, been invited to their homes. Most seemed to want to convey a European sense of style and elegance and Old World charm. Chamber music. Antique automobiles. Pipes and tweeds and fond, fond memories of dear Firenze. But Chesterton Vineyards was different. It was rooted squarely in the Rough Riding mold of Teddy Roosevelt. Immense, solid, sweeping. Opulent beyond vulgarity, bellowing the crude triumph of the pioneer spirit, and not the least damn bit apologetic about it, either.

Rogelio escorted me through the spacious entrance area and down a long wood-paneled hallway that led off to the left. We chatted softly in Spanish while we walked. Paintings hung on both sides of the hallway walls. Vast landscapes of the craggy West. Portraits of no-nonsense forefathers. I glanced at my watch. Three minutes to ten. No matter what else might transpire, Frank Matson could not hold tardiness against me in the chew-out session to come.

Rogelio led me into the last room on the right, announced it as the North Parlor, and said that Mr. Matson would be with me soon. *Ahorita mismo,* to be exact, which is the Spanish way of saying so soon it could practically be this exact, selfsame, precise moment. I didn't know about the Napa Valley, but in Mexico *ahorita mismo* usually involved a wait of anywhere from an hour to a couple of days. Then Rogelio left me there alone, closing the door behind him while backing out, just like in the movies.

I took a look around. It wasn't exactly a kick-off-your-shoes, toss-me-your-underwear type of room, the North Parlor. Solemn.

Formal. Filled with antique doodads and Oriental vases and tiny, brittle chairs with spindly legs that begged not to be sat in. The heat was turned up too high, and a cloying smell hung in the humid air, saggingly sweet, as though a dozen ripe gardenias had recently been ground into the blue-gray upholstery. It wasn't the kind of room where you'd expect to find a lion's head mounted over the fireplace, but there he was. The King of Beasts—stuffed, stitched, contoured into artificial ferocity, roaring his one silent extended roar down onto the North Parlor's matching china and fussy trinkets.

I was braced for ten o'clock. It came and went. So did ten-fifteen. And so did ten-twenty and ten twenty-five and ten twenty-eight and ten-thirty. *Ahorita mismo,* like Rogelio said. I twiddled my thumbs. Paced the North Parlor. Watched my much-heralded long fuse burn steadily shorter.

Fortunately I'm good at constructively killing time. I used the half-hour to reassemble the starting lineup of the 1963 San Francisco Giants, jingle all the loose change in both my front pockets, figure out which actors in *The Great Escape* actually escaped at the film's end, and, as the clock struck ten-thirty, nail down Bashful as the last of the Seven Dwarfs. Exhilarating stuff, yes, but the thrill of victory has limited staying power. Fifteen more minutes, I told myself, and after that I didn't give a damn what the crisis was. I was gone.

I yawned, blinked away the tears. An expensive, handmade photo album was prominently displayed on the coffee table. It had "Safari—Kenya" embossed on the front in gold. The cover was as coarse as tree bark, the spine a smooth piece of driftwood, the pages held together by thin leather straps in a manner meant, I suppose, to convey the rustic nature of Africa. If Kalahari tribesmen kept photo albums, they'd look like this.

I'd been carefully avoiding the thing for each conscious minute of the half-hour wait, knowing that the bloody demise of my friend above the fireplace was no doubt chronicled within. Despite being as tough as rusted nails, I'm still one of those people who never wholly recovered from the death of Bambi's mother, and I contend to this day that *Old Yeller* should've been rated R and placed high on the shelf out of the reach of children. But I'd given Matson his fifteen bonus minutes, and it was either the photo album or naming the twelve actors who comprised the Dirty Dozen, so I pulled up the sturdiest chair available, set the Kenya book on my lap, and began leafing through.

Inside was a series of ten-by-fourteen-inch color shots of a burly, hairy-chested white guy and his diminutive, black-as-midnight African assistant kneeling before an assortment of dead animals. I figured the Great White Hunter to be Frank Matson. We'd never officially met, but Phillip had painted a pretty vivid picture of his bullying stepfather, and this guy looked the type. He squinted into the harsh Serengeti sun through slitted, ball-bearing eyes, the stub of a cigar jutting from his mouth, holding the animals' heads up by the backs of their necks so we could see them better. He was maybe fifty years old, but a youthful fifty. There was a clenched, hard-ass look on his face. Don't tread on me.

I turned the pages, one after the other. Every photo was more or less like the one that went before. Same backdrop. Same pose. Same expressions. Only the grim inventory of dead animals, heads yanked up for the cameraman, varied from picture to picture. There wasn't a genuine smile to be found anywhere in the album, and as I neared the end I had the odd feeling that the last photo would be the white hunter holding up the lifeless head of the diminutive black assistant.

"You Parker?"

The voice startled me. A man stood in the doorway, twirling amber liquid in an almost empty highball glass. He wore faded jeans, light brown cowboy boots, and a sky-blue turtleneck. There was a little more puffiness to the face, perhaps, but no doubt about it. This was the same flinty, unsmiling character who'd slaughtered his way through the animal kingdom.

"Yes," I said, standing up. "Quinn Parker."

I held out my hand but we weren't shaking hands. He walked through my extended arm like it was a turnstile at the ballpark and moved purposefully to the opposite wall, opening a cabinet and pulling out a bottle of bourbon.

Though Matson was a few inches shorter than my six-two, he more than made up for it in wingspan. His shoulders went from here to there, solid as the side of a beer truck. He topped off his drink and headed back in my direction, using his forefinger as a stir stick. Frank Matson had been in the room less than a minute and had uttered a grand total of three syllables, but there was an aggressive, confident, in-your-face virility about the man that was immediate and undeniable. I felt myself automatically on the defensive.

"I'm surprised we haven't met before this," I said. "For one reason or another I never—"

Matson started shaking his head halfway through my sentence, face puckered against the initial jolt of the undiluted booze. "Look, Parker," he said. "Right off, because I don't have the time. I don't like you. I never even *met* you before and I don't like you. So let's park the break-the-ice bullshit and get on with it."

I felt my posture slightly improve. Spine a bit more erect. "However you want it," I said.

"That's how I want it." Matson leaned against the wall and twirled his drink. "First of all," he said, "you got me at a disadvantage."

"No kidding?"

He ignored that. "You've been Phillip's shrink for how long now? A year?"

"Ten months."

"Ten months," Matson repeated. "Long time."

"Some clients take longer than others."

"I bet they do." Matson took a healthy gulp of his drink. Two more like that and he'd need a refill. "What was Phillip's problem, anyway? Or is it unethical for you to talk about it?"

"Phillip's problem wasn't a secret. He suffered from agoraphobia."

"What's that?"

"From the Greek, meaning 'fear of the marketplace.' Fear of the outside world."

"Never heard of it. How the hell can somebody be scared of the whole world?"

I took a deep breath. "What's the problem, Mr. Matson? On the phone you said there was serious trouble."

Matson shook his head. "I'll get to the trouble later. Right now I want you to bring me up to speed on some of the stuff that's been going on around here."

"For instance?"

"For instance how did you and Phillip get hooked up in the first place."

"I was put in touch with Phillip through Dr. Lohr. He'd been a patient of hers."

Matson looked blank. "Dr. Lohr?"

"Angela Lohr," I said.

Still blank.

I said, "It was my understanding you met with Dr. Lohr several times regarding—"

"Oh, yeah," Matson suddenly nodded, remembering. "Yeah, yeah, yeah. *Doctor* Lohr." The way he pronounced "doctor" left no doubt he didn't think much of the title, or Angie's right to use it. "That was a helluva long time ago. Why did Phillip switch over to you?"

"Phillip didn't actually 'switch.' Dr. Lohr and I work together. She's a clinical psychiatrist who specializes in phobic disorders. Phillip went through the first stage of his therapy with her."

"But it wasn't working?"

"It was working fine."

"So why you, then?"

"Phobias can't be cured at the side of an analyst's couch, Mr. Matson. Not completely, anyway. At some point the patient has to actually go out and confront whatever it is in the real world that's causing the fear. So after Dr. Lohr feels she has done all she can in the office, she contacts me about ... practical application."

"Practical application?"

"That's right."

Matson mulled it over. "Meaning if I'm afraid of snakes, you what? Throw a cobra in my lap?"

"Exactly."

It was kind of a nice image, actually. I took a moment to savor it.

Matson smiled down into his bourbon. "Outdoor phobia therapist," he muttered. "Only in California. So, anyhow. Ten months go by and during all this time, what? You two sit around and talk about his deep, dark problems?"

I closed my eyes. Slowly opened them. "Mr. Matson, earlier this evening I had to listen to you yell at me on the phone. Then I spent an hour driving up here in the middle of the night, abandoning a perfectly good parking space a half-block from my apartment. A half-block. If you knew my neighborhood you'd appreciate what I'm saying. Then I had to sit at the front gate while your crackerjack security guard refilled his stapler, and finally I had the pleasure of sitting in this room another half-hour waiting for you so we could have our ten o'clock sharp meeting which got under way at roughly twenty till eleven." I took a deep breath. "I'm trying to be nice, but it's getting harder and harder. So I suggest that if you have something to tell me, you'd better just spit it out."

Matson stood there for a moment, nodding his head and looking at me with something that almost resembled admiration. Almost. "That was quite a speech, Parker. You rehearse it?"

"I had a lot of time on my hands."

Matson set his drink down on the fireplace mantel and tucked in his shirt, a whole new start, like now we'd cracked through the niceties and finally understood each other. "You want me to spit it out?"

"Please. And if it concerns Phillip, he should be down here with us."

"That so?"

"I'm just playing by the rules, Mr. Matson."

"That's real white of you, Parker, but the fact is Phillip can't come down and join us."

"Why not?"

"Because Phillip's disappeared. Gone. Vanished. Poof!"

I took a moment to think about what Matson had said. "Since when?"

"This afternoon. Left the house after lunch and nobody's seen or heard from him since. We've called every place we can think of. Abby—" Matson pointed at the ceiling. "She's upstairs worried sick. Won't even get out of bed."

Abby was Abigail Chesterton, Phillip's mother. She and I had developed a nice relationship over the course of Phillip's therapy, and I found myself wishing she were in the room to balance things out.

Matson reached for his drink, took another swig, then pulled up short. Examined his glass. Peered at the amber liquid as though somehow it had changed flavor between gulps and he was wondering who the hell was responsible.

"So okay," Matson said distractedly, putting his drink aside. "Now it's your turn."

"My turn for what?"

"True confessions. You were the one just talking about playing by the rules. Come on. Let's have it."

"I don't know what you're talking about."

Matson looked pained. "Don't bullshit me, Parker. You and Phillip've been huddling up twice a week for ten months and you don't have a clue where he went? Phillip never told you any of his secrets?"

"Phillip's secrets are Phillip's secrets, Mr. Matson. What he and I talk about during therapy is not out there for general consumption. Besides, aren't you hitting the panic button a little early?"

"Aren't I what?"

I shrugged. "Phillip isn't some teenager with a skateboard. He's a twenty-three-year-old adult. And from what you say, he's only been gone about ten hours."

Matson's gray eyes got a little grayer. He suddenly looked exactly like the guy in the Kenya book, yanking up the heads of the animals he'd killed. "What makes you such an expert on missing persons? They got disappearance timetables in phobia school?"

"Detailed ones. We memorize them during our sophomore year."

For a split second Matson looked as if he were going to lunge across the coffee table and throttle me. But then he checked himself. Smiled. Went back to his drink, this time sipping. When he spoke again his voice was soft, controlled, tenderly malignant. "You got a hell of a bedside manner, Parker. This an attitude you cop for all your clients?"

"No, sir. Only for those who request at the outset that I park the 'break-the-ice bullshit.' And just for the record, Mr. Matson, you're not a client of mine. Phillip is."

A long, stalemated silence filled the North Parlor. Our meeting was not going particularly well. Matson rotated the drink glass in his palm. Around and around and around, an inch at a time, jerky, abrupt, like the hand of a clock, snapping off the individual seconds. Then he suddenly polished off what was left of his bourbon, tugged at his turtleneck, and looked irritated. "This room's like a fucking steambath. Abby's blood can't take the cold. Abby's blood can't take *anything* anymore. Come on. Let's do our talking in the backyard."

Matson turned and walked toward a door at the far end of the North Parlor. I hesitated.

"Let's go!" he barked. "Now!"

I sighed, casting a glance at the lion silently bellowing from his position above the fireplace. Look out for the rifle, the lion seemed to say. Look out for the long slender tube of metal that spits bullets and neutralizes the pounce. It got me. Don't let it get you.

Rifles comes in all shapes and sizes, so I took the unspoken advice to heart. Then I turned and followed Frank Matson out the door at the far end of the North Parlor.

= 2 =

The door led out onto a large, rectangular stone terrace. The cold night air felt good. The terrace was bare except for a few potted plants and a handful of wicker chairs scooted up to a circular redwood picnic table. From our slightly elevated position you could look out on a tennis court, dog kennel, croquet lawn, lap pool, and five-car garage, all bathed in the pale glow of the full moon. There was enough manicured acreage to the left, right, and beyond to comfortably hold a small golf course.

The backyard.

Matson headed on a brisk, slouch-shouldered diagonal across the terrace toward the croquet lawn. All I could see was the back of his neck, tendons taut as elevator cables, jaw muscles working overtime. I didn't like the feel of it and trailed a safe distance behind.

In the middle of the terrace Matson suddenly slammed on the brakes, whirled around, and took three sharp, menacing steps in my direction. Face red, fists clenched. His attitude toward me was firming up, so I stopped and waited for him to come to me. Less of a collision that way.

"Just what kind of a moron do you take me for, Parker?" he shouted. "You don't think I know what's going on? About Phillip and this tramp he's sleeping with? Suzie Fong or Wong or Kong or whatever the hell she's calling herself?"

Ahh …

The fog lifted. The mystery revealed. Phillip had finally done it. He'd told the family about Suzie, and the disclosure had set off an earthquake or two. I knew that it would, and Phillip knew that it would. For this reason Phillip's Third World, wrong-side-of-the-tracks girlfriend had been the closest of closely guarded secrets for the last few months.

"Phillip's love life is his own business, don't you think?" I said.

"No," Matson shouted. "I *don't* think! Take a good look around, Parker!" He swept his arm across the grounds, the mansion, the swell of rolling vineyards that hit the horizon. "In case you hadn't noticed, we're not exactly Ma and Pa Kettle out here. Phillip's love life carries about a twenty-million-dollar signing bonus with it. And you know as well as me the kid isn't in any kind of shape to be making decisions about getting married."

"Married?"

"Goddamn right."

"He told you he was getting married?"

My genuine ignorance of the marriage angle seemed to give Matson some leverage. "You didn't know?" he said in a cavalier fashion. "Jeez. Looks like even trusted phobia therapists don't get in on all the juicy details. Yeah. Phillip's gonna walk down the aisle with this woman. Me and Abby got the joyful news over lunch."

"I'll believe that when I hear it from him myself."

Matson wasn't one to sustain a cavalier pose. He moved close, right up in my face, stale bourbon breath filling my nostrils, forefinger jabbing me hard in the chest.

"I'm not going to ask you again, Parker," he said. "You clam up about this and you got trouble you never dreamed of before. Where is he? And where does this Suzie woman live?"

Every third word or so Matson jabbed me with his finger, hard, and I was getting sick of it. About the fifth or sixth poke I grabbed him by the wrist and pushed his hand away. "I think our meeting is over, Mr. Matson. I'll call you if I hear anything."

Violence always takes me by surprise. Especially when it takes place on the edge of a manicured croquet lawn in the genteelest portion of the genteel wine country. When I turned to leave, Matson reached out and grabbed me by the elbow and yanked me back hard, dislocation hard, the way an abusive parent will wrench the arm of a resistant child. No warning. No preliminary clichés about how would I like a fat lip or knuckle sandwich or anything else. He just balled his fist, reared back, and launched the punch.

The fleshy blur came up at me like a surface-to-air missile. I leaned back and almost avoided it. The punch caught me high on the forehead and I backpedaled four or five steps trying to keep my balance before crashing over the wicker chairs and onto the redwood picnic table. The table tipped at a forty-five-degree angle and a heavy glass ashtray slid off and shattered on the stone terrace. I ended up sitting on my ass on the cold stone next to the chunks of broken glass. Everything was whirling in the pale moonlight. My left eyebrow burned like hell. I tried to touch the spot where it burned, but my hand had trouble locating my head.

Before I could regain my senses, Matson charged over to the upended table and clamped his powerful hands around my shirt collar and literally threw me halfway across the terrace. I was airborne awhile, then landed hard and ended up with my neck bent against a potted plant. Matson advanced on me. I scrambled to my feet and waited for him.

I box to keep in shape. Nothing serious. Strong men don't blanch and fair maidens never swoon. But two or three times a week I *do* pack my duffel bag and journey to Newman's Gym in the heart of the Tenderloin to lace up the gloves and throw vicious punches at big, inert bags that can't hit me back. Every once in a while I shelve my natural cowardice and spar with an up-and-coming heavyweight named Roscoe Laughinghouse. Roscoe is black, muscled, with a shaved head and ten wins in ten fights as a professional, all by knockout. I don't spar with Roscoe to see who'll win. I climb in the ring with him because it's a more interesting way to stay in shape than pedaling a stationary bicycle. Why he spars with me I don't know. Maybe to practice against my reach advantage and discover at what new angles a flailing, head-over-heels white boy can go crashing out of a boxing ring. But it's all in fun and Roscoe never consciously hurts me, and in small, significant ways the boxing routine has made me tougher, faster, and not easily sucker-punched. Not twice in a row, anyway, and especially not by a fully dressed guy in his fifties who'd been washing down his lunch all day and night with room-temperature bourbon.

Matson came at me in a boxer's crouch of his own, chin tucked low, both fists up near his face, making tight little circles in the air.

"Where is he?" Matson said.

"Take it easy."

"I said where is he? You want more? Hunh? You want more I'll give you more! I'll put you in fucking *traction!*"

Frank recocked, let the left hand fly this time, and I leaned easily out of the way. Without the element of surprise his left hook was as slow and telegraphed as one of those five-stage haymakers John Wayne threw in the movies while drawling out a paragraph of scripted dialogue. The punch whistled past my chin and I pivoted and dug a medium-hard left hook into Matson's stomach. A wheeze, a slow-motion drop to one knee, and the war was over. He knelt there, gagging, a sliver of saliva seeping from the side of his mouth. It hung from his lips like melted cheese, forming a little liquid bubble on the cold stone between his knees.

I started to help him up, but Matson wasn't in the mood for

charity. As soon as I touched him he lunged at me, clutching at my hips, tearing, clawing, trying to drag me down onto the terrace floor where he could use his weight to better advantage. I kept my feet, but he had a death grip on my waist and wouldn't let go. We staggered around awhile like two drunks on the dance floor, then I saw him groping with his left hand. In the next instant I saw what he was reaching for. The largest and deadliest shard of glass from the broken ashtray. I tried to kick it away, but my foot wouldn't quite reach. He clutched it, raised it, fumbled for a better grip.

Imminent disembowelment quickens the senses. I brought my knee up in a hard, swift motion and cracked Frank Matson solidly on the jaw. His teeth rattled like the scatter of billiard balls, and his eyes emptied out.

Matson let go of my waist and the shard of broken glass at the same time and sagged. I backed away so he could sag unobstructed. Frank's face slowly went down, like a deflating rubber doll, down, farther down, until his forehead rested flat against the stone terrace floor. His powerful back surged with heavy breathing.

I kept retreating till I was sure I was out of Matson's strike radius, then started putting myself together again. Torn shirt, a few buttons missing. Scraped elbow. Could've been worse. I checked the area around my left eyebrow for blood but there wasn't any. Then a set of ground-level floodlights snapped on and a sliding glass door farther down the terrace flew open. Rogelio raced out as fast as his seventy-year-old body would allow him to race. His eyes were wide and alarmed.

"It's okay," I said. "It's over."

While Rogelio stood there the door opened again and Abigail Chesterton hurried out. She wore a nightgown and bathrobe and her soft gray hair trailed behind her, long and loose and very fine, like cobwebs from the attic.

"Who is that?" she said, shielding her eyes from the glare of the floodlight. "Quinn? Is that you, Quinn?"

I nodded my head at the folded-up body on the terrace floor.

"I'm sorry, Abigail. Mr. Matson called earlier this evening and asked if I could come up."

"Frank called you?"

"He's been drinking and lost his temper," I said. "That's all."

Abigail looked from Frank to me and then back to Frank. The surprise was wearing off. She was putting it together.

My trivializing of Matson's rage got his attention. He slowly lifted his forehead from the floor and straightened his upper body. Deflate, inflate. Blood was leaking from the corner of his mouth, and his right hand was cradled palm up in his left hand like a wounded bird, curled and swollen and waiting to die. Only drunks and amateurs throw bare-fisted punches at somebody's skull.

Abigail turned to Rogelio. "Stay here with Mr. Matson. Don't let him move."

Rogelio nodded. I didn't see how he could keep Frank Matson from moving without the aid of a stun gun, but no matter. First things first and worry about details later.

I followed Abigail back into the house, through the North Parlor, and along the wood-paneled hallway I'd gone down earlier with Rogelio. We ducked into a large, brightly lit bathroom at the end of the hall, and Abigail immediately went to work treating the abrasion on my head.

I looked into Abigail's face as she swabbed my forehead with astringent. She was older than Matson, closer to sixty than fifty, but retained the kind of aristocratic, fine-boned beauty that money can't necessarily buy, but can certainly preserve. Her face was long and thin, like a Modigliani woman, with sensuous, vaguely disapproving lips. Her eyes were dark blue, almost colorless, and her chin came to such a pointed tip it looked like it would be sharp to the touch.

"I should have known something like this would happen," she said at last. "I should have called you immediately and warned you."

"Mr. Matson said Phillip's disappeared."

She nodded. "Since lunch."

"What happened?"

"Frank and Phillip got into a terrible argument."

"About Phillip's girlfriend?"

Abigail paused. "Frank told you?"

"I'd rather hear your version."

Abigail put more astringent on the cotton pad and talked while she whisked at the edges of my abrasion. Her story didn't vary significantly from what little I'd learned from Matson. Phillip had told them about Suzie. That they were deeply in love and were planning to get married. Frank exploded midway into the confession and everything went to hell. Phillip bolted from the table, and that was the last anybody had seen or heard of him.

I wanted to ask more, but suddenly we could hear Matson shouting and banging around at some unknown corner of the house. Abigail froze for a second, then stepped up the tempo of my facial repair.

"There," she said. "That will stop any infection. Now go quickly. I'll call you first thing in the morning when things have settled down. We'll talk then, okay?"

"Okay."

I didn't need my arm twisted. The world was full of weapons, blunt or otherwise, and Frank Matson was in the mood to use any number of them on me. Abigail stuck her head into the hallway to make sure the coast was clear, then waved her hand for me to follow. She quickly led me out the main entrance and saw that I got into my van, all the while looking over her shoulder. She wrapped her bathrobe around her more tightly and put a cold white hand on my wrist.

"Is Phillip with you, Quinn?"

"No."

"You can tell me," she said, leaning closer. "I won't say anything to Frank. You have my word."

"I'd tell you the truth about this, Abigail. I haven't seen Phillip since our last session, three days ago."

"If you *do* see him … if he shows up …"

"I've got a guest bedroom," I said. "He'll be fine."

"Thank you, Quinn." She looked at me, managed a weak smile, and squeezed my wrist a little harder. "You'd better go."

I started up the van, and Abigail hugged herself against the December chill and walked back up onto the front steps. I wheeled down the cobblestoned road and watched her in my rearview mirror. Her white, vulnerable body grew smaller and smaller in the moonlight until at last she simply dissolved into the rust-red masonry of the mansion, and was gone.

3

I passed back through the security station, and Ted gave me a kind of half-wave, half-salute. It must have been an automatic response to all exiting vehicles, because as soon as it registered who I was, his expression went flat and his hand went down. Ted's expression went even flatter when he saw the bandage on my head. I waved back to him anyway, and he watched me with his sternest five-dollar-an-hour-security-guard look until I pulled back out onto Glenville Road and drove away.

I didn't drive very far. A half-mile, then I did a U-turn on the quiet street and headed back in the direction of the Chesterton estate. Just before the security gate I cut the engine, put the van in neutral, and coasted soundlessly to a grassy shoulder maybe thirty yards away from the entrance. This way I was shielded from Ted Wonciar's eagle eye, but could still see anybody going in or out.

I put on the emergency brake and moved over to the passenger side of the van where I could stretch out my legs. I figured the odds were at least fifty-fifty that Phillip would calm down and come home to his own bed tonight, and there was no way in hell I was going to let him walk into the drunken, human buzzsaw that was Frank Matson. I'd keep my vigil in the cold and dark. Quinn Parker, the full-service phobia therapist.

An hour quietly drifted by. Glenville Road existed primarily to connect a couple dozen extremely wealthy families with the rest of civilization, and for a full sixty minutes not a single car passed in either direction. I sat in the dark and thought about Phillip. Pale, gentle Phillip. No wonder he had problems coping with the real world. A stepdad like that, a neighborhood like this. Up and down Glenville Road reality was kept safely at bay. You picked it up by the scruff of the neck whenever it intruded and gently redeposited it back where it came from. There were no little stores in this part of town. No gas stations or phone booths or roadside fruit stands. Nothing. Just gates and mansions, gates and mansions, with an occasional country club thrown in to break the monotony. All evidence that the world conducted its unclean business through such tainted concepts as buying and selling had been completely and thoroughly removed. Fear of the market-place, indeed ...

A little after midnight I heard the sound of an approaching automobile. The engine seemed revved at an especially high pitch, and I looked back and forth before realizing that the sound wasn't coming from Glenville Road. It was coming from the direction of the Chesterton estate itself. Headlights suddenly illuminated the bushes to my right, and in the next instant a black Corvette roared out of the Chesterton gate and made a tire-squealing left turn on Glenville Road, skidding in the dust and gravel, and was gone.

I cranked up the van and took off. I didn't have a chance to see the driver, but it had to be Matson. I kept my headlights off initially so he wouldn't be suspicious, but it was a ridiculous precaution. The Corvette aired it out and was completely out of sight before my van could even get up to speed.

Three miles down the empty road I was about to give up and head back when I saw the Corvette waiting at the main intersec-

tion with Highway 49. It was trying to make a right on the red
light, but an automobile in front of it hogged just enough of the
right shoulder to keep the Corvette from edging by. I slowed,
downshifted, and timed my approach to the intersection to coincide with the green light.

Then we were off and running again. Matson was now out on
the four-lane main artery leading from Napa to the Bay Area.
Traffic was a little thicker, and the threat of the Highway Patrol
kept him from rocketing away from me again.

We went south for five or six miles, then the Corvette turned
off onto a smaller county road and picked up speed. I followed
as best I could. After a few miles the road narrowed, degenerat-
ing into a two-lane blacktop, rutted with weather damage,
scarred by potholes and numerous half-assed attempts to repair
them. Traffic thinned to nothing. We were in a hodgepodge
neighborhood of discount gas stations, boarded-up hamburger
joints, and ratty trailer parks, and the Corvette began to pull away
again. A black dot on the asphalt horizon, barely lit by fading
moonlight. Then not even that.

I kept going anyway. The road started up into the hills, weaving and climbing through increasingly narrow canyons. A faded
signpost identified the road as Route C, and people lived up
here. Their names were scrawled on the ramshackle mailboxes at
the side of the road in various degrees of unreadability. Up from
the mailboxes I caught an occasional glimpse of shantytown cabins, mobile homes, and dilapidated RVs up on blocks. Crushed
beer cans littered the roadside. The entire area reeked of domestic violence, restraining orders, and probation violations.

For five minutes I maneuvered the sharp twists and turns of
the canyon road. No Corvette, no Frank Matson, no anything. I
was about to pack it in when I turned a corner and slammed on
the brakes. My heart was in my throat. The Corvette was right
there, a hundred feet in front of me, at a complete standstill in
the middle of the road.

Damn! He'd known I was following him from the start, and
now he'd lured me to a spot where he could do something
about it.

But no. The Corvette suddenly accelerated rapidly away, then braked again almost immediately. Accelerated. Braked. Accelerated. Braked. Five or six times, in short, spasmodic bursts, like the house-by-house start and stop of somebody delivering newspapers from a car window.

I kept the van in first gear and coasted safely behind. Was it possible that he hadn't seen me? Or was this the slow, gradual reeling in of the hooked fish? A little slack to pull me in farther? I inched forward in the darkness, one eye on the rear-view mirror. At the bend of a horseshoe-shaped curve the Corvette seemed to find what it was looking for and swerved sharply to the left and headed up a dirt road.

I stayed put for several minutes, then slipped the van into gear and cautiously picked up speed. I eased around the bend of the horseshoe curve and took a look. The Corvette was parked in front of a small, off-white mobile home that sat up on a man-made ledge of land about twenty yards back from the canyon road. There was a nameless mailbox with the number 1824 on it in big, stick-on black letters. No other cars, and no sign of Matson himself. I drove on by without slowing down, hoping to hell I hadn't been spotted.

I kept going on Route C, thinking that it might loop around and eventually pick up one of the larger roads heading back to Napa. But three miles later it petered out into a gravel road with a chain hooked across it and signs nailed on every available tree. The signs were rusted and pocked with bullet holes. Private Property, No Trespassing, Don't Come in Here or We'll Kill You. I'd reached the end of the line.

I got my van turned around, and on the way back I slowed and took another look at the mobile home. Matson's car was still parked in the driveway. No sounds, no light from the window, no activity at all. I thought I saw a face in the window, but given my state of mind it would be almost impossible for me *not* to have seen a face in the window.

I kept going back down Route C until I picked up the main road heading toward Napa. I resumed my watchdog spot outside the gates to the Chesterton estate, but nothing happened. Matson didn't return, and Phillip didn't show. Maybe he'd sneaked in while I was out chasing the Corvette, but I doubted it. At two in the morning I rubbed the lack-of-sleep burn from my eyes and decided to go home. The likelihood of all hell breaking loose between now and dawn was small, and besides, Ted Wonciar was at the ready. He had a gun, a nametag, and a stapler filled to the brim.

I fired up the engine, took one last look at the brightly lit entrance gate to Chesterton Vineyards, and pointed my van back in the direction of San Francisco.

=4=

Hank was already sitting at the breakfast table when I dragged myself out of bed at nine the next morning.

"Huevos rancheros," he said without looking up from the sports page. "Left some in the pan for you."

"Thanks."

I lifted the lid and took a peek. There are variations on the huevos rancheros theme, but this was not variation. This was mutation. Whatever was in the pan had thickened over time and congealed into something more closely resembling day-old road-kill than eggs and salsa. I put the lid back on and opted instead for some coffee. I took my mug and stood for a minute at the dining-room window, peering through the fragrant steam at the Golden Gate Bridge, three miles away.

I was several hours short of requisite sleep, but after the previous night's adventures on Glenville Road it felt good to be home. For the past half-dozen years home has been 1464A Union Street, high on the top floor of a blue and white three-story Victorian with bay windows, hardwood floors, and emphatic lack of elevator. It's fifty-four steps from the bottom of the stairs to the top of the stairs, which might not seem like much unless you do it seven or eight or ten times a day, often with groceries or laundry or the weight of the world on your shoulders. But I try not to complain. Aztec priests scaled pyramids that were almost as bad, and they were rumored to be a group of very old men.

"Where were *you* last night?" Hank said.

"I was about to ask you the same thing."

Hank pushed away the sports page. "Took the boys over to Berkeley for some ice skating."

"Sounds wholesome."

"Pat Boone all the way. Afterward Cort was curious about what a college looked like, so we took a stroll around campus. I pointed out the buildings. Cort wanted to know what you learned in college and I told him very difficult things. Know what he said?"

"What?"

"'Like cartwheels, Daddy?'" Hank laughed, remembering it. "Isn't that great? Cartwheels! Hell, why *not* cartwheels? Around the kindergarten yard that's about as difficult as things get."

I yawned and rubbed my face. "Kids say the darndest things."

"Shame on you, Quinn," Hank said, swiveling his chair around to face me. "You're losing your humor."

Hank Wilkie is five feet eight inches of slender, pale, transplanted New Yorker. He has a nice angular face with a strong jaw and fine brown hair combed straight back from an expansive forehead. Hank is a professional comedian, and his work as a stand-up comic consistently generates enough money to live fairly well twelve weeks out of the year. Reconciling the other forty weeks with this unfortunate economic fact is what keeps Hank's life interesting.

"Looks like you've been trying a few cartwheels of your own." Hank smiled. "What happened?"

"I had a rough night."

"You and Molly expanding your repertoire?"

"As a matter of fact, I didn't even see Molly last night."

"You sure as hell saw *somebody*."

There would be no drinking coffee in peace this morning. After three months I still wasn't used to Hank Wilkie futzing around the apartment. Normally I live alone, but these were not normal times. One morning back in September Hank had shown up on my doorstep, suitcase in hand, announcing that his eight-year marriage to Carol was over. Done. Kaput. Lost at sea in an unexpected squall.

Of course, this announcement was unacceptable. Hank and Carol are my best friends in the world and they have two great kids who—when not fretting over the difficulty of cartwheels— call me Uncle Quinn and draw elaborate crayon pictures on my birthday. People like that are required by state and federal law to live happily ever after. I intended to explain all of this to Hank as soon as he was receptive.

Meanwhile, I was giving him shelter and monitoring the phases. For the first few weeks he simply wandered my apartment in a catatonic daze. Fork abandoned in half-finished meals. Single-syllable answers to all my cautious questions. Great, long intervals of time stretched out in the drape-closed dark of the guest bedroom, door shut, adrift in a lobotomized silence, staring up at the ceiling and watching which way the strands of cobwebs blew.

That was the Zombie Mode. It was quickly followed by Victim Mode, which in turn gave way to Angry Mode, which eventually led to his current stage, the Byronic Mode, characterized by a determination to bestride the earth, have dazzling women in every port, fight side by side with brave peasants in noble revolutions, and generally do all he could to demonstrate to Carol what a mistake she'd made in throwing such an extraordinary man out of the house. Hank Wilkie might be my closest friend, but he could be an extremely trying roommate.

"Come on," Hank said. "Let's have it. You show up at the breakfast table with a purple golf ball attached to your head. What happened?"

I set down my cup of coffee and moved over to the answering machine next to the kitchen phone. "This happened."

I pushed the playback button and let Hank listen to the lengthy message that had been awaiting me when I stumbled up the fifty-four steps at three that previous morning. It was Phillip, calling to tell me in a panicked voice what I'd already just learned the hard way. He'd told his mother and stepfather about Suzie. His stepfather had gone berserk. He was afraid to return home. Feared for his life. The message ended with Phillip urging me to call him, but in typical Phillip fashion, he left no number. The machine beeped three times and I hit the stop button.

Hank still had his hands linked behind his head. "Phillip," he said. "That's the kid up in Napa you've been counseling, right?"

"Phillip's not really a kid anymore, but yes. He's the one."

"Doesn't sound good, does it?"

"No."

Hank unlinked his hands and leaned forward on the chair, elbows on knees. "Let me take a wild guess. You went up to Napa last night?"

I nodded.

"And had a conversation with the distressed stepfather?"

I nodded again.

"And this stepfather converses with what? Fists? Baseball bat? Monkey wrench?"

"Fists."

"Did you converse back?"

"Yes."

"Who won the argument?"

"I did."

Hank smiled. "Wish I could've been there."

I went back out into the kitchen, picked up the spatula, and poked at the huevos rancheros. I was as hungry as hell, and my resolve to not touch Hank's mystery dish was weakening. I separated the least harmful-looking chunk of foodstuff and nibbled at it. "How many hours has this been sitting here?" I asked.

"Longer the better," Hank said, wandering into the kitchen. "Flavors mix all together."

I tried a second bite. Hank watched me eat and shook his head. "Disgusting," he said. "Right out of the pan. And with the *spatula* no less."

"I intend to destroy both utensils after I finish, so it doesn't matter."

Hank poured himself some more coffee and rested his haunches against the drainboard. "Where do you suppose Phillip is now?"

"Anybody's guess."

"What's your guess?"

I shrugged. "My guess is Phillip's with Suzie."

"Suzie being ...?"

"His girlfriend."

Hank looked perplexed. "You mean that's what all this panic is about? Phillip told his folks about his girlfriend?"

"It's a little more complicated than that."

"How come?"

"Phillip is Phillip Chesterton," I said. "If that last name rings a bell it might be because you've seen it plastered on high-priced wine labels from sea to shining sea. Chesterton Vineyards. Chesterton Cellars. Chesterton Premium Reserve. Chesterton *everything*. Suzie, on the other hand, is Suzie Wong. *Not* of cinematic fame. If this Suzie Wong's name rings a bell, it's because you've seen it on her nametag when she waitresses the graveyard shift at Denny's."

"Not what the folks had in mind for a daughter-in-law?"

I shook my head. "Not even close. Abigail just wants Phillip to be happy, and I'm sure she could live with it. The problem is Frank Matson."

"The stepfather?"

"The stepfather. For starters, Suzie is Asian. That's strike one, two, and three right there. Pack up the tent and go home. Suzie's also older than Phillip. A good ten years older, easy."

"You've met her, then?"

"Let's just say I was in her presence once, for ten minutes."

Hank shrugged. "So if you think he's holed up with his girlfriend, why don't you give her a call? See if he's there."

"I don't have her phone number."

Once upon a time I had it, just like once upon a time I had her address. But I'd gone through Phillip's file last night and couldn't find it. I'm an organizational nightmare.

"Back to the demerits," Hank said. "She's Asian and she's old. What else?"

"Suzie's been married before and divorced before," I said. "Possibly more than once before. There's a little confusion about that. Suzie is also dirt-poor and has no real prospects in life beyond serving chicken-fried steaks and mashed potatoes at one coffee shop or another."

"No prospects?" Hank said, eyebrows arched. "I don't know, Quinn. Seems Phillip Chesterton is an *excellent* prospect, if you get my drift."

"The thought's crossed my mind, Hank." I dug the spatula in the reddish glop and tried some more. Not bad. Not bad at all.

"But you still think her motives are pure?"

"I don't know what her motives are. I don't know if she even *has* a motive. I only know Phillip's desperately in love with her."

"Who else knows about this girlfriend?" Hank said.

"Nobody. It's been like the Manhattan Project from day one. Secret meetings. Hush-hush all the time."

"What for?"

"Suzie's ground rules. She was afraid the family would blow the whistle on things if they knew."

"Not an unreasonable fear," Hank said.

"Maybe not, but all the secrecy drove Phillip crazy. Poor kid. First good thing to happen in his life and he couldn't share it. I was the one who kept urging him to come clean. To talk it over with Suzie. Be proud of his choices." I looked over at the answering machine. "So he came clean. Looks like that turned out to be a great piece of advice."

"And what about the stepfather?" Hank said. "He likes to talk with his fists and what else?"

"A real sweetheart. Former Green Beret. War hero. Did time in a North Vietnamese prison camp. Super gung-ho type."

"What happened to Phillip's real father? Divorce?"

"Died in a plane crash about five, six years ago. Then Abigail married this Matson character right away. God only knows why. Let's just say Phillip and his wicked stepdad didn't get along and leave it at that."

The phone rang. Hank answered while I made further inroads on my hunger, then he held the receiver to his chest and said it was for me. As I approached he silently mouthed the word "Abigail."

I took the phone. We talked for a few minutes, with Abigail doing most of the talking. Phillip was still missing. Not only that, but late last night Frank had gotten a phone call from somebody and went racing off. He hadn't come back home and Abigail was scared to death. Before Frank took off he'd gone into his study for a moment, and when Abigail checked it later, the pistol he kept hidden in his desk drawer was gone.

Then she broke off and all I could hear was her muffled sobbing. It was the gentle, unraveled cry of a small child who has been incomprehensibly wronged in a way no child should ever be wronged. I asked if she wanted me to come up and she said yes. She wanted me to come. There was no pretense in her voice. No artificial posturing about how my presence wouldn't be necessary. I told her to sit down and try to relax. I was on my way.

I returned the receiver to its cradle and stood there a moment, staring off into space.

"Trouble?" Hank said.

I nodded. "Looks like Frank Matson's disappeared now, too."

"The stepfather?"

"Yep."

"They're *both* gone?"

"Apparently."

"Jesus ..." Hank shook his head and thought about it. "Maybe someone ought to check the Chesterton backyard for a sinkhole."

"Maybe they should."

"So what do we do next?" Hank said.

"*We?*"

"Look at your head," Hank said. "You're going to need some backup muscle."

"Hank ..."

He shook his head. "Not debatable, Quinn. If anything happened to you I'd never forgive myself. I'd be sick. I'd be grief-stricken."

"You'd be out free room and board."

"I was getting to that."

I mildly protested, but Hank wouldn't let me off the hook. It was a bright, sunny day, Hank pleaded, full of foolish hope. I reminded Hank of his long-standing abhorrence of bright, sunny days, but he wouldn't be dissuaded. His new life would never have a chance to get untracked if he didn't take field trips once in a while. He went off down the hall to get his jacket. End of discussion.

5

I t was an easy drive up. Traffic was light, and we were on the
outskirts of Napa inside an hour. I decided to swing by Route
C first. Hank's theory of a backyard sinkhole was a good one,
but the dilapidated mobile home at the bend of the horseshoe
curve was a likelier starting point.

The canyon was dim and dank. The rutted asphalt glistened
with a light sheen of wetness, and the barks of the trees were
black with absorbed moisture. I turned on the defrost and wiped
the inside glass with the palm of my hand. There was the same
uninhabited feel of the night before. No people, few cars, only
sporadic lights showing from the tucked-away cabins.

"Frank Matson came *here?*" Hank said.

"Yes."

"By himself?"

"So far as I know."

"Hmmm."

I glanced over at Hank. He was stroking his chin, thinking
about it.

"That was a portentous 'hmmm,'" I said.

"Did you ever think that maybe Frank was only having some tension alleviated."

"You mean a woman?"

Hank shrugged. "Why not? A little between-the-sheets slumming with a low-rent girlfriend? Must happen all the time out here with the decadent rich. If I were rich and decadent I'd do it."

"No you wouldn't. And neither did Frank Matson. Not last night, anyway."

"How can you be so sure?"

"Because Frank had a mouthful of chipped teeth and probably a broken hand. I don't know about you, but for me that would be a romance killer."

Hank turned sideways in his seat and looked at me. "Chipped teeth and broken hand?"

"That's right."

He whistled softly and reached over to feel the bulge of my biceps. "I'm impressed."

"You ought to be," I said. "Now just hold that thought awhile."

We drove in silence. The canyon grew narrower. The tree cover thicker. Small pockets of morning fog still hovered at the base of the trees.

"I don't like this," Hank said.

"Don't like what?"

"*This*. The forest primeval. Didn't your mother ever tell you the story of Hansel and Gretel?"

"So start leaving bread crumbs."

"That's just it," Hank said. "Leaving bread crumbs didn't work. Birds came down and ate the crumbs and ... ah, never mind."

The horseshoe curve suddenly appeared before us. "This is it," I said.

I slowed to a crawl and took a look at the mobile home. The Corvette wasn't there. The driveway was empty.

"Okay," Hank said. "He's gone. Now let's get out of here."

"Hold on a second."

I pulled onto the gravel roadway and parked in front of the house. Cut the engine and waited. Lack of cars didn't necessarily mean lack of people, and the good folks out here seemed the type who settled problems with unleashed pit bulls and loaded shotguns.

After a minute I got out, slammed the van door shut as a final calling card, and walked slowly toward the mobile home. Hank reluctantly followed. The house was set on cinderblocks a couple feet up off the ground, with three uneven wooden steps leading to a flimsy-looking front door. I knocked and waited. Nothing. Knocked again and waited. A squirrel scampered down from a tree and looked at me. Cautious was cautious, but we had nothing to fear. Nobody at this address was home.

"Let's check around back," I said.

We angled around behind the mobile home. The property was backed up against a wall of scrub and brush that turned into a severe slope of canyon wall. 1824 Route C was a solitary place even for this solitary setting. There were two windows on the rear of the mobile home, each the size of jumbo cereal boxes. No drapes, so I stood on tiptoes and cupped my hands to the glass of one. Hank looked through the other.

"Empty," Hank said. "Not a stick of furniture."

"Same here. Let's go inside and take a look."

"Do what?"

I went back around to the front and tried the door. It opened easily and swung slowly inward of its own accord. I quickly stepped inside, and Hank was right behind me.

The place was deserted. No furniture at all. Just cheap gray wall-to-wall shag carpeting, with a kitchen of sorts to the left. To the right a hallway led ten or fifteen paces to a small, doorless bathroom. The air had that distinct and peculiar chill of long abandonment.

"You must've made a mistake about the house," Hank said behind me. "Why would Frank Matson come here?"

I stood for a moment in the middle of the living room. The

roof was splotched with rain damage and the carpet below was discolored in spots where the rain had come in. What I generously deemed a kitchen was little more than a warped drainboard, an unplugged two-burner hot plate, and a mini icebox that didn't look big enough to accommodate a six-pack of soda pop. Hank was right. Maybe Frank had seen me tailing him and had simply used this driveway to hide in till I went away.

"I'll wait in the van," Hank said. "Keep an eye out."

"Suit yourself."

He left and I went down the hallway and took a look at the bathroom. The toilet was of the no-seat, no-lid variety, like a toilet in a prison cell. The porcelain bowl was bone-dry and stained a dull, permanent yellow. A wobbly sink jutted from the wall at crotch level, fixtures hopelessly corroded, and to my right was a curtainless shower compartment the size and shape of a smallish phone booth. A rancid smell hovered over the area.

I turned away and took a deep breath of non-bathroom air. At least Hank's illicit rendezvous theory had been dispelled. Nobody was going to rush to this dump for a stolen evening of erotic splendor.

There were two doors off the hallway to the right as I came back out toward the living room. Both were wide open, and I poked my nose in the first and then the second. The first room was empty.

The second wasn't.

I took a moment to let things settle. Let my thought processes untangle, straighten out, and reconnect. A mattress was on the floor. It was stripped bare, ratty and worn out and oozing stuffing at the corners. But that's not what had stopped me. I was looking beyond the mattress, at the flat expanse of the opposite wall.

Starting at a point approximately head level and then flaring out in a circular direction was a wild and almost festive spray of brownish-red. Left, right, and upward. Arterial confetti that had stuck and held. A shattered crimson halo extending almost to the roof, with syrupy, downward, solidified drippings where the red was thickest.

I moved closer. The stains on the wall were already dry, but where it had pooled down below, in the roots of the shag carpeting, the fluid was still sticky, viscous. I knelt at the discolored area. It had the consistency of schoolhouse glue, and the smell was the unmistakable smell I remembered from my six short months of pre-med years ago. Blood. The metallic, coppery smell of freshly spilled blood.

The room got colder. Somehow a little less empty. I stood quickly and resisted the foolish urge to look over my shoulder, this way and that. Instead I walked steadily back down the hall and out the front door. Hank was leaning against the van, arms folded across his chest.

"Can we go now?" he said.

"We can call the police now."

Hank stared at me, then at the mobile home.

"Down the hall," I said. "First room on your left."

Hank went back into the mobile home. I got in the van and waited. He came out a minute later and climbed in next to me. "Let's get the hell out of here," he said. "Now."

There was a small grocery store about five miles down the road. I pulled in and placed a call to the Napa Police, told them what I'd seen and where I'd seen it, and the dispatcher said that I should go back to the mobile home and wait. It was a county matter and an officer from the Sheriff's Department would be there shortly.

We drove back and waited, both of us leaning against opposite ends of the van, hands in our pockets, ankles crossed. Hank was reconsidering his new life of danger and excitement. I was thinking about what I was going to say when the police arrived. Figuring what dance steps would be required to keep Phillip's name out of it.

Brilliant strategies weren't coming to me, so I took a stroll down to the mailbox. See if there were magazines or letters so I could put a name with the mobile home. The little metal door was almost rusted shut and I had to pull hard to open it. There were three dead spiders, long-curled, resting atop a clump of papers. I swept them aside and leafed through the mail. Sweepstakes contests. Tire sales. A yellowed flier announcing pizza promotions from the previous summer. At the bottom was a computer software catalog. I looked at the mailing label. It was addressed to Frank E. Matson or current resident. I tucked the mail back where it was, even replacing the dead spiders, and walked up to Hank.

"Anything interesting?" he said.

"Catalog with Frank Matson's name on it."

"So he kept this place on the side."

"I don't think so."

"Why not?"

"When I followed him up here last night he didn't seem to know where he was going. Stopped and started, like he was trying to find an address."

"Didn't you say he was drunk?"

I shook my head. "Not *that* drunk."

A tan Napa County sheriff's car came slowly around the bend. I walked halfway out to the canyon road and signaled it over. The squad car pulled up behind my van and a young officer got out. He glanced at Hank and walked up to me. The officer had on a tan uniform to match the car, no hat, and Dumbo the Elephant ears made to look even floppier because of an especially harsh basic-training haircut. He had a creamy complexion and rosy cheeks and I had a hard time not imagining him selling Bibles in his spare time. He held a clipboard loosely in his right hand.

"Mr. Parker?" he said.

"Yes."

He referred to the clipboard as though he'd forgotten his mission on the drive out. "You reported the discovery of blood on the premises?"

"That's right."

"Why don't you show me."

I led the patrolman past Hank and into the mobile home and took him to the middle bedroom. I pointed to the spatter of blood on the wall, and the spot where it had gathered on the floor. He knelt before it, just as I had done before him. The gesture had the grotesque resonance of a religious rite. A genuflection at a holy shrine.

"Is this your residence, sir?" the officer asked, standing and facing me.

"No," I said. "I live in San Francisco."

He nodded and went down the hallway, sticking his face into the other bedroom and glancing at the doorless bathroom. Then he came back out, not looking overly concerned. Something told me the local authorities were accustomed to finding spilled blood out on Route C.

"What is your connection with this residence then, sir?" the patrolman asked.

"The husband of a friend is missing," I said. "I thought he might have come here."

"Why's that?"

"I saw him drive out here last night. His wife called me this morning and said he was missing."

The patrolman took out a pocket-sized notebook. "Can I have the name of this missing individual?"

"Frank Matson."

His eyes darted up. "Hunh?"

"The missing person is Frank Matson. He's married to Abigail Chesterton. They live—"

"I know where they live," the patrolman said. He was standing very, very still, looking at me with different eyes. "Wait right here," he said.

I did, and he went out to the patrol car and got on the police radio. He talked into the receiver and never once took his eyes off us.

For the next twenty minutes the officer stayed in his car while Hank and I stood around. He nervously fiddled with knobs and switches and buttons the way newscasters shuffle paper to fill up dead time at the end of a broadcast. He'd gotten his instructions. No more chit-chat until reinforcements arrived.

After a while an unmarked four-door olive-green Dodge sedan veered around the corner and tucked in behind the squad car. It had a flashing light on the hood, but no siren. The man who got out wore civilian clothes. Beige slacks, pale yellow Izod golf shirt, expensive loafers. He didn't have a tennis racket in his hip pocket or designer sunglasses hiked up on his forehead, but otherwise it was your basic country club look. The young cop immediately quit rearranging the cigarette stubs in the patrol car ashtray and clamored out, full of purpose. He met the second man halfway and together they walked slowly in my direction, the young cop doing all the talking and the other man listening and nodding and scrutinizing the gravel driveway.

"Good luck," Hank said.

They whispered final instructions to each other and the young cop drifted away. The second man approached me.

"I'm Detective Davis," he said. "You're the guy who called?"

"Yes."

"The one who says he's looking for Frank Matson?"

"The one who *is* looking for Frank Matson."

The clothes might have been country club, but up close Detective Davis was anything but. He was about forty years old, five foot ten, with a tough, wiry body and a prematurely gray stubble of hair that couldn't decide if it was going to be a crew-cut or not. Not would be a better choice. The skull beneath was rough and misshapen, like a dented bullet casing, and a number of tiny nicks and scars showed through the close-cropped hair. He had an iron-gray mustache trimmed sandpaper-short, a square jaw, sharply angled cheekbones, and a mouthful of teeth so uniformly perfect I wondered if they hadn't been purchased. He held his face at an angle, as though suffering from a permanent low-grade headache; slight squint to the eyes, wrinkles in the forehead, corners of the thin mouth turned up in a kind of prolonged wince.

"Show me what you found," he said.

I led him to the bedroom, and Davis crouched before the

bloodstain and rubbed his chin. Then he stood and put his hands on his hips and looked at me.

"You say you're a friend of Frank Matson?" There was challenge in his question. Suspicion.

"I'm a friend of his stepson."

"Phillip?"

"That's right," I said, a little surprised. "You know the family?"

Davis didn't answer. He kept his hands planted on his hips and surveyed the room. Then he turned and went back outside and I followed. Davis walked over to the squad car and said something else to the young cop and then came back in my direction.

"All right," he said. "What makes you think this dive has anything in the world to do with Frank Matson?"

I gave Davis the two-minute version of events leading up to the discovery of the bloody rug. I skimmed over the fact that Phillip had disappeared and said nothing at all about Suzie Wong, so the recap had a walking-on-eggshells feel about it, and I could see Davis wasn't buying it.

"Besides," I said. "There's mail in the mailbox with Frank Matson's name on it."

"You checked the mailbox?"

His suspicion intensified, and I immediately wished I'd kept my mouth shut. Full disclosure is never a good idea.

"Let me get this straight," he said, wincing his permanent wince. "You saw Frank Matson drive out to *this* place?"

"Correct."

"When?"

"Last night."

"What time last night?"

"Between midnight and one."

"Midnight and one ..." Davis repeated. Then he flashed a glance Hank's way. "You along for this midnight ride, too?"

"No."

"Then what're you doing here now?"

"Now?" Hank said.

"That's right!" Davis half-shouted. "*Now!* Now means now. It's a one-syllable word so I can't make it any simpler."

The skin on Hank's face tightened up a bit. I cringed. Not Tolerating Bullshit from Jerks was one of the subheadings of Hank's brave new life, and I was afraid he might choose this moment as a time to showcase it.

"Hank's a friend," I said. "I asked him to join me this morning."

Davis let his glare linger on Hank for a few extra seconds, then turned in my direction. "How come you happened to be hanging around at the stroke of midnight last night to see all this happen?" Davis said.

"I had an appointment with Mr. Matson earlier in the evening. We left the house about the same time."

"And you just decided to follow him around?"

"He was driving very fast. Recklessly. He'd been drinking and I was concerned."

"Concerned," Davis repeated. Then he pointed at my head. "That lump on your head have anything to do with your appointment?"

I didn't say anything. Neither did Hank. Detective Davis suddenly didn't want to waste any more time with either one of us. He said to give my phone number and address to the patrolman and to stay available during the next couple of days in case he needed to ask some questions. Then he turned and went back up the three rickety stairs into the mobile home.

After the young cop wrote down our vital statistics, we got in the van. Hank was fuming, rattling off obscure one-syllable words that Detective Davis couldn't begin to know.

I wasn't paying attention. I was thinking about Abigail. She was up at the house, waiting for us. Wondering what was taking so long. Waiting for comfort, for understanding words, for good and hopeful news. Jesus …

"Hold on a second," I said. "I'll be right back."

I got out of the van and went back into the mobile home to ask Detective Davis how he wanted to handle this. Should I mention what we'd found to Abigail, or was he planning to contact her, or what?

I went down the hall and found Davis still in the bedroom, hands clasped behind his back, standing in front of the spatter of blood and studying it as though it were a painting in a museum. I cleared my throat and said his name, but he didn't react. The detective just stood in front of the reddened wall and stared, and I didn't bother calling out his name again.

= 6 =

There were a number of other cars already parked in front of the Chesterton mansion as we drove up. A white, late-model Volvo. A sky-blue BMW convertible with the top down. A utility vehicle with pruning shears and bags of topsoil in the back. A black Mercedes with the license plate CHESVIN 1.

Rogelio answered the door and for a moment seemed unsure of what to do with us. He was befuddled and flustered and ended up leading us into a small anteroom that fed off the entranceway to the left. It was a strange little room, different from the rest of the house. Modern and sterile, with that plush, temporary feel of an airport VIP lounge. Three couches formed a triangle around a circular coffee table, and an attractive young woman was sitting on the farthest couch. She had very long, very blond hair, and a tan that was deep, dark, and legitimate. She was strictly business. Briefcase. Portfolios. Eyes that looked like they could go cold or warm depending on what it took to close a deal. She was dressed in a manner to blast open boardroom doors and then not get thrown out for a while once she was in. She wore a short white cotton skirt and a clinging white cotton blouse and generated enough electricity—static and otherwise— to levitate a football.

We nodded at each other the way people do in an elevator, then Rogelio said he would be back in a moment and drifted off in that silent, evaporative way of his.

"The waiting room is filling up," the woman said.

"Who are you waiting for?" I said.

"Mr. Matson."

Hank and I nodded diplomatically and kept our mouths shut. It wasn't our place to tell her that we'd probably just seen Frank Matson's cranial fluid doing a Jackson Pollock imitation all over a mobile home wall.

"And you?" she said.

"We're here to see his wife."

The woman smoothed back a strand of blond hair. "Hope you have better luck than I'm having."

"You have business with Mr. Matson?" Hank said.

"I'm his wine broker," the woman said.

"Who told you to wait?" I said.

"Who told me?" The woman seemed puzzled by the question. "The butler did. Why?"

"Just curious."

Rogelio was either senile or one hell of an optimist. We were silent awhile, and in the silence I heard Abigail's voice drawing nearer, then stopping just outside the door.

"Excuse me a minute," I said.

Hank stayed put while I went out into the entranceway. Abigail was talking to Rogelio, and when she saw me her face went heavy with apology.

"Quinn!" she said. "For goodness sake! How long have you been kept sitting here?"

"Just arrived."

Abigail shook her head, exasperated, and moved quickly to

greet me. She wore a flowing lemon yellow dress that trailed across the floor like a bridal gown. Rogelio used the opportunity to beat a hasty retreat.

"I *told* Rogelio to take you directly into the music room," she said.

Abigail extended her right hand, and I took it in both my hands and held it a moment. Her fingers were cold and brittle, but given recent events she looked remarkably poised.

"Come on," she said. "There are some people here I would like you to meet."

"A friend drove up with me this morning," I said. "I hope you don't mind."

"Absolutely not!" Abigail said. "Your friends are always welcome here. Bring him along."

I opened the door to the waiting room and Hank stood and I introduced him to Abigail. They shook hands, Abigail insisted that we both stay for lunch, and benign pleasantries filled the air for a while. When it came time to move on, Hank said for us to go ahead, he'd join us in a few minutes. He gave me a secretive wink and we left him there in the room with the woman in white.

Abigail linked her arm in mine and we headed off into the depths of the mansion. She leaned against me as we walked.

"How are you holding up?" I said.

"I go in and out."

"No word from Frank or Phillip?"

Abigail shook her head. "No. Nothing."

"You said on the phone that Frank had gotten a call after I left."

"Yes."

"Do you know who it was?"

"Rogelio answered the phone," Abigail said. "Not me. I was in the bathroom trying to wrap Frank's hand. I was going to take him to the hospital for X-rays."

"So Rogelio answered and gave the phone directly to Frank?"

"Yes."

"What was the conversation like?"

"There was no conversation," Abigail said. "Frank just listened. Never said a word. When he hung up the phone he was white. Pure white. He just sat on the edge of the bed and stared off into space. I knelt right down in front of him, but it was like he didn't even see me. Then all of a sudden he bolted up and took off."

"And you think he took his gun?"

"I'm sure of it," Abigail said. "He went into his study and came out right away and got in his car."

"And the gun was missing from its usual spot when you went back to check?"

Abigail nodded. She sighed, shut her eyes, let the frail weight of her body lean into mine. "I don't know what to think anymore, Quinn. I *can't* think."

"Did Rogelio recognize the caller?"

"He said he didn't."

"Man or woman?"

"Rogelio thinks a man."

"Thinks?"

Abigail shrugged. "He said the voice was strange. That it didn't sound like a normal voice."

We were drawing nearer to the music room and the friends she wanted me to meet. There was no quick, graceful, and uncomplicated way to let Abigail know what I'd seen out on Route C. I decided to hold off for a while. If we were staying for lunch I'd have time to find the right opening. Not now. Not with her arm linked through mine, a fragile hope still on her lips. Not with friends to meet.

My trained eye recognized the music room before Abigail had a chance to announce it as such. The two dozen instruments gave it away. There were harps and cellos and bright, shiny cymbals. Violins mounted on pedestals. Paintings on the wall of court musicians entertaining royalty. Yellowed musical scores preserved under glass. To the left a man sat at a grand piano, doodling with the keys. Another man stood by his side, listening, peering down over his companion's shoulder like a diligent music instructor. Beveled windows looked out onto a grove of trees. The leisure class at their leisure. Tranquil, pastoral, tea-garden British.

When we came into the room, the man at the piano quit tinkering around and quickly hustled up to greet us. He beamed a game-show host smile and smoothed imaginary wrinkles from his lap.

"Leslie," Abigail said. "I'd like you to meet Quinn Parker."

"Leslie McCall," the man said. "It's a pleasure to finally meet you after all this time. Phillip and Abby talk the world of you."

We shook hands. Leslie McCall was a dapper, fiftyish gentleman of neither/nor sexuality, dressed sharply in loafers, no socks, chino pants with a khaki open-necked shirt, and a bright red ascot. A smallish man, with smallish, birdlike features. His thinning silver hair was definitely bottle-induced, and he carried himself with the proud rigidity of a duke in exile. Unlike that of the woman in the waiting room, Leslie McCall's tan was as artificial as the silver in his hair, and a little roll of inappropriate belly spilled over his belt line. He held his mouth in a slight pucker when he talked, as though prepared for a kiss, and his voice seemed to come at you sideways, from some deep corner of his throat.

"Leslie has been a dear, dear friend of mine since forever," Abigail said.

"*Before* forever," Leslie corrected, never taking his eyes off me. "I came rushing over as soon as I heard. My gosh, I've known Phillip from the time he was a baby, toddling around in loaded-up diapers."

"Leslie!" Abigail said. "Right before lunch!"

"Well, it's true."

They exchanged smiles, and then Abigail clasped her hands together and announced that she had to hurry to the kitchen and make sure the lamb was coming along. Leslie said no, no, no, she wasn't hurrying *anywhere*. She was to sit back down and relax and let other people worry about things. But Abigail would have none of it and turned on her heels and veered back toward the kitchen. As she drifted out of sight Leslie's smile faded.

"She's been like this all morning," he said.

"Like what?"

"Perpetual motion. She's afraid to stop for half a minute because everything will gang up on her."

Leslie kept his eyes on the spot where she'd exited, and when I didn't say anything he exhaled deeply and shook away his momentary preoccupation.

"Well!" he said. "Enough of that. We all handle these things in our own way, I suppose."

We went over to the piano and Leslie introduced the other man as Holt Riolo. Holt was about six feet tall, with evidence of a hard, solid body beneath the loose confines of his black silk shirt. I put his age at about forty or forty-five. The top three buttons of the shirt were undone, and he had the kind of smooth, contoured muscle definition you see in professional athletes. His face was clear and boyishly handsome and had none of those signs of dissipation that inspire trust. His thick dark hair was trimmed short.

"Good to meet you," Holt said.

Leslie resumed his seat at the piano and began idly plunking one key, then another. "Abigail will doubtlessly refer to Holt as my 'companion' or 'sidekick' or some such thing," he said. "But in the interest of accuracy I'll tell you now that he is my lover."

Leslie paused and looked up at me, waiting for a reaction.

"Fine." I shrugged.

"It's not a problem for you?"

"Why should it be a problem?"

Leslie relaxed. "I'm sorry, Quinn. I suppose I'm still a little paranoid about the subject around here. Frank Matson was not the most tolerant individual when it came to alternative life styles."

"Somehow that doesn't shock me."

Leslie smiled. "You met him, then?"

"Once. That was sufficient."

Holt walked over to the beveled windows. "Look at that pool," he said. "You could hold a swim meet in that thing."

"Forgive Holt's oohing and ahhing," Leslie said. "This is his first visit to the Chesterton compound. Frank was forced to tolerate me because I was Abby's friend. But that privilege was not extended to any of my deviant comrades."

Holt was still staring out in the direction of the pool. "Do you think Abigail would mind if I took a swim later?" he said.

"Yes," Leslie said. "Abigail would mind if you took a swim later."

"What for?"

"For one thing, we don't have time," Leslie said. "For another, we're here to comfort, not party. And if Frank *did* come back and saw you splashing around out there, he'd burst a vein, drain the pool, and have thirty of his Mexicans scour the damn thing with disinfectant. Besides, I thought you wanted to see the winery."

"Naw." Holt shook his head. "Another day."

Leslie gave me a long-suffering look. "The fickleness of youth."

"What winery?" I said.

"Chesterton Vineyards," Leslie said.

"The wine operations are here on the property?"

"Just over the hill," Leslie said. "You've never been?"

"No."

He stood and lowered the lid on the piano keys. "Then our dilemma is solved."

Leslie went off to tell Abigail of our plans and returned a few moments later. "We've been given thirty minutes of special dispensation by the woman of the house," he said. "Let's go."

= 7 =

We went out onto the front steps, and a few minutes later one of the handymen drove up in an electric golf cart. He got out and handed Leslie the keys, and we took off cross-country.

Leslie was not the type who had to be prodded into conversation. He leaned back and drove with his right wrist draped over the steering wheel and talked. He was a journalist by trade, and for the past decade had been the editor of a local daily newspaper called the *Napa Observer*. But that was just a job. Wine was his true passion, and the last few years had been spent trying to fuse the two disciplines. In addition to his newspaper job, Leslie managed a small winery nearby for a consortium of East Coast businessmen, did some free-lance consulting work for some other wineries, and was a regular contributor to several national wine magazines.

"Abigail seems fond of you," I said.

Leslie smiled, steered the golf cart down a narrow dirt fire road that wove through the vineyards. "We're fond of each *other.*

When I said we went back before forever, I wasn't exaggerating. Our families in Boston have been friends for, Jesus, three generations. At *least* three generations. In fact, I was the one who introduced her to Darryl Chesterton. Ushered at their wedding. She's the closest friend I have in the world. It rips me apart to see her in the pain she's in now."

"What was Darryl like?"

"Great man," Leslie said. "Truly a great man. Exceptional. Darryl met Abigail back in Boston, swept her off her feet, and took her out west, here, to the family wine business and the land of milk and honey. They kept pestering me to come out, too, but I never would."

"Why not?"

"For one thing, I couldn't afford it. My family wasn't all that rich to begin with, but once they found out my sexual preferences ... the gig was up. They disowned me and concentrated their time, energy, and money on their heterosexual offspring. I was so broke at one point I remember adding tap water to my shampoo bottle to make it stretch. Anyway, one freezing New England afternoon in the dead of February I came trudging home from my miserable job and looked in my mailbox and there was a round-trip plane ticket to San Francisco. Abby and Darryl sent it, completely out of the blue. That was twenty-four years ago and I never went back home, not even to visit. Still have the return portion of the ticket. Framed it and hung it on my office wall."

"Phillip talks about his father all the time," I said. "He's still not over his death."

"None of us are. Right over there is where it happened. Just beyond the tree line."

Leslie pointed to a strip of concrete on an elevated piece of land perhaps two hundred yards away. "That used to be the runway. His plane got about five hundred feet up and then came straight down."

I kept my eyes on the strip of concrete as the golf cart pulled further away. It was rutted now and overgrown with weeds.

Leslie temporarily lost his talkative bent, and we drove the rest of the way to the winery in silence.

The architectural motif of Chesterton Vineyards was identical to that of the main house. Massive, gloomy, plenty of carved stone and tangled ivy. There were three primary structures; two smaller buildings flanking one enormous central building. Trucks were parked here and there, and a half-dozen workers milled around outside.

"Now that's how a winery is supposed to look," Leslie said as we approached. "Like a castle. Like a cathedral!"

Leslie parked the golf cart out front, and we walked the final fifty yards. The heavy, elaborate masonry and ornate decoration were evocative of a bygone era. One half-expected to swing open the doors to a festive chaos of plump, drunken men; women crushing grapes with skirt hems held high; and children shooting slingshots at each other while dogs pranced and barked. A bustling, scurrying, eighty-six-proof version of Santa's Little Workshop.

But the exterior was deceptive. When Leslie pushed open the double doors and we stepped inside, it was strictly space-age technology. There were no wine-stained floors or handmade barrels plugged up with corks. The containers were of stainless steel, with tubes and interconnecting cylinders crisscrossing from one end of the room to the other. There were a number of smallish tanks scattered about the room, but the area was dominated by four huge metal vats that reminded me of something a refinery would use to haul around gasoline. Each tank was ten feet high, twenty feet long, and perhaps five feet wide.

Two guys who looked like Lockheed engineers were walking from vat to vat, reading instrument panels and making notations in notebooks.

"Where's the little ol' winemaker?" I said.

Leslie laughed. "Under house arrest. This is the future, Quinn, like it or not. Test-tube wine."

We strolled around, but there wasn't much to see. Stainless steel tanks look pretty much alike. A set of metal stairs led up to a kind of narrow mezzanine section that rimmed the entire periphery of the building. There were large framed photos along the elevated walkway, demonstrating the various stages of wine-making, from planting to harvesting to fermentation and eventual bottling.

"They conduct tours here?" I said.

Leslie shook his head. "Used to. Frank cut that out."

"Why?"

"Said it disrupted production."

"Did it?"

"Of course not. Glenville Road's too far off the beaten path to draw enough tourists to disrupt anything. Point is, research shows the average Joe doesn't remember one winery from another. He can only buy what's on the grocery shelf back home in St. Louis, so that was that. Frank focused on marketing and distribution. Channeled his energies into reaching the grocery store owner."

"Was he right?"

Leslie shrugged. "Sure he was right. But that didn't make him right."

"Come again?"

"Our dear Mr. Matson was no King Lear." Leslie smiled. "Frank *always* reasoned the need."

We spent another couple of minutes meandering around. Leslie showed me the Cabernet vat and the Chardonnay vat, showed me the small spigots at the bottom where the vintage was tasted from time to time. Then we went outside and stood next to the golf cart. The air was crisp and cool, the pale December light soft on the leaves in the trees. I breathed in deep the distinctive moist earth smell of the wine country. Leslie took a pack of cigarettes from his shirt pocket and lit one.

"Trying to quit," he said. "You smoke?"

"Never got started."

"Smart man." He drew deeply, squinted into the sunlight. "The cancer part of it doesn't bother me. We all die of something. It's what the tobacco does to this." Leslie tapped his tongue with his finger. "The palate. Wine tastes different to a nonsmoker. It's criminal that I do this. Criminal."

We fell silent again. Leslie smoked his cigarette like a man who cherishes his vices, criminal or not.

"What do you think has happened to Frank Matson?" I said at last.

"Frank?" Leslie drew from his cigarette. "I think Frank's dead."

"You sound pretty sure of yourself."

"I am."

"Why?"

"Law of probabilities," Leslie said. "Too many people have wanted him too dead for too long a time. It was inevitable. That, and Frank would never just go off at night and not come back. Abigail said she's had to cancel two very important meetings this morning."

"Uncharacteristic?"

"Un*precedented*," Leslie corrected. "Frank Matson might have acted like Neanderthal man most of the time, but when it came to keeping schedules he was as fussy as a Swiss watchmaker. If you had a party starting at eight o'clock, Frank's headlights would come swerving into the driveway at seven fifty-nine. I used to tease him about it but he didn't think it was funny. Said it was because of all those years in the prisoner-of-war camp where everything was done on a rigid schedule. He was a big war hero, Frank. You knew that, right?"

"Phillip mentioned it."

"No," Leslie said, shaking his head. "Something's happened to the old boy. Somebody's finally done him in. Abby knows it, too. She just won't face it."

"Who would want to kill Matson?"

"There's a phone book up at the house. We can go through it together column by column when we get back."

"Seriously."

"I'm *being* serious," Leslie said. "If you wanted to kill Frank Matson you would have to queue up at the end of a very, very long line."

"Who'c be at the front of the line?"

"Me," Leslie said. "Phillip. Matson's overworked, underpaid field workers. Anybody in any of the small wineries around here who've been crushed underfoot in the name of rebuilding the Chesterton empire. Matson was a staunch no-growth advocate, so you've go a big group of contractors and construction people out here who would love to have his head on a plate."

"Frank Matson? No growth?"

Leslie smiled. "Don't worry. It had nothing to do with preserving the environment. Frank just had his stake in paradise and didn't wart any more competition. When you stop to think, it's really quite remarkable how the man was able to alienate so many different people for so many different reasons."

A flatbed truck rumbled around the corner and a half-dozen Mexican workers jumped off the back, laughing and talking energetically in Spanish. Lunch break.

"What do you suppose Abigail saw in him?" I said. "Was he after her money?"

Leslie shook his head. "That's what everybody around here thought, but no. Frank had a stash of his own. Big stash, by most yardsticks. Plunked a million dollars of his own money into Chesterton Vineyards when the operations needed modernizing."

"A million dollars?"

"One point one, to be exact." Leslie watched my reaction and smiled. "You look surprised, Quinn."

"I am. Impression I always had was that he was a blue-collar guy who fell into something good."

"Oh, he was blue-collar, all right," Leslie said. "But with Frank Matson, blue-collar was a state of mind, not a bank account. He wanted to be accepted into this society and they wouldn't have him."

"Not even with his one point one?"

Leslie softly smiled. "I said Frank was rich by *most* yardsticks. Not *these* yardsticks. The wealth out here put poor Frank to shame. He was way out of his league and he knew it. Last week, for instance. I went to a party just a few miles down the road.

Huge bash. Gigantic. All outdoors, five hundred people, bands everywhere you looked. The works. When I arrived, a woman took my invitation and handed over a key. Everybody with an invitation got a key. Know what they were for?"

I shook my head.

"Golf carts," Leslie said. "Five hundred guests, five hundred golf carts, so we could conveniently get from one end of the party to the other. The host leased them for just this one night."

"Amazing."

"This same host, last year his wife died and five retail establishments in San Francisco went down with her. Shoe store. Clothing store. Catering service. A couple others I've forgotten. Bankrupt, just like that. Her patronage *alone* had kept them all afloat for three decades. I'm telling you, Quinn. The wealth out here boggles the senses. One point one is pocket change. Except that he was the head of Chesterton Vineyards, Frank Matson was a bit player all the way."

"I'm surprised he wanted to play at all," I said. "Frank Matson struck me as the type who'd thumb his nose at all this society business."

Leslie shrugged. "People are funny. You saw the dog kennels up by the main house?"

I nodded that I had.

"Well, that was a perfect Frank Matson–ism right there. His prize dog." Leslie grinned, remembering it. "A while back Frank got it into his head that he was going to breed show dogs, which was fine except for the fact that he didn't know the first thing about breeding show dogs. It was the idea of it. Going to the shows. Subscribing to dog-breeding magazines. Anyway, Frank thought how complicated could it be? You slap two expensive mutts together and let them do what comes naturally. So he paid a fortune for a German shepherd bitch, built a fancy kennel, got ready to breed the female with a top shepherd over in Cotati."

"Why do I sense things didn't work out?"

Leslie laughed. "It was a disaster! Some low-life mongrel from the farm across the way snuck in one night and humped the living bejesus out of his prize female. Frank had a fit. Screamed that this street dog raped his dog, ruined the next litter, maybe gave his shepherd sexual hangups because now the dog didn't seem to want to fuck at all anymore. He was going to call the cops. Sue for damages. Abby called me, so I went over to the house and sat Frank down and explained to him, first of all, that his dog hadn't been raped."

"It hadn't?"

Leslie gave me a look. "Quinn, have you ever tried to rape a one-hundred-and-twenty-pound German shepherd who doesn't want to be raped?"

"Not since the last office party."

"If you want your face to remain unshredded, I wouldn't try it. In point of fact, it can't be done. It is exceedingly difficult to do much of *anything* to a powerful, full-grown German shepherd unless the powerful, full-grown German shepherd wants you to do it. I explained to Frank that if this other dog climbed on board it was because the female let him, that they were consenting doggie adults, and he should either build a better fence or invent a canine chastity belt if he wanted to keep such things from happening in the future. That was the end of Frank's dog-breeding phase."

Leslie put out his cigarette. "Better be getting back. I think we've just about used up our thirty-minute allotment."

We climbed into the golf cart and drove back to the main house. The white Volvo was gone. Leslie parked the golf cart out front, and we stood for a second at the entrance to the mansion. Leslie gave me a curious look. A look I hadn't seen before.

"I've been doing all the talking, but you know something, don't you, Quinn?" He stared at me as if trying to get right up under my eyelids.

"You'll have to be more specific than that."

"You know what I'm talking about." He smiled. "You know where Phillip is."

I shook my head. "No, I don't."

"Then you know something about Frank."

There was no point in being secretive. The police were probably swarming the mobile home and it would be big news soon enough. "Matson drove to a mobile home late last night, and this morning there was blood on the walls. The Sheriff's Department is already on the scene."

Leslie nodded while I spoke, staring at a spot about halfway up my chest. "You were there when the police arrived?"

"I was the one who called it in."

"Who's the investigating officer?"

"Detective Davis."

Leslie winced. "Does Abby know yet?"

"I'm going to tell her after lunch."

"Don't let her hear it from Davis."

"You know him?"

"Oh, yes."

"And?"

Leslie shook his head. "Too complicated to get into right now. Here."

Leslie dug into his wallet, pulled out a small white business card, and handed it over. It had his name, Leslie R. McCall, a Napa address, a phone number and a fax number. A glass of wine was drawn in the upper right-hand corner, a cork and corkscrew in the upper left.

"Let's keep in touch with each other," Leslie said. He wasn't smiling anymore. "If Frank turns up dead and Phillip stays disappeared, this is going to get ugly in a hurry. Frank was an asshole drinking buddy with half the cops on the force—*especially* with Davis—and everybody knew Phillip and Frank hated each other. You and me, we're on Phillip's side. Abby's side. But there are other elements out here who are going to lick their chops and start sharpening their teeth. Davis will send the bloodhounds after Phillip, and when they find him they'll tear him to bits, guilty or not."

"What do you want from me?" I said.

"If you hear something you think I should hear, let me know," Leslie said. "That's all. I'm a newspaperman. I don't reveal sources, and I'm in a position to give Phillip some good press if the heat is turned up."

I nodded and tucked the card in my wallet. "I'll keep you in mind."

"And if I hear something, I'll let you know. Tit for tat."

"Can we start the tit for tat now?" I said.

"Now?"

"I just told you about the blood out on Route C. What can you tell me?"

"Fair enough," Leslie said. "What do you want to know?"

"I'm open to anything."

"All right." Leslie put his hands in his pockets, thought for a moment. "You asked earlier about Abigail and what she saw in a character like Frank Matson."

"That's right."

"I'll give you a hint."

"Do hints count in tit for tat?"

"This one does."

Leslie looked off at the horizon and narrowed his eyes, trying to summon something up from the depths of memory. "'My father once gave me some advice. "Whenever you feel like criticizing any one," he said, "just remember that all the people in this world haven't had the advantages that you've had."'"

Leslie refocused on me. "There's your hint, Quinn. The opening paragraph of one of our greatest novels. Now we're even. Go home and think about it."

"I'll need more than that."

"You'll get more, Quinn. In good time you'll get more. More than you can handle, probably." Leslie took a deep breath and let it out. "Lots of skeletons rattling in lots of closets out here. I'm thought of as a snake in the grass in some circles, but that's okay. People can think what they want. They can lock the closet, double-bolt, post a guard. But all doors have a crack at the bottom, and that's my advantage."

"Advantage?"

"Snake in the grass," Leslie said with a wink. "Does wonders when you need to slither under locked closets. Stay in touch."

8

Lunch was going to be served in the main living area, on
flimsy TV trays scooted up to a cluster of armchairs. It struck
me a little odd, given how the Chesterton mansion seemed
littered with dining rooms and breakfast nooks and picnic tables
from one end to the other, but Abigail had her eccentricities, and
apparently this was one of them.

Leslie and Holt weren't staying for lunch. They had a prior
commitment that simply couldn't be broken. Leslie grieved the-
atrically and Abigail assured him that she understood completely.
They held each other's hands and the apology, apology-accepted
routine went on for a while. At one point Holt caught my eye. He
smiled and shook his head at the excessiveness of it all. Abigail
walked them to their car while Hank and I waited in the living
area.

"Thought we'd lost you," I said.

"Couldn't leave Vanessa in that cold, lonely waiting room
alone."

"Vanessa?"

Hank nodded. "Vanessa Powell. I mean, Frank stood her up. Abigail didn't invite her to lunch ..."

"Your compassion knows no bounds."

Hank smiled. A half-hour's worth of Vanessa's long, blond, undivided attention had helped to dispel recent events out on Route C. "She didn't believe I was a stand-up comic," Hank said, "so I did my new routine for her."

"Which new routine?"

"Great men in menial jobs. Beethoven bagging groceries. Paper or plastic, the whole bit. Hemingway the bellhop. D. H. Lawrence seating people at Sunday brunch, with the menus tucked up under his arm. That was Vanessa's favorite. The D. H. Lawrence."

"Sounds like the two of you hit it off," I said.

"She's a wine broker."

"I remember."

"Did you know that the average American drinks only nine liters of wine annually?" he said.

"No I didn't."

"It's the truth."

"I believe you."

"Nine lousy liters." Hank sadly shook his head. "In France they drink over *eighty* liters a year."

"That's a lot."

"Italy, too. Portugal. Lots of places. But not us. Hell, no. We'd rather guzzle watered-down beer than enjoy a fine bottle of wine." Hank exhaled loudly and let his gaze drift around the vast room. "I guess this is where they park the 747 when it rains."

I nodded. The living room *was* enormous, even by Chesterton standards. The 49ers could practice their two-minute drill here, no problem. Montana to Rice down the sidelines for thirty yards. Vaulted ceilings, sturdy construction, a fireplace with more square footage than some apartments I've lived in. Yet for all its cavernous size, the room had many of the confining qualities of the North Parlor. The same sense of stifling inactivity, of ventilated heat jacked up too high, of yawns and carpeted stillness and the sound of clocks ticking in the expensive air.

It was hard for any one object to dominate a room like this, but the closest contender was a heavily framed oil that hung above the fireplace. I strolled over for a closer look. It was a portrait of a dour, unpleasant-looking character from the nineteenth century. A silver plaque identified the man as R. K. Chesterton, patriarch of the clan, founding father of Chesterton Vineyards.

He didn't appear to have gotten many belly laughs out of life, R. K. Chesterton the First. The mouth was administered like the swipe of a scalpel, with thin lips clamped firmly together as if hiding evidence of bad teeth. He had bushy white sideburns and the ruddy face of a confirmed outdoorsman. In his stern brown eyes was that innocuous look of not-too-bright single-mindedness that sometimes results in the accumulation of exorbitant monetary wealth.

R. K. Chesterton and I stared at each other. There certainly wasn't much resemblance to Phillip. The man glaring down from the century-old canvas wouldn't have had one spitful of tolerance for a frail, sensitive great-great-grandson like Phillip. Hungry? Eat a rat! Polio? Walk it off!

Rogelio came in with a small wrench, got down on his knees next to the flimsiest of the eating trays, and reached under to tighten a bolt. I told him I'd do it and he gratefully handed over the wrench.

I tightened all three trays, Rogelio trailing after and testing them by placing both hands on top and wiggling. He nodded his approval and I gave him back the wrench.

"Can I ask you a question, Rogelio?"

"Of course."

"Abigail said you answered the phone last night," I said. "The call for Mr. Matson that came very late."

"Yes."

"What did the caller say?"

"That he wanted to talk to Mr. Matson."

"That's all?"

"No," Rogelio said. "I told him Mr. Matson was asleep, and the man said it didn't matter. It was urgent. The man said to tell Mr. Matson that it was about the office space on Pilkow Street."

"Pilkow Street?"

"Yes."

"And did you tell Mr. Matson?"

"Yes."

"What did he do?"

"It was like this." Rogelio let his open palm drop slowly across his face as if to signify a complete personality change. "He was a different man."

"What *is* Pilkow Street?"

Rogelio shrugged. He didn't know.

"And you said the caller was a man?"

"I think," Rogelio said. "But maybe a woman."

Abigail suddenly reentered the room. Rogelio clutched his wrench and left without another word.

A maid brought out the roast lamb. Hank and Abigail and I talked about peripheral things. Diversionary things. Forget-about-how-the-men-in-your-life-are-vanishing things. Abigail mentioned the tough times in the wine industry, and Hank was off and running. He launched into a convoluted harangue about Lee Iacocca. The details were sketchy, but the gist of it was that Iacocca owned a wine estate in Italy and was importing wine to this country under his own signature, competing with our domestic market and thus undercutting an industry already in serious economic trouble. This from Mr. Patriotic! This from Mr. Buy American! Abigail shook her head at such hypocrisy.

"Have you ever heard of the 'presumptive' level of drunkenness?" Hank asked.

Abigail and I said yes in unison, but we might just as well have said no because Hank was going to tell us anyway.

"Presumptive drunkenness isn't even legally drunk," Hank said. "It's on the way to *being* drunk, or coming *down* from being drunk. A guy my size would reach it by drinking two glasses of wine in an hour! Two! Knowing that, are you going to order another bottle of wine at a restaurant?"

"No," I said.

"Top off the glasses of your dinner guests because the mood is right?"

"No."

"Of course you wouldn't," Hank said. "Never mind that only two percent of all drunken driving arrests are made on people who have been drinking wine and wine alone. Ninety-eight percent of the drunks on the road got that way from beer or hard stuff."

"Is that right?" Abigail said.

"A cold fact." Hank nodded. "And not only that, the California government is thinking about slapping on a special wine tax to fund drug abuse programs! *Drug abuse!* Like savoring a fine Chardonnay has anything to do with junkies sticking needles in their veins!"

Hank was getting worked up, so I concentrated on my roast lamb. Vanessa and Hank had been talking, and I braced myself for a long ride home learning the minutiae of wine brokering.

When lunch was finished, I asked Abigail if it would be possible to take a look at Phillip's bedroom. The question seemed to take her by surprise, but she recovered quickly and said of course. His room was upstairs.

We pushed our trays aside and went out into the foyer and up the swirling, hourglass-shaped staircase. Wide at the bottom, cinched in close toward the middle, then flared back out wide again as you neared the second floor. Curving hallways swept away to the right and left. We went left.

Phillip's bedroom was all the way at the end, occupying the northeast corner of the mansion. Abigail stood outside in the hall talking to Hank while I strolled the room. It was austere, as I thought it would be. A single bed; a large, nearly empty closet; and a small dresser. No television. No stereo. Nothing electronic at all except for a small reading lamp and digital alarm clock at the side of the bed. The walls were bare. It was the plain and simple living space of an agoraphobic. Antiseptically clean. Strictly controlled. There was no cluttered cubbyhole where the world might sneak in undetected and get a foothold.

"I always tried to get Phillip to make his room more cheerful," Abigail said from the doorway, "but he had his own ideas."

"Did Phillip pack anything before he left?" I said. "A bag or toothbrush or anything?"

Abigail shook her head. "No. He bolted straight from the dining table to his car."

"Which car did he take?"

"His own."

"The white Mazda?"

"Yes."

I nodded and continued my spot check. I don't know what I was expecting to find. Too many childhood hours curled up in bed reading Sherlock Holmes had continued to make me believe in the obscure clue, the single incriminating leaf of esoteric tobacco wedged between the floorboards. But nothing presented itself, and I turned and walked away.

"I keep forgetting that you haven't seen the whole house before," Abigail said as we headed back out into the hallway. "Let me give you the grand tour."

We followed as Abigail led us from one room to the next. Movement, as Leslie said. Perpetual motion. She showed us the guest bedroom next to Phillip's, then another guest bedroom, then a third. There was a library and a reading room and then a game room with pool table, vintage jukebox, and antique pinball machines. This was the room where we lost Hank. He vanished into the game room like a kid in a candy store. Abigail and I continued on alone.

The master bedroom was the last room on the right. It was predictably huge, with a mammoth four-poster bed dominating the right side of the room. The color scheme was purple, with an emphasis on fluffiness and comfort and soft, rounded edges. I couldn't picture Frank Matson spending much time in here. An antique rolltop writing desk was against the far wall. To the left a C-shaped satiny sofa was tucked up close to a cozy fireplace. The walls were covered with paintings, mostly seascapes evocative of the New England coast, with craggy-faced fishermen in rain gear pulling at their nets. The opposite wall was dominated by an enormous window that looked out on the rolling grounds and the narrow cobblestone road leading to the Glenville Road security gate. Two small doors flanked the four-poster bed. One led to a bathroom, the other opened into a well-stocked walk-in closet.

"The room used to be completely different," Abigail said. "Darker and heavier. Pleasantly gloomy, if you know what I mean. But when Darryl died I changed everything. Started over from scratch."

I wandered the room, hands in my pockets, and looked at the framed photos on the desk. Most were retouched, turn-of-the-century pictures of loved ones long dead. Grandma as a baby. Wrinkled Aunt Penelope back when she was a hot tamale in the Roaring Twenties, decked out in flapper regalia and striking a ribald pose. There was a black-and-white shot of a youthful, college-era Abigail, leaning against a Studebaker, smiling seductively and showing an inch or two of come-hither cleavage. I studied the photo. She had cool, assessing eyes. Accessible and unapproachable at the same time. Her smile said no holds barred, once it was agreed that you'd be allowed to hold in the first place. Abigail saw me lingering on the photograph and she plucked it away. "Enough of that one."

I moved on. In the center of the desk was a color snapshot of Phillip in high school, with the ridiculous hairstyle that everyone seems condemned to have in high school. But the largest photo by far was set off by itself and showcased in an ornate metal frame. It was of Abigail and Frank Matson on a sailboat in San Francisco Bay. The water was rough and they were laughing and Frank was holding her tight. In the background you could see the Transamerica Pyramid, and there was a brisk, windblown, wildly happy feel to the moment.

"That was when we got back from our honeymoon," Abigail said, smiling and looking over my shoulder. "We had so much fun that day. Frank was such a healing person after Darryl's accident."

I nodded. I didn't want to see Frank's happy, loving face, or to learn about what a healing person he had been. The memory of our North Parlor meeting was still too vivid. I preferred to remember him as Frank Matson, raper of the land, oppressor of the poor, voracious killer of Born Free wildlife. The bully boy who'd caused Phillip to turn and run and leave no trace. Hearing about his good points only confused my desire to dislike the guy one hundred percent.

"How did you and Frank meet?" I said.

"At a fund-raiser in San Francisco," Abigail said, still gazing at the sailing shot. "When Darryl died, I set up a scholarship fund in his name for disadvantaged students. Education was always an important thing to Darryl. Frank was at the fund-raiser and we met and, well … one thing led to another." Abigail's voice trailed off unconvincingly.

"Does Pilkow Street mean anything to you?" I said.

"Pilkow Street?" Abigail thought for a second, mouthed the syllables silently to herself, then shook her head. "Pilkow Street. No, it doesn't mean a thing. Why?"

"Rogelio said the caller last night mentioned Pilkow Street on the phone. Office space on Pilkow Street."

Abigail continued to shake her head. "This is the first I've heard of it."

"Does Frank have an address book?" I said.

"I really don't know. Frank kept most of his addresses and that sort of thing on his computer."

"Which computer?"

"The one in his downstairs office."

"Can I take a look?"

Abigail hugged herself, bit her lower lip. "I don't know, Quinn. If Frank came home and found out somebody had been going through his office things …"

I told Abigail I understood, and she looked relieved that I wasn't going to press the issue. I went back to the sailing photo, picked it up, looked at the smiling faces.

"What do you suppose triggered Frank yesterday?" I said.

Abigail shook her head. "I've asked myself that same question, Quinn. Over and over and over again."

"Was it the booze?"

Abigail shook her head. "He wasn't the most pleasant drinker in the world, but I've never seen him the way he was yesterday. Never." Abigail paused. "You knew that Frank fought in Vietnam?"

"Yes."

"Did you know he spent time in a prisoner-of-war camp? Almost five years?"

"Phillip told me."

"They did bad things to him there," Abigail said. "Frank wouldn't talk about it. Not the details. I'm not trying to find excuses, because there is no excuse for racism, but ... I think Frank was especially upset because Phillip's lady friend was Oriental. All those years as a prisoner, being tortured. He was funny about it. Our landscape man was Chinese, and Frank fired him one day for no reason at all. I don't know, Quinn. I'm grasping at straws. It's the only thing I can think of."

We both heard the approaching car at the same moment. I moved to the window and could see Detective Davis's drab green sedan easing around the final curve of the cobblestone driveway. It pulled up behind my van. Davis got out, glanced at my vehicle like it was a can of trash the dogs had knocked over during the night, then headed toward the entrance.

Abigail was beside me, peering down from the window. "I know that man," she said. "He's from the police. He and Frank are friends."

Abigail turned to leave, and I reached out and stopped her. Held her by the shoulders and squared her so that she was forced to face me. The gesture alarmed her, and her eyes were all over mine. Huge. Engulfing.

"What's going on, Quinn?"

"There's something I haven't told you, Abigail. I was going to wait till we were alone—"

"Haven't told me? What haven't you told me?"

"Last night I saw Frank when he left the house."

Abigail blinked. "I don't—"

"He drove to a mobile home about ten miles from here. This morning I checked the mobile home before coming here." I paused. "There's been some sort of accident."

Downstairs we could hear the doorbell ring, then voices as Rogelio let Detective Davis in. Abigail looked past me, in the direction of the voices. There were footsteps, then a deferential tap on the half-opened bedroom door. Rogelio leaned his head in. "A man to see you, Mrs. Chesterton."

Rogelio had a card in his hand, but Abigail didn't bother with that. She brushed past me and slipped through the door with speed I would not have thought her capable of. Rogelio looked at me, shook his head grimly, and followed after.

I went out onto the balcony and joined Hank, who was already standing looking down at Detective Davis. "Guess who's here," he said.

"Come on."

Hank and I headed down the stairs. Detective Davis was standing in the foyer talking to Abigail and paid no attention to us as we approached. He had a pocket-sized notepad in his left hand, a ballpoint pen in his right. Abigail was white-faced before him. I stood beside her and she turned in my direction.

"He wants to know Frank's blood type," she said.

"You're sure that it was B negative?" Davis said, still ignoring me.

"Yes," Abigail said, turning back to face him. Her voice was wooden. Mechanical. "B negative."

"Because most people don't remember a thing like that off the tops of their heads."

"I'm sure."

Davis wrote it down, but he was still dubious. "Do you have any documents in the house that would verify that, Mrs. Matson?"

It was the first time I'd ever heard Abigail referred to as Mrs. Matson. She was always Abigail or Abby or Mom or Mrs. Chesterton. Never Mrs. Matson.

Abigail assured him the blood was B negative, and Davis

bulled on with the rest of his questions. Which car had Frank taken when he left? Did she have prior knowledge of the mobile home on Route C? Had Frank said anything to her before he left? Abigail responded in a flat monotone. The car was the black Corvette. She didn't know anything about a mobile home. Frank hadn't said a word before he left.

Davis nodded, clicked his pen, and hooked it back in his shirt pocket. He told Abigail he might have more questions a little later, turned, and headed out the door.

"Hold on a minute," I said to her. "I'll be right back."

I caught up with Davis just as he reached his car. He leaned against the hood and folded his arms across his chest and waited for me.

"What was the point of that?" I said.

"Point of what?"

"That." I hooked my thumb in the direction of the house. "Hi, how are you doing, don't want to alarm you but what's your missing husband's blood type?"

"You telling me how to do my job?"

"The woman's upset," I said. "Her son's disappeared and now her husband's vanished. You could've quickly gotten the blood type information from medical records. Insurance forms. A dozen other places."

Davis kept his arms folded across his chest, smiled an unpleasant smile. "You know, I finally clicked on who you are, Parker. Frank used to talk about you. You're the phobia guy, right? The one who sits around and talks with Phillip for a hundred bucks an hour."

I didn't say anything.

Davis leaned closer. "If I were you, Parker, I'd spend less time being Sir Galahad defending the ladies and more time thinking about what's going to happen to your ass if you don't start telling me the truth. Frank Matson was a friend of mine, so I've got what you'd call a personal interest in this one. Clam up on me and I'll give you a new phobia to think about. Fear of getting your balls kicked up into your throat. And I'll do it. Don't think I won't."

Davis abruptly turned and got in his puke-green car and drove away, bouncing down the cobblestones at a too-high speed, leaving only the smell of his bad exhaust in the crisp afternoon air.

I went back in the house. Abigail hadn't moved an inch from where I'd left her.

"I'm sorry you had to hear it this way, Abigail."

She leaned into me and I held her a moment. Hank pointed at the door, indicating that he would wait outside, and I nodded.

We stood for a while in the foyer like that, swaying slightly. The bones of her back felt breakable under my hands.

"I knew something terrible had happened," she said. "I knew."

"Let's wait to see what happens," I said. "The blood might not be B negative. And even if it is, you should check to make sure you remembered right."

Abigail broke the embrace and wiped from her eyes the remnants of what had been silent tears. "I'm sure about the blood type," Abigail said. "Phillip was B negative, too."

The room grew stiller. "Phillip?"

Abigail nodded. "I remembered because the doctors said they could donate blood to each other in an emergency. They said we were lucky because B negative was kind of rare. That was the word the doctors used. Lucky."

= 9 =

t was early afternoon when we swung down out of the Marin hills and onto the north entrance of the Golden Gate Bridge. The December sky was clear and cold and pale, pale blue. The Pacific below was a flat gray table. Traffic thickened, and by mid-span things had slowed to a ten-mile-an-hour crawl. I wondered what it was this time. Roadwork. Fender-bender. New guy working the toll booth. It doesn't take much to disrupt the plans of ten thousand people. I downshifted, stretched the kinks out of my back, and sighed.

"Look at this," Hank muttered. "Bumper to bumper at two in the afternoon. Why do countries spend so much money on guns and bombs? Give me a couple dozen stalled cars and I could rule the world."

"Write the Pentagon."

Our drive home from Napa had been silent and introspective. I was thinking about Pilkow Street, the gun missing from Matson's study, and B negative blood. Matson *and* Phillip's B negative blood. Hank was lost in his own troubles. He began to get that lost, confused, where-is-my-teddy-bear look again. He didn't give a damn about Lee Iacocca's wine estate or Vanessa Powell's struggles in the wine-brokering business or what she might look like out from underneath all that clinging white cotton. Suddenly he was just a guy with a great wife and two wonderful children and the whole thing was threatening to go glug.

In fifteen minutes we were clear of the logjam, speeding down Doyle Drive, past the Palace of Fine Arts, and onto Lombard. A dozen or so miserably timed lights, right on Van Ness, another quick left on Union, and we were home. I double-parked in front of the apartment and kept the engine idling.

"You're not coming in?" Hank said.

"I'm going to try to find Suzie Wong."

"You know where to look?"

"Sort of. I lost her address, but I think I remember how to get there."

He sighed heavily, climbed out of the van. "I was thinking. Maybe Carol and I should just go ahead and get a divorce."

"That's a complicated exit line, Hank."

"I mean it," he said. "We should get divorced. For the kids' sake."

"The kids' sake?"

"Sure. At least then they wouldn't feel like freaks at school. Held up to daily ridicule and shame because they come from a stable and loving family. No. It's better that Carol and I just call it a day."

I took a deep breath. "We'll discuss your divorce later, when I'm not double-parked. Besides, you're never going to know what to do about Carol unless you start seeing other women. What's the story with Vanessa?"

"Vanessa?"

"The vixen wine broker, remember? Did you get her number?"

"No."

"Why not?"

"I don't know." Hank looked miserable. "I'm bad at making the first move."

"I hate to tell you this, Hank, but by my count Vanessa Powell made the first *five* moves before you even said a word."

Hank sighed. Stared off into space. "I'm just not very good at this."

"Look," I said. "If you're feeling shaky, don't start with the Vanessa Powells of the world. There'll be nothing left of you in the morning but bones and tooth enamel. Ease into it. Think of assistant librarians. Grade-school teachers."

Hank smirked at me. "Shows what you know about women. I dated a grade-school teacher once back in New York, and she packed a wallop I bet Vanessa Powell only dreams of."

"You know what I'm saying."

"Fine," Hank said. "We'll do it your way. First thing tomorrow I'll go out and start pounding the pavement and try to trump up some meaningless affair that in the end will just make me feel cheap and dirty."

"Who knows?" I said. "You might like the part where it leads up to being cheap and dirty."

"You're a great help."

"Do me a favor," I said. "Eat a healthy dinner and stay out of the wine bin."

Hank nodded that he would, but the nod didn't have much conviction. He shuffled up to the door, and I waited till he demonstrated proficiency with the front door key. Then I accelerated away across town toward the Castro District. Toward Phillip's girlfriend.

It took some backing and forthing before I pinpointed Suzie Wong's apartment. I'd only been there once before, two months earlier, during a blustery San Francisco night of gusting rain and malfunctioning windshield wipers. Hill Street near Noe. The address was scribbled on a piece of paper somewhere in my office files, but I didn't have time to scavenge for it. I vaguely remembered a broken red awning out front, and that was how I ended up finding her again. The awning was still red and still broken. I parked around the corner, locked up the van, and started walking back.

This session didn't promise to be any easier than my visit with Matson. My one and only meeting with Suzie Wong had not been a rousing success. For weeks all I had been hearing from Phillip was this new, wonderful woman in his life. The *first* woman in his life, really. Not just in a physical sense he said, neck reddening, eyes averted, but in *every* sense. Phillip had met her at the De Young Museum where he did volunteer work. Suzie had come up to him with a question about one of the exhibits, he'd answered, and things had proceeded from there.

As the weeks went on, Phillip's conversation in therapy became increasingly peppered with references to Suzie. But when I suggested one afternoon that the three of us might go out to lunch, the fizz went out of Phillip's exuberance. His expression darkened. No, he said, that wouldn't be a good idea. Suzie didn't want to meet his friends or his family. Not yet. There would be disapproval, she said. Outsiders who didn't understand would whisper in Phillip's ear, trying to drive a wedge between the two of them. No. There could be absolutely no mention of her to friends or family, and certainly no direct contact. That was a rule, firm and unbreakable.

So when Phillip made an independent decision a few weeks later that I was the exception to the rule, it didn't go over well with Suzie. After one of our afternoon sessions he suggested that I drop in on them at her apartment that night during dinner on some flimsy pretext of returning something important that had been left at the office. Anything. A briefcase, say, filled with important museum papers.

Though my curiosity was high, I was inclined to nix the idea. Suzie would be upset regardless and I didn't want to ruin things for Phillip. But at the same time there were doubts of my own that needed satisfying. As Frank Matson had said, the Chestertons weren't Ma and Pa Kettle, and Phillip's devotion did come with a nice, plump, eight-digit stipend attached. All those zeros and commas and decimal points can attract less than noble types, and I thought it might be a good idea to meet the elusive Suzie Wong in person.

So I went. Dropped in on the dinner-in-progress the way Phillip had diagrammed it. Suzie didn't buy the forgotten museum papers gambit for one nanosecond. I was checking her out, clear and simple, and she sat absolutely motionless at her end of the dining table, brittle as porcelain, until I left. She never stood, never touched her food, never said a word. Her microwave eyes burned me up one side and down the other, and when I finally turned my collar to the wind and rain and headed back out I knew no more about Suzie Wong than I did before I went in. Maybe less. The experiment was a disaster, and Phillip never suggested that we do anything of the sort again.

I rang Suzie's buzzer, took a deep breath, and waited. There was activity on the other side of the door. It cracked open a half-dozen inches and Suzie's face appeared in the wedge of dimly lit space.

"Suzie Wong?"

"What do you want?" she said.

"You probably don't remember me, Suzie. My name is Quinn Parker. Phillip Chesterton is a client of mine and we met here about—"

"I know who you are," she said curtly. "What do you want?"

"Something's come up. A problem."

"What problem?"

"Can we talk for a minute?"

Suzie hesitated. She was holding the edge of the door firmly with both hands, like I was a stormtrooper about to kick it back into her face. I heard movement behind her, down the hallway, but Suzie's eyes gave no indication of anything amiss.

"What problem?" she repeated.

"Phillip's disappeared."

She kept silent, waiting for me to continue.

"I just came back from Napa," I said, "and his family is concerned. Phillip left the house yesterday and hasn't come back and I thought he might have come here."

"You talked to his family?"

"That's right."

"His mother?"

"No. The stepfather."

Suzie took a moment to think about it. Then she nodded abruptly. "I'll get my coat."

She disappeared back into her apartment, closing the door in my face. I listened closely. There was a noise. The almost imperceptible metal click of someone gently relocking a door. Nothing an unsuspicious person would notice, but I wasn't unsuspicious. I thought she might be hightailing it out the back, but a minute later the door reopened and she was with me, pulling on a heavy, black, knee-length coat.

"Let's walk," she said.

Suzie led me down to Dolores Park. Now that I was seeing her in daylight and out from behind the candlelit dining table, I was surprised by how small she was. Petite, verging on bony, with a flat, oddly expressionless face. Severe lips and eyebrows that were two razor-thin scratches of black pencil and nothing else. Her fingernails were long and painted fire-engine red. She had a built-from-the-ground-up feel, reconstructed each morning before the bathroom mirror, yet you could see in her face vestiges of what once must have been youthful beauty. Now there was only one truly extraordinary feature left to Suzie Wong. Her hair. It was thick and black and fell in a tumbling, cascading, sumptuous pile to a point well below her waist. Volcanic. Breathtaking. Head-turning. I had a hard time imagining timid, faltering Phillip caught up in the fragrant tangle of it. Or maybe I was just envious.

When we reached the park she paused, took a pack of cigarettes from her purse, and lit one. She drew from it deeply, then tossed back her hair and looked me in the face. Her eyes were cold, hard marbles. Merciless eyes. Interrogator's eyes.

"When did you say Phillip disappeared?" she said.

"Yesterday afternoon."

"And you think he came here? To see me?"

"Did he?"

She shook her head. "No."

"You can tell me the truth, Suzie. I'm not going to report back to the family."

"I already told you no."

Suzie wrapped her coat tighter and moved to a wooden bench that looked out on Mission Dolores. I sat next to her. She had her legs crossed, working the cigarette, flexing her free hand as though trying to dispel muscle pain. The angle of her body was slanted to the left, away from me. A protective stance.

"How come this stepfather is so worried, anyway?" Suzie said. "He never cared about Phillip before."

"I don't know. Maybe he feels responsible."

That drew a cynical laugh.

"I need your help, Suzie. Phillip left a message on my answering machine last night and he sounded scared as hell. Do you have any idea where he might have gone?"

Suzie shifted further on the bench. She practically had her back to me. Then she turned her head to look at me over her right shoulder. It was not a pleasant look. "You need my help?"

"Yes."

Suzie paused, looked down at her bright red fingernails. "I have a question for you, Quinn Parker."

"Okay."

"When Phillip told you about me ... what did you think? The truth."

"I was happy for him."

"Bullshit."

"It's not bullshit," I said. "But I won't lie to you. I also advised caution."

"Caution?"

"That's right."

"Would you have advised caution if I'd been white? Young? Rich?"

"Phillip was extremely vulnerable around the time he got involved with you," I said. "I only wanted to protect him."

"From what? My lies?" Suzie dropped her cigarette to the pavement and crushed it with her heel. "I told Phillip everything at the start. Who I was. My past. All of it. Didn't he tell you?"

"He said you emigrated from Thailand."

"Emigrated," Suzie said distastefully. "I suppose that is one way to put it."

"What's another way?"

Suzie reached into her purse and extracted another cigarette and lit it. "You have a lot of money, don't you?"

"What does that have to do with anything?"

"I know you have money. Phillip told me so. A power tool or something blew up in your hand and the company paid you lots of money. Right?"

"That's right," I said. "I have some money. But I didn't always, and I certainly don't have money like Phillip has money. What's the point?"

"The point is I don't have money. My family in Thailand is very poor, and a poor young girl there does not have many options. You can stay in the fields all your life and try to keep from starving. Or you can go to Bangkok and become a prostitute. Or, if you get lucky and are pretty, you can marry someone who will change things for you. I was pretty, so that's what I did. When I was a little girl I saw the movie *The World of Suzie Wong,* and I thought Nancy Kwan was the most beautiful woman I ever saw. I wanted to be her more than anything else in the world. So I changed my name and did it. Got married."

"Who was the man?"

"Just a man. It happened by mail. He was in Los Angeles. The agency sent him a photograph and he wrote back to say he liked me, but wanted to see a picture of me with no clothes on." Suzie brushed back a strand of hair. "So I did, and after that he flew me to the United States."

"Where you got married?"

"Yes." Suzie stared down at her shoes. "He was terrible. Old and fat. Smelled bad. His fingernails were yellow and his teeth … I guess I should have asked to see a picture of *him* with no clothes on. Anyway, he was never going to have a woman again unless he purchased one, so he purchased me."

"I'm sorry."

Suzie shook her head. "No reason to be sorry. It was a fair deal. I escaped my life in Thailand, and he got a wife."

"What happened then?"

"He beat me up a lot, but I waited so I could learn English better and hide some money for myself. Then one day I left. He went to the liquor store, and while he was gone I called a taxi and left the house. Took the bus to San Francisco and never went back."

"He didn't come looking?"

"What for? There are thousands of girls where I came from. Prettier, younger, cheaper than me. It's a buyer's market."

A couple walked slowly past the bench, and we fell silent till they were out of earshot. If Phillip had known all this, he had done a thorough clean-up job before passing the information on to me. It made me uneasy. I wondered where else he had reworked the truth. Suzie looked over at me and smiled. "Don't feel pity, Quinn Parker. I was lucky. I got out."

"Is that all that matters? Getting out?"

Suzie shrugged. "Crawl before you walk, walk before you run. Because I got out I met Phillip."

Another pocket of silence came over us. Suzie worked her cigarette and followed the progress of the couple who had walked past. The man was pointing to Mission Dolores and explaining something to the woman.

Suzie turned to face me. "What will happen if Phillip doesn't come back?"

"The police will get involved. The family will hire their own investigator, if they haven't already. But for right now Frank Matson is concerned about keeping it quiet."

Suzie nodded. A vacant nod. She was off thinking about something else. I gave fleeting thought to telling her about the mobile home, but decided against it. Then she snapped alert and looked at me. Hard. So hard I could almost feel her cold marble eyes right up against my bones.

"If I tell you something about Phillip," she said carefully, "is that considered confidential?"

"Depends."

"On what?"

"On what it is you tell me."

"Why?"

"If you tell me Phillip has a bomb and is going to blow up the Civic Center tomorrow at noon, I can't keep that confidential."

"It's nothing like that," Suzie said.

"Then what is it?"

"Confidential?"

"Suzie ..."

She leaned back on the bench and drew from her cigarette.

I took a deep breath and let it out. This umbrella of patient-therapist confidentiality was widening and widening, and I had to be careful about letting it stretch too thin. It was one of the easier ways of getting your license yanked. But Suzie was firm. She wasn't going to utter one more syllable about Phillip Chesterton unless I agreed to her terms.

"Okay," I said. "As long as it doesn't involve a crime, what you tell me will be kept confidential."

"Promise?"

"Promise."

"No matter what?"

"No matter what," I said. "Go ahead."

"I saw Phillip last night." Her eyes locked onto mine. Stayed there. Didn't waver.

"Where?"

"Here. My apartment. It was very, very late. I was asleep and he woke me up. He was frightened, shaking. I'd never seen him like that before. He said he had a bad argument with his stepfather and was afraid."

"Afraid of what?"

"That his stepfather might try to kill him."

"Had Phillip been threatened?"

Suzie lifted her shoulders. "I don't know. Maybe, but I don't remember. It was so late, and I was half-asleep."

"Then what happened?"

"Nothing," Suzie said. "He left."

"The truth, Suzie."

"I'm telling the truth."

"Is Phillip in your apartment now?"

Her face stiffened. "I already told you. He left."

"Just walked out the door at three in the morning?"

"No. He stayed the rest of the night with me, then I drove him to the airport."

"In your car or his?"

"My car."

We fell silent. Now it was Suzie's turn to scrutinize me. Did I believe her? Would I still keep my vow of silence? Her eyes darted from one part of my face to another.

"Suzie ... if Phillip's in danger the police should be notified."

"No."

"Phillip's safety is—"

"No!" Suzie stood, leaned over me, and put a bloodred fingernail an inch from my throat. "You swore to me! You swore!"

I glanced around. Other people in the park stopped what they were doing to watch.

"Calm down, Suzie."

"I *won't* calm down! You *swore* to me!"

"Okay," I said. "Relax. I gave you my word and I'm going to stick to it. Just take it easy."

The fingernail stayed where it was. "No lies to me."

"No lies," I said. "But sit down tonight and think about it. Here's my number." I took a card from my wallet and handed it to her. "If you change your mind, or if you hear from Phillip again, please call me. Phillip isn't just a client to me. He's a friend."

Suzie glanced at my card, then slipped it into her purse. I could drip honey all day and all night, but she didn't trust me anymore. Her initial instincts had been right. I was the white wealthy therapist of the white wealthy Phillip who had just returned from a fireside chat with the white wealthy family. No question where my loyalties resided. I'd sworn confidentiality to her and then tried to hedge, and Suzie's attitude toward me changed with the finality of a whistling guillotine. I'd been added to the dungheap of people and events that had conspired from birth to ruin her life, and there would be no more help coming from her. Suzie Wong had spoken her last.

"I told you everything I know," she calmly said. "Now don't come back to bother me ever again."

"Suzie …"

"I mean it. Never again."

She turned and walked briskly away, hands shoved deep into the pockets of her winter coat, head down, fabulous thick black hair spread across her back by gusting wind.

I sat on the bench and watched Suzie go. No sense chasing after or kicking in doors or scouring apartments. Suzie Wong was not a stupid woman. Our stroll to the park had served a number of purposes, not the least of which was to buy time. She'd walked her walk and talked her talk, and whoever had been in her apartment a half-hour earlier was by now ancient history. Traceless, vanished, never happened.

I sat on the bench a few more minutes, watching the young couple kiss and lean into each other, then I got up and headed back toward the van.

=10=

My encounter with Suzie Wong did not leave me feeling all warm and snuggly inside, so when I got back to my apartment I went into the office and started digging around for Phillip's file. I wanted to refresh myself on exactly how and when the Chesterton heir met the Bangkok catalog girl. My office hadn't been cleaned in a while and I wasn't having much luck. I pulled open this file drawer and that, muttering deletable expletives under my breath, and vowing never to let things get this disorganized again.

I heard Hank's bedroom door open, and he sauntered in and stood there in the doorway, watching me at my labor. He cradled a glass of red wine in his right hand.

"Dozed off for a second," he said. "Had a hell of a nightmare."

"Forget about Lee Iacocca."

"The nightmare happened to concern Carol," Hank said.

"Carol's not nightmare material."

"She was this time," Hank said. "I was back home somehow,

standing in a corner of the living room like a ghost nobody could see, and I was watching the new man in Carol's life."

"What new man?"

"The new man in my nightmare," Hank said testily. "Can I please finish?"

"By all means."

"The kids, they were tugging on this guy's robe and calling him Daddy. He was puttering around the kitchen like he owned the place, fixing coffee. Then he and Carol started playing around, pinching each other, grabbing little handfuls of tush. You know how couples do sometimes while fixing breakfast?"

"Sort of."

"Anyway, Carol and this man couldn't wait. They left the bacon to burn and the kids to their cartoons and hurried back to the bedroom and I floated down the hall with them and watched it all. How they fought to get each other's robes off. The kissing. His mouth on her breasts."

I kept quiet and continued digging through the files. Hank's self-pity hadn't leaked onto the hardwood floor yet so I let him wallow in it for a few moments longer.

"Lips moving down the hollow of her neck," he said. "Brushing over her nipples. Lingering. Grazing."

"I get the picture."

"Suddenly the whole bedroom was crowded with people. Well-dressed people, like opening night at the opera. And they were applauding wildly, watching all of it. They were throwing bouquets of flowers on the bed right in the middle of it all, hitting the guy in the ass, screaming for more."

"Enough."

"And it wasn't like Carol was trying to fight it," Hank said. "Hell, no! Just the opposite. She craned back to give him total access, holding the headboard with both hands while this guy—"

"Hank!"

Hank stopped, sighed your basic audible sigh, and took a sip from his wineglass. Then he turned his attention to me. "What're you looking for?"

"Phillip's file."

"It's right there on your desk."

"That's his current file. I'm looking for the old one."

Hank swirled the wine and smelled the bouquet and held the glass up to the light, almost like he knew what the hell he was doing. "I was thinking about what you said this afternoon about having a cheap and meaningless affair."

"Yeah?"

"What ever happened with Denise?"

Denise was a woman I used to date in Palo Alto. An actress. Fun. Attractive. It was my one reluctant shot at matchmaking for Hank. "I called her."

"And?"

"She hasn't called back yet," I said.

"When did you call her?"

"Two months ago. I get the feeling she's involved."

"What did you say about me?"

"I said I had an unusual friend who was interested in going out with her."

Hank positioned himself to look more clearly into my face. "'Unusual' friend?"

"What's wrong with unusual?"

"It's hardly what I'd call a ringing endorsement. You could have said 'delightful,' 'handsome,' 'interesting.' But *unusual?* Unusual could mean anything. Ted Bundy was unusual. Adolf Eichmann was unusual. No wonder she never called back."

"Truth in advertising, Hank."

Hank sulked and I flipped through files. "Find Suzie?" he said at last.

"Found both Suzies."

"Both?"

I briefly recapped my encounter with Suzie while Hank leaned against the wall and sipped his wine. When I finished, he shrugged his shoulders. "Math was never my strong suit, but I still only count one Suzie Wong."

"Like this," I said. "On the one hand you have this meek,

barefoot girl from the rice fields who signed up for an Asian-women-seek-romance thing and managed to parlay her good looks into a marriage by mail. Bared her breasts and smiled for the camera and some sleazeball bought her. Miserable business, but it's a flawed world. So from the Bangkok auction block she goes to Los Angeles for further use and abuse before escaping to San Francisco, where she lands a job waitressing at a coffee shop. That's Suzie Number One."

"Who's Number Two?"

"Number Two is the Suzie Wong who walked with me to Dolores Park. The two personalities didn't jibe."

"Why not?"

I closed a file drawer and sat there. "I try not to think in stereotypes, but ..."

"Let's have it," Hank said. "Your narrow-mindedness is safe with me."

"Well ... one of my stereotypes is of how a Thai peasant girl who has been miraculously rescued from the clutches of lifelong poverty behaves in a strange country. She's quiet. Obsequious. Deferential. Her eyes are kept lowered and her wants kept simple, lest she fall out of favor and find herself shipped back to where she started."

"I harbor the same stereotype," Hank said. "Suzie Number Two wasn't like that?"

"Definitely not."

I leaned back and tried to explain to Hank the gutsy, aggressive toughness of the Suzie Wong who'd walked with me to Dolores Park. To convey the gritty instinct for survival so cold it might have been carved into her DNA with a penknife. I thought of the contentious way she smoked her cigarette. How she flicked the match away while it was still burning. Her no-nonsense manner of crossing a street, heels clicking, head bobbing. The way she'd spat out the word "bullshit" in my face. The lethal red fingernail held an inch from my neck. And her English was disturbingly perfect. Not something a barely literate homeless waif from Thailand would pick up from daytime soaps while playing obedient housewife to a drunken, abusive bum in Los Angeles.

"Not only that," I said, "but there was someone in the apartment with Suzie when I knocked on the door."

"Phillip?"

I shrugged. "Maybe. There was noise in the hallway and she locked the door when she went to get her coat so I couldn't barge in."

Hank frowned. "Why would she want to hide Phillip from you?"

"I have no idea. Maybe she thinks I'm in bed with the family and would blow the whistle on the two of them. I just don't know."

"Do you think there might have been another man in the apartment?" Hank said.

"Another man?"

"Sure. If Suzie were two-timing Phillip, you'd be the worst person in the world to discover it."

I mulled it over. Another man. Someone who had to be hurried out the back door, pulling at his pants and yanking his zipper, before the phobia therapist saw the infidelity and wised Phillip up. It was possible. For Suzie Wong, poised to marry the heir to the Chesterton fortune, any dalliance could prove to be a very, very expensive indiscretion.

"I don't know," I said. "All I want right now is to find Phillip's file."

The file wasn't there, which pissed me off because I knew it *was* there. Somewhere. I slid shut the final drawer on the final cabinet and let myself fall back on my butt, and there I sat in the middle of the office, surrounded by the debris of my disorderly life. "That's it!" I said. "Tonight's the night!"

"For what?"

"I roll up my sleeves and tackle this goddamn mess once and for all."

Hank smiled benevolently. "By my unofficial count that makes twenty-three goddamn-once-and-for-alls this year."

"Tonight it happens."

The phone in the dining room rang. Hank signaled for me to stay where I was and headed down the hall. Then he was back, ducking his head into the office. "It's Molly."

I pushed myself up and wandered down the hallway with Hank right behind me.

"Where've you been?" she said.

"Long story."

"Good. That means we won't be short of dinner conversation tonight."

I sighed, shifted the receiver to my other ear. "Can't make it tonight, Molly. How about tomorrow?"

"Tomorrow's impossible for me," she said. "What's the problem tonight?"

"My office needs straightening up."

There was a long pause on Molly's end. "I'll pretend I didn't just hear you say that," she said. "Comb your hair and get over here. I'm fixing my top secret recipe for chicken Marengo. Got a fire in the fireplace. Eggnog with spiced rum ..."

Hank was watching me carefully, a little smile on his face. I cleared my throat and reiterated to Molly in a firm voice that I *had* to get my office organized. I'd been putting it off and putting it off and it simply couldn't be put off any longer. To postpone yet again would be to dash the last remaining bit of self-respect I had left. I'd be unfit for any decent human endeavor. Marriage. Personal fulfillment. The fathering of children. With all of that gone there would be nothing left for me except a career in politics, and for Quinn Parker the campaign trail held no thrills. Hank sat on the arm of the armchair and gave me a thumbs-up.

Molly listened, bemused, till I finished. Then she cleared her throat and dug deeper into her bait box. It was a shame about my cluttered office, she said, because the evening wasn't going to be *only* food and drink. There would be witty conversation, offbeat humor, and steamy carnal pleasures. Or steamy conversation, witty humor, and offbeat carnal pleasures. Or offbeat conversation, steamy ... well, I got the idea. Adjectives and nouns

combined in the most wondrous ways, and she was in an accom-
modating mood.

"Not fair," I said.

"*All's* fair in love and war," she said. "Especially when I've
already marinated the chicken."

"What time," I said.

"Eggnog starts flowing at five o'clock. See you then."

She hung up and I hung up, and Hank sat on the arm of the
living-room armchair, looking down into his wine.

"What are you doing?" I said.

"Listening."

"Listening to what?"

"Whether the sound of resistance collapsing in an almost-
empty apartment makes any noise," Hank said. "It's called the
Zen of Capitulation."

"Her daughter's spending the holidays with her father," I
explained. "Molly's lonely and she doesn't have free time like this
very often."

Hank shrugged. If I was comfortable with such weasely,
spineless behavior, then who was he to comment? Instead he
held the glass of wine up to the light and swirled it again and
watched it some more.

"That's a glass of wine, Hank. Not an ant farm. Molly needs to
know about Phillip anyway."

"What for?"

"She was the one who hired him at the De Young. When he
doesn't show up for work she's going to start to wonder."

"Wait a second. Molly *hired* Phillip?"

"Back in September. Phillip felt he was strong enough to try a
part-time job and I asked Molly to give him a shot. She went out
on a limb for me and it worked out." I glanced at my watch. "I've
got to get ready."

"Yep," Hank said, putting down his wine. "Me, too."

"What for?"

"Remember last month when you told me to sign up for adult
education?"

"I did?"

"So I could meet women ...?"

"Oh, yeah."

"Well, I took your advice. Beginning tonight, I'm a student again."

"No kidding?"

Hank nodded. "The sessions have been going on for a month, but they took my money anyway and said I could jump in."

"What are you taking?"

Hank held up three fingers. "Comedy in Film. Human Sexuality. History of Norwegian Music."

"Pretty grueling workload," I said. "And you with neither slide rule nor computer."

"What's that supposed to mean?"

"Sounds to me like you're trying to maximize the possibility of meeting Nordic bombshells who like sex and laughter."

"I thought that was the whole point."

Hank followed me to my bedroom and sat on the end of the bed while I changed my clothes. Vanessa had told him the story of how wine was discovered, and he related the details to me while I pulled on pants and shirt. It involved a king in ancient Persia who loved grapes, but someone in the palace kept stealing them. So the king figured if he put the grapes in a jar labeled "poison" nobody would touch them. The king spent so much time worrying about his grapes that he started to neglect the women in his harem. One of the women got depressed and decided to kill herself. She went rummaging through the royal closet, looking for a weapon, and stumbled on the jar. The king had forgotten about the stash of grapes, and over time they'd fermented. The woman said her good-byes to the world and drank the poison. When it didn't kill her she drank some more, and when that didn't kill her she drank even more, and finally ended up polishing the thing off. The wine made her feel so good she decided life was worth living after all. Not only that, she wised the king up and they fermented another batch, and she took him out back and shared some with him. The woman wasn't neglected anymore.

We both agreed it was a good story, but couldn't agree on the moral. Hank said the moral was simple: Don't neglect your harem. I said his brain had been twisted by three months of celibacy, and that the *real* lesson of the story was that just because a jar is labeled "poison," don't be afraid to drink. Hank said I had no future as a school nurse and withdrew into his room. I grabbed a jacket from the closet and headed down the stairs.

Molly's apartment was on Cole Street in the Outer Haight, formerly one of the great old flophouse neighborhoods of San Francisco that had in recent years fallen victim to the mixed blessing of "restoration." In my heart of hearts I knew it was fine, admirable, and civic as hell that citizens of a city wanted to roll up their sleeves and refurbish decaying buildings to their former splendor. But this sensation was inextricably tied up with a wariness of people with eager faces and paint brushes and sandpaper. You might as well stencil "Triple the Rent" across their well-intentioned foreheads, and before you know it you have a city filled with one kind of people: those who can afford to pay triple the rent.

Molly lived on the bottom floor of a pointy, turreted, three-story Victorian. There was a front porch with a swing and a backyard with a garden. I parked across the street in the gathering winter twilight and sat there awhile. Molly's living-room window was bright behind the pulled curtains, and I could almost feel the warmth of the fireplace clear out into the street.

I'd met Molly Dexter seven years earlier when we were both working for ExecuClimb, a consulting firm with offices in downtown San Francisco. It was a small, flashy little company that played perfectly into most people's notion of how flaky, indulgent Californians made their hot-tub money. The idea behind ExecuClimb was that top corporate executives were just little boys and girls who grew up to be important men and women but would never realize the full extent of their capabilities unless they crawled back through time and got reacquainted with the child within. For a stiff fee, ExecuClimb would haul out the long-discarded toy box and reconnect these power brokers of business and finance with their lost childhoods. Gag-making, but at the time I was stone broke and desperately needed a job. I sent in a résumé, and before I could change my mind I was hired as one of ExecuClimb's consultants.

Molly joined the company two weeks later. She had just graduated from Berkeley with her BA in art history, and given the torrent of sensational jobs available to art history majors, she was hired as the new ExecuClimb receptionist.

Molly Dexter made quite an impact. Twenty-two years old, tall and robust and brimming with energy, she had an exuberant, all-over-the-place pile of blue-black hair; small, upturned nose; and large oval eyes that were almost too blue. A wild, exaggerated, Caribbean blue, as though filled in by an overzealous child who had chosen the most outlandish color in the crayon box. She had great long legs and a saucy, hands-on-hips attitude, and to watch her sweep across the office in the direction of the water cooler was to bring ExecuClimb's productivity to a temporary standstill. Desire hung, prehensile, from the edge of every male employee's desk.

My work space was up near the front and I had a chance to watch as one by one ExecuClimb's male contingent got up the courage to adjust their ties, approach her station, and take their best shots. Whenever this happened Molly would push herself away from the desk, lean back in her swivel chair, and squint up at the man in question as if to bring the bullshit more clearly into focus. But it was all done with a smile, no hard feelings, and she gracefully sent each home-run candidate trudging back to the dugout with Strike Three! ringing in his ears.

Fortunately I was involved at the time and was thus spared the temptation to add my name to the list of men who had tumbled in the dust. Molly and I just smiled and exchanged cautious hellos and that was it. But we also detected in each other's eyes the heretical glint of an ExecuClimb nonbeliever, and as time went on we began to share lunch hours and coffee breaks.

I found another job in six months but continued to keep in touch with Molly after I left. She hung in there with ExecuClimb for another year, but then budgets all across the city were cut, and fiscally conscious, stressed executives decided to hell with the child within and went back to handling their anxiety in the good old-fashioned way: chewing out underlings and having three-martini lunches. ExecuClimb cut their own staff by half, then by half again, then finally closed their doors for good. A touchy-feely comet streaking across San Francisco's trendy corporate skies, doomed to flame and fall and become, ironically, a kind of neglected toy itself.

Molly spent her new time as an unemployed person by falling in love, getting married, and having a baby. Her husband, Noel, was an insurance executive in Oakland and had plenty of money, so the financial pressure was off. In between bottles and diapers, Molly dusted off her BA and managed to wangle volunteer work at both the De Young and the Legion of Honor. She sufficiently impressed enough people that when an assistant curator job at the De Young came open, it was offered to her. She jumped at it.

Our respective lives grew more complicated, and visits dwindled to the standard three or four get-togethers a year. Christmas and New Year's parties, Super Bowl festivities, Fourth of July barbecues. As her marriage worsened and finally collapsed, Molly drifted farther and farther from the dynamic woman who'd first burst into the sterile, self-important world of ExecuClimb and shook things up. At parties she would find a corner to sit in, chat politely with those who bothered to seek her out, then leave early.

It was only in the past year that Molly seemed to be recapturing some of what she had lost. She divorced Noel, fought for and was awarded primary custody of her daughter, Crystal, and began to see that when one's world collapses there are other worlds that rise up to take its place. Better worlds, usually.

I walked across the street and rang the doorbell, and Molly answered immediately. She was wearing tennis shoes, gray sweat pants, and a red 49ers sweater. Her long dark hair was tied up with a rubber band and there were loose strands hanging out at strange angles.

"You shouldn't have dressed up," I said.

She kissed me hard on the lips and pretended to straighten the nonexistent collar of her 49ers sweater. "How's that?"

"Much better."

She kissed me again and I held her as she let her lips drift down to my neck.

"Is the steamy carnal stuff going to start already?" I said.

Molly laughed a soft, throaty laugh. I breathed in the fragrance of her blue-black hair. "Now that you're here I can confess," she said.

"Confess what?"

"I left one small detail out of my sales pitch on the phone today."

"What's that?"

"I'm sure you'll understand. I mean, I *had* to get you over here."

"What detail, Molly?"

She nibbled on my collarbone. "Our steamy, witty, etcetera evening has to be wrapped up by seven o'clock."

She quickly tried to plant another kiss to neutralize me, but I backed away from it. "Seven o'clock?"

"Sorry."

"But that's in two hours!"

"We'll just have to compress the pleasures," Molly soothed. "That's all. Might be kind of fun. There'll be an illicit feel to it. Like you're a businessman about to hurry home to his wife but I'm the woman you really love."

"I'll be hurrying home to Hank Wilkie," I said.

"Pretend he's your wife."

"There are limits to the imagination."

Molly gave up on the kisses, took me by the hand, and led me into the living room while I complained. I asked what was so special about seven o'clock, and she explained that a major exhibit of Tibetan art was due to open at the De Young Museum. As the assistant project supervisor, she had the job of overseeing the dusk-till-dawn uncrating of the exhibit. Simple as that. I protested, but Molly was unbudgeable. That was why she was dressed in her grubbies. An evening of dirt and nails and sawdust lay in front of her.

I can manage a staggeringly good pout when required, but Molly was unimpressed. She told me to put my lower lip back where it belonged and look upon the evening as a challenge.

"After we eat we can make love right here in the living room," she said. "In front of the fireplace."

"On the hardwood floor?"

"I'm all out of bearskin rugs," she said. "Come on, Quinn. Show some spirit. Once Crystal gets back the spontaneous love-making comes to an end."

"How can it be spontaneous when we're already scheduling it?"

"While Crystal is gone," Molly patiently explained, "we'll plan our spontaneity well in advance."

We went through the living room and into the kitchen. All four burners on the stove were going, and it smelled wonderful. My resolve to continue pouting weakened.

"Rum in your eggnog?" she said.

"Make it a double."

I lifted the top off the largest pan and took a deep breath.

"What do you think?" Molly said.

"I'm almost ready to forgive you."

"Chicken Marengo à la Dexter." Molly turned from the refrigerator and handed me my drink.

"What is chicken Marengo?"

"After Napoleon's victory at Marengo, this meal was prepared from what the French soldiers scavenged nearby."

"Scavenged?"

"Uh-huh."

I made a face. "Sounds iffy."

"The spoils of victory," Molly said. "Napoleon liked it so much he had his chef prepare it from then on after every battle. It's a fun dish because every chicken Marengo's a little different."

"Each victory carries different spoils?"

"Exactly," Molly said. "Ran across my recipe this morning and thought of you."

"Guess it's only natural that I would bring Napoleon to mind."

Molly smiled, let her eyes drift down to my waist. "Don't leave yourself open like that, Quinn. A nastier woman than me would have taken a cheap shot."

Molly poured out some rumless eggnog for herself, and we clinked glasses. She looked at my forehead. "Speaking of battles ..."

"You noticed."

"Head bandages have a way of standing out," she said. "Is this part of that long story you mentioned on the phone?"

I nodded.

"Feel like telling me about it?"

"After dinner."

Molly rolled her eyes at the cloak-and-dagger and turned back to fiddle with something on the stove.

We ate in the dining room with linen napkins and the good china and two candles. Dinner at Molly's was usually a scoot-around-the-kitchen affair, with Crystal and her gaggle of six-year-old friends running around and cartoons in the distance and the telephone ringing. But this was nice. This was almost like romance.

Despite being on the clock, we ate a slow, measured dinner. Her chicken Marengo did indeed set a new world indoor record for being unputdownable, and afterward we lingered at the table and drank coffee and talked while the candles burned lower.

"How long is Noel going to have Crystal?" I said.

"Ten days."

"When did he pick her up?"

"Yesterday. Only he didn't exactly pick her up. I drove her over to his place in Oakland."

"I thought it was his turn to do the ferrying about."

Molly sighed. "It was, but he was running late at the office and called to say he was sending over a driver and ... I don't know. I didn't think Crystal should have to start her holiday by having some strange guy from the office driving her over in a strange car."

"It's none of my business," I said, "but—"

"You're right," Molly said. "It's none of your business."

"But if it *were* my business I'd be forced to say that he's jerking you around again."

"Quinn." There was an edge to Molly's voice. "We said we weren't going to argue about this anymore. Just because we're eating Napoleon's favorite meal doesn't mean we have to battle it out."

"You're right," I said. "End of subject."

Noel, Molly's ex-husband, was an ongoing sore point with us. He was charming and handsome, and had grown wealthy at the insurance game. But the same qualities that made him such a success in business made him a failure at home. The ambition. The need to win. He was cruel and manipulative and frighteningly cold at his emotional center. At least that was my knee-jerk assessment. Noel was currently badgering Molly about taking over custody of Crystal. She'd already won one battle in court but he'd found a loophole to challenge her again, and the process was gearing up. He had a legal team that would've cozied up to Hitler, a lot of patience, and great reserves of money with which to wait Molly out. It wouldn't be the first time that a moral truth was starved into submission by an imbalance of cash, and Molly was worried. I kept telling her she should fight fire with fire, and she kept telling me that any perceived nastiness on her part would only erode her position as a responsible, loving mother. We never made any headway on the Noel issue, and we weren't going to tonight.

We cleared the plates, went into the living room, and sat on the rug in front of the fireplace.

"Okay," Molly said. "Dinner's done. Explain the bandage on your head."

I stretched out, propped myself up on one elbow, and gazed into the fire. "You're a big reader, aren't you?"

Molly looked puzzled. "Yes," she said. "I'm a reader. Minored in English literature. Art history major, English lit minor. Relentless practicality all the way down the line. What do my reading habits have to do with your bandaged head?"

"I heard a quote the other day that's supposed to be the opening of a famous novel."

"What's the quote?"

I squinted, trying to remember. "'My father once told me that when you feel like criticizing somebody, just remember that they haven't had the advantages you've had.' Something like that."

"It's from *The Great Gatsby*," Molly said matter-of-factly. "Why?"

I sat up straighter. "Are you sure?"

"Sure I'm sure. Hold on."

Molly pushed herself to her feet and disappeared down the hallway. She came back a few minutes later with a paperback in her hand. She tossed the book into my lap and resumed her stretched-out position in front of the fireplace. "Fitzgerald's one of my favorites. In fact, I've been lobbying at the De Young for a year to have an exhibit with the theme of Paris in the twenties. Not just all the fabulous art, but a kind of multimedia thing with photographs and quotes by Hemingway and Fitzgerald. Maybe even pipe in some music. Stravinsky. Ravel. It'd be wonderful, but the De Young's too stodgy to do it. You say 'multimedia' and they automatically think of basements in Greenwich Village."

I opened up the book and read the opening passage. It was what Leslie McCall had quoted out in front of the Chesterton mansion earlier in the day.

"So what's the big deal about *The Great Gatsby?*" Molly said. "You're acting really strange tonight. Quiet. Ready to skip sex with me so you could tidy up your office. You okay?"

"Something's happened to Phillip."

"Phillip? *Our* Phillip? Phillip Chesterton?"

I nodded. "He's disappeared."

Molly's expression darkened. "Since when?"

"Yesterday."

"What happened?"

"He and his stepfather got into an argument about something and he took off."

We were silent awhile. Then Molly glanced up at my forehead.

I nodded. "The stepfather thinks I know where Phillip is. When I didn't tell him he lost his temper."

Molly pressed me for details, but I feigned ignorance. I saw no reason for her to know about bloodspatter or missing weapons or the mounting tension up on Glenville Road. Not yet, anyway. I downplayed the whole thing, making it sound like a domestic argument that got out of control.

"Poor Phillip," she said.

"He'll be okay."

"Is there something we can do? What about his mother?"

"There's nothing to be done right now," I said. "I wasn't even going to tell you, but I knew you'd start wondering when Phillip didn't show up for work."

Molly turned and looked into the fire. Her mood had sobered significantly. I moved close and reached behind her and removed the rubber band from her hair. The thick black locks fell over her shoulders.

"If memory serves," I said, "we had a spontaneous lovemaking session penciled in for this time slot."

Molly turned from the fire, and a soft smile lit up her face. "We did, didn't we?"

When Molly said we'd have to compress our pleasures, she wasn't kidding. I was soothed, eggnogged, fed, and bedded in record time, the way it might have happened to a dazed, blinking Buster Keaton in one of those hurry-up silent comedies of yesteryear, with ragtime piano banging out musical accompaniment. Despite the rat-a-tat-tat schedule, our lovemaking was particularly nice. The concern about Phillip added to the urgency of her lovemaking, and I even entertained the foolish notion that Molly would say the hell with it. Throw caution to the wind and dally in front of the fireplace till seven-thirty, quarter to eight. But no. True love might be true love, but the De Young Museum was still the place that issued her a paycheck. So at the stroke of six fifty-nine I was kissed, helped into my jacket, and lovingly shown the front door.

I wasn't in the mood to go straight home, so I headed out to the Coronet on Geary and caught a movie, then burned off the remainder of my restless energy nursing a beer out at Leon's in the Sunset District. I listened to the wind blow off the dark Pacific and talked sports with Leon, and at the stroke of eleven I finally got in the van and pointed it home.

My apartment was dark and quiet when I got back. No sound from behind Hank's shut door, not a squawk from Oscar the parrot. Lola the cat came down to greet me on the landing, and I picked her up and carried her quietly down the shadowy hallway.

As I walked along the hall I stopped and nudged open the door of the guest bedroom. Hank was back from school, out cold, face buried in his pillow. An empty bottle of wine lay sideways on the floor next to the bed in authentic skid-row style. Apparently his first night of Adult Education had not produced a consenting female adult in his life. He snorted, adjusted his head on the pillow, and grew still. God only knew what tormented images were churning through that fevered brain. Another nightmare, probably. House burned down, children all gone. Carol dancing the Dance of the Seven Veils in tear-away black lingerie, preparing to take on the national soccer team of Argentina, one by one.

I quietly shut the door and carried Lola with me out to the dining room. There were two messages blinking red on my answering machine. I rinsed and refilled Lola's milk bowl, got a bottle of Dos Equis beer from the refrigerator, then came back out into the living room and pushed the playback button.

"This is Detective Davis calling for Quinn Parker," the voice said. "We found something and you need to be in my office at eleven o'clock tomorrow. That's Friday, eleven A.M. And I don't want to hear how you can't make it, because you're making it or else."

There was a pause, like he was fishing around for newer and better threats, then he hung up. There was a loud click as his message ended, then a beep, and then the second message, which turned out to be nothing. A few seconds of windy silence, then the loud, clumsy, amplified rattle of a phone being returned to its cradle.

I retrieved my beer from the dining-room table and stretched out next to Lola on the kitchen floor, propped up on one elbow, watching her drink. Small pink tongue, little white milk droplets on the tips of her whiskers. They hung there, perfect liquid spheres. She drank, and I watched. Thursday night fascinations.

"I hate that answering machine," I said to her.

Lola paused to look at me, then turned her attention back to the milk.

"Miserable invention. If I was half a man I'd yank the goddamn thing out by its scraggly roots and Frisbee it right out the window."

I drank from my beer, listened to the sounds of cars racing up Van Ness Avenue.

"Yep, Lola," I said, tapping the side of her dish with my bottle of beer. "'Tis the season to be jolly. Molly's ex is putting her through the wringer. Hank and Carol have broken up. Phillip's vanished, Abigail's a wreck, and tomorrow morning I have to deal with Detective Davis. So what do you say?" I tapped her dish again. "Let's you and me drink to all the good news."

Lola glanced up at the sound of the bottle clinking her dish for the second time. Once was once, but twice meant I might keep on doing it, and that would be annoying. We stared at each other for a couple of seconds, and for a moment I halfway thought that in her mysterious, feline intelligence Lola knew exactly what I was saying. Get up off the floor, her expression seemed to say. Quit wasting your time stretched out here on the linoleum telling your problems to the household pet. Detective Davis is one tough SOB, and you're going to need your strength.

I never argue with Lola when she's right. I stood, dumped the rest of my beer down the drain, and went to bed.

= 12 =

Hank was already up and about the next morning. Shaved, showered, shampooed, and cologned. He was straddling one of the dining-room chairs, leafing through the sports section of the *Chronicle*.

"Hey, hey, hey!" he said. "Look who's finally up. Coffee's already made."

I wandered into the kitchen, poured myself a cup, and took a seat across from Hank at the dining-room table.

"You're awfully chipper this morning," I said. "Higher education must agree with you."

Hank just smiled, found an article that interested him, and began reading.

"Which class was it last night?" I said.

"History of Norwegian Music."

I sipped my coffee and watched a tanker slowly inch its way toward the Golden Gate Bridge. The sky was overcast, the bay below the color of asphalt. "There's enough Norwegian music to fill up a semester?"

"Of course there is," Hank said, still reading. "If you weren't so provincial, you'd know that Norwegian music is so vast it has to be broken down into four major categories."

"I'll bite. What are the four major categories of Norwegian music?"

"Grieg, of course."

"Of course."

"Pre-Grieg."

"Naturally."

"Post-Grieg. And reaction to Grieg." Hank read his article. "That's four."

"And did you bribe a seat assignment next to the woman of your dreams?"

Hank grinned a tolerant grin. "Too bad Gunnhilde isn't here. She'd find your attitude amusing. I'll have to tell her about this tonight on our dinner date."

"Gunnhilde?"

"Gunnhilde von Edlund. Of course, it's just plain Hilda to her friends, close associates, and future inexhaustible bedmates."

"You're not serious."

Hank looked up. "About what?"

"You already met someone? First night out of the blocks?"

Hank lightly shrugged. "That old Wilkie magic. Thought we'd do French. Maybe take her to Christophe's over in Sausalito. Of course, you'll have to extend me a small, temporary loan. I'll pay you back. You know I'm good for it."

"Exactly how old is this student?"

"Why?"

"Just curious how far you've sunk. Does she absentmindedly twist strands of hair and look blank when you mention Watergate?"

Hank tsk-tsked and shook his head. "Student? I would never involve myself with a student. Gunnhilde von Edlund is no girl. She's a woman. She's the professor."

"You've got a dinner date with your professor?"

"Might have to borrow your good suit, too."

My curiosity was high, but time was getting on and Detective Davis was waiting for me up in Napa. I showered and dressed and left Hank sitting there at the table, basking in the glow of his unexpected success.

Detective Davis had his office in a white, two-story Spanish-style building a couple of blocks off Napa's main plaza. It had a red tile roof and colorful, flower-bearing vines of purple and yellow that snaked and curled and clung to the walls. The place had a manicured, showcase feel that reminded me of the boyhood homes of U.S. presidents, well-maintained by the chamber of commerce, with guided tours and brochures for tourists.

The woman working the reception desk was not the type to put the nervous at ease. She was a thick, grizzled, thirty-years-in-the-trenches buzzard with copper-colored, Brillo Pad hair and a face like a baseball mitt. She was just sitting at her desk, staring straight ahead, both hands out flat on the desk, palms down. I told her who I was, and she jabbed a stubby finger at an intercom panel on her desk and lowered her face to the speaker.

"Quinn Parker to see you."

The voice came right back. "Send him in."

The woman pointed at a hallway that led off to the left. "Last door on the right."

I thanked her, but she didn't say I was welcome. She simply resumed her motionless, palms down, straight-ahead pose.

The door to Davis's office was open, and I stepped in. It was a small rectangular room, shadowy, with the cool, pleasant mustiness of old adobe. Shades were drawn on both windows. An illustrated Ducks Unlimited calendar hung on the wall behind the desk. Men with rifles pointed skyward, with three doomed, retreating ducks flapping their wings like hell. The calendar wasn't a critical item in the office. It was an autumn scene, still touting October.

Detective Davis was sitting behind a gray metal desk, head bent to the task of putting his signature at the bottom of a pile of papers. He wore a short-sleeved shirt, and the veins in his arms were pronounced. His complexion in the filtered morning light wasn't great. Chalky, washed-out. A slate-gray, flesh-and-blood extension of the desk itself. He scribbled, went to the next page, scribbled, went to the next page. I passed the time counting the nick marks on his skull.

"Have a seat, Parker," he said at last.

I pulled up a chair, and Davis signed the final paper with a flourish and shoved the stack to the side. He leaned back in his swivel chair and looked at me for the first time.

"Didn't know if you were going to show."

"I got your message last night," I said.

"Should've called me and confirmed."

"It was late."

"Should've called me anyway." Davis leaned forward and started drumming his fingers on the desk. They were blunt, blocked-off fingers, shaped by years of desk-drumming. "Today your birthday, Parker?" he said.

"My what?"

"Your birthday?"

"No," I said. "It's not my birthday."

"Let's pretend it is anyway," Davis said, "because I already went ahead and got you a present."

"What sort of present?"

"The best present I could ever give you, that's what," Davis said. "What I'm going to do is pretend that you and me haven't even met before. We didn't see blood on a wall anywhere. That friend of yours didn't mouth off to me. We didn't talk about Phillip. Nothing. Starting right this moment you got a clean bill of health. That's your present."

"Why do I need a present like that?" I said.

"Because yesterday afternoon we found Frank Matson's car," Davis said.

"Where?"

"Stashed down in a ditch about a half-mile from the murder scene. No body, but there was blood all over the trunk and fender. Lab reports came back, and the blood from the wall and the blood from the trunk match. B negative, both. That means Frank Matson's case is now officially a homicide, and you're up to your neck in it."

"Because I called it in?"

"No," Davis said. He leaned forward and spread his hands out on his desk, wide, the way schoolchildren do when tracing fingers and thumbs. "Not because you called it in. Because of this bullshit story of yours about following Frank out to the mobile home in the middle of the goddamn night." Davis paused. "Birthdays only come around once a year, so don't fuck with me on this. I want to know exactly what happened the night he left the house."

"We've covered this ground before," I said.

Davis took his splayed hands off the desk and leaned back in his chair. My birthday present had been withdrawn. "Clamming up like this isn't going to make it any easier on Phillip. It's going to make it *worse*."

"Phillip didn't kill Frank Matson."

"He didn't?"

"No."

"Then who did?"

"I don't know," I said, "but Phillip didn't. He's not capable of murdering a person in cold blood."

Davis smiled condescendingly. "Killers are *never* capable of killing anybody, Parker. Until they do it, of course."

"What motive did Phillip have to kill his stepfather?" I said.

"Motive?" Davis half-laughed, incredulous. "Motive is the least of my problems! Chesterton Vineyards has about thirty million motives. They're green and have George Washington's picture on the front."

"Phillip has his own trust fund," I said. "A sizable one. He doesn't need to kill for money."

Davis picked up a paper clip and began playing with it, bending the prongs out. "I read a poll once, Parker. They asked a bunch of people how much money it'd take before they'd kill

someone. Not one person would do it for five bucks. For a thousand bucks a few people kicked in. For a hundred thousand
bucks a whole lot more people joined the party. Jack that offer
up to a cool million and I bet you'd start looking at the mailman
funny. Chesterton Vineyards is worth thirty or forty million dollars, and with Frank Matson gone all of it funnels straight over to
Phillip. Half the goddamn PTA'd sharpen their carving knives for
that kind of cash."

I didn't say anything. Davis got all the prongs bent out and
tossed the paper clip away. "You know what's bothering me,
Parker?"

"What?"

"It's crazy, but I can't get it out of my head. The mailbox out
at the mobile home."

"What about it?"

"You said you looked at the mail, right? Saw Frank's name on
the envelopes?"

I nodded.

Davis shook his head. "When I took a look there were some
dead spiders sitting on top of the stack. How'd you look at the
mail and not move those spiders?"

"You're very observant. I moved the spiders and then put
them back."

"Put them back?" Davis said.

"That's right."

"What'd you do that for?"

"I don't know why I did it," I said. "We all do strange things
from time to time. You just sat there and ruined a perfectly good
paper clip."

Davis smiled. If I hadn't known better, I would have said he
looked at me with admiration. The begrudging admiration a parent might feel for the black-sheep child who at least shows more
spunk and persistence than the rest of his siblings.

"The problem with the mailbox thing is that it doesn't make
me trust you so much," he said. "Makes me think you're covering
your tracks."

"Then why did I say anything about the mail to begin with?"

Davis shrugged. "I don't know. Maybe so you'd look helpful and trustworthy. I don't have a clue what you're about at all, Parker."

"We're not getting anywhere this way," I said. "Since you don't believe my version of events, why don't you tell me yours?"

Davis pointed at himself. "You want *my* opinion?"

"Why not?"

"Okay," Davis said. "Here it comes. Some of this might ring a bell, so listen up."

Davis stood and went over to one of the windows and opened the shades a touch to let in some sunlight.

"Phillip and Frank had an argument over lunch earlier in the day," he said. "Phillip stormed out and Frank got worried. He called you up to the house because he figured you were Phillip's therapist and knew where the kid went. You didn't tell him anything and went back home. Then late that same night he gets a phone call from Phillip. Phillip tells him to meet him at the mobile home and when Frank gets there, Phillip blows him away. He drives the body somewhere, dumps it, brings the Corvette back because he has to drive his own car away from the murder scene. When things calm down Phillip can't believe what he's done and calls you because you're his therapist and everything'll be confidential. So you drive out to the mobile home first thing next morning and see that Phillip was telling the truth. Since you're such a loyal son of a bitch you blow smoke in my face for a while until Phillip can get his story together and arrange for a good lawyer." Davis stopped and looked at me. "How am I doing so far?"

"How did you know about Matson's late-night phone call?" I said.

"Just got back from a visit with Abigail Chesterton, that's how."

"Why do you assume it was Phillip?"

"Butler said the voice was strange." Davis shrugged. "Couldn't even tell if it was a man or a woman."

"So?"

"So it means one of two things. The butler *did* know who was calling but didn't tell me because he was trying to protect the caller. That'd be Phillip. Or the voice wasn't normal because it was being disguised. Why the hell disguise your voice unless you think somebody might recognize it, and there's a real short list of people who had the Chesterton unlisted phone number *and* whose voice would be recognized by the family servant. That'd be Phillip, too."

"Did Abigail tell you Frank took a gun from his study before heading out?"

Davis nodded. "A .38 caliber revolver. I've fired the gun myself."

"Don't you think a man who grabs a gun and heads out into the night might be intending to use it on somebody? Who's to say Frank Matson wasn't on his way to kill somebody, not to be killed?"

"A man also grabs a gun when he thinks he might be in danger," Davis said. "Maybe Frank went to see if the gun was still there, and it wasn't. Phillip knew where that gun was, too. We can 'maybe' this thing to death, Parker. The blood on the wall was B negative. Frank Matson's blood type."

"It was Phillip's type, too," I said.

That stopped him. Davis stood very still. The smirk that had been such an important part of his personality for the past fifteen minutes went flat. He watched me very closely. "What are you talking about?"

"Phillip and Frank had the same blood type. Both were B negative."

"I can check that out in ten minutes."

"Abigail told me. I wouldn't mind having it confirmed myself."

Davis glared at me. "Last chance, Parker. Where's Phillip Chesterton?"

"No idea."

Davis waited a second, then he pointed his bony head at the door. "Beat it. I'm sick of looking at you."

That was all the coaxing I needed. I stood, put the chair back where it had been, and went to the door. My hand was on the doorknob when Davis barked out for me to hold it a goddamn second.

"Something I forgot to ask you about, Parker," he said, moving out from behind the desk and up to where I stood at the door. "What did you and Frank talk about out there on the terrace?"

"Frank wanted to know how to find Phillip."

"Nothing else?"

"Nothing else."

"What about Suzie Wong?"

I relaxed my grip on the doorknob.

"Didn't think I knew about her, did you?" Davis said. "Frank filled me in. Called me that afternoon when he was trying to track down Phillip. Asked me if I could help him locate a woman named Suzie Wong."

"Have any luck?"

Davis shook his head. "No. But I'm betting you did. Phillip told you all about her."

"Whether he did or didn't doesn't make any difference," I said. "What goes on during therapy is strictly confidential."

I knew the word "confidential" would bring the color to Davis's face, and he didn't disappoint.

Davis said, "According to the butler, you and Frank tossed some punches out there on the patio."

"Frank was drunk. He lost his temper."

"Rumor is you stretched him out pretty good with a hook to the jaw."

"To the stomach, and it was in self-defense."

"Stomach?"

"That's right."

Davis squinted as though confused, rubbed his lower lip. "You mean like this?"

Before I could react Davis twisted his body to the side, planted his feet, and slammed his right fist hard into my abdomen. My legs went numb and I fell to my knees. I tried to breathe, but couldn't.

Davis knelt beside me and angled his face so he could look into my eyes. "I don't think you appreciate what a good friend Frank Matson was to me," he said. "Guy survives five years in a Vietcong prison camp, five fucking years in a bamboo cage, for what? To come back here and have some fucked-up stepson put a bullet in his head?" Davis moved his face even closer. "And if you think, Parker, that I'm going to sit here now and listen to wacko Phillip's goddamn *phobia* therapist tell me about client privilege, you better think again. You're a lying son of a bitch and I'm going to fry your ass just as bad as I'm going to fry Phillip's when I find him."

Davis finished his speech and stood up. All I could see were his shoes. His voice came from way up in the direction of the ceiling. "That punch was from Frank, by the way. He owed you one."

The shoes walked away and the door opened and closed, and I was alone in the room. I rolled over onto my side and lay there for a couple of minutes, in the fetal position, taking shallow breaths of gradually diminishing pain. After a while I was able to pull myself to my feet, brush off my clothes, and go out into the hall.

No Davis. No undue alarm. It was as though nothing out of the ordinary had transpired. The hatchet-faced receptionist just sat behind her desk and watched me exit into the bright sunny skies of the wine country.

= 13 =

A blue BMW convertible was parked along the curb right in front of the sheriff's building. Leslie McCall was sitting behind the wheel. He had a smile on his face as I approached.

"You're walking a tad gingerly this morning, Quinn," he said.

"I'm making progress. Only a few minutes ago I was crawling gingerly."

Leslie laughed. "Congratulations. You've just become a part of the proud tradition of people limping out of meetings with Detective Davis."

I stood next to the car and looked down into Leslie's face. "How did you know I was here?"

"No secrets in this town. Come on. Hop in and I'll buy you lunch."

I went around to the other side and eased in beside him, and Leslie fired up the engine and pulled away. "How did you like Davis's secretary?" he said.

"Sparkling personality."

Leslie nodded. "Rumor is she supplements her income by working weekends guarding the gates of hell."

"How can she tell which job is which?"

Leslie laughed and kept driving. We turned right at the first intersection and headed into the heart of town, circling the main plaza once and then taking the main road going east. Leslie wore sunglasses and was dressed in beige from top to bottom, like a southern gentleman. His silver hair glinted in the sunshine. "You in a hurry?" he said.

"Not particularly."

"Good. There's some minor crisis at the office I need to take care of first, then I thought we could go out to my winery and eat there, at the house. What do you say?"

"Sounds good."

The *Napa Observer* occupied three small rooms in an L-shaped office complex on the outskirts of town. We parked in a little slot that said "Mr. McCall," and I followed Leslie through the door. It smelled of ink and newsprint, just like a newspaper office should. Two older women were leaning over some documents that were spread out on a drafting table, and they called Leslie over immediately.

"Deadlines," he muttered. He pointed to a room that led off to the right. "You can go in there and look around if you want, Quinn. This shouldn't take more than ten or fifteen minutes."

I went into the room Leslie indicated while he huddled with the two women. An empty desk and a layout table were pushed up close to the shuttered windows, and beyond them oversized bookshelves had been built into the walls. The shelves were filled to capacity with dusty bound copies of old editions of the *Napa Observer,* one month's worth of newspapers per binder. I selected a volume from the middle of the wall and took a look.

The *Napa Observer* was a smallish paper, about the size of a large coffee-shop menu and never more than thirty or forty pages. Half the newspaper was devoted to classified ads. I put the volume back and moved down the wall to the summer of 1987. Darryl Chesterton had died in July or August, I couldn't remember which. I took down the binders for both months and sat on a couch near the window and flipped through until I found it.

August 5, 1987. The headlines were in the kind of large black print generally reserved for assassinations or the outbreak of war. "Plane Crash Claims Darryl Chesterton!" The story took up the entire front page, and there was a photo of Darryl at the bottom left. I'd never seen his picture before and was expecting something dignified, conservative. A chairman of the board type. But this man looked just the opposite. He had the face of a guy who might have put frogs in teachers' desks and instigated panty raids during summer camp. Boyish. Mischievous. A full head of light, wavy hair, narrow face, and sparkling eyes.

I sat for fifteen minutes with the binder on my lap and read the coverage of Darryl's death. Phillip and I had never discussed details of the tragedy, and I was curious. The accident was as freakish as an accident could be. Somehow the wrong type of gas had been put into the underground tank out on Chesterton's property, and when Darryl fueled up that afternoon in August he unwittingly loaded his single-engine Cessna with high-octane jet fuel. The plane reached an altitude of five hundred feet, sputtered, and came straight down.

There was little mention of Phillip or Abigail, which made sense. Leslie McCall as editor would have done his best to keep them out of the glare of publicity. The funeral on August 10 had a photo of the mourners at graveside. Abigail in black, a teenage Phillip standing next to her with his chin down and his hands clasped at his waist.

"Ready to go?"

It was Leslie, sticking his head in the room. I put the binder back in its spot and followed Leslie out to the main room. The two women had apparently left for lunch and we were alone. He went from door to door, making sure they were locked.

"Crisis averted?" I said.

"Late-breaking news," Leslie said, nodding at the red-penciled layout sheet he'd been working on with the two women. "When you asked yesterday about people who wanted to kill Frank Matson, I forgot to mention the Pomo Indians."

"Indians?"

"They have a reservation up here, and they want to put in a bingo parlor. It's a fiasco, but big news. This morning the tribe got the go-ahead to start laying concrete. The whole county's up in arms." Leslie exhaled and shook his head. "Sad, isn't it? I'm for Native American rights as much as the next guy, but nobody wants to see five hundred diesel-spewing buses come up here every week and spit out a bunch of inner-city bingo fanatics. Anyway ... a few weeks ago Frank made some typical Frank comment about keeping them in their teepees. Chief of the tribe demanded an apology, but nothing came of it."

Leslie secured a window that had been left open, slapped his hands free of dirt, and nodded. "Done! Now let's get outta here!"

We went out the front door, and Leslie took out his keychain and flipped through the keys.

"How *did* you know I was up here today?" I said.

"Called your apartment," Leslie said. "Talked with your friend Hank. Said Davis had a surprise for you."

I nodded. "They found Frank Matson's car a half-mile from the murder scene with blood all over the trunk. Blood type matches Frank's."

"I know," Leslie said. He found the key he wanted and locked the door, yanked it to be sure, then put the keys away. "Usually Davis stonewalls me about any kind of police business, but this he leaked as fast as he could."

"Why?"

"He wants everybody to know about it. Get the media to play up the fugitive stepson angle right away." Leslie squinted into the bright sunshine, fumbled around his shirt pocket for his sunglasses. "I don't know, Quinn. Looks bad for Phillip."

"I didn't know Davis and Matson were such good friends," I said. "Davis is really taking this personally."

Leslie shrugged. "I'd be friends with Frank Matson too if he cut me a big fat check every month."

I watched Leslie adjust his sunglasses. "Davis is on Frank's payroll?"

"Not officially," Leslie said. "No 1099 tax forms changing

hands. But, yes. Davis is most definitely riding the Matson gravy train."

"In exchange for what?"

"Favors. Perks."

"For instance?"

"For instance if Frank didn't like something I was writing in the newspaper, I'd have to watch out for Davis. Keep both feet in the crosswalk. Make sure my parking meter always had plenty of quarters. But messing with me was just minor harassment. What Frank wanted was for Davis to use his influence in bigger areas. Labor problems. When the immigration people did their periodic rousting of illegal aliens, Chesterton Vineyards was always remarkably spared. The other wineries out here would lose a third of their workers right before harvest and have to start scrambling like mad, but good old Frank always had a stable work force."

"How long has this been going on?"

"How long?" Leslie finally got his sunglasses on the way he wanted, and together we strolled over to his car. "It's been going on for about five years, Quinn. It's been going on ever since Frank Matson murdered Darryl Chesterton."

=14=

N ot that I have any proof," Leslie said. We were out on the main freeway headed south, going back in the general direction of Glenville Road. "But Frank killed Darryl. He killed him just as sure as we're sitting here now talking about it."

"I was reading about it in your newspaper just now."

"I know you were," Leslie said. "Over two hundred binders are on that wall, and August 1987 is the one I have memorized. I could pick it off the shelf blindfolded."

"How in the world could wrong fuel get into his tank?"

"Simple," Leslie said. "Darryl had his own pumps out on the property and bought his fuel from a local jobber. The kid driving the fuel truck came out and dispensed gas from the wrong tank in the truck. Innocent mistake."

"Weren't the police suspicious?"

"There was an investigation, sure, but what was there to investigate?" Leslie turned to face me as he talked. We were up to speed now, but his silver hair seemed lacquered to his head. Not a single strand fluttered in the sixty-mile-per-hour swirl of the convertible. "The kid made a terrible mistake and that was that. Pulled out hose number one instead of hose number two. Afterward there was the typical outcry for safety features to prevent that sort of thing from happening again. You know how it goes. The kid was just a teenager. Local boy, high schooler on a summer job. The insurance company didn't like the smell of it either, believe me. But they started getting bad press about badgering the grief-stricken kid so they tossed in the towel and paid up. Two and a half million."

"So why automatically murder?" I said. "Why couldn't it have simply been an accident like the kid said? Sounds plausible enough to me."

"The *im*plausible stuff happened later," Leslie said. "Frank Matson came on the scene almost immediately. He married Abby before Darryl's corpse had a chance to cool and started going to work at Chesterton Vineyards as if he had that two and a half mil already earmarked for upgrades and renovations. And just for the hell of it I kept tabs on the anguished high-school kid."

"His standard of living improve?"

Leslie gave me a knowing smile. "The boy was so torn up he moved down to Santa Cruz and comforted himself with a new Trans-Am and a condo on the beach. I turned over all the cushions on all the couches, but couldn't see where he suddenly got cash like that."

Leslie took the turnoff after the Glenville Road exit and we began weaving through the rolling hills. They didn't have anything as bourgeois as a four-lane highway in this neck of the woods. The streets were imported chunk by chunk from Europe—winding, weaving, perfect for a car like this, top down, sun on your forehead.

We drove in windy silence for another ten minutes until Leslie suddenly downshifted and wheeled the BMW sharply off the main road and into the empty parking lot of a small winery. A sign identified the winery as Shrader-Cox Vineyards. Leslie parked and cut the engine.

"This is it," he said. "My small slice of heaven."

We got out and went around to the side of a Tyrolean-style building to the tasting room entrance. Like a lot of small wineries in the area, Shrader-Cox felt more like someone's indulgent hobby than a serious business endeavor, and the tasting room reflected this attitude. Swiss chalet motif, paintings on the wall, shelves filled with books, ferns in the corners. A glass counter ran along the length of wall to the left, and beneath the glass was an antique corkscrew collection. To the right was a refrigerated display case filled with gourmet cheeses, imported crackers, and exotic bottled seasonings. Five or six oak barrels were placed in the center of the room, functioning as tables to handle the anticipated overflow of wine tasters. But crowd control wasn't a problem on this day. I suspected crowd control wasn't a problem any day. Shrader-Cox wasn't doing much business.

Leslie spoke to a bored, sullen-looking man who was working behind the counter and gumming a half-smoked cigarette. The man yawned and nodded and I followed Leslie back out to the car.

"I've told him not to smoke on the job," Leslie said. "Pisses me off."

We angled around the building and came to a stop in front of a wooden gate. Leslie got out and swung the gate open. There was a padlock hooked onto a chain, but it was old and rusted and only there for show. Then he climbed back in the BMW and we started down a narrow, one-lane gravel road.

The road skirted the uneven base of a steep hill that rose and sloped away to the left. To the right were vineyards, horses grazing in green meadows, and a pond shining blue and glassy in the middle of an open field.

"New York consortium owns all of this," he said. "Tax haven for a few dozen doctors and dentists. I manage it for them, oversee the winemaking, make sure the hired help gets paid, jack it up with some free publicity in my wine columns. In return I get a rotten salary, free room and board, and the company car." Leslie smiled and gently stroked the dashboard of the BMW. "Things could be worse. The way I see it, they're freezing their asses off commuting to Penn Station and I'm sipping wine in the sunshine. Balances out."

Leslie slowly followed the gravel road another couple of miles. We rounded a bend and a ranch-style home suddenly appeared before us. Solid white, with a white picket fence, some geese wandering around, and wisps of gray smoke drifting from the top of a brick chimney. Around back was a long, narrow swimming pool. The home was surrounded by a grove of enormous, sheltering oaks. A beat-up looking Buick Le Sabre was parked out front, and a Jeep was tucked around the side of the house.

We parked and got out and I saw why the Buick looked beat up. It *was* beat up. The vehicle had been vandalized by someone with time on his hands and energy to burn. The driver's side window completely bashed out. Large cracks in the others. There were long, deliberate scratches running from one end of the automobile to the other. A half-dozen healthy dents pocked the roof, and a misspelled "faggit" had been gouged into the hood. A swastika was scrawled onto the trunk. Leslie and I walked past the car without comment.

The front door opened and Holt Riolo came out onto the porch. He watched us come up the steps, wiping his hands with a towel like some faithful pioneer wife, steadfast and brave even though the hills were known to be filled with Comanches.

"Lunch guest, honey," Leslie announced. "Make room for three."

"Very funny."

Holt and I nodded to each other and the three of us went into the house together.

The living room was surprisingly large, flat, low-ceilinged, with the furniture positioned at odd places in the room. The couches and chairs and tables faced in haphazard directions, like stones in a Japanese rock garden. Props in a play by Beckett.

"Lupe needs to talk to you right away," Holt said.

"Let Grover handle it."

"Grover's not here."

"What you mean he's not here?"

"Just what I said." Holt shrugged. "He's not here."

"Where the hell *is* he?"

"I don't know where the hell he is, Leslie. He's not here. He hasn't been here. All I know is Lupe's got a problem and he has to talk to somebody about it."

Leslie rubbed his eyes. "Did Lupe say what it was about?"

"No. He's out in the east field, waiting for you."

"Come on, Quinn," Leslie said. "Let's take a walk."

We went back out onto the front porch and started walking out into a furrowed vineyard.

"Nothing but problems, this business," he said. "It's as bad as running a newspaper, except you lose money faster."

"Who's Grover?"

"Grover's the guy who's supposed to be handling the problems when I'm doing other things. 'Supervisor,' I think he calls himself. I don't know, Quinn. You get into this originally because you love wine, the tradition, being a part of the noble chain, but you end up getting migraines over the business end of it. You find yourself watching the twenty-four-hour Weather Channel at night instead of enjoying life."

"What got you interested in wine to begin with?"

Leslie thought about it for a while, and as we walked a slow smile tugged at the edges of his mouth. "It wasn't really an 'interest' that was cultivated, Quinn. Not in the traditional sense. It was more like something that came crashing down on me. Like one of those divine calling cards that the old mystics write about."

"The Calling of St. Leslie?"

Leslie grinned. "Exactly. I knew wine was going to be the passion of my life the moment Signora Capelli sent me down into the large vat with the pitchfork."

"Back up. Who sent you where? With what?"

"I went to Europe between my sophomore and junior years in college," Leslie said. "This was before my family cut me off. I went to learn Italian, and by sheer chance I ended up living with the Capelli family. They were vintners, not that that made any difference to me. They could've been bricklayers or farmers or bank executives for all I cared. I was in Italy to learn Italian, and spent all my time in my room working on irregular verbs. Until Signora Capelli presented me with the pitchfork, that is."

"To do what?"

"During the harvest the destemmed grapes are put in this huge vat. There's a little door at the bottom that can be opened to let the grapes feed out of the vat and into a press. But at some point the force of gravity stops and then you have to go down there and start shoveling the last of the grapes manually toward the opening with a pitchfork. Sounds easy enough, but you can't believe the sensation. The carbon dioxide is so powerful you have to breathe through a tube. There's a brick at the bottom of the vat so you know when you've shoveled all the way. To be handed the pitchfork by Signora Capelli was tantamount to being adopted into the family. When I finally climbed back out, gasping for air, half the village was standing there cheering. Sisters, uncles, cousins, friends, the local butcher. I still have the brick from that vat. The family gave it to me as a memento."

We kept walking through the rows of grapeless, wintry vines. A brown-skinned man was up ahead, bent over some irrigation piping.

"Okay," Leslie said. "There's Lupe. Hold on a second while I see what the big problem is."

I waited while Leslie went on to have his conference. There was a pleasant, smoky quality to the cool air. Silence. Calm. A curious sensuality to the gently rolling hills. No wonder everybody wants to retire early and come here to do this. No wonder there was a worldwide wine glut. No wonder everybody was going broke.

Leslie was back in five minutes, shaking his head. "That's that."

"Nothing serious?"

"No. Dirt gets in the irrigation system sometimes and clogs the pipes. This is terrible soil, you know. Gritty and loose. Feel it."

I knelt down and sifted some of the dirt through my hand. It had a pebbly, granulated feel.

"See what I mean?" Leslie said.

"Sure do."

"The worst soil produces the best wines," Leslie said. "Just another of the many ironies of this business."

"Why's that?"

"Large grain makes for good draining. Full of minerals. What we're standing on here used to be part of one of the finest wineries in the whole valley. LaGue Brothers. Chardonnays so wonderful they used to be served at the White House during the Carter years. Anwar Sadat drank wine from this field. Brezhnev. Billy Carter himself probably knocked off a case or two and peed it in the Rose Garden."

"What happened?"

"Two years ago they bellied-up and had to close shop. Auctioned off the tanks and barrels. Dumped the unbottled vintage into the ground as fertilizer. The New York group I work for bought this section, but that was all. The rest of the vineyards were plowed under, and now it's a golf course. Robert Louis Stevenson called the wine of this region 'bottled poetry.' Climb the top of that ridge and you'll see the new legacy. Sand traps. Ball-washing machines."

"If LaGue Brothers was so successful," I said, "how did it go out of business?"

Leslie smiled a tight, bitter smile. "The square tomato put LaGue Brothers out of business, Quinn."

"The what?"

We turned and began to walk back in the direction of the house. "A few years ago I took a trip to Mexico," Leslie said, "and I saw this strange-looking red vegetable in the open-air market. Imagine my shock when I found out it was a tomato. My companion explained that having lived in the United States all my life, I'd never really seen an authentic tomato before. In this country we were dealing entirely in hybrids. Working toward the square tomato, was the way he put it. Sturdy. Resistant to disease.

Something that in the most wonderful of all possible futures could be stacked like building blocks in uniform boxes. Of course, in pursuit of the square tomato we lose both flavor and distinction. The square tomato syndrome applies to the wine industry too, Quinn. Reduce wine to something functional, unexceptional. Never great, never bad. Just a product to be shipped out by the truckload with a maximum of efficiency. Frank Matson was at the forefront of this movement. That's why you see some of the fine old wineries going broke."

"But won't there always be a market for fine wines?"

"Sure," Leslie said. "So Chesterton Vineyards and the other big boys fill that premium wine gap themselves by ignoring the appellation system and cranking out labels reading 'vintage' or 'estate bottled' and slapping them on their own unexceptional wines."

"They can do that?"

"Absolutely. The Bureau of Alcohol, Tobacco, and Firearms rumbles once in a while about enforcing the *Appellation Controlée* laws of France, but nothing ever comes of it. Frank Matson was absolutely ruthless with the backroom stuff. He had so many weapons at his disposal."

"What kind of weapons?"

Leslie puffed out his cheeks as though exasperated as to where to begin. "The most recent was scanner data."

"What?"

"You know," Leslie said. "Those bar codes printed on food containers and magazines that the cashier passes over the scanner at the checkout line. Rings up the amount automatically?"

"Sure," I said. "What about them?"

"Most supermarket chains and liquor warehouses in this state won't even stock a wine now if it isn't bar coded. Period. The wine companies that do have bar coding have a great marketing tool to see what sells and what doesn't, and where. Scanner data has taught us a lot of things we didn't know before."

"Such as?"

"Such as to sell more wine you don't lower prices."

"No?"

Leslie shook his head. "Just the opposite. Discounting wine is the *least* efficient method of selling. Heavy promotion with flashy displays is what sells wine. It was scanner data that finally told us this, and the big companies like Gallo and Sebastiani and Chesterton who can afford bar coding learn this stuff first and they don't necessarily share the information with us little guys. I tried for years to get the independent wineries around here to form our own trade union so we could pool resources and bar code our own wines, but it never panned out."

"Why not?"

Leslie shrugged. "Too much turnover. New faces all the time. People come to the wine country, try it. Some stay. Most leave. Usually they paid a small fortune just to buy the land and they're not in the mood to shell out more for marketing tools. Plus a lot of these little boutique wineries you see out here are owned by retired professional people who don't always understand the values of marketing. People like Frank Matson, of course, did everything they could to reinforce this confusion and fear. Sometimes I wonder why I even try, Quinn. Sometimes I wonder what's the point."

The house loomed on the horizon, and we walked the last few minutes in silence. The sun was out, so we ate lunch on the back terrace overlooking the pool. Holt had prepared a kind of beef stew in a large ceramic pot, and Leslie went down to the cellar to get a bottle of wine he'd been saving for a special occasion. We ate and drank and talked.

Holt was curious about my career as a phobia therapist. He'd majored in psychology in college, but nothing had ever come of it. For the past dozen years he'd been running the family feed and grain business in Willits, fifty miles north, but over the summer he'd sold out and was ready to start a new life in the wine country. He said that if I ever ran out of patients, Willits had a whole town full of homophobics in desperate need of therapy. Or prison terms.

"See my car out front?" he said.

I nodded that I had.

"Three guys did that in broad daylight, right out in front of my house. I watched the bastards from the kitchen window. I mean, what was I supposed to do? Go out there and fight three drunks who were armed with screwdrivers and knives?"

"I prefer Holt in one piece," Leslie said, "so I suggested he move down here in more civilized country."

That was fine, but Holt had a premonition that he was soon going to get restless with the passive good life down at the end of Shrader-Cox's gravel road. He was used to working sixty hours a week and swimming two hundred laps a day, and he needed to be more active. Leslie waved a hand at the pool and told Holt he could swim all he wanted, but that didn't wash. Holt wanted to start up his own small business in town. The three of us speculated on the types of businesses a town like Napa needed but didn't have yet. There weren't many, but the few we came up with didn't appeal to Holt. Throughout the course of our lunch, geese wandered up to the table and then wandered away. Holt threw them scraps from his plate. He wasn't happy. There was trouble at home.

I turned to Leslie. "I solved your riddle, by the way."

Leslie looked blank. "What riddle?"

"The quote from the novel. It's from *The Great Gatsby.*"

Leslie smiled. "Well done."

"I can't take credit. I have literate friends."

"How well do you know the novel?" Leslie said.

"Details are sketchy."

Leslie shook his head. "Details aren't important. I'm talking about the themes. Obsession. Vengeance. Long-deferred lust that goes criminal." Leslie cleared his throat, settled back in his chair. "What were you doing, Quinn, in the spring of 1968?"

"Too long ago," I said. "Why?"

"Well, in the spring of 1968 Abigail Lawton—soon to be Chesterton—was a dashing woman in her early thirties. In the spring of 1968 she also fell in love for the first time in her life. The only problem was the guy. He was poor, something of a roughneck, and all the crowbars in the world were not going to pry open the doors that would give him access to the blue-blood world of Abigail Lawton. So they fell briefly together, were torn apart by circumstance and family pressure, and Abby went on shortly thereafter to marry Darryl Chesterton. Picture beginning to clear?"

I nodded. "The roughneck was Frank Matson."

"None other."

"Then what happened?"

"Frank did what men have done since time immemorial when spurned by love," Leslie said. "He went to war. Enlisted in the army and headed off to Vietnam as men before him might have impulsively joined the Foreign Legion. Seeking adventure. Running away from troubles at home. The story was romantic and timeless. The stuff of great books. That's why I gave you a literary clue, because that's what we have here, really. Jay Gatsby and Daisy. Obsessive love. Jealousy. Revenge. Murder."

"Matson killed Darryl Chesterton to get Abigail back?"

"Exactly."

I sat and thought about it a moment. "Why wait twenty years?"

"Why did Gatsby wait? Because he couldn't come back to her the way he was before," Leslie said. "Frank Matson needed money. His own stash of wealth. It took him twenty years to get it."

"How does an army grunt make one point one million dollars?"

"It was easy," Leslie said. "Once he stopped being an army grunt."

"Explain."

Leslie leaned forward. "Frank Matson went to Vietnam in 1968. In the spring of 1969 he disappeared while out on patrol. Six years later he turned up in Saigon with this swashbuckling Rambo story about how he escaped a POW camp and waded through perilous rivers at night to get back to safety. Saigon was in the process of falling to the North Vietnamese about the time Frank showed, but instead of coming back to the States, our boy went the other direction."

"Which direction?"

"Best I've been able to tell, Cambodia. Thailand, too. And Singapore. Somewhere in there. He simply vanished in the postwar chaos before turning up in San Francisco in 1987."

"With a million dollars."

Leslie smiled. "Million and change."

"Where do you suppose he got it?"

"He went in broke and came out rich, so your guess is as good as mine. Drugs, maybe. Or weapons. Boom market for guns and bullets when governments collapse. Frank was a Green Beret and had specialized skills. Access to classified information."

"Where did you get *your* information?"

Leslie wagged his finger at me. "Unh-unh. A newsman never reveals his sources, Quinn. You should know that."

The phone rang in the house and Leslie said that he'd get it. Holt watched him walk back into the house.

"Don't get him started on Frank Matson and the missing years," he said.

"Why not?"

"I'm sick of it." Holt lowered his voice. "Just between you and me, Quinn, I hope this Matson character *stays* disappeared. I hope he's dead as a doornail so we can bury him and get on with things."

"Leslie's preoccupied with Frank?"

"*Preoccupied?* Leslie's *obsessed* with all this. We've only been together a year, not even that, but I don't even want to think of the money he's spent finding out all this stuff. Digging up dirt, tracking down bank records. Fuck it. He talks about Gatsby and sips his wine like he's on top of things, but it's more like *Moby Dick*. What's-his-name chasing after the great white whale."

"Captain Ahab."

"You got it," Holt said, lowering his voice even more. "Captain fucking Ahab. Don't let the nice house and BMW fool you. He's broke as hell. Tapped out. The people back East who own this spread are ready to unload. I'm the one sitting around here taking the phone calls. When I said I wanted to get a job downtown it's not because I'm bored out here. I *like* this! But we need the money and Leslie won't face up to it. He just won't. Every cent Leslie's earned in the past year has gone into this Matson fixation. One time we got in a fight about it and I told him the same thing I just told you. That he was like Captain Ahab chasing the white whale all over hell and back. You know what?"

"What?"

"Leslie took it as a *compliment!*" Holt leaned back in his chair. "Laughed his ass off! From then on whenever he got some new piece of dirt on Matson he'd smile and say he was off to sharpen his harpoon. I'm sick of it. I never even met the guy, but I hope Frank Matson's dead. Maybe then it'll finally stop."

The screen door swung open and we fell silent. Leslie came out and stood by the table. His face was flushed.

"That was Abigail," Leslie said.

"Now what?" Holt said.

Leslie turned to me. "Remember that steel vat filled with Cabernet I showed you at the winery, Quinn? The one with the spigot at the bottom?"

"Sure."

"It's gone bad. All of it. Thousands of gallons."

"What happened?"

"Taste went bad and they sent off a sample to the lab. The results just came back. Something's in there."

"What?"

"They don't know," Leslie said. "But whatever it is, it's leaking blood."

=15=

A half-dozen official vehicles were out in front of the Chesterton winery. Three police cars, two ambulances, and an emergency van with red and blue lights flashing.

We were riding in the same golf cart as the day before, Leslie driving, Holt sitting next to him, and me in back. The field workers paused and leaned their dark hands on shovels and hoes and watched us hurry by. Curious. Impassive.

A flatbed truck with a hoist was backed up flush to the double-door entrance to the winery, and a dozen or so laborers milled around outside. Leslie pulled the golf cart up next to the flatbed and parked.

Inside it was oddly quiet. Three men were standing on top of the middle stainless steel fermentation tank. There was a faint, acrid smell of burned metal, like some welding had been going on. The hoist from the flatbed truck outside was securing a pulley contraption hooked to a metal bar at the top of the fermentation tank, and another man was tugging on it to make sure it was holding tight. The pulley rope hung loosely down into the tank.

Several uniformed men moved around the floor of the winery, now and then breaking the silence with shouted instructions to the three men on top. Detective Davis stood in the middle of it all. He had his back to me and didn't seem to know I was there. That was fine with me. Davis was talking to an overweight man with a florid face and curly red hair. The overweight man was extremely agitated. He kept shaking his head and running his fingers through his hair.

I turned to Leslie and whispered. "Who's Davis talking to?"

"Jack Paquini," Leslie said. "The winemaster."

Davis nodded at something Paquini said, and out of the corner of his eye he saw me. The transformation was immediate. His face twisted like a hand towel being wrung dry and he marched up and jammed his chin right up into mine.

"What in the hell are you doing here, Parker?"

"The family asked us to be here," Leslie said.

Davis whirled on him. "Well I'm telling you *not* to be here! Get the hell out! Now!"

Davis took one step back and tried to gather himself. He was trembling. A light sheen of oily sweat covered his stubbled face, and the stick deodorant underneath his armpits had congealed into a clammy white paste and soaked through his shirt. He wasn't bluffing. People usually don't froth at the mouth when they're bluffing. Holt played it smart and went outside immediately. Leslie and I stayed where we were. Davis took one step toward us and then a man on the top of the steel tank shouted, "Here it comes!"

Everything stopped. All movement, all sound. The motorized hoist groaned to life and the rope that had been immersed in the wine went taut with the weight of its catch.

"Keep it steady!" someone shouted.

"Slower!"

"I said *steady,* damn it! Slow the fuck down!"

Davis faded away from us. Everything faded away. All you could hear was the sound of the two men grunting as they straddled the opening and steadied the hoist. Then the body rose from the top of the steel container.

At first it didn't look like anything. A huge limp sponge, nothing else, saturated and spilling a river of red as it rose toward the rafters. Then as the wine drained away you could start to see features. Arms, legs, hands. What was left of the shot-away face. My fists clenched involuntarily, and for a moment there was no oxygen left in this world to breathe. The hoist jolted to a stop and the corpse rocked, steadied, then slowly turned a full 360 degrees, as though surveying the empire it once ruled. On the second slow orbit there was no mistaking the body. It was Frank Matson.

Everyone stood transfixed. All but one. To my left I could see Paquini the winemaster start to go. His eyes gave a little flutter, the batting of moth wings, like a fluorescent light flickering on, flickering, flickering, but not quite making it. Then his knees bent slightly, his butt went out, and he went down in a kind of slow-motion corkscrew action. The thunk of his head hitting the floor was the only sound in the vast, cavernous room, but nobody bothered to look. Paquini just hit and lay there, and the silence went on without him.

16

The man operating the hoist had an instinct for tidiness even under these gruesome circumstances. He paused for ten or fifteen seconds of drip-dry while the slowly revolving body was still positioned over the opened vat. No sense spilling excess wine on the floor. The tow rope had been secured to a harness fastened onto Frank Matson's hips and now he hung in the air, stomach-down, like a half-folded ventriloquist's dummy. When the excess wine had drained from Matson's body, the corpse was levered out away from the stainless steel drum and lowered slowly to the floor. Two paramedics waited for their cargo with a plastic body bag.

Nobody yet seemed aware that Paquini the winemaster was out cold on the floor. He lay there flat on his back, palms up and fingers gently curled. His pudgy legs were splayed straight out, shoetips pointing due north and due south.

Detective Davis faltered a second, reaching out with his right hand to steady himself against a wall that wasn't there. Then he moved slowly toward the two paramedics who were inserting what was left of Frank Matson in the body bag. He knelt at the corpse. I saw him put his hand on a soggy shoulder and leave it there.

Leslie and I looked at each other. It seemed the right time to go back outside and not get in Davis's immediate line of vision. The dozen Mexican laborers who'd been rubbernecking had vanished. A soft breeze rustled the tops of the trees. I was vividly aware of the branches above me, strong and pliable, of the breeze and the sound it made in the leaves. Holt was leaning against the golf cart, and by the look in his eyes he had caught a glimpse of Frank Matson, too.

The double doors to the winery suddenly opened wide and there was a lot of activity. The cadre of police had recovered from being shell-shocked and were now full of officious hustle-bustle, directing traffic, clearing obstacles, looking stern and intolerant of gaping bystanders. The two paramedics brought the body out and put it in the back of their vehicle. One chewed gum and the other rested his clipboard on Matson's stomach. Just another day on the job for them. They climbed in the van and drove away. Beneath the tires the gravel crunched its indiscriminate crunch, and for all the trauma displayed they might just as well have been a couple of Roto-Rooter men driving off to the next plugged toilet.

Paquini was next out, wobbly on his feet, face the color of watered-down kindergarten paste. He was assisted by two sheriff's deputies who flanked him on either side, hands cupped under his collapsing armpits to hold him up. Paquini was a load, and the deputies were struggling. They led him to a squad car and he stretched out in the backseat.

Davis was last out. I was braced for anything. Screams. Handcuffs. Flying fists. But he was scarily composed, smoking a cigarette with no discernible tremble to the fingers. Calm. Almost thoughtful. He rubbed the back of his neck and walked up to Leslie.

"Know where Frank's office is up there in the main house?"

Leslie nodded.

"Good," Davis said. "I want you and Parker to wait for me there. I'll be up in a minute. Don't either one of you two go running off." Davis paused, then looked over at Holt. "Who's he, anyway?"

"He's with me," Leslie said.

"Then I want to talk to him, too."

Holt shook his head and stared at the ground. He looked miserable. He'd left the drunken car vandals of Willits only to encounter this.

Back at the house Leslie showed me where Matson's office was and then went off with Holt to find Abigail. He was going to tell her in a simple, quiet way what the police had found. He was her closest friend. He was the one who should do it. This was one piece of news, goddamn it, that she was *not* going to hear from Detective Davis.

Frank Matson's office was large and comfortable. Except for a wall filled with somber, probably unread books, there was no pretension here. No dog-breeding magazines on the coffee table. No decorative pipe racks on the lamp tables or Kentucky Derby lithographs on the wall. The desk was simple and functional. A well-stocked bar was to the left of the desk, and to the right a computer was built into a compartmentalized area against the wall. The only concession to boardroom intimidation was an oval table of dark, polished wood occupying the center of the room. It had a dozen expensive-looking chairs scooted up to it, and I half-expected to see nameplates in front of the individual seating positions. Secretary of State. Secretary of Defense. Ambassador to the Court of St. James's. On the far wall, opposite the desk, was a large-screen television set, sixty-inch screen at least, with surround-sound stereo speakers, VCR, satellite control box, and descrambler boxes on shelves above.

The house was very silent. I closed the door of the office, edged my way around the desk, and booted up Frank Matson's computer. I didn't need a password to gain access to his files, which was good news and bad news. Good, because I could browse through them at my leisure. Bad, because if they hadn't been secretly coded, there probably wasn't much to see. There weren't many directories, and his address file was easy to find. I pulled it up on the screen and scanned from A to Z looking for Pilkow Street. Or Pilkow Avenue. Or Pilkow Boulevard or Pilkow Place or Mr. and Mrs. Pilkow. But nothing showed. Frank Matson's computer, as far as I could see, was entirely Pilkow-free.

I turned off the computer and reopened the office door so people wouldn't think that I was the type to go scavenging through another person's computer files. As I opened the door I heard a terrible sound. The sound of someone throwing up. Normally somebody being sick is their own business, but these retchings were huge. Volcanic. Wall-shaking. I wandered down the hall and stopped before the bathroom door where the sounds were originating. I hesitated, then tapped on the half-opened door.

"You okay in there?"

Another titanic regurgitation.

I pushed the door open a little further. It was Paquini the winemaster, curled up around the porcelain, clinging to the bowl with both arms as if his very life depended on it.

"Are you okay?" I said.

"Leemee alone!" Paquini choked. He kicked ineffectively at the door to slam it shut. The kick missed, but I got his intention. I backed out and closed the door tight. Inside Paquini groaned pitifully, almost like a plea for mercy, then heaved again. This wasn't just throwing up. This was what it sounded like when you're being worked over by the Uruguayan secret police.

I went back to the office and waited. Ten minutes later Paquini staggered in.

"Jesus, God ..." he muttered, collapsing into one of the armchairs. "Good Jesus God ..."

"Can I get you anything?"

Paquini shook his head. "What a thing. Were you down there?"

"Yes. I saw it."

"*Saw?*" Paquini shot me a look. "*Saw?* How about *drank?*"

"You drank from the wine vat?"

"I sucked down a half a *carafe* of that shit yesterday trying to figure out what was wrong! Just talking about it ..." Paquini's abdomen shuddered and his mouth quaked open and for one terrible second I thought he was going to projectile vomit all over the rug. But he somehow regrouped. Held it together. He gagged, choked back the rising bile, and sank deeper into the contours of the armchair.

"You drank out of the wine vat?" I said.

"Didn't I just tell you that?" Paquini moaned.

"But why?"

"It's my job!" Paquini said. "Standard procedure. Every morning I go by, sample the wines, see how they're coming along. Yesterday I knew that Cabernet vat was funny. Knew it! Taste was off, and not off for the usual reasons. I couldn't figure what the hell had gone wrong." Paquini shook his head mournfully. "Normally it's oxidation or too much oak or too much sugar or something. So I stood by that goddamn tank and downed three whole glasses of the stuff, trying to pick it up. Nothing. So I send a sample to the lab and what happens? It comes back showing fucking *brain fluid!*" Paquini shook his head, clamped his mouth shut. "Oh, no!"

He bolted from the room, and I had five more minutes of solitude. Then he was back.

"That better be the last of it," he said. "I can't take any more. I'm dying. I'm going to puke out my fucking spleen. Poor Mr. Matson. Jesus ... I can't believe it. Dead. Dead, just like that!"

"You were his winemaster?"

Paquini nodded. "Mr. Matson was a good guy. The best. Poor son of a bitch. Now what's going to happen?"

"You two got along?"

"We got along super," Paquini said defensively. "Why?"

"I got the impression he wasn't too popular."

"Who gave you that impression?"

"Almost everybody I talk to."

Paquini lost interest in his nausea for a second and gave me a sharp, sideways look. "Who are you, anyway?"

I told him, and Paquini nodded. "That explains it. Phillip hated Frank. If that's where you've been getting your information it's going to be all twisted around."

"Others echoed Phillip's sentiments."

"Like who?"

"Others."

Paquini glanced at the door. "Like your buddy in the golf cart? Leslie McCall?"

I kept quiet.

Paquini winced, grabbed his stomach, and belched loudly. "You read his newspaper ever?"

"No."

"He thinks it's the goddamn *New York Times* but for everybody else out here it's a joke. He's got this wine column he writes. People call it 'Sour Grapes' because all it is, is McCall up on his soapbox whining about how everybody else did him wrong. That winery he's managing is about to go Chapter 11 and he had to blame somebody. Frank was the guy he blamed."

"Shrader-Cox is going bankrupt?"

Paquini nodded and gave me a thumbs-down signal. I wanted to follow up on this but we were interrupted by the arrival of Detective Davis. He was subdued and all business. He took a seat at the polished oval table. "Where's McCall and his boyfriend?"

"Upstairs with Abigail."

Davis shook his head disgustedly and asked a suddenly obsequious Paquini a few questions about sequence of events. Paquini answered with exaggerated, bootlick politeness. Davis wrote in his notebook and then told Paquini he could leave, but to stay available for further questioning in the next couple of days.

Paquini stood, lingered, cleared his throat. "Detective Davis ..."

Davis looked up, irritated. "What?"

"About how much longer do you think your people will be here?"

"My people?"

"The police."

"What the hell's the difference?" Davis said.

Paquini tried to smile. "It's the Mexicans we got working for us. Some of them … well, they don't have their papers in order and half my work force already headed for the hills when your officers arrived. They probably won't come back and if there are going to be cops swarming the—"

"Your wetbacks aren't my problem," Davis snapped. "This is a homicide investigation."

Paquini flinched, mumbled something deferential under his breath, and walked out of the room on unsteady legs.

Paquini had no sooner exited than another man entered the room. He introduced himself as Harlon Kendrick and explained that he was in charge of security for Chesterton Vineyards. Kendrick was tall, dark, and handsome without distinction, like those soap opera doctors who always have K Mart stethoscopes dangling around their necks. Davis asked some pointed questions and Mr. Kendrick kept his poise even though in the back of his mind he had to be thinking about security of a different sort. Job security.

There were three separate access roads into the property, Mr. Kendrick explained. Only the main entrance from Glenville Road had a manned guard station. The others were controlled by electric gates, coded for access by a card that was in the possession of the family. Of course, that was only to stop vehicular traffic. A person on foot could sneak into the property at almost any point on the grounds. There were, after all, thousands of acres of Chesterton land. Perhaps with gun towers and barbed wire and roving helicopters you could secure the area completely, Mr. Kendrick said, but that was a bit impractical. He paused so that we could all have the chance to chuckle at his tension-breaking humor, but Davis didn't chuckle. Kendrick quickly reattached his look of grave concern.

What about alarms, Davis asked? Kendrick cleared his throat. He was comfortable with this question and eager to answer it. There were alarms at various points in the winery itself, including motion detectors, but they were often turned off. Turned off, Davis said. What for? Wine operations, Kendrick explained, tended to be a twenty-four-hour-a-day process, so motion detectors weren't terribly practical. There were two night watchmen who patrolled the grounds, but yes, he supposed it was possible for someone to have snuck in and put a body in the vat without triggering an alarm. Davis thanked him cynically for admitting the possibility of that which obviously had already happened. Mr. Kendrick said he would help to the full extent of his abilities, that Detective Davis should not hesitate to call him if further assistance was needed, blah, blah, blah, and then headed out the door.

That left Davis and me in the room alone. I wondered where Leslie was.

"Feels like we just talked, Parker," he said.

"We just did."

"I don't suppose in the last three hours you've cleared your head on this issue of where Phillip went."

"You can slug me in the stomach all you want," I said. "Your guess is as good as mine."

Davis nodded in a congenial manner, clicked his pen, and reattached it to his shirt pocket. He folded the tablet and got up and started walking toward me. I felt my body tense, but he simply brushed on past me and left the room without another word. It was a scary gesture. Far more menacing than if he'd just hauled off and punched me again. Detective Davis had made some sort of decision about me, and it wasn't good.

I lingered in the office. Went to the window and looked out. A few of the maids were standing on the terrace, talking excitedly to one another in rapid-fire Spanish. Farther out were small groups of Mexican workers from the vineyards. Word of the grisly discovery was spreading, and they were watching the house, talking among themselves. I could read their lips from a quarter-mile away. Every cop and fireman and siren-screaming vehicle in Napa County had come to roost at Chesterton Vineyards in the past couple of hours, and maybe it was time to quietly lean the shovel against the nearest tree and head to Washington for the apple-picking season. If Paquini hadn't lost his entire work force before, they were going to be history very soon.

I turned from the window and wandered over to the large-screen television and simply stared at the blank screen for a while. It was gradually occurring to me that maybe the meeting was over, and I wondered what to do next. Then Leslie was suddenly standing in the doorway.

"Well," he said. "That's done."

"How's Abigail?"

"Not great. But at the same time it's not like she was sitting around waiting for good news. The doctor gave her a sedative." Leslie wandered into the room. "Did I manage to avoid Davis?"

"Yes."

"He talk to you?"

"Yes."

"And?"

"He was calm and nice and didn't say much."

"Watch yourself," Leslie said. "That's a sure tip-off he's rolling out the heavy artillery."

Leslie pulled out one of the chairs from the large oval table and slumped into it. "I left out an important detail this afternoon when I was telling you the Gatsby story, Quinn. I wasn't going to tell you, but now that Frank's dead I don't see why not."

"What detail?"

Leslie paused, looked around the room as if to confirm that it was empty. "What I tell you here doesn't go any further, right?"

"Not if you don't want it to."

"I'm not telling you this because I get off on spreading gossip. You're Phillip's therapist. Maybe this might help you when you're trying to make sense out of things later on down the road."

"Okay."

Leslie exhaled loudly and linked his hands behind his head.

"Before Frank Matson enlisted and went to Vietnam he got Abigail pregnant. Darryl quickly married Abigail to keep scandal to a minimum. They came out here and raised the child as their own." Leslie paused. "The man you just saw fished out of the wine vat was Phillip Chesterton's father."

17

L eslie and Holt gave me a ride back to my van near the Sheriff's Department. We didn't say much except to confirm that
we would keep in touch. Proximity to Davis's office seemed
to make them jittery, so we said good-bye with a minimum of
fanfare and they accelerated quickly away.

I didn't go straight home. When the world stops making
sense you get back to basics, so as I approached the exit to Jack
London State Park, I made an impulse decision to go there
instead. The first excursion I'd ever taken with Phillip at the start
of our therapy had been a trip here. We'd toured the museum,
wandered the winding trails down to Wolf House, had a picnic
up on the grassy hillside overlooking Jack London's grave and
the gently rolling Napa countryside. This was the spot where our
initial trust was formed, and in some foolish way it suddenly
became crucial that I retrace earlier steps if I ever hoped to
reconnect with Phillip. I try not to be mystical about these things,
but I didn't know what else to do.

I bought my ticket to the museum and stared at the yellowed

documents preserved under glass. I wasn't inspired. Normally the preserved-under-glass evidence of dynamic lives inspires me, but not today. If anything, the sheer density of Jack London's life started making me rue the relative sparsity of my own. So I left the building after a couple of minutes and instead walked down the steep dirt trail leading to the remains of Wolf House.

As I walked I thought of Frank and Phillip. Father and son. In retrospect these things always seem obvious. Frank Matson's abnormal frustration over the shortcomings of his "stepson." The fact that they shared the same unusual blood type. Phillip's utter lack of physical resemblance to the framed portrait of old man Chesterton. It cleared up the mystery of why, after twenty years, Abigail still had such strong ties to her former lover. But why had they kept it a secret even after Darryl Chesterton had died? Did Abigail think it would be too much for the already-frail Phillip to deal with? Or were there other reasons? Was I still far, far, far on the outside, trying to scratch my way through the first of many layers?

It was a bit of a hike down to Wolf House, and the visitors thinned out. I turned a corner of the trail and could see the rocky shell of the remaining structure. Wolf House was to have been Jack London's dream home, but it burned to the ground shortly after completion, and now only the high carved rocks remained, reaching up toward the tops of the surrounding redwoods like a kind of frontier Stonehenge. I leaned against the cool rock and thought of Phillip.

Where was he, and why hadn't he made an effort to contact me again? Was he still alive? Frightened? Oblivious? Or had he been put into a situation that prevented him from contacting others? I found myself thinking of Suzie Wong. Suzie of the half-truths and locked doors and threatening gestures. Suzie who seemed to fit with the convenient perfection of tracing paper over Phillip's life: loving the same paintings, adoring the same music, sharing the same vision. She was due for another visit, and this time the mild-mannered phobia therapist wasn't going to be as congenial.

I wandered around to the north side of the ruined house, and that's when I noticed them. Two men in their early twenties. I'd actually noticed them earlier, up at the museum. They didn't have flat noses and cauliflower ears, but neither did they look like the types who would visit a literary landmark. Both men wore plain white T-shirts and jeans and had the bunched-up musculature of weight lifters. They spoke to each other and pointed to the house, but it was mannered. They were more interested in me than in Jack London.

I went off on the path that led another quarter of a mile to Jack London's gravesite, and after an appropriate thirty-second pause, the two guys started up the path behind me. A family of three was in front of me and I stuck close to them. They were German. The man took photographs of the grave and then we turned around en masse and headed back toward the house. The two men passed me going in the other direction. They had their eyes unnaturally focused straight ahead.

As soon as we passed each other I put a little spring in my stride and placed the German family in between me and the two men. I glanced back and they'd already done a one-eighty well before reaching the gravesite.

There was a bend in the trail where visual contact was interrupted for a few seconds, and that was where I broke into an all-out run. The trail dipped down and up and down again, and startled visitors stepped aside as I rushed past. I looked back once, and that's all it took. The German father was sprawled on the ground, trying to gather up his photographic equipment. The two muscle boys were running as fast as they could in my direction. They were faster runners than me.

I scrambled up over the hill and then left the trail completely, thrashing into the tree cover cross-country back in the general vicinity of the museum. It was rough going. Branches and tangled ivy and thick underbrush. I stopped at one point to listen. Nothing. Just my labored breathing and the rustle of startled lizards heading for higher ground. No T-shirted men. Their line of vision had been blocked when I left the trail, and I might have gone anywhere.

For ten minutes I struggled through the underbrush. Then I

heard voices straight ahead. Friendly, neutral, Johnny-quit-pick-ing-your-nose voices. I emerged from the tree cover, scratched and dazed and sweating. I was on the eastern edge of the park-ing lot. A family who'd been on their way to the museum saw me emerge from the shadows and looked at me disapprovingly. They'd heard about San Franciscans. I tried to smile but the mother just cupped the heads of her two small children and hur-ried along.

I walked quickly and steadily toward the van. I chanced one glance behind me, but the two guys were nowhere in sight. I'd lost them, but they'd be hurrying back to the parking lot. I felt in my pocket for the van keys. I didn't want to have to waste pre-cious seconds fumbling around for the right one once I reached the van. The relief was short-lived. As I closed in on my van I saw him. This third guy wasn't even trying to be sneaky. He was sitting on my front bumper, waiting in the sun. He had a goatee and was playing with it. His eyes were closed and he had his head tilted to get the most of the afternoon rays. I walked past him and kept going, out of the parking lot, around the twisting two-lane road that led back to the town of Glen Ellen.

The park ranger at the entry station watched me leave. He smiled and we nodded to each other, but he was suspicious. As soon as I was around the bend I got out in the middle of the road and flagged down the first car heading back into town. The driver honked at me, swerved, and accelerated away. The kids in the backseat turned to watch me. The next car did the exact same thing. The boys in the T-shirts would be getting back to the parking lot by now. I broke into an easy trot.

I heard a third vehicle coming around the bend. I stopped and waved. It was a Jeep with a man and a woman and it stopped for me. I told the man I'd run out of gas and needed a ride into Glen Ellen. They told me to hop in. By Glen Ellen they trusted me enough to agree to take me into Sonoma, and by Sonoma they said what the hell. They were going to San Fran-cisco anyway. They'd take me all the way into the city.

I was dropped off at the corner of Lombard and Gough, next

to a Budget car rental office. I thanked the young couple from the bottom of my heart and went in to rent a car. Once that was done I went to a pay phone a few blocks down Lombard and called Hank at the apartment.

"Oh," he said. "It's you."

"You don't have to sound so excited."

"Thought it might've been Gunnhilde canceling out." Hank took a deep breath. "I'm nervous as hell."

"I'm not trying to minimize your problems, but here's how my day's gone so far. Frank Matson's body was found this afternoon up in Napa. Then on my way home I stopped by Jack London State Park and some men with unpleasant intent followed me."

"What men?" Hank said.

"No idea. My guess is they're working for Davis. Just watch yourself around the apartment. Keep an eye and an ear open."

Hank was quiet a moment. "I will."

"What time are you going out?"

"Dinner reservations are for eight."

"I might not see you then," I said.

"Where are you going?"

"I'm going back over to Hill Street and figure out which of the two Suzie Wongs is real."

Hank told me to be careful, and that he'd keep a candle burning in case I got home late. I told him to give Gunnhilde my regards, then hung up and climbed in my rented car.

=18=

pulled up to the broken red awning, rang the doorbell, and got ready. If Suzie gave me the six inches she'd given me before, I was going to jam my foot in the opening and make it twelve. No more benefit of the doubt. Suzie was going to invite me into her apartment—either graciously or otherwise—and tell me every single thing she knew about Phillip's disappearance. Then I was going to have a look around. Period.

A few seconds passed. I rang the buzzer again, waited, then again, this time leaning on it for a good long time. In door buzzer language it said: I'm going to sit here and do this and drive you crazy until you get it through your head that it would be simpler for both of us if you just came to the door and let me in.

"Hey!" A voice behind me. "Hey! Knock it off!"

A man was walking up the sidewalk toward me, shaking his head, a frown on his face. "Don't do that," he said. "Ruins the doorbell, you keep pushing on it like that."

"I didn't know if it was working," I said.

"What're you talking about?" the man said. "I can hear it all the way down the street. It works fine. Everything in there works fine, if that's what you're worried about."

The man was in his late twenties, heavyset, with a round face, shaggy blond hair, and work overalls. He was carrying a box filled with brushes and paint cans. "I can't believe it," he said. "You're here about the apartment, right?"

"Pardon me?"

The man put down his box and pulled a key chain from the depths of his overalls. "Ad in the paper hasn't even come out yet. This city, man, what a grapevine. Unbelievable."

I watched him flip through his keys and didn't say anything.

"Who told you about the place?" the man said. "Warren?"

"The woman who lives here told me."

"Suzie?"

"Yes. Suzie."

"Suzie told you she was leaving?"

"That's right."

The man shook his head. "You rate a lot higher than me, pal."

"Are you the manager?"

The man nodded, selected a key, and opened Suzie's door. "I'm Kevin. Wasn't going to start showing this place till Monday, but since you're here already go ahead and have a look. I have stuff to do in there anyway."

I went in first and Kevin trailed after, lugging the box of paint paraphernalia with him.

"Obviously the walls are gonna get a new coat," Kevin said. "And in the bathroom the shower's getting new fixtures. Other than that, what you see is what you get."

I stood in the middle of what used to be Suzie's living room, trying to keep my brain from racing, arm wrestling my demeanor to keep it relaxed and casually inquisitive.

"She didn't take her furniture?" I said.

Kevin looked at me curiously. "Apartment comes furnished," he said. "Suzie didn't tell you?"

"No."

"That a problem?"

"No," I said. "Furnished is fine."

Kevin came up and stood next to me, hands on hips, shaking his head. "When she cleared out, man, she cleared out. Boom. Sayonara. Middle of the goddamn night."

"She win the lottery?"

"Who knows? You and her friends?"

"Not really," I said. "We met at a party a couple weeks ago. Suzie was intending to move out and I said I was looking, so …"

"Weird chick," Kevin said, picking at some paint that had dried on his knuckle. "Okay. I don't know what she told you she was paying, but it's going up, naturally. Nothing to do with me. Outfit over in Oakland owns this and what they say goes. You know how it is."

I nodded that I knew how it was. "How much?"

"Nine hundred a month, first and last, five hundred damage deposit. So twenty-three hundred, total, to move in. That gonna be a problem?"

I lifted my eyebrows. "I don't know …"

"Thought I'd better tell you now," Kevin said. "That's a lotta dough, right off the bat."

"Sure is."

"Of course, if you want to do it like Suzie, the landlord might give you a better deal."

"How did she do it?"

"Six months' rent in advance."

I peered at Kevin. "One lump sum?"

"Cash on the table," Kevin said. "If you did it that way the landlord'd probably go eight hundred, eight twenty-five. Don't quote me, but they might."

I couldn't keep the astonishment from my face. "Suzie Wong put down a half-year's rent in advance? That must've been—"

"Five thousand something."

"We're talking about the Asian woman with the long hair, right?"

"Right." Kevin looked at me funny. "What's the matter?"

"I'm just a little surprised. She told me she was broke. That she worked as a waitress in a coffee shop somewhere, living on tips."

"I don't know *what* her job was," Kevin said. "All I know is she laid down cash money. I don't ask questions. Maybe she sold drugs on the side. I told you she was a weird chick. In and out all hours of the night."

We fell silent, and the silence went on just a tad too long. I felt Kevin staring at me. He was slowly coming to sense that I wasn't there to rent the apartment. But he shelved his suspicions and went ahead and showed me the rest of the rooms anyway. I examined closet space and asked about utility bills and did all the innocuous, standard things an apartment hunter does. Kevin was a trusting sort of human being and by the end of the tour I think he was back to believing me. I looked carefully for signs of Phillip's presence, but there were none. I knew there wouldn't be. Suzie, if nothing else, was thorough.

At the end of it Kevin walked me back out to the Hill Street sidewalk and said he'd have to have a decision one way or the other real fast. Ad was coming out Monday, which meant that by Wednesday or Thursday it'd be rented. Even at nine hundred bucks this was a good deal. Nice area, close to a lot of things.

"What about parking?" I said. "I have a van."

"There's no garage," Kevin said. "That's the only bad thing, but it's usually not *that* big a hassle to find a decent spot. I park on the street and almost always get it within a block or two. What you ought to do is check with the people who live across the street. Mr. and Mrs. Fuentes. Nice folks. Older couple. Suzie rented their garage. I don't know for how much, but it's probably cheap."

"Mr. and Mrs. Fuentes?"

"Right there." Kevin pointed. "Brown stucco house. Tell them I sent you. They know me."

I thanked Kevin for his help and he said it wasn't anything. Then I took a chance and wondered in an offhand manner if Suzie had left any kind of forwarding address, just in case I took the place. A thank-you note would be in order. Kevin shook his head.

"Nope. Nothing. She even has five more weeks left on her prepayment but last night she said to forget it, to go ahead and rent it out. I asked her what if her plans changed and she wanted to come back, that I'd keep it free through January like it says in her lease. She said no. She wasn't coming back. There wasn't much doubt in her voice about that." Kevin made a palms-down, outward motion with his hands, like an umpire making the safe signal at home. "Suzie was outta here. When that woman left, she was gone."

I rang the buzzer at the brown stucco house and waited. Eight steps took you up to the front door. Below and to the right an asphalt driveway dipped under the house to a single-car garage. The garage door was closed, and a sign was nailed to it. A cartoon policeman brandishing a billy club, and the words in bright red—"Don't even *think* about parking here!"

An elderly Hispanic woman answered the door and stared at me through the screen door. She was heavyset and shuffled about in half-disintegrated bedroom slippers. She wore glasses and a rust-red robe with small purple flower patterns, and there was a kind of instinctive friendliness in her face. A television droned softly in the background.

"Mrs. Fuentes?" I said.

"Yes?"

"My name is Quinn Parker." I turned and pointed at the apartment building across the street. "There's a chance I'll be moving across the street there and Kevin, the apartment manager, said I should talk to you about the possibility of renting your garage for my car."

"What?"

I repeated what I'd just said, only slower.

"Oh, no." She smiled apologetically. "The garage already rented."

"To Suzie Wong, yes?"

Mrs. Fuentes adjusted her glasses and squinted to see me better. "Yes, we rent to Suzie."

"That's why Kevin sent me to you," I explained. "Suzie's left the city. It's her apartment I'm going to be moving into."

"Suzie left?"

"Yesterday."

"We don't know nothing about that," Mrs. Fuentes said.

"It was pretty sudden."

Mrs. Fuentes nodded. We stood there like that for five or ten seconds, looking at each other through the tight webbing of the screen door. She wasn't sure whether to trust me.

"Better go check," she said at last. "I think Suzie's car still there."

She went back into the house and returned a minute later holding a key. We went down the steps to the sidewalk and then down again to the garage door. The exertion had Mrs. Fuentes breathing heavily, so I unlocked the garage and lifted it open.

When they said one-car garage, that's what they meant. One car. Not one car and some tools on the wall. Not one car and a trash can in the corner. One car. With some Vaseline and a shoehorn you could just barely squeeze a single midsized automobile into the dank parking space below the Fuentes home. It almost looked hacked out of stone, the place where cave dwellers discovered the secret of fire. Phillip Chesterton's white Mazda was parked in the Fuentes garage.

"This is not Suzie's car," Mrs. Fuentes said.

"No?"

She shook her head. "This is *not* Suzie's car."

"Maybe she let somebody borrow her space," I said.

Mrs. Fuentes wagged her finger and her normally pleasant face grew stern. "Is against the rules. Suzie know all about that. No cars in here but her car."

Mrs. Fuentes showed me why. There was a door at the rear of the garage that led to the house. Sometimes they forgot to lock the door and they didn't want strangers coming in and out of the garage.

While she talked I edged in close to the driver's door. Mrs. Fuentes's suspicion began to drift in my direction.

"You know what maybe happened," I said. "Suzie might've bought a new car. She's a friend of mine and I remember one year she changed cars three different times."

Mrs. Fuentes was too sweet a human being to see me for the liar I was. She just lifted her shoulders as if to say who knows? "Nobody said nothing to me."

"Door's unlocked," I said. "Do you think we should check the registration?"

I let Mrs. Fuentes make the decision. She thought about it a second. "Okay."

I leaned in the car and gave the front and back seats a quick once-over. Nothing was out of the ordinary. Nothing shoved under the seats. I reached over and popped the glove compartment and leaned down to take a look. It yielded glove compartment things. Registration papers. A badly refolded road map. A screwdriver. Sunglasses in a dusty carrying case and a thin metal instrument to measure tire pressure. I pushed the map aside, and when I did I saw the gun. The handle was toward me. I covered it again with the road map and closed the glove compartment. Then I casually locked all the doors so Mr. and Mrs. Fuentes could not go snooping around on their own.

"No registration papers," I said, crawling back out. "Strange."

Mrs. Fuentes looked even more concerned. "My husband is at work ..." she said aimlessly.

"Maybe Suzie borrowed the car," I said. "Why don't you lock up the garage and I'll try to find out. There's no rush about me using the space."

Mrs. Fuentes nodded uneasily and we went outside. I reached up and rattled the garage door down. As it clattered into place the cartoon of the policeman and his billy club stared me straight in the face, nose to nose, inches away.

I thanked Mrs. Fuentes and she waddled back up onto her

porch and on inside. I walked to my rented car and could feel Mrs. Fuentes watching me. When I climbed behind the wheel I saw that she was standing just inside the living room, peering at me from behind the protective webbing of the screen door. Just standing there, waiting to see what I was going to do. I started up the car and eased away from the curb and didn't give her another glance. Mrs. Fuentes was not as trusting as I'd originally thought.

Smart woman.

═19═

Hank and Carol Wilkie used to live together in a cozy, three-bedroom home on Woodland Avenue, a tree-lined oasis of peace and calm just in back of the U.C. Medical Center. Used to. Now it's just Carol and the two boys. Woodland Avenue is a neighborhood where kids leave their bicycles out on front lawns and games of cowboys and Indians spill from one yard to the next. There's a suburban feel to the place, a Midwest sense of barbecue smoke and men doing the yard work on Sunday mornings before hunkering in with beer and football. A family place in a city that increasingly has very little to do with families. After the day's events I was desperately in need of a dose of its wholesomeness, and I found myself driving there from Suzie's apartment without having made a conscious decision to do so.

I pulled in behind Carol's car in the driveway, climbed the patio steps, and rang the doorbell. There was no answer, but I could hear the vacuum cleaner humming inside, so I knew she was there. I waited till the vacuum cleaner shut off and then buzzed again. Her footsteps clicked briskly down the hallway, then the door opened and Carol stood before me. Carol is five-six, with short black hair and a nice, tight, athletic body. Close-set eyes, olive skin, dazzling white teeth. She smelled of sweat and hard work. The T-shirt was wet at the small of her back, and when she stepped out onto the porch and drew my head down to give me a kiss her lips were salty. She held the kiss a fraction longer than normal, then released me.

"Maybe we ought to go inside," I said. "Don't want the neighbors to get the wrong impression."

"Getting the wrong impression is the primary function of a neighbor," Carol said. "Anyway, we Italians have a noble history of conducting our personal business on the front steps."

She smiled, and the trip mechanism that causes people to fall hopelessly and disastrously in love was almost triggered.

Carol and I used to date back in the old days, but our budding romance never really got beyond the hand-holding stage. When I casually introduced her to Hank one afternoon in Golden Gate Park, that was the end of that. Still, there are times when we look at each other and the air is suddenly sharp with the risky scent of what might have been. We went into the house, and I followed Carol down the hall. "How's the crew holding up?" I said.

Carol put out her hand, palm down, and wiggled it like an airplane trying to steady itself. "So-so."

"Kids doing okay?"

"They still think Daddy is on some kind of trip, even though they see him a lot. When the time comes I'll figure out what to say."

"How about you?"

"Me?" Carol laughed a weary laugh, turned to face me, and struck a high-fashion-model pose in her jeans and T-shirt. "What do people usually do when their marriages fall apart? They throw themselves into their work. Coffee or beer?"

"Coffee'd be great."

"Boys are in there watching television if you want to say hi."

I went into the living room and said hello to Cort and Matty.

They were stretched out on the floor, completely absorbed in the flickering television screen, and didn't react. It was a critical moment in the movie, so I quietly plunked down on the couch and watched a couple minutes of the film with them.

The movie was circa 1962, and was about two young children lost in the jungles of India. A beast had been terrorizing the village and the children had intervened, and now the animal was after them. I found myself drawn into the story. It was fun to sit and watch a movie filmed in an era when society didn't feel compelled to portray a rampaging Bengal tiger as a misunderstood creature who massacred entire villages only because it had been mistreated. The tiger was deadly, the kids were frightened, and in the end they weren't going to make friends and come to a mutual understanding about our fragile ecosystem.

The Christmas tree was up, filled with ornaments and tinsel and rough-hewn decorations the boys had obviously made in school. Toys were on the floor. Parts of a plastic train set. Lincoln Logs. One of those parachute men who never work because the lines get tangled up. I picked up the parachute man and methodically began smoothing out the snarled lines.

The toy I was monkeying around with, the kids on the floor, the Christmas tree in the corner blinking its lights ... suddenly it came home to me how very sad this breakup was. Hank and Carol had been having troubles of one sort or another for several years. I knew that. But in the months before the separation it seemed as if they'd turned a corner. Lots of public affection. Private moments. Secret, loving glances that I'd noticed out of the corner of my eye.

Now, as I sat in the living room untangling the parachute man, the tenderness seemed false. A lead-in for something that had nothing to do with love, like those Three Stooges routines where Curly dumbly stands there while Moe moves his chin a half inch there, a quarter inch here, tilting his jaw, soothing him with honeyed words, all the while positioning him so that the bone-crushing punch to come will land with maximum effectiveness. It didn't matter that the breakup was couched in comforting and hopeful words: time out, temporary breather, distance to gain perspective, and so on. The fact remained that Hank's toothbrush was now in my bathroom and there were two small children living in an emptier home, tugging on Carol's skirt and wondering what had happened to Daddy.

Carol came out with two steaming mugs just as I smoothed the last of the tangled parachute lines. She put my mug on the side table. I tossed the plastic parachute man up into the air, and he floated down just the way he was supposed to. Carol gave me a small round of applause, but the lines were already in the process of retangling.

Carol suggested to the boys that they go into their room to watch the last of the movie, and they clamored to their feet and went thundering down the hall. She shook her head and turned off the television and sat cross-legged on the rug in front of me.

"So how's Hank doing?" she said.

"Sleeps two hours, broods two hours. Like that."

"I mean really."

"You know Hank. He can't decide whether to carry a cross through Union Square or start his woman-in-every-port stage. I don't take any of it very seriously."

"Woman in every port?" Carol said. "How does Hank intend to finance getting from one port to the next?"

"The details haven't been worked out."

"Is he seeing anyone?"

"Not really."

Carol gave me a look. "'Not really' isn't the same thing as no. I'm a big girl, Quinn. You can tell me."

"He's going out on his first date tonight."

"Really?"

"Really."

Carol looked off toward the Christmas tree as if it didn't matter much. "What's her name?"

"Gunnhilde von Edlund."

"Come on!"

I nodded. "That's her name."

"Gunnhilde von Edlund," Carol repeated. "What does she do on weekends? Churn butter and sing to the goats?"

"Let's not be petty, Carol."

"No," she said. "Let's not."

"Besides, *you're* seeing someone, so you can't really blame Hank."

Carol pointed at her chest. "Me?"

"Hank's having exceptionally vivid dreams these days about another man living at the house."

"Uh-huh," Carol said cautiously. "Tell me more."

I crossed my legs and peered up at the ceiling. "Nothing much to say except this mystery man makes love to you a lot. Or he's made love to you once, a lot. Not sure which."

"Either way's fine," Carol said. "What else?"

"That's it. Of course, there was a lot of stuff about lips and breasts and arching backs. The usual. A great number of people at bedside cheering the two of you on."

Carol cupped her coffee mug in both hands and took a sip. "I could do without the audience, but so far, so good. What did this guy look like?"

"Hank didn't say, but knowing his capacity for self-torment I'd say he's no doubt a mixture of Sean Connery and David Niven."

"My kind of mixture." Carol smiled and glanced at the Hoover Upright in the corner. "So was all this arching and coaxing going on before, during, or after I did the vacuuming?"

"In Hank's dreams I don't think you vacuum anymore."

"Too busy making love?" Carol said.

"That and trying to replace your shredded lingerie."

Carol shook her head and reluctantly started laughing, and I laughed with her. We were probably the only two people on earth who truly understood about Hank being Hank.

"Okay," Carol said. "Enough about me and my torrid love life. Is it okay Hank being there?"

"It's fine."

"And what about you?"

"Me?" I said. "Well, my morning started with a homicide detective slugging me in the stomach. Then I learned about a five-year-old plane crash that really turned out to be a murder. Then I saw a body being lifted out of a ten-thousand-gallon tank of Cabernet Sauvignon. Then a couple of thugs tried to ambush me at Jack London State Park. What else? Oh, yeah. I stumbled on the probable murder weapon in the glove compartment of my client's car. The client, by the way, who vanished into thin air a few days ago and is now the object of a statewide manhunt. That's how my day's gone."

Carol just stared up at me from her cross-legged position on the floor. "This is a joke, right?"

"No joke."

"Then you'd better fill in some of these blanks."

I sighed and shook my head. "I don't want to bother you with this, Carol. That's not why I came by."

"This may sound cold," Carol said, "but all I've done for the past three months is think about my own problems. Listening to somebody else's would almost be a relief. So let's have it. Start bothering."

I leaned back in the couch and ran the events of the past few days by Carol. All of it, with no amendments, no curveballs, leaving out only the detail of Frank Matson being Phillip's true father. Leslie had asked me to keep the information to myself. Carol listened intently, interrupting once in a while to have a point clarified or more background filled out. She knew when I was skimming over something and wouldn't let me get away with it. By the time I finished my tale, Carol Wilkie knew as much about the Phillip Chesterton case as I did.

"What do you think has happened?" she asked at last.

"I don't know, because I don't know if Suzie was telling me the truth. I only see three possibilities for Phillip in this, and they're all bad. One, he killed his stepfather. Two, he didn't kill his stepfather but he's still in deep trouble because he ran and the police are going to eat him alive when they eventually find him."

"And three?" Carol said.

"That Phillip's dead. His blood was B negative, too. Frank Matson could have been rushing off to the mobile home to kill somebody just as easily as to be killed. One body found doesn't mean there won't be another."

"You don't really believe the first possibility, do you?" Carol said. "That Phillip murdered his stepfather?"

"No," I said.

"Why not?"

"It wasn't in him, that's all."

"A jury's going to want more than that."

I thought about it for a second. "Phillip and I took a trip last September," I said. "Flew down to Cabo San Lucas."

"I remember."

"It was kind of a celebration he threw for himself in honor of landing the museum job. I remember on the flight down he would hardly eat his food. Know why?"

"Why?"

"Because he was afraid of putting pressure on the fold-out tray table."

Carol wrinkled her nose. "What?"

"He didn't want to disturb the person sitting in the seat in front of him. Phillip worked on that chicken breast like he was defusing a bomb. I don't see somebody like that walking up point-blank and squeezing the trigger of a gun and blowing a chunk of Frank Matson's brain all over the side of a wall. I don't care how much he hated his stepfather. An act like that from Phillip would be unimaginable."

Carol drew her knees up to her chin. "I don't want to rain on your parade," she said, "but your airline anecdote doesn't help things. Sounds like the personality profile of somebody who suppresses and suppresses and then finally erupts. And anyhow, just because something is unimaginable doesn't mean it won't happen. I've at least learned that in the last few months."

"It's not all personality profile," I said. "Some of it's real basic. Frank Matson weighed at least two hundred pounds. Phillip goes a very bookwormish one-forty. How did he lug that kind of weight to the top of the wine vat? Besides, Phillip knows the routine out there at the winery. If the idea was to stash Matson's body in a place where it wouldn't be found for a while, he could have done a lot better than a wine container that is taste-tested on a daily basis."

We fell silent. Focused on our coffee, listened to the shouts of children from the yard across the street.

"Only one person truly scares me in all this," Carol said at last.

"Suzie Wong?"

"Exactly. How did Phillip meet her?"

"Like I told you before. He met her at the De Young Museum."

"But I mean how *exactly*? What were the circumstances?"

"I don't know. She asked him a question about a painting or something."

Carol shrugged. "I think you should try to find out. See if the meeting was as accidental as everybody claims, or whether Suzie had Phillip lined up in the cross hairs. Is there anybody who'd know?"

"Maybe."

"Well ...?"

I looked at the phone. "Can I make a quick call."

"Go ahead."

I reached over and set the end table phone on my lap and dialed Molly Dexter's number at the De Young Museum. She answered on the fifth ring and breathlessly identified herself.

"You doing jumping jacks?" I said.

"Who is this?" Curt. Impatient.

"It's Quinn."

"Oh." Softer, but not by much. "Hi, Quinn. What is it?"

"Is this a bad time to talk?"

"The *worst*. This is the night."

"The night?"

"The Tibet exhibit," Molly said. " Remember?"

"I completely forgot."

"The doors swing open in exactly two hours and nothing's ready. Can this keep till tomorrow?"

I rubbed my forehead. The Tibet exhibit had been big news in San Francisco for weeks. The Dalai Lama himself was going to be there, along with a big Hollywood movie star, and it was rapidly turning into *the* social event of the winter season.

"Phillip's in trouble, Molly. A lot of trouble."

"Is he with you?"

"No. He's still missing."

There was a pause. "What aren't you telling me, Quinn?"

"I'd rather not talk about it on the phone," I said. "Can you come by the apartment tomorrow?"

"No, hold on," she said. "This sounds important. Let's talk tonight. I'm thinking." Momentary silence. Stressed voices in the background. "I'll get you an invitation," she said at last. "Don't ask me how, but I'll get you one. It'll be waiting at the desk by the main door. Look for me in the first big exhibit room to the left. Around seven o'clock. Can you get here by then?"

"Absolutely."

"Dress is formal, you know."

"I'll rent a tuxedo."

Molly said she'd be looking for me, then hung up without a good-bye.

I put the receiver back in its cradle and looked at Carol. She unfolded her legs and pushed herself to a standing position. "Tuxedo?"

"Appears I'm going to the bash at the De Young tonight."

"Not the Tibet thing?"

"Yes."

Carol whistled a slow, impressed whistle. "My, my. That's the toughest ticket in town. A true friend would scalp it out front for a lot of money and come back here with the proceeds and take the vacuum lady to dinner."

"Don't tempt me."

I wandered in the direction of the front door, and Carol trailed me out. "Thanks for letting me talk," I said.

"Any time."

We stood on the porch and Carol waved to a man who jogged by. He waved back, doing a lousy job of not scrutinizing me.

"Everybody knows that Hank's gone," Carol said. "The neighbors are curious."

"Hank'll be back."

Carol shook her head. "I never thought I'd hear myself say this, Quinn, but I'm not sure that I want him back. And it has nothing to do with loving him or not loving him. I'll always love Hank. But when you were just talking about Phillip and how he was on the plane to Mexico, you know what I flashed on?"

"What?"

"How the flight attendants tell you that if the cabin should depressurize that you should tend to your own oxygen needs first, then help your children." Carol looked me directly in the eyes. "That's the way I was starting to feel about being a mother and a wife. I couldn't do much for other people if I couldn't breathe myself. Something had to give, and it couldn't be my kids. So it was Hank."

We held hands silently out on the porch for a second, then Carol exhaled and slapped on a smile. "Enough of that," she said. "Say hi to the Dalai Lama for me."

"Will do."

"And tell Mr. Hollywood that I thought his last movie sucked eggs."

I closed my eyes as if trying to commit her instructions to memory. "That's hi to the Dalai Lama, suck eggs to the movie star."

"Right. Don't get them confused."

I walked down the wooden steps to the driveway and got my keys out. Carol stayed on the porch.

"I've never seen you in a tux," she said.

"I'll have Molly take a snapshot."

"Make it black," she said. "White's for summer."

"Yes, ma'am."

"And no ruffles. It isn't prom night."

"I know I'm not a fashion plate, Carol, but give me *some* credit."

"Just making sure."

I got in the rented car and started it up. "Any messages for Hank?"

She shook her head, then changed her mind and nodded yes, she *did* have a message. She leaned down further, as close as she could to the open passenger window.

"This mystery guy," Carol said. "The one who gets my back to arch and breasts to heave?"

"Yeah?"

"If Hank sees him again, go ahead and send him on over."

We exchanged thumbs-up and I headed back toward the center of town, in search of a tuxedo.

20

knew parking was going to be impossible, so I left the rental car and took a taxi from my apartment. Even so, the snarl of traffic leading into Golden Gate Park was such that I opted to get out early, pay the cabbie, and walk the final mile and a half.

I wasn't prepared for the size of the crowd waiting outside the De Young Museum. Several thousand people at least, milling about under the harsh glare of television spotlights. Platoons of frustrated blue-suited cops hustled this way and that in the chilly night, trying to get vehicles to move, to keep gawkers at bay. At the edge of the Music Concourse a half-dozen news vans were parked, technicians up on the roofs working with lights and cables, reporters reviewing notes and blowing into their hands to keep warm. In the distance a siren screamed, and a small group of Chinese protestors wielding unintelligible signs chanted from behind police barricades. The museum itself was off to my right, well-lit, heavily guarded, and curiously remote, like the dictator's palace trying to weather a proletarian uprising. I adjusted my cummerbund and kept walking. Just another dull Friday night art opening in the city.

My tuxedo apparently counted for something because people tended to step back out of the way and let me through. There was a formidable line of defense at the entrance to the museum. Five beefy San Francisco police in leather jackets covered all possible assaults from the right, left, and front. I walked up to the cop in the middle and he asked to see my invitation. His nose was running and the tips of his ears were bright pink and patience had ceased being one of his virtues. I explained that I didn't have my invitation with me, exactly. The cop wondered where it was, exactly. I pointed over his shoulder and said it was waiting for me up at the main entrance, and he gave me a pained, weary look. This was probably the tenth time he'd heard that ploy tonight and it meant he would have to walk all the way up there, find nothing, and then come all the way back. Prelude to a heave-ho. He stayed rooted in place to see if I would change my story, and when I didn't he turned and trudged slowly up to the main entrance.

A minute later he came back with a surprised look on his face and said, yeah, there actually *was* an invitation waiting for me. He asked for some identification so I showed him my driver's license and he looked it over carefully, reading all the small-print information with a tiny flashlight. I was bracing myself for a frisk, strip, and deep-cavity search when the cop handed my license back and waved me on. Permission granted. I was free to proceed on through the hallowed gates and mingle with the chosen few.

I passed through the portals and took a deep breath. The chosen few numbered close to a thousand. They packed the huge rooms to the left and front, shoulder to shoulder and nose to nose. I declined the glass of champagne immediately foisted upon me by an eager young woman with a tray and began edging my way through the clusters of people. Molly was where she said she'd be, in the first room to the left. She was standing with a young man, listening to him talk, nodding her head and smiling a barely maintained smile. She saw me and waved.

When I reached her she leaned to kiss me, and the man she

was talking to reluctantly angled his body so as to admit a third party.

"You made it," Molly said.

"Momentarily. I think they're still going over my dental records at the front desk."

Molly laughed and introduced me to the other man. His name was Mika something, from Finland. He had a glacial handsomeness, trim and remote and rimmed with frost. We talked idle pleasantries for a minute or two, and when Mika saw I was hunkered in for the duration, he grudgingly drifted off.

"What's it like outside?" she said.

"The peasants are up in arms again," I said. "Tanks in the streets, Molotov cocktails. The usual."

Molly forced a smile and nodded her head in the direction Mika had gone. "Thanks for the rescue."

"Dull?"

Molly shook her head. "Not at all. Mika is quite interesting, as a matter of fact. He drives race cars. Not that boring around and around nonsense, but endurance things, all over the world. Malaysia. Baja California. He's going straight from here to France to race the Paris-Dakar."

"All that and an art lover besides?"

"Let's just leave it at 'lover,' period," Molly said. "That's why I needed rescuing."

"A little flirtation never hurt anybody," I said. "I'm not the jealous type."

"You're not the problem," Molly said. "I'm worried about Noel. Flirtation can hurt a lot when you're trying to maintain custody of your child." She scanned the crowd. "It wouldn't surprise me at all if he had a spy here tonight, watching me, documenting everything."

"You're being paranoid, Molly Dexter."

"*You're* being naive, Quinn Parker."

"And we said we weren't going to discuss this anymore."

"You're right." Molly paused and looked me straight in the eyes. "What's going on with Phillip?"

"No easy way to say it, so I'm just going to lay it out. His stepfather's been found murdered and Phillip is the primary suspect."

Molly's hand went to her mouth, and there was a sharp intake of breath. "Oh, my God!"

"I know. The body was fished out of one of the fermentation tanks at the family winery this afternoon."

Molly looked off in the distance, tried to blink away her shock. "How ... how did you find out about this?"

"I was there when they pulled the body out."

Molly's eyes locked on me. "You were *there?*"

I shook my head. "It's a long story that I can tell you later. Right now I need to ask you something important. Were you aware that Phillip had a girlfriend?"

"Phillip? No."

"Well, he had one. A *serious* girlfriend, and she's mixed up in this somehow. Phillip claimed he met her here, at the museum."

Suddenly another woman intruded on our conversation. She had a De Young nametag on her blouse that identified her as Sarah, and after a quick, insincere apology for the interruption, she began telling Molly about a problem that had come up. An irate couple wanted to meet the Dalai Lama and weren't taking no for an answer. Sarah lowered her voice. The couple were the so-and-so's, and the reverential way Sarah whispered it left no doubt they were heavy hitters. Molly said she'd handle it in a moment. Sarah said it was *ur*gent, with an emphasis on the first syllable. Molly's face tightened and she said she would handle it in a *mo*ment, emphasizing a first syllable of her own. Sarah shrugged an it's-your-funeral shrug, turned, and was immediately swallowed up by the crowd. Molly pressed her fingers against both temples and closed her eyes.

"Headache?"

"Not all the pills in all the pharmacies in all the fifty states ..."

"What can I get you?"

"Nothing."

"Sure?"

Molly nodded. "These are the kind I just have to ride out. But let's get back to Phillip. You said he met his girlfriend here?"

"So he claims."

Molly slowly shook her head, a bit dazed. "I'm just ... I'm at a loss. This is all news to me."

"You never saw him with anyone?"

"No."

"Try to think. Phillip said he used to rendezvous with this woman here quite a bit. Her name is Suzie Wong. She's Asian. Small. No more than five-two. Mid-thirties ..."

Molly continued to shake her head. "No. I mean ... Phillip was always so painfully shy."

"I don't think he'd be lying—"

"Wait," Molly interrupted. "You said an Asian woman?"

"That's right."

"Not the one with the incredible hair?"

"Yes," I said. "That's her."

"That's his *girlfriend!*" Molly tried to assimilate the fact. "He never said a word!"

"When did you first notice her?"

"I have no idea," Molly said. "I really don't. A few months ago. Three, four. We have our regulars at the museum just like a restaurant has its regulars at the coffee counter, and I guess at some point I was more or less aware that she was becoming one of our regulars. I'd see her wandering the halls, looking at the paintings. And that fabulous hair! It was impossible *not* to notice that."

"But never Phillip with her?"

"Once or twice maybe, explaining something, but that was his job so it didn't strike me as odd. He did that with a lot of peo-ple." Molly's look of wonderment faded, replaced by concern. "You say she's involved. How?"

"Not sure yet. At the very least I'm convinced she knows where Phillip is, but I don't have a handle on her. She says she's a waitress but pays her hefty rent six months in advance. Murky background."

"What did you want from me?"

I shrugged. "Trying to get a fix on how they met. Whether it was an accident, or if Phillip was ambushed. And I'd like to know what kind of car she drove."

"Why?"

"Phillip's car is in her garage, which makes me think they took off in hers. I could go back and ask the couple who rented the garage space, but they're suspicious enough as it is ..."

Molly shrugged her shoulders helplessly. "Sorry. I can ask around if you want. The security people are on the floor a lot more than I am. Maybe they saw something."

We were quiet a moment. I didn't see the point in telling Molly about the weapon in the glove compartment. People jostled us. Now and then a couple of Buddhist monks would slide by in their robes, shaved heads glistening. People stared at them with a mixture of wonder and awe, like they were movie stars disembarking from limos on Oscar night.

Sarah, the same woman who'd interrupted us before, was suddenly back in our faces with a well-dressed, middle-aged couple in tow. Sarah ignored me completely this time and introduced the couple to Molly as Mr. and Mrs. Whatever, prominent donors and longtime friends of the De Young. The man had a scrunched-up, rodent sort of face and was pissed as hell. His wife seemed embarrassed by the commotion and was scanning the area for a nice, big potted plant to hide behind. Introductions completed, Sarah beat a hasty retreat.

Rodent Face immediately launched into a tirade about all the money he and his family had given to the museum over the years and how the least—the *least!*—he expected was a small dribble of preferential treatment from time to time. Not much. Just a dribble. Just a little eensie-weensie eyedropful every once in a great, great while. Was that too much to ask?

The harangue went on and on. Molly patiently listened to the vented bile, nodding, trying not to show her headache. Part of her job tonight was to gracefully inform people who'd donated big bucks to the museum that they could not automatically get in a conga line with a thousand others to glad-hand with the spiritual leader of Tibet. But this information wasn't getting through to Rodent Face, and after a few minutes of his high-pitched whining I excused myself so Molly could work her delicate diplomacy unencumbered. There was appreciation in her eyes, but her expression told me not to wander far. She and I hadn't finished talking.

I had a change of mind about the complimentary champagne, so I snatched a glass from a tray and spent some time milling about, looking at the exhibit. The Tibetan art wasn't my cup of tea, so I cut it short after ten or fifteen minutes and headed back to see how Molly was doing.

Incredibly, Rodent Face was still there, still arguing. He was sweating now, the shoulders of his jacket bunched up around his neck. I tucked myself back into the group but nobody acknowledged my reappearance, not even Molly. Her countenance was showing the strain, and she was locked in on Rodent Face.

"Who gives you the right?" Rodent Face was saying, jabbing a finger in Molly's direction. "Who the hell gives *you* the right? That's what I want to know! Why am I having to stand here and argue with some ten-buck-an-hour-assistant, for Christ's sake! *That's* what I want to know! Can somebody explain that to me?" Rodent Face turned to the nearby minglers with his arms extended. "Anybody? Anybody know the answer to that?"

Molly didn't answer. Her jaw was set and her eyes were shimmering with suppressed anger. Rodent Face ceased his appeal to the indifferent masses and turned on Molly.

"Did it ever occur to you who pays your salary, whoever you are?" he said, reaching out to tilt her nametag so he could read it. "Molly Dexter? Did it ever occur to you?"

Molly flinched at the sudden, aggressive proximity of his hand to her breast. "Don't touch me," she said.

"Don't what?"

"Don't touch me."

"I didn't touch you."

"Just don't."

Rodent Face let his mouth drop open, then turned to do his appeal-to-the-audience shtick again. "She says not to—"

"That's enough," I said.

Rodent Face slowly turned to face me. "What?"

"She said not to touch her. I'll take it one step further and tell you to shut your mouth and drift away."

"Quinn!" Molly snapped.

Rodent Face looked disbelievingly at his wife, then at me. He had a big nose, bunched-up eyes, and an unpleasant five o'clock shadow even though a nick on his jaw indicated he must have only just shaved. The wife was dishwater blond and Social Register bland, hair yanked back in a severe bun, face buffed to the unnatural shine you see on newly varnished bowling lanes. She was taller and bigger than her husband, thick and rustic, with lifeless eyes and a large, flat forehead that you could almost see your reflection in.

"Who the hell," Rodent Face said, "are you?"

"Quinn," Molly said. "I'll handle this."

"I only—"

"Quinn!" Her eyes were flashing and there was color in her cheeks. "I *said* I'll handle it."

Fine. The crush of celebrity-sniffing humanity was starting to get to me anyway, so I took my glass of champagne and began working my way slowly to the silent and empty east wing of the museum. I thought of Rodent Face and rued the restrictions civilization places upon us when it comes to dealing with jerks. It wasn't right. In a more highly evolved society I would have been allowed to pull his trousers down to the floor and force him to waddle out of the De Young to the laughing, finger-pointing ridicule of thousands.

I ended up in a small room in the most distant corner of the museum. It had an expatriate theme, the exhibit consisting of paintings by nineteenth-century Americans who had turned their backs on the United States to live and work in Europe. There was a bench in the middle of the room and I sat there. Initially the silence was louder than the chaos I'd fled, but then it gradually became true silence. Deep silence. Almost a meditation, and before long I was lost among the restful water lilies and rainy European streets, feeling the melancholy of all these painters who had left their own land to paint others. Lost, seeking, displaced. The Quinn Parker Room.

Time passed.

"Somehow I knew you'd be here."

The voice brought me, blinking, back to the present. Molly was standing in the doorway, arms folded across her chest, smiling.

"You okay?" I said.

"I'm fine. A headache that could bore through wood, but I'm fine."

"What happened with that charming gentleman?"

"I found his teething ring and sent him on his way."

Molly strolled into the room and sat down on the bench next to me, thigh to thigh, shoulder to shoulder.

"Sorry for the knight-in-shining-armor routine," I said.

"You should be sorry. Same old Quinn. Have lance, will travel."

Her perfume was spicy and her blue-black hair shone beneath the bright lights.

"Why aren't you out there looking at the exhibit?" she said. "Mr. Box Office just made his appearance."

"I already looked."

"Not your style?"

I shrugged. "I guess I'm not Buddhist material."

"Why not?"

"I'm real bad about letting go of worldly things."

"Do tell?"

I nodded. "I still die a little inside when I think of how Bobby Richardson caught McCovey's line drive to end the 1962 World Series."

Molly softly laughed and leaned her shoulder against mine. "You don't give the Buddhists nearly enough credit," she said.

"Probably not."

"*Definitely* not."

A soft din of distant applause echoed through the museum and filled our momentary silence. "I've got to get back," Molly said. "Crowd control's going to be a problem very soon."

"Okay."

"Can you stay awhile?" Molly said. "I'll only be another hour or so, then we can go home together."

"An hour?"

She bent her head, leaned up under me, and kissed me softly on the lips. "Don't let my deeply spiritual interior fool you," she said. "In actual fact I'm just the woman for a man who likes to cling to worldly things."

"Haven't I clung to your worldly things enough in the last six months?"

"You've got a one-track mind," Molly said.

"Thanks. You can't believe what I went through to get rid of the other tracks."

I returned her kiss, and there we sat on the bench in the expatriate room of the De Young Museum, necking like high-school kids, while off in the distance the Dalai Lama spoke and the people applauded.

21

woke up and realized I was alone in bed. Lola had taken Molly's place beside me, curled into the rumpled sheets and pillows, yawning and licking her tail and daring me to do anything about it. Down the hallway I could hear the sound of bathwater running. I dragged myself out of bed and pulled on my pants and tapped on the bathroom door.

"Molly?"

"Come on in."

I went into the bathroom and shut the door behind me. Molly was stretched out in the tub, taking a bubble bath. It's not a large bathtub and Molly is a big girl, so she had her feet propped high on the wall above the faucets, showing a long delicious taper of legs that disappeared into the bubbles.

"You keep Popeye the Sailor bubble bath in stock?" she said.

"Hank's kids spend the night once in a while," I said. "Obviously you don't linger in bed these days."

"I don't linger *anywhere* until the Tibetan road show moves on to Los Angeles," Molly said. "I've got to clean up and get back to the museum right away."

"This morning?'

"That's right."

"You're kidding."

"Sorry."

"It's—" I looked at my watch, "not even eight o'clock."

"There's a breakfast for the mayor and various dignitaries. Don't fight it, Quinn. Just accept that for the next few days all of us remotely connected to the De Young Museum are indentured servants."

"Great."

Molly shut her eyes and eased down further into the water. "I haven't taken a bath in years," she said. "Funny how you can stop doing something you love and not even realize it. When I was a girl I always took baths. Used to get in the tub when it was empty and lie there while it filled up. Found it erotic."

"Erotic?"

Molly nodded. "Like bleeding all over, but without the pain."

"Delightful."

I offered to scrub her back but Molly said she didn't want us to start something that we couldn't finish. So I went out to the kitchen and got the coffee going. In ten minutes Molly was out, dried, dressed, and hurrying down the stairs with a mug of strong black coffee.

I pulled on some clothes and walked her to her car. She kissed me and said she'd give a call later in the day and I watched her drive away. Then I went to the Silver Platter on Van Ness and picked up the morning *Chronicle* and flipped through it while climbing the fifty-four steps. I rapped on Hank's closed door, then opened it and stuck my head in.

"Rise and shine," I said. "Up, up, up, up, up. Got some questions for you."

Hank was stretched out on top of the covers, hands linked behind his head, ankles crossed. The room was dark, but as my eyes adjusted I realized he was completely dressed and wide awake.

"Thanks for knocking, Quinn," he said. "I want you to feel right at home."

Hank wasn't alone. Another form took shape in the darkness. A woman, in bed next to him, sound asleep. She had a pillowful of tousled honey-blond hair and wore a blouse and skirt and nylons.

"Whoops," I said, backing out and closing the door. "So sorry."

I went out to the kitchen and poured myself a cup of coffee. Okay. Hank Wilkie was in bed, fully dressed, with a woman, also fully dressed. There was no doubt a perfectly good explanation for that, and I would hear all about it soon enough. I put it out of my mind and sat in the dining room's bright December sunshine and read the account of Frank Matson's murder.

I don't know why I ever harbored the hope that a high-profile millionaire hauled from the bottom of a ten-thousand-gallon vat of vintage Cabernet Sauvignon would slip by the *Chronicle* editors unnoticed. On the contrary. The story was right there in big bold letters on the first page. The article spared no details. Phillip Chesterton was named as the prime suspect, and a statewide search was currently under way.

I read the article three times, then shoved it away. After a while there was activity behind Hank's door and he came shuffling out. His clothes were wrinkled. He got a cup of coffee and poured himself a bowl of cereal and joined me at the dining-room table.

"Morning," I said.

"Morning."

I picked up the entertainment section of the paper and began reading a movie review. Hank dug his spoon into the Cheerios and nosed around for the sports page. The silent seconds ticked by, and a few minutes later the door to the guest bedroom opened again and the woman with the honey-blond hair came out cautiously and stood in the hallway. Her red skirt and white blouse were lined with irregular creases, and there was a ten-inch run in her nylon stockings. She was a big-boned woman, but not heavy. Forcefully attractive. Chiseled features and dramatic dark eyebrows and breasts that demanded your immediate and complete attention. "Hi," she said.

I said hi. Hank got up and joined her in the hallway and they exchanged one of the most stilted kisses I've seen this side of great-aunts with great-nephews.

"Can I take a shower?" she asked him.

"Sure," Hank said. "Here. Let me get you set up."

The two of them ducked into the bathroom. Hank reemerged a moment later and scooted up to his bowl of soggy Cheerios. Another minute of silence.

"Want to hear your horoscope?" I finally said.

"No."

"It applies."

Down the hall we could hear the shower water coming on. The sliding of the shower curtain.

"Gunnhilde?" I said.

Hank nodded, continued to eat his cereal.

"Not that it's any of my business," I said, "but the bedroom part works a lot better when you take your clothes off."

Hank's spoon stopped at his lips, and he gave me a look. "Thanks for the technical advice. How was the Dalai Lama?"

"He was fine. How was your hot date?"

"Hot date ..." Hank shook his head. "I don't know, Quinn. This isn't me. I'm not cut out for this."

"Cut out for what?"

"Dating." He looked back at the bathroom, then leaned closer, confidential, and his voice dropped to a semi-whisper, as though Gunnhilde might hear our conversation above the roar of water and shut doors and thirty feet of hallway. "She passed out on me last night."

"Where?"

"Right here in the living room!" Hank snapped his fingers. "Just like that."

"How?"

"I don't know how! She had a few glasses of wine and the next thing I know she's gone! Lights out!"

"Why don't you start at the beginning," I said. "You went to Sausalito and had dinner at Christophe's ..."

"Right," Hank said, "Christophe's. That went okay, except it turns out Hilda's a vegetarian. The kind who won't even eat chicken or fish. So as soon as I ordered the coq au vin she started in. Asked if I'd ever been to a chicken farm. I said no. It was a good thing, she said, because I'd be horrified. They cram the chickens into these wire cages. And it's not like chickens don't have a social sense. They do. There's a natural hierarchy, the pecking order we always hear about, but the hierarchy starts to break down after about ninety chickens. Up to ninety the chickens can figure out where they stand in the scheme of things. The world makes sense. But go past ninety and they start to get nervous. Guess how many chickens are in the average chicken warehouse."

"More than ninety?"

"Eighty *thousand!* Crammed in like that they go berserk. Literally berserk. Start to kill and cannibalize each other. So the farmers hack off their beaks, a *very* painful process incidentally, so they can't kill each other. But half the time that means they can't eat or drink very well either and a lot of them slowly die of starvation. Not that hunger bothers the farmers. Chickens aren't fed for the final thirty hours of their life because the feed stays in the animal's digestive system and doesn't have a chance to convert into flesh, and since chickens are sold by the pound, the last few meals a chicken eats are a waste of money. Have you ever heard of force moulting?"

"No."

"It's light deprivation followed by intense, around-the-clock lighting. Shocks the chickens into thinking they've experienced a change of season and they become more productive. Those that can still move, that is. The chickens are so crowded in their cages that their toenails grow around the wire mesh at the bottom and the feet have to be cut off. Farmers solve this problem by cutting off the toes of the chicks when they are a day or two old."

"She told you all this?" I said.

"The minute I ordered!"

"That must have set a nice tone for the evening."

"Gunnhilde said it wasn't just the chickens. It was *us*. That the chickens absorb all this dementia into their flesh, and when we eat of the same anguished flesh the torment is passed on to us. It's absorbed in our flesh and we start to go insane ourselves."

I nodded. "Dinner sounds like it was a rousing success. Then what happened?"

"We drove up to the Marin Headlands and sat there for a while looking over the lights of the city and talking."

"Not about food, I hope."

"No. About her trouble with orgasm."

My coffee cup stopped at my lips. "Pardon me?"

Hank shook his head. "The only way she can satisfy herself is with the massage thing in her shower, and even then it takes a while. Sometimes a half-hour or more. The hot water runs out and then it gets cold, which just makes it harder. She's nervous about what the people in the next apartment are thinking."

"She told you this on your first date?"

Hank waved it off. "That's Gunnhilde. She would have told all this to the guy working the Golden Gate tollbooth if it wouldn't have backed up traffic. Gunnhilde believes in complete honesty all the time."

"Does she believe in water conservation?" I said. "Somebody should let her know we're in the middle of a drought."

"There are droughts," Hank said. "And then there are droughts."

As if on cue the shower in the bathroom turned off and the pipes in the old Victorian groaned. Hank glanced down the hallway, then turned back to me.

"Anyway ... we came back here for a nightcap. It was only around midnight, and even with the chicken business the evening had gone pretty well. So she had two quick glasses of wine and passed out, boom, right over there on the couch. I don't know if you noticed, but Gunnhilde's a load."

"Why didn't you just leave her there?"

"Because she's allergic to cats," Hank said. "That's why. And the goddamn couch is full of Lola's hair. So I dragged her onto my bed. I didn't feel like snuggling with you, and I'm not crazy about cat hair, either. I was careful to sleep on top of the covers and keep my clothes on so she wouldn't wake up in the middle of the night and think I was trying to take the place of her Water Pik."

"Welcome to the singles world," I said.

Hank shook his head. "Know what I kept thinking last night while all this was going on?"

"What?"

"How Carol would have laughed if she could have seen it! Carol! I'm out on the town with the Scandinavian bombshell of my dreams who's telling me about her orgasms and all I'm thinking about is Carol! The woman who tossed me out of the house!"

"There'll be other dates," I said. "Saner ones."

Hank looked utterly weary at the prospect. "I hope not. Besides, I can't *afford* to date. Christophe's about killed me. I've got some money stashed away, but that's for Cort's dental work next month. What am I supposed to say to the next woman I take to dinner? Please don't order that appetizer because my second-grader needs his molars cleaned?"

The bathroom door opened and Gunnhilde flashed by in a blur of flesh tone, blue towel, and billowing steam, disappearing into Hank's bedroom.

"Enough about my love life," Hank said. "What's going to happen with Phillip?"

I sighed, refocused. "I don't know. The questions are piling up."

"What sort of questions?"

"Who called Frank Matson that night? What does Pilkow Street mean? Who was hiding in the apartment with Suzie when I went to see her? Where is Suzie now? Who were those men at Jack London Park and why were they following me? How come that mobile home was registered in Frank Matson's name when he obviously was heading up Route C for the first time?"

"Is that so important?"

"Sure it is," I said. "Means someone must have gone to the

trouble of connecting Matson to that house a long time ago. A little premeditated for an upset stepson who supposedly committed a crime of passion."

At that moment Gunnhilde came slowly, sheepishly down the hall. She'd smoothed out her blouse and skirt.

"I'm going to go now," she said.

Hank stood. "I'll walk you to the car."

Gunnhilde said that it was nice to meet me and the two of them headed down the stairs.

I took the opportunity to clean up. Put the dishes away and dumped the last half-inch of the coffee down the sink and rinsed out Lola's milk bowl. Fifteen minutes later I heard the front door open and close and Hank trudged up the stairs. I was finishing up the last of the dishes by the time he reached the kitchen.

"Are you ready for this?" Hank said.

"What?"

"She likes me! Says I'm the first guy who really took the time to listen to her and didn't start pawing her right away. And she thought it was sweet that I kept my clothes on all night."

"I thought that was sweet, too."

"You're not getting this," Hank said. "She wants to see me again."

I shrugged, dried my hands on the towel looped through the refrigerator door. "Good."

"Good? This isn't good! This is Gunnhilde, the chicken-coop and Water Pik woman! What am I supposed to do?"

"What you're supposed to do is give Gunnhilde another chance," I said. "Only this time order tofu and tell her about *your* sexual problems."

"I don't have any."

On that fictitious note Hank announced that he had some errands to run downtown and waved good-bye. He wasn't that upset about having a second shot at Gunnhilde. There was interest in his eyes.

I spent the morning doing mundane apartment things. Laundry. Garbage. Changing the newspaper sheets in Oscar's parrot cage and fixing him up with a new grain mixture. Sunflower seed, hemp seed, large millet seed, white millet seed, peanuts, and a healthy dose of canary seed. But Oscar isn't picky. He'll also settle for smoked pheasant.

A couple hours later Hank came back with a shopping bag from Macy's tucked under his arm. He disappeared into his bedroom before I could inquire. New clothes, no doubt, to match Gunnhilde's specifications. He didn't want to give me a chance to comment.

Shortly before eleven o'clock the door buzzer sounded and I headed down the fifty-four steps and opened the door. Abigail Chesterton stood before me. She had a metal strongbox in her hands.

"I didn't know where else to go, Quinn," she said. Her voice was shaking, and her eyes were red.

"What's happened?"

She cradled the strongbox as though it were a newborn baby. All she could do was shake her head. Some of my unanswered questions were about to be answered.

22

Abigail stepped through the doorway. She'd been to my apartment several times before, but now she appeared disoriented and hesitant, like a child wandering into the pre-school classroom for the first time. She was wearing the same bright yellow, ground-trailing summer dress she'd been wearing the day Hank and I had eaten lunch with her up in Napa. She held out the strongbox and I took it from her.

"What's this?"

"Is there someplace we can talk, Quinn?" Upstairs Hank was bumbling around in the bathroom. "Someplace private?"

"Sure," I said, trying to clear my head. "There's a café around the corner."

"Leave the strongbox here," she said. "Put it in a safe place."

I told Abigail to wait a second and I took the heavy metal box upstairs. I unlocked the wall safe in my office and put it there. Hank was brushing his teeth and stepped out in the hallway to give me a silent, inquisitive look. I shrugged and pointed downstairs. He returned my shrug and went back into the bathroom.

Abigail and I went to La Parroquiana, a small café around the corner on Polk. It had a dozen tables inside and six out on the sidewalk, and was a nice place to have coffee except for the vacuous New Age music that played incessantly. We sat inside where it was private. The waiter took our coffee order and disappeared.

"You must be surprised to see me," Abigail said. "The new widow, out and about."

She tried to smile away her pain, but failed. Instead her eyes went to the tabletop and stayed there.

"What is it, Abigail?"

She swallowed to regain control of herself. "Rogelio brought the strongbox to me last night. Frank gave it to him a few months ago. Rogelio was under strict instructions to give the box to Detective Davis if anything should ever happen to Frank."

"Davis?"

Abigail nodded. "Rogelio doesn't trust Detective Davis, so he gave it to me instead."

"Rogelio's instincts are good," I said. "What's in the box?"

Abigail opened her purse. "You'll have time later to see for yourself." She took a plain white envelope from her purse and handed it to me. "This came with the strongbox. Read it."

I took the envelope and looked at her.

"Go ahead," she said. "Read it now."

I opened the envelope. A single handwritten page was inside.

Bill—If you're reading this it's because I'm either dead or I don't give a damn anymore. Whatever reason, it won't be good. Been putting this together for a while so you can nail this little bastard down the road if I can't. Don't know how McCall got all this stuff, but I'll feel better wherever I am right now if I know that the son of a bitch is getting his. As one last favor please make his life as miserable as he's made mine.— Frank

I read it again, slower this time, then looked up at Abigail. "McCall? He's talking about Leslie?"

Abigail nodded.

"What does it mean?"

"It means," Abigail said in a quivering voice, "that for most of the past year my best friend has been blackmailing my husband."

She stared down at the untasted coffee and her eyes brimmed with tears. Then the emotion subsided.

"Whatever's in that strongbox supports this?" I said.

Abigail nodded. "I mean, I think it does. Half of it made no sense to me. Nothing makes any sense anymore." She spoke in a wistful fashion, as if including her own life with Phillip's, and dead Darryl's, and now dead Frank's, too.

There was nowhere else for the conversation to go. We sat silently for a minute or two while our coffee grew colder and the anemic New Age music harmlessly wafted by. Then Abigail stood and abruptly excused herself. I stood with her but she said no. She wanted to be alone.

"All I want you to do is look through the material in the strongbox," she said. "Look through it and tell me what you think. What you think I should do."

Then she turned away and walked back out onto Polk Street. I watched her go. She moved with a pigeon-toed, rest-home frailty well beyond her years. The bright yellow summer dress did nothing but serve as a painful contrast to just how unsummery her person had become. It trailed along the ground behind her like tattered bunting from a finished parade, and then she was gone.

Frank Matson had been a military man. If somewhere along the line I'd forgotten that, the contents of the strongbox reminded me. There are some unpleasant rules that govern in times of war, and one of those rules is to not leave anything of value to an invading army. Farmers burn their fields, factory workers sabotage their machines, the Russians all but burned Moscow to the ground rather than give it to Napoleon. And Frank Matson had done the same thing to Leslie McCall. He had rigged Leslie's blackmail scheme with an explosive of his own. A posthumous calling card. A time bomb from the grave, set to be activated with the first shovelful of dirt landing on the coffin.

I had the papers of the strongbox spread out across my desk. I'd been at the documents for the entire afternoon. Bank statements mostly. Telegrams. Phone records of long-distance calls, and long dull recitations of funds being transferred from one numbered account to another. Not the thrilling stuff of tabloid journalism, though there were a couple of interesting finds in among the boredom. One was a packet filled with surveillance-type photos of Detective Davis handing a briefcase to a man I'd never seen before. There was no accompanying documentation, but the picture must have meant enough to Frank Matson on its own. The other piece of paper that got my attention was a letter. An official communication from the government of Cambodia to the Bank of Zurich confirming the executions on January 11, 1982, of two people named Paul Wilson and Nguyen Nyu for the crime of espionage. But other than that the strongbox was mostly filled with pages of figures and not much else.

One thing, however, was startlingly clear. Leslie McCall was extracting hefty payments from Frank Matson for something that had happened in Frank's past. Less clear were the specifics of what Frank Matson had done that Leslie'd uncovered. Maybe Leslie didn't have the details. Or Frank had chosen to destroy the evidence before the strongbox went on to Detective Davis. Or perhaps Abigail herself had done some pruning. Maybe she'd been selective in what she wanted me to see.

It was five in the afternoon and my eyes were beginning to fail. I pushed myself away from the desk with a sigh and went down the hall toward the dining-room table. Hank was sitting there bent over the classified section of the *Chronicle,* circling various items with red ink. He was spruced up and ready for his follow-up date with Gunnhilde. I went into the kitchen and began throwing together a Dagwood sandwich from various leftovers in the refrigerator.

"How does this sound?" he said without looking up. "San

Francisco, two-bedroom, excellent location near BART station, ethnic diversity, ten minutes to downtown. Three hundred fifty dollars a month."

"'Ethnic diversity'?"

"That's what it says."

"I don't know. That's kind of like 'city of contrasts.'"

Hank nodded. "In other words, convenience store holdups."

"Afraid so."

"Great." Hank pushed the newspaper away. "So how am I ever going to find a decent apartment with my finances?"

"How come you're looking for an apartment?"

"You've got real cute dimples, Quinn, but I can't live with you forever."

I put my sandwich on a plate and joined Hank at the table. "Why don't you just stay on here a little while longer till you come to your senses about Carol and then move back home where you belong?"

"I'm serious," Hank said.

"So am I."

He exhaled and looked forlornly out the dining-room window at the Golden Gate Bridge. You could see the shimmering glint of cars inching across toward the city. "You know what my problem might be, Quinn?"

"Uh oh."

"I'm not thinking big enough."

"Big is expensive, Hank. In this city, *small* is expensive."

"I'm not talking about an apartment," Hank said. "I'm talking about the bigger picture. I mean, this is an enormous change in my life. A *huge* change! What am I doing responding to this crisis by scrounging around in the cheap column of the classifieds? Maybe I've got it all back-asswards." A dreamy sort of smile formed on Hank's lips. "Brazil ..."

"Please ..."

"Why not?" Hank turned and faced me. "Why the hell not? Rio! Ipanema! Go down there and dive in headfirst. For once in my life really go crazy! Dance till dawn every night and lose myself in a sea of bodily fluids!"

I held up my sandwich. "Do you mind, Hank? I'm trying to eat."

"Sorry."

"And anyway ... I appreciate your exuberance, but forget about Rio."

"What for?"

"For one thing, it's more expensive in Brazil than it is here. For another, you can go HIV-positive by simple eye contact down there. These days bodily fluids are best kept to oneself. Or shared with someone you know and love. Like Carol."

Hank's eyes lost that fanatical glow. His shoulders slumped, and he stared dejectedly at the open newspaper. "You're right. And they're not going to do anything about it, are they? They're just going to fuck themselves into extinction."

I stopped in mid-chew. "If I may borrow a buzzword from my profession, why don't you internalize this conflict until you have it resolved."

"Thanks."

"What time's your date tonight?"

"Six."

"Why so early?"

"We're going to catch a movie before dinner."

"You sound less than delirious."

Hank shrugged.

"I saw Carol yesterday," I said.

"Yeah? How is she?"

"Fine. Looking really good."

"She always looks really good," Hank said.

"I know. What I meant was she looked really good even for someone who always looks really good."

Hank gave me a look. "I know what you're trying to do but it's not going to work. Carol's the one who issued *me* the walking papers, remember. And you didn't see her at the end. You never read the note she left me. Forget it. If that's the way she wants it, that's how it'll be."

I decided to drop the subject. Hank looked at his watch, exhaled loudly, and got to his feet. "Five-twenty," he said glumly. "T minus forty minutes and counting. Gunnhilde lives over in Larkspur, so I better take off."

"Don't order the glazed ham."

"Was thinking more along the lines of steak tartare."

"Perfect."

Hank tromped off down the stairs and I made another stab at finishing my sandwich. It went down easier without Hank's bodily secretions to deal with.

I spent a restless evening alone in the apartment. Molly was at the De Young, there was nothing on television, I was in between books. I almost called Carol, but knew that we'd end up spending the whole night talking about Hank, and I'd had my Wilkie quota for the day. So I got out the miniature Nerf football and played field goal with Lola. It's a dumb pass-the-time game. I try to flick the ball with my forefinger through the uprights of the dining-room chair, and Lola leaps high at the last minute to bat the ball away. Lola doesn't find it dumb. Lola could do this till the Cubs go to the World Series. So we sat and did it for a while, and when she opened up a sixty-five to thirty-eight lead I quit keeping score and declared her the winner.

Around nine o'clock I went back into the office and began gathering up the various papers from the strongbox. But when I opened the lid I noticed something. A square, rigid envelope, four inches by four inches, that had lodged itself flush against the wall of the strongbox and had gone overlooked. I wiggled it free and opened the envelope, and a photograph fell out.

It was a grainy, dog-eared, black-and-white shot of a young Frank Matson in a Hawaiian shirt, straw hat, and that familiar, clenched Great White Hunter grin of his I remembered from the safari album. He was sitting at an outdoor café, but it wasn't a posh setting. The street was made of dirt, and a pig rooted around in the background. Tropical palms in the distance. A man sat in the chair to Matson's right, his face in three-quarter profile. A woman sat on Matson's lap, her arms linked around his neck. She was peering down at Matson with a reluctant grin on her face, as if about to scold him for having told an off-color joke in mixed company. She was Asian. Very young, good-looking, stunning hair. There was no mistaking Suzie Wong's hair. On the back, in pencil, was written "Pilkow, Cambodia. 1971."

23

Hank was up early the next morning. There were no women, dressed or otherwise, in the bedroom or bathroom. He looked a little glum so I told him I'd buy him breakfast.

We drove out to Mel's on Geary and took a booth at a window facing the street. The decor of Mel's is 1950s carhop, but this morning the employees seemed to be overdoing it. Every single waitress, without exception, was chewing gum. It smacked of orchestration. Report to work, punch in, put on the apron, toss in the gum so as to further enhance the bobby socks, Teen Angel feel. Change was in the air, and it didn't bode well.

I scanned the menu. "What're you having?"

"With cheese."

"What?"

Hank turned his menu around and pointed at the bottom. "Right there. It says, 'With cheese, add fifty cents.' After last night with Gunnhilde that's all I can afford."

"I'm buying breakfast," I said. "Go ahead and order something to put your cheese on."

Hank reopened the menu.

"I take it your evening was less than successful?" I said.

"Accurate assumption."

"Don't worry, Hank. Things'll be better in the next life."

"Next life ..." Hank pushed aside the menu and began absentmindedly flipping through the jukebox selector attached to the table. "There'd better not be a next life. Reincarnation scares the hell out of me. With my luck I'll come back as a bug. First insect suicide on record. A grasshopper strung up from the top of a sunflower, blade of grass around his throat, kicking the clod of dirt out from under him."

"What happened? You order chicken again?"

Hank shook his head. "No. Gunnhilde noticed that I was still wearing my wedding ring and wondered why. I said I was still married, that's why. She said it made her feel funny, and wondered if I could take it off, just for the evening."

"Did you?"

"Hell, no," Hank said. "Remember when Carol and I went on our honeymoon?"

"Hawaii, right?"

Hank nodded. "The Big Island. First afternoon there I went down to the beach and lost my wedding ring. Very first day of the honeymoon! Suntan oil or something, the damn thing just slid off my finger and I never felt a thing. Had to go back to the hotel room and tell Carol, and she started crying. The lost ring really nailed her. I could tell she saw it as a bad omen. Carol's more superstitious about those things than she'll ever admit to."

"So what you're wearing now isn't the original?"

"Let me finish," Hank said. "So when Carol quit crying she asked where I'd been sunbathing and we went down to the beach together and I showed her. We sifted the sand but couldn't find it. I finally gave it up and went back to the hotel room and didn't see Carol for hours. For all I knew she was on her way back to California. Then at dinner that night Carol got a funny look on her face and said she had a present for me. There it was, in her purse!"

"Your wedding ring?"

"The very one, all wrapped up in a gift box, like I was getting it for the first time. She'd spent the entire afternoon out there on the beach, raking through a twenty-foot diameter of sand with her comb! Every square inch! Next morning I went out to the beach early and you could see the patch of raked sand. The circles she'd made." Hank's throat was tight with emotion. "I wanted to excavate that plot of sand, Quinn. Dig it up, take it on the plane back with us. Keep it forever in some roped-off portion of the backyard."

"I think that's exactly what you should do," I said.

Hank shook his head. "Too expensive."

"Damn the expense. And how come I haven't heard that story before?"

"The removal of my wedding ring has never been an issue before," Hank said. "Anyway, Gunnhilde didn't think it was such a great story. I kept my ring on and she kept her clothes on and that's the end of that. Still a nice lady in her own bizarre way. I almost started liking her. She should've been my wacky younger sister."

The waitress brought our breakfasts and we began to eat. "How about you?" Hank said. "What was Abigail's visit all about?"

I told him. At the end of my tale I took the Pilkow photograph from my shirt pocket and showed Hank what the young Suzie Wong looked like.

"Poor Abigail," he said at the end of it. "She's getting hit from all sides."

"Leslie McCall's the one bothering me. Last night I lay in bed and played the what-if game."

"What if what?"

"What if Frank Matson had decided not to pay any more blackmail money? What if Frank decided to call Leslie's bluff? What if Leslie decided that Frank Matson had to die?"

Hank frowned. "You think Leslie killed Matson? That mousy little guy with the bad toupee?"

"Leslie wears a toupee?"

Hank shook his head. "You've got a great eye, Quinn. What else makes you think he killed Matson?"

I shrugged. "Leslie didn't seem especially concerned that Frank was going to show up at the house while Holt was promenading around. Leslie knew about the blow-up between Phillip and his stepfather, so maybe he saw an opening. Dead Frank, missing stepson, evil Detective Davis straining at the leash. Leslie would have had the unlisted phone number and he would certainly have disguised his voice to Rogelio. And it would not have been difficult for an intimate friend of the family to have gotten his hands on a coded access card to slip past the electronic gates."

Hank nodded while he ate. "And Suzie?"

"I don't know. All this photograph proves is that Suzie and Frank knew each other in the past, and Leslie discovered it. It doesn't necessarily mean Leslie knew about Suzie Wong out here."

"But if he did," Hank said, "doesn't it make sense that the two of them were working together?"

"I choose not to think that way."

"Why not?"

"Because Phillip's life gets more precarious that way."

Hank shook his head. "You're making me say the 'D' word."

"Which is?"

"Denial."

The "S" word took over for the rest of our breakfast. Silence. Then I drove back home, got my boxing gloves, and went down to Newman's Gym so that I could hit something.

Two days passed. I tried to call Abigail several times but she was never there, and for one reason or another was not returning my calls. I used the dead time to take care of some problems. I called Jack London State Park, pleaded with them not to tow my van, and promised that I'd be up in the next day or so to get it.

I did some legwork of my own, but nothing came of it. Called every airline flying out of San Francisco and Oakland to see if a Phillip Chesterton had made reservations in the past couple of days. He hadn't. An entire afternoon was spent canvassing a ten-block area around Suzie's apartment, showing residents and shopkeepers and passersby Phillip's photograph, hoping for a flicker of recognition. Gumshoe stuff, but I wasn't a gumshoe and didn't get much cooperation. Most of the people veered away from me as I approached. Those who bothered to look just cast a quick glance at the photo and said no, they hadn't seen him. The few who did take the time to listen to my spiel had some burning issue of their own they wanted to share with me. Central American politics. The Most Holy Swami Satchinanda. How the Tri-Lateral Commission, working in conjunction with visiting space aliens, had conspired to spread the AIDS virus. I put the photo back in my wallet and gave up.

Frank Matson's murder stayed on page one for two days. Side by side pictures of Phillip and Frank, with a summary of the long-existing hostility between the two. The mobile home out on Route C was confirmed to have been registered in Frank Matson's name, and there was speculation that he might have been using it for some less than legal business. An all-out search for Phillip was under way, and casual reference was made to the young Chesterton heir's long history of "mental instability."

Television latched on, too. Channel Five sent a crew up to Napa, and they broadcast their initial report live from the stone entry gate at 100 Glenville Road. Even Detective Davis got some air time, briefly interviewed on the steps in front of his quaint Napa office. He talked about Phillip as though his guilt were a foregone conclusion. Public Enemy Number One, but not to worry. The Sheriff's Department always got their man. There was an Old West feel about the thing. A sense of posses and six-shooters and tumbleweed showdowns, of long-simmering personal vendettas played out on a lawless landscape. Watching the news, one thing became painfully clear. When Phillip was found, Davis was going to do his best to lynch him. You could almost hear the God-fearin' townspeople in the background, hammers clacking, hastily erecting wooden gallows in the town square.

One fact I was overlooking in all this was Phillip's agoraphobia. If he *had* run, he wouldn't have run far. Or he'd have run to an understandable place. Somewhere he'd been before. Phillip and I had taken four overnight trips together during the past ten months. Maybe he'd gone back to one of those places. It was worth a shot.

Of the four trips, three were in California. I pulled the phone over to the dining-room table and called the hotels one by one. A ski lodge in Lake Tahoe. A downtown hotel in Los Angeles. A bed-and-breakfast place on the Mendocino coast. None of them showed a Phillip Chesterton currently registered. I explained that he might be using a different name and gave a brief physical description, but the false name business only served to make the various reservations clerks get nervous and less talkative.

The fourth trip had been the one to Mexico Carol and I had talked about. A five-day junket to Cabo San Lucas at the tip of the Baja Peninsula. An old friend of mine from my Peace Corps days in Guatemala, Jimmy Kamamoto, owned a restaurant in town and lived on a sailboat, and he took us fishing and snorkeling every day.

I called the restaurant and spent a few minutes catching up with Jimmy. Sure, he remembered Phillip. The shy redheaded kid who ended up landing the biggest marlin of the week. No, he hadn't seen him since our visit. But it was the holiday season and the town was jammed full of tourists, so it was not inconceivable that one more gringo could get lost in the shuffle. I asked Jimmy if he could keep an eye open and maybe discreetly ask around. Jimmy said no problem. Discretion came naturally to those of us who'd spent time in Central America. I told Jimmy I'd send a photo to refresh his memory, and Jimmy said a free dinner was waiting for me when and if I ever came back down again.

I took my photo of Phillip and walked down to a printing shop near Fisherman's Wharf. I had four copies made, then hopped a cable car downtown and sent the pictures Federal Express to the three California hotels and to Jimmy in Mexico.

After the four packets went off I had some time on my hands, so I wandered around North Beach for a while and ended up eating a solitary dinner at a new Italian restaurant on Grant Street. I was a little early, but they weren't doing much business and the proprietors stood at the cash register, playing with their knuckles, looking worried. A youngish couple, late of stockbrokering and middle managing, now wondering why they'd quit their dull but steady white-collar jobs to put up with this uncertain, fiercely competitive grief.

The winter sun set in a hurry and the fog was rolling in. The foghorns boomed to each other out in the cold, dark bay. I finished off my glass of wine, turned my collar to the gusting mist, and walked the fifteen blocks back up and down Russian Hill, toward home.

The Christmas lights were on along Union Street. I wasn't in the mood to go back to the apartment, so I kept walking down Union Street till I hit the Metro Theater. I didn't care what was playing. All I wanted to do was sit in the dark and be alone for a while. I decided three blocks away that I'd watch whatever was running. Back-to-back screenings of *The Way We Were*. A Charlton Heston retrospective. Anything.

I bought a ticket for the seven o'clock show, thus violating my firm policy of never going to a movie that promises to make me "stand up and cheer!" I took a seat in the center of the near-empty theater and sat through one-hundred twenty-eight minutes of Hallmark pablum. A beautiful woman who gets a disease but overcomes the hardship to win the piano competition. The disease eventually kills her, but all the primary characters learn something important about themselves because of the ordeal. I sat there with the bag of popcorn clutched between my legs, and when the film was done I felt neither cheated nor rewarded. It was roughly six dollars' worth of movie, like a restaurant omelette usually works out to six dollars' worth of eggs and potatoes.

The apartment was empty when I got home. I called the Chesterton house and the ubiquitous Rogelio answered on the fourth ring. He sounded relaxed. Off the clock and taking it easy. Utensils clattered in the distance, and I pictured him sitting in the kitchen with his collar loosened, enjoying an end-of-the-day brandy and gossiping in Spanish with one of the maids.

Abigail was asleep, Rogelio said, but my call reminded him of something. Mr. Matson's funeral was going to be held the next day at eleven o'clock, and Abigail wanted me to be there. After the funeral, there would be a reception back at the house, and I was welcome to bring someone if I wanted. I told Rogelio I'd be there, then called Molly and told her answering machine about the funeral, and if she wanted to come I could use the company.

Time passed. An hour. Two hours. Then I was aware of something. It tugged suddenly at the edge of consciousness. Lola. I hadn't seen her all day. Not today, and not last night. Lola can be as antisocial as the next cat, but her personality is one that demands you acknowledge her antisocial behavior. She'll always promenade her bad attitude in front of you for a couple minutes before slinking off, just to let you know she's being antisocial. If it were within her powers to slam a door behind her, she would. But for the last thirty-six hours she had been nonexistent.

I went down the hall, calling her name, whistling softly. Nothing. I cracked open Hank's door but she wasn't there, either. Bathroom, no. Office, no. I finally went into my bedroom and called her name, and there was a scuffling sound in the closet.

I slid the closet door open all the way and there she was, huddled in the corner with my shoes and loose golf balls. Her eyes were wide and fearful. I knelt down and held my hand out to her. She wouldn't come.

Lola and I had played out this scene once before, in another closet in another apartment. At that time Lola's owner lay on the bed, savagely murdered, and Lola, as the only witness, cowered in the dark until I was able to coax her out and bring her home to live with me. Time had passed and the memory slowly faded, but now that same look was in her eyes. The same fear. She'd seen something.

I left Lola where she was and rose very slowly. I went back

out into the hallway, stood at the top of the stairs, and listened. Then I methodically went from room to room, checking closets and looking under beds. I checked the wall safe. The strongbox was there. The apartment was empty.

The front door had been double-bolted when I'd come home, so there had been no entry there. The only other way to get into my apartment is to climb the back stairwell and come through the auxiliary door that leads off the living room. It's a door I almost never use except to get to the roof.

I grabbed a flashlight and took a look. There were scratches on the outside doorknob. Big ones, clustered around the keyhole. They looked like fresh scratches, but it was hard to tell. They might've been months old. Years old. Under normal circumstances I don't pay close attention to my apartment doorknobs.

I clicked the flashlight off, came back into the empty apartment, and stood for a moment in the utter stillness of the living room. The mind plays games. Suddenly the apartment had the undeniable feel of a violated space, and there was nothing I could do to shake the feeling. Someone had been here. Someone had done something.

Lola was still reluctant to come out of the closet. Finally I had to reach in and pull her quaking body out with one hand and stroke her trembling fur until she began breathing normally again. For the rest of the evening she didn't eat or drink. When it got late enough I finally went to sleep. But not Lola. She just sat at the edge of my bed, eyes wide open, watchful and wary.

=24=

Molly called first thing in the morning and said she'd be by to pick me up at nine-thirty. Last night was the last of the Tibetan exhibit and the heat was off. The plan was to drive up to Napa in Molly's new car, then after the funeral and reception swing over to Jack London State Park and pick up my van.

Frank Matson's funeral was being held at a cemetery in a part of Napa that was new to me, and Rogelio's directions weren't very precise. After three wrong turns we pulled into the parking lot of a convenience store. Molly waited in the car and I stood in line behind a man in mud-caked blue jeans who was buying fifty lottery tickets at the register. He had long, snarled hair, a tattoo of a minotaur on his right shoulder, and he didn't smell real great. There had been a three- or four-week carryover of the jackpot and California was in the grips of one of its periodic spasms of lottery fever. The payoff currently stood at over thirty million.

Fifty lottery tickets take a while to process. I looked out the window at Molly. She tapped her watch and I shrugged my shoulders. Tattoo's family was waiting for him in the car next to

Molly. It was a broken-down Ford Galaxie, the color of unbrushed teeth, held together by Band-Aids and baling wire. Mom was up front, staring straight ahead at the dashboard in a kind of desolate, dead-eyed stupor that is hard to achieve without surgical assistance. Three malnourished kids were in back, climbing over each other and throwing things. The kids didn't know it yet, but their warm meal to cold meal ratio was about to take a turn for the worse. Daddy thinks he's going to win thirty million dollars. Daddy'll bet this week's food budget on it.

Tattoo finally finished his transaction and shuffled out the door. I stepped forward and asked the old man behind the cash register for directions to the cemetery, and on the back of a brown paper bag he drew a map for me that was so detailed I could almost see the cracks in the sidewalks. I thanked him and off we went.

The graveyard was a few miles north of town, on the slope of a lush, green hill. There were a number of people milling about the entrance to the cemetery when we drove up. Some had cameras, and there was a single news van from a Napa television station. Why not? The circumstances of Frank Matson's death so far had been nothing short of spectacular, so maybe the trend would continue. An unexpected gunfight erupting as the coffin was lowered, bullets ricocheting off the tombstones, people diving for cover. Film at eleven.

Molly parked the car and we hurriedly walked to the outer edge of a small gathering of mourners on a ridge at the eastern slope of the cemetery. The services were already under way, and a priest was talking.

We discreetly tucked ourselves into the crowd and listened to the benign platitudes. I scanned the crowd. An older, well-heeled group. There were some fold-out chairs at the foot of the grave, where Abigail, Leslie, and several elderly women sat. I watched Leslie closely. He looked appropriately somber and had his hand resting gently on Abigail's knee. His head listed to the side, a contemplative tilt, gaze skyward at sixty degrees as though digesting each and every laudatory syllable the priest was intoning. Ah, yes. So true. So very, very true.

I recognized Detective Davis among the crowd. Paquini the winemaster. Holt. But that was about it. The bone-dry lack of grief among the other fifty or so mourners convinced me they were business associates, doing the proper thing but secretly pleased that a hard-nosed competitor had fallen by the wayside. No sniffling or wadded handkerchiefs in this crowd. Even Abigail was dry-eyed. She sat in solid black, veil pulled back, face white as chalk, looking ninety years old.

At last the priest closed his book and stepped back and asked if anyone wanted to say anything about the deceased before the body was returned to the earth. Silence. Eyes darting back and forth like you used to do in school when the teacher asked for volunteers to solve a problem on the blackboard. Nope. Nobody wanted to say anything.

So the order was given and the casket went down into the freshly dug earth. Abigail stood and, escorted by Leslie, walked to the edge of the grave, and dropped something in with the coffin. I couldn't tell what it was. Something small and light. A flower, maybe. Or a final note.

A dignified silence followed while Leslie led Abigail to the black stretch limo waiting at the entrance to the cemetery, but once they drove off the mood changed completely. I wouldn't call it festive, exactly, but there was a great deal of loosening of ties and greetings exchanged and thoughts turned to other matters. One woman passed by me and I overheard her complain to her companion that she had been burping tuna all day long. The companion recommended Maalox Plus, and the woman said that was an excellent idea, she'd give it a try. Frank Matson's funeral was not the stuff of great tragedy.

The post-funeral reception was going to be held back at the Chesterton mansion, so our three dozen cars formed a convoy and proceeded with a full police escort. It seemed a little elaborate, and I wondered whether this was standard procedure or whether Detective Davis had pulled some strings.

Molly was more than happy to let me drive. The Dalai Lama and company had pulled up stakes the night before and headed off south to terrorize a museum in Los Angeles for a while, and Molly was a burnt-out case.

I almost didn't recognize the front of the Chesterton mansion as I drove up. Good-intentioned well-wishers had been forklifting artificial cheerfulness over to the house ever since the "accident," off-loading it on the doorstep where it sat, unnoticed and unwanted. Wreaths and bouquets of every shape and size were piled on both sides of the door, and I could see Rogelio in his bright white suit, wandering among the tangled foliage like a florist salesman at a going-out-of-business sale. He was talking heatedly to one of the maintenance men, hands thrown up in the air as if to say: What the hell am I supposed to do with all of this?

A tremendous buffet was set out on the back terrace, with sumptuous piles of fresh fruit and seafood and case after case of Chesterton wine. Abigail was nowhere to be seen. Leslie McCall passed by once in a while, but he was not his usual, mingle-at-a-moment's-notice self. He seemed troubled and distracted. Going through the motions. I wondered whether Abigail had confronted him about the strongbox. Or whether he had detected something different in her manner himself.

The wine went faster than the fruit, and the decibel level of the mourners increased significantly. I saw Holt sitting alone on the outskirts of the festivities, quietly eating from a paper plate. He was the new kid on the block, the feed-and-grain guy from Willits, and this wasn't his crowd. Detective Davis made a point of avoiding me. I thought it would be the other way around, with him right up in my face with more balled-fist questions about Phillip's whereabouts. But no. He kept his brass-knuckles personality to himself. Whenever I crossed a room in his direction he would turn his back to me, or walk away, or find a new conversation cluster to join.

I finally cornered Leslie near the entrance to the kitchen,

where he was instructing a maid where to take a new tray of food. He smiled as I strolled up.

"Looks like the party's a hit," I said.

"I knew they'd all get drunk," he said, "but I didn't think this fast."

"Where's Abigail?"

"Resting upstairs." Leslie looked out the window at the rollicking mourners and shook his head disgustedly. "According to Herodotus, all important Persian matters were discussed twice in council—once sober, and once while drinking. This is why."

"Revelation of character?" I said.

"That," Leslie said, "and the fact that truth comes at you from different angles."

We were silent a moment, then I popped it. "Does Pilkow Street mean anything to you?"

Leslie held it together pretty well, considering. But at the mention of Pilkow Street there had been a slight flinch from the neck up, as though he'd just taken a mild slap to the face.

"Does *what* mean anything to me?"

"Pilkow Street."

Leslie shook his head. He was back in control now, but the gears were going underneath. "No. Why?"

"The night Frank Matson died, somebody called the house and mentioned Pilkow Street."

Leslie tried to maintain his look of benign befuddlement, but his concern deepened. His eyes lost their focus. Just then Molly came up beside us, and I introduced the two of them. Leslie wrenched himself out of his thoughts and forced a smile. Mild chitchat ensued, and when he found out she worked at the De Young he asked if she had been involved in the recent Tibet exhibit. Molly started to tell him of the trials and tribulations, and Leslie kept saying, "I can just imagine," over and over again. His color had gone bad, and his eyes kept drifting from Molly to where they'd been when I mentioned Pilkow Street. They were frightened eyes.

I left the two of them and found a stool off by myself and

worked slowly on a paper plate of cold cuts. After a few minutes Holt came over and sat next to me.

"Mind if I join you?" he said.

"Not at all."

"Leslie doesn't want to have much to do with me these days," Holt said, "so you're the only friend I've got here."

"He does seem a little subdued."

"He's subdued with me, too," Holt said. "Only a lot louder."

"What's going on?"

Holt shrugged. "Search me. Last night all I did was bring up the fact that Abigail didn't seem to be doing so well and Leslie freaked. Yelled at me so loud he woke the geese up. Told me I could take my worthless ass out of *his* house if that's the way I thought about *his* friends. He wasn't even making sense."

"Everyone's under a lot of stress about this," I said diplomatically.

Holt shook his head. "Unh-unh. With Leslie it's more than that. Remember when we were talking about Captain Ahab going after the whale, sharpening up his harpoon?"

"I remember."

"What I'm thinking is the whale just got buried and now Leslie doesn't know what to do with himself."

"Maybe he'll find another whale," I said.

"Yeah!" Holt said. "Like me!"

I studied Holt's profile. There was a skeletal aspect to his face that I hadn't noticed before. Skin stretched tight to the bone, ligaments and tendons in his throat taut and very pronounced. The eyes were deep in their sockets. I'd underestimated his age by a good ten years, and his Willits routine of swimming two hundred laps a day suddenly seemed less like fitness and more like rehabilitation. A recuperative process.

"I don't know, Quinn," Holt said at last. "I think I made a mistake moving down here. Things were fine when I had my own place, but this ..." He shook his head. "Last night Leslie was pacing back and forth out in the living room, crying like a baby. Every time I tried to talk to him about it he just snapped my head off. When two people care about each other they're supposed to talk, right? Well, forget it. I don't need this grief."

"You're moving out?"

Holt nodded. "For a while. I haven't told Leslie yet, so keep a lid on it, okay?"

"Of course."

We sat quietly for a few seconds, playing with the food on our paper plates. "I'm no literary genius," Holt said at last, "but this Ahab character ... he *was* crazy, right?"

"Right."

"Ended up killing his entire crew, didn't he? Sent them all to the bottom of the goddamn ocean?"

"All but one."

"One lived?"

"Ishmael. The man who tells the story."

Holt thought about it. "That's a hell of a comfort. I wonder which one of us is going to be the one. Who's going to be the sole survivor of all this."

Abigail eventually made a brief appearance, and the mourners all put down their plates of food long enough to gather around and offer their condolences. I watched from a distance. She smiled bravely and shook hands dutifully, and the mourners drifted, one by one, back to their food. I gave her a hug and that was that. She logged her required ten or fifteen minutes, then headed back to her bedroom.

The party broke up an hour later for the same reasons most parties break up. The food and the booze ran out. Detective Davis left without having said a single word to me. His neglect was far more sinister than his previous strident concern, and it made me uneasy. Negotiations had broken down, his silence seemed to say, and now there was nothing to do but make sure the cannons were oiled and the gunpowder fresh. The heavy artillery, as Leslie had warned.

Molly and I stuck around after everybody else left. A platoon of maids began cleaning up, and I sat on the armchair near the door and looked at the stack of telegrams that had been put in the box next to the guest register. Frank Matson may not have been popular, but his unceremonious exit from this world had gotten a lot of response.

Molly said she needed some fresh air and went out back to take a walk. I sat in the chair and idly read the telegrams. They were standard fare, except for one. It was from a Vicki and Jeff Lowery: "Please accept our profound sympathies in your time of grief. Without your husband's generous and constant support, we could not have come as far as we have come. Mr. Matson was as fine a man and soldier and friend as anyone could want to have. He will be missed." The telegram originated in a place called East Chandler, California.

Abigail was suddenly in the room. She had changed out of her funereal black and wore comfortable slacks and a light blouse. She looked much better. Relieved that the mob had cleared out.

"Where's your ladyfriend?"

"She went for a walk out back."

Abigail nodded.

I held up the telegram from Vicki and Jeff Lowery. "Do you know who these people are?"

Abigail took the telegram and read it, her lips moving and brain straining against the effects of the sedative. "No. But Frank knew many people I didn't."

"It sounds like they might have served in Vietnam together. He refers to Frank as a soldier."

Abigail handed back the telegram and nodded. "Perhaps."

"It also sounds like Frank might have been sending them money?"

"It's possible."

"I wonder why?"

Abigail gently shrugged. "Frank was a generous person. He helped many people. But quietly. Not with a lot of fanfare. You saw him at his worst, Quinn." Abigail paused. "I'm going to miss him."

"Where is East Chandler?"

"I don't know."

We sat quietly for a moment. Then Abigail cleared her throat and looked about the empty room. "Did you have plans for the rest of the evening?" she said.

"Not really. Why?"

"This is going to be a very lonely house tonight," she said. "I'd like it very much if you and your ladyfriend ... I'm sorry. I've forgotten her name ..."

"Molly."

"Molly," Abigail repeated. "I'd like it very much if you and Molly would be my guests tonight. There's plenty of room, and it would be nice to have some talk and life ..."

"Let's go ask Molly."

"Yes," Abigail said. "Let's."

And so we did. Abigail took my left hand in her right and did not let go. She led me out of the living room and onto the bright sunny terrace, her fingertips linked with my fingertips, Scott and Zelda slipping through yet another mansion, two youthful drunken debutantes who had extracted themselves from the clutches of an insufferable party and now were going to explore the world.

25

It had been a strange enough day without having to endure the complicities of a near full moon, but there it was. High and bright and waning in the ink-blue Napa sky. I sat by myself out on the back terrace, head back in the lawn chair, legs stretched out. It was ten o'clock. Invitation accepted, Abigail had gone to bed and Molly had wandered off to explore some region of the house. A soft breeze blew up from the south, rustling the leaves of the trees and casting agitated gray shadows across the empty croquet lawn. The wickets were still in place from some incomprehensible time in the past when people gathered at the Chesterton mansion to enjoy the frivolities of life, not to deal with the vanished and the dead. The balls and mallets were scattered on the manicured grass, and I wondered why I'd never noticed them before.

I heard the door slide open behind me and Molly appeared to my right. She had changed into a sweater, jogging pants, and sneakers. She had two snifters of brandy in her hands and handed me one.

"Forgive my presumption," she said.

We clinked a toast to the blessed absence of people wanting to meet the Dalai Lama or any other bald-headed spiritual leader and then Molly settled into the chair across from me.

"Know who you look like?" she said.

"This ought to be good."

"Citizen Kane."

"Please …"

"I'm serious," Molly said. "Out here all by yourself, deep in troubled thought. Mansion in the background and tennis courts everywhere, but all the money in the world can't buy you happiness."

"A man without his sled?"

"Maybe that's it."

We were silent a moment, listening to the wind in the trees. "Where have you been?" I said.

"Rogelio showed me around the house, then Abigail told me to go ahead and raid the guest closet." Molly plucked at the shoulder of her sweater. "How do you like my evening wear?"

"Very fetching."

"Wait till you see the nightgown I found."

Molly's blue-black hair shone in the night, impossibly dark, twice the depth of the sky itself. Her face was pale and seemed especially soft in the white light of the moon. Her hands were in her lap, slender fingers interlaced. Delicate wrists. Breakable-looking.

"Want to hear a confession?" she said.

"What?"

"Today was my first funeral."

"Really?"

Molly nodded. "When I was a girl I swore that I'd never go to one. Ever."

"Why such strong feelings?"

"My grandfather's coffee cups."

I rubbed my eyes. "It's been a long day, Molly. I don't think I'm up for a parable."

"This is an easy one." Molly smiled. "My grandfather owned a coffee shop in Rice Lake, Wisconsin, and I used to waitress there when I was a teenager, during summer break. It was the kind of place where half the time the customers took their own plates back and put them in the sink. The regulars had their own per-sonalized coffee mugs. There must've been a hundred of them. 'This is Bill's mug,' 'This is Dusty's mug.' They were all lined up on a rack near the cash register. When a customer died my grandfather took his mug off the rack and put it in a wooden tomato crate in the back storage area. Never threw one away. It was like a graveyard, that tomato crate. Like where the elephants go and everything dries up but their tusks. It gave me the creeps, all the dead people's cups back there in the storage area. The edges still stained brown by the coffee. The handles worn where their fingers were." Molly paused. "Every time I had to go in the back to get something and I saw those retired coffee cups with all the names … I don't know."

"So now you avoid funerals?"

"Funerals and waitressing."

Molly smiled, got up, and came over to my deck chair. I scooted over to make room and she stretched out next to me, putting her head on my chest. We held each other like that for a while.

"What's happening tomorrow?" she said.

"You need to run me over to Jack London State Park so I can get my van, then I'm going over to East Chandler."

"Where's that?"

"According to the map it's about fifty miles from here. Off Interstate 5 down in the valley."

"What are you going there for?"

"Do you really want to know?"

Molly thought about it a second. "Actually, I don't. I've got problems enough."

"I thought the Buddhists headed south."

"I'm talking about Noel."

"Noel?"

Molly sighed. "I just called home to check my answering machine and there was a message from him. Apparently Crystal used the word 'bitch' about something and now he wants to know just what kind of a household I'm running."

"Ignore him."

"I can't ignore him. He has a team of lawyers sitting around *waiting* for me to ignore him. Except they don't call it 'ignoring.' They call it 'negligence' and it gets tucked into their child custody file."

I shook my head, held Molly a little closer. "Can I ask a personal question?"

"You've seen me in my underwear," Molly said. "Ask me anything you want."

"What was good about Noel?"

"How do you mean?"

"You were married five years," I said. "There must have been something good that kept you hanging in there that long. Something the two of you had in common besides a child."

"Things in common ..." Molly shifted her head on my chest. "Let's see. We both thought Shemp was the funniest of the Three Stooges. How's that for glue to hold together a marriage?"

"I was asking a serious question."

Molly sighed. "Can we not talk about Noel tonight?"

"Fine," I said.

"That was a pissed-off 'fine.'"

"Let's drop it."

We were silent for a while. A long while. The kind of brooding, hunkered-down-in-your-seat silence that starts to take on a momentum of its own.

"You're mad now, aren't you?" Molly said.

"About what?"

"Noel."

I shook my head. "How about if I answer your parable of the coffee mugs with one of my own?"

"Go ahead."

"I'm thinking about a village in Mexico. It's in the middle of the Chihuahua Desert. Hot, dusty. Perpetual drought. But once a year, on the hottest day of summer, every man, woman, and child in the town comes to the main square with a pail of water and they dump it into the earth."

"Why would they do a thing like that?" Molly said. "Seems self-defeating."

"They're just making a statement, that's all. What the gods have chosen to make scarce they are not afraid to occasionally waste."

"So why are you telling that story to me?"

"It applies," I said. "Your ex-husband is making your life scarce. Don't be afraid to throw some water in the ground once in a while."

"Or in his face?"

I smiled. "Wherever you think it would do the most good."

Molly pulled herself to a sitting position and looked at me. "Abigail asked if we wanted two bedrooms made up, or one. I told her one, but if we continue this line of talk we're going to get into a fight and then I'll have to tell Rogelio to get out another set of bedsheets."

"Then I vote for ending the conversation."

"Smart man." Molly stood and gathered up the half-finished brandies. "Let's go to bed."

We went back into the quiet, darkened house and climbed the stairs. Our room was next to the game room, and was a little on the formal side. A big, heavy king-sized bed with a massive headboard of carved wood. Severe, no-nonsense dressers and a framed still-life on the wall that had a lot more still to it than life.

Molly sat on the edge of the bed and looked around. "Bet this room's never seen a pillow fight."

"Safe bet." I picked up a small cushion from a chair in the corner and tossed it in her general direction. She grabbed it and let the gentle force of it take her back full-length on the bed, flat on her back, legs dangling over the edge.

"There was rumor of a nightgown ..." I said, easing down on top of her.

Molly took my face in both her hands and kissed me on the lips. "I'll show it to you in the morning."

And so we made love on the big, gloomy bed. Quietly. Carefully. It was a way Molly and I had never made love before. Not the core-oblivion of deep passion. Not profound intimacy. It was something different. The talk of Noel had altered things. Our lovemaking was a gliding, shifting polygraph test, measuring each other, searching with lips and hands across the landscape of each other's bodies for hidden bits of evidence that, once found, would help us say what we hadn't yet said to each other in the world beyond the bed. That our love was real. That our futures might be the same futures. That what we were doing now was not going to merely be a footnote to be browsed for reference when we found ourselves in other beds, with other lovers.

It ended strangely, with very little lingering tenderness. Molly rolled to her side of the bed and I stayed on mine. The test was over and the wires had been detached and put away. I kissed her on the shoulder and she reached up to touch my head, and within minutes she was asleep.

I was not so lucky. I stared at the ceiling and thought of Frank down in the soft wet earth. Wondered what was awaiting me over the hills in East Chandler. I remembered Leslie McCall, and the expression on his face when I'd mentioned Pilkow Street. It wasn't shock that I might have discovered his blackmail scam. It was something else. The look mirrored a deeper fear. Something that leapfrogged far beyond mere worry at having been found out.

It was warm in the room. It was always warm in the Chesterton mansion. Molly groaned from time to time, shifted her sleeping body, moved this way and that in search of comfort. She eventually kicked off her covers, then her sheets, and finally lay nude on her stomach, one knee drawn up, a whisper of sweat on her back. I didn't have the willpower not to stare at her exposed body, and for some reason my gaze felt like violation. So I reached down and softly draped a thin sheet over her.

Not so long ago I would have drunk it in. Turned and gazed

and let my eyes feast till they could feast no more. Then in the morning I would have told Molly about it and she would have given me hell for not waking her up so more than just eyes could have been pleasured. But it was different now. What should have been a simple, incidental pleasure now had the resonance of voyeurism, and that bothered me. Our relationship was shifting. White water was just around the bend.

Modesty took a backseat to comfort and Molly kicked the sheet off again. So I turned from the undulating flesh and concentrated instead on my hormones lighting up the far end of the room like the Aurora Borealis. Then the firestorm died out and I fell asleep.

I had a strange dream. I was a contestant on the old "Let's Make a Deal" with Monty Hall, dressed up like a giant parrot, trading away one emotion for another, watching the curtains rise and fall and feeling like I never possessed anything. When the show was over another show immediately started, and I did the same thing all over again. America couldn't get enough, and the taping never stopped.

I woke once in the middle of the night. Way off in the dark a dog barked at something and then was silent.

26

East Chandler was a small, windblown, three-pack-a-day freeway town on Interstate 5 midway between Sacramento and the Oregon border. It was the kind of place where tractors rumble down Main Street, men see no reason to take off their baseball caps while at the dinner table, and the calendar of social events revolves around the annual demolition derby. You could see that once upon a time agriculture made East Chandler run, but not anymore. When the bottom fell out on the American farmer the townspeople turned instead to the four-lane interstate for sustenance, working the two dozen fast-food, fast-gas establishments that clung to the concrete underbelly of the freeway like barnacles. As far as I could tell there was no Chandler for East Chandler to be east of, but there wasn't panic in the streets over the discrepancy, so I didn't dwell on it.

I pulled into the parking lot of a bright, garish coffee shop named Wally's. Jam-it-down-your-throat happiness was the motif at Wally's, complete with artificial flowers and winding yellow brick road and a footbridge over a pool of rancid water where travelers were supposed to toss dimes and nickels for good luck. On the outside lawn there was a fiberglass statue of a beaming fat kid who looked like he was going be arrested in a Greyhound toilet stall one day when he grew up. The kid held a hamburger in one hand and an ice-cream cone in the other. Even the letters of the sign announcing the restaurant as Wally's were happy, tilted at odd, bouncy angles, as though the construction workers themselves were so caught up in the general mirth and merriment of Wally's they were unable to hang the letters on straight.

There was a pay phone inside the lobby and I glanced through the white pages, looking for Vicki and Jeff Lowery. They were listed as living on Maple Avenue. No street number. Just Maple Avenue. I asked the young girl working the cash register where Maple Avenue was and she was helpful to a fault. Maple was the one after Oak, but before Elm. If I hit Elm, I'd gone too far, and if I hit Webster, then I was *really* too far.

I found Maple Avenue without much problem and parked the van alongside a lawn where a large man was working on a pickup truck. He was bent over the engine, three inches of butt cheek showing, a can of discount beer propped on the front fender. A toddler in soiled diapers stood next to him, peeling dried snot from his dirty face, staring at me with big, wary, coal-miner eyes. The pickup windows were festooned with stickers of the American flag, and across the back bumper was a bright Day-Glo sticker that read "Foxy Grandma on Board." I looked to the heavens and silently prayed to please not make this the residence of Jeff Lowery.

As I approached, the toddler got scared and clung to his father's leg and started wailing as if I'd just stuck him in the butt with a rusty weeding tool. The man straightened up from his work on the engine. He was chewing what looked to be a whole pack of gum at the same time. It was yellow.

"Afternoon," I said.

"Afternoon."

"Wondering if you could help me."

"Sure thing."

The toddler continued to wail. The tears mixed with the dried snot and the mixture moved in a thick, goopy descent down his face.

"I'm looking for Jeff and Vicki Lowery," I said. "Someone said they lived on this street, but I'm not sure exactly what house."

"That's them right over there," the man said, pointing to a green house at the end of the block. "Jeff's got himself a recycling business around the end, in the alley, so he's probably back there."

"Green house?"

"That's the one."

"Thanks."

"You bet."

The toddler finally realized that all the wailing in the world wasn't going to make his dad bludgeon me to death with his wrench, so he shut up. I climbed back in my van and nudged it farther up the block.

I rang the doorbell on the green house but there was no answer. I wandered around back and found the alley separating the houses of Maple Avenue from the houses of Oak. Behind the green house was a high, chain-link storm fence built on coasters so you could slide it open and shut. It was open now. There were two large Dumpsters, one filled to the top with flattened cans, the other half-full of bottles. A bundle of rolled cardboard stood to the side, taller than me and twice as thick. Swarms of hornets and flies circled the Dumpsters, and their soft hum was the only sound at this end of Maple Avenue.

A man was sitting at a small, low desk that had been set out in the middle of all this. He was bent over an accounting log of some sort, scribbling figures, adding columns. The man was in his mid-forties, prematurely bald, with only the finest of blond hair still holding on to the side of his head. There was a burnished look to his skin, polished and unevenly dark, like a piece of furniture improperly stained. He had dark eyes and a long, straight nose. His Adam's apple was very pronounced and located high up in his throat. I approached the desk and the man looked up at me.

"Jeff Lowery?"

He put down his pen. "Who are you?"

"My name's Quinn Parker. I'm a friend of Frank Matson's."

His face relaxed. "You're a friend of Frank's?"

"That's right. You *are* Jeff, yes?"

"I'll be goddamned!" The man smiled. "I'm Jeff Lowery!"

"I'm glad I found you."

Jeff stood and dragged another chair over to his table. "Sit down."

I did, and Jeff closed up his log book and leaned close. "How is Frank?" he said.

"How *is* he?"

"Yeah! I haven't seen him in a long, long time." There was a lack of focus in Jeff Lowery's eyes. Something was wrong. He wasn't entirely with me.

"Frank's fine," I said at last.

"Good," Jeff said, nodding as though I'd confirmed something he'd always known but nobody else would believe. "Doing real good. That's good."

We were silent awhile, and Jeff kept nodding his head. A sheen of moisture covered the inner wall of his nostrils, like a dog who was sick, and every ten or fifteen seconds he threw a knuckle in the direction of his leaking nose.

"We put bombs in the hogs," he suddenly said.

"Excuse me?"

"Me and Frank, over in Nam. We put bombs in the hogs."

"Bombs in the hogs?"

Jeff lifted his arm and drew a line through his armpit. "Right there. Make a little incision, bring down the flap of skin, put the bomb in. Heat-activated sucker. Sew it up, then turn the hogs loose back in the jungles and when the Cong would capture them and roast 'em ... boom!"

"You and Frank did this?" I said.

Jeff squinted at me as if remembering all of a sudden that he wasn't talking to himself. "What?"

Then there was a voice behind me. "Can I help you with something?"

I turned around. A small, thin woman was standing in the alley. She was pale and had light brown hair that hung straight down past her shoulders. It was wet, like she'd just gotten out of the shower.

"This is Frank's friend," Jeff said, quickly standing up.

"Are you Vicki Lowery?" I said.

"Yes I am," she said. "Who are you?"

I introduced myself and Vicki asked Jeff if it would be okay if she and I had our own private talk in the house for a few minutes. By way of answer Jeff reopened his log book and immediately went back to scribbling figures in the columns.

"Come with me," Vicki said, and I followed her around front. She did not invite me into the house. We stood on the front porch in full view of the other houses on Maple Avenue. She was an attractive woman in her own way, with the look of someone who might once have been described as effervescent. But something had happened to put the fire out.

"You're a friend of Frank Matson's?" she said.

"I'm a friend of Frank's stepson."

"His stepson?"

"Phillip Chesterton."

Vicki looked at me awhile. "He's the one the newspapers say killed Frank, right?"

"The newspapers are wrong. That's what I wanted to talk to your husband about. I saw your telegram at Frank's funeral yesterday."

Vicki shifted her weight and looked uncomfortable. "Let's go inside."

The living room was clean and simply furnished. Vicki sat at one end of the couch and gestured for me to sit at the other end, and we both turned sideways to face each other.

"Why did you come here?" she said. "We don't know anything about Frank's personal life."

"Your husband served with Frank in Vietnam, didn't he?"

"So?"

"I think Frank died because of something that happened over

there. I thought perhaps your husband might be able to shed some light."

"You saw what Jeff's like," Vicki said. "I don't think he can help you very much."

"Was it the war?"

"Yes. He got shot in the head."

"I'm sorry."

"I didn't tell you that so you could be sorry. I just told you so you'd know. Jeff was a good soldier, a Green Beret."

"I gather from the telegram that Frank Matson has been helping you out?"

"Every month he sends a check for five hundred dollars," Vicki said.

"Why?"

"Jeff got shot looking for Mr. Matson when he disappeared that night," Vicki said. "Jeff never talks about it. Maybe he doesn't remember. After a while I quit asking and just put the money in the bank. It helped us a lot. Not proud to say it, but my first thought when I heard that Mr. Matson was dead was how the five hundred dollars was going to stop coming every month."

We were silent a moment. Then Vicki pulled back the strands of her wet hair and focused on me.

"What do you want from Jeff? Specifically?"

"I'd like to ask him a couple of questions. Show him a photograph and see if he can identify someone. That's all."

"And if he doesn't want to do it, you'll go?"

"You have my word."

Vicki thought about it, then nodded. "Okay. But if he doesn't want to do it, you go. And if it bothers him, you go. No standing there arguing about it in front of him."

"Deal."

We went back out to the alley and approached Jeff. He was still hunched over the log book, furiously writing down figures. The recycling business in East Chandler didn't warrant such a fevered pace. Jeff Lowery spent his afternoons scribbling gibberish.

"Jeff, honey," Vicki said. "This man would like to ask you a couple questions. Is that okay?"

"About Frank?"

"Yes," Vicki said. "About Frank."

"Sure," Jeff said, pushing away the log book. "What kind of questions?"

I knelt down near the desk so Jeff and I could be eye level. "I heard that Frank was captured while out on patrol."

Jeff nodded. "That's right."

"Were you there?"

"I was there," Jeff said. "March 21, 1969."

"What happened?"

Jeff's eyes lost their intensity. The question was too vague, it encompassed too much.

"He got captured," Jeff said. "Him and the others."

"What others?"

"Paul and Wade."

"They were in your platoon?"

"Detachment," Jeff corrected.

"Paul and Wade were in your detachment?"

"Yes."

"And they were captured along with Frank Matson?"

"Yes."

"What were Paul and Wade's last names?" I said.

Jeff paused. Below the table his right knee was going up and down at a furious pace. He stared down at the rows of figures and blinked. "Wilson and Davenport," he said.

"Paul Wilson and Wade Davenport?"

"That's it," Jeff said. He was smiling, and there were tiny beads of perspiration on his forehead despite the chill December day. "Paul Wilson and Wade Davenport."

I remembered the name Paul Wilson. He was the man named in Leslie's blackmail packet. The man who was executed by the Cambodian government in 1982.

"That's enough questions," Vicki said.

"Can I have him look at one photograph?" I said.

"Let me see it first," she said.

I took out the black-and-white shot of Frank and Suzie Wong in Pilkow. Vicki glanced at it, nodded, and handed it back to me. I gave it to Jeff and he stared at it for a while.

"That's Frank," he said, smiling. "Look at that shirt. Frank always liked wild shirts. And that other guy, that's Wade."

"Wade Davenport?" I said. "The one who got captured with Frank?"

"Yep."

"What about the girl sitting on Frank's lap?"

Jeff looked at the photo harder. The sweat was obvious on his brow, and his right leg was going up and down so fast it was banging the bottom of the desk. "No," he said.

"You don't recognize her?"

"No."

"Was her name Suzie Wong?"

"No."

Vicki stepped forward and took the photo out from under Jeff's eyes and handed it back to me. "I'm sorry, Mr. Parker, but that's enough."

I put the photo in my shirt pocket and stood. Jeff Lowery had the strained breathlessness of a runner who had overextended himself.

"Thank you very much for your help, Jeff," I said. "I appreciate it."

"Tell Frank hi," he said. "Tell him I say hi. He'll remember me. The bombs in the hogs."

"I will."

I made the gesture to shake Jeff's hand, but he was already fumbling with the binding of the log book, trying to get it open and return to the world of meaningless figures. He wasn't with me at all. He was gone. Gone as the barrel slipping over the falls at Niagara.

I drove back out to the freeway and stopped at Wally's again to use the phone. The cashier remembered me and asked if I'd found Maple Avenue okay. I told her I had.

I called the Chesterton house first and the one time I wanted to talk to Rogelio, somebody else answered. A maid. I asked for Rogelio and waited while she went to get him. Rogelio was on the line a moment later and I asked him if he knew how to operate a computer. I might just as well have asked him if he could quote me labor statistics from post-Soviet Russia. Rogelio said he had never turned on a computer in his life, so I told him he was in for a new experience. He was to switch over to a cordless phone and go into Frank Matson's office and wait for further instructions.

I waited till Rogelio was sitting in front of the monitor, then I talked him through it. The procedure was painless, and within five minutes he had accessed Frank Matson's address file. I had him look for Paul Wilson. There was no Paul Wilson. I didn't think there would be. According to the documentation in the strongbox, Wilson had been dead over a decade. Then I asked Rogelio to look for a Wade Davenport. I spelled it out and heard the tapping of computer keys and then Rogelio said yes, there was such a person in the address file.

I had Rogelio carefully give me the address and phone number and then I talked him back out of the depths of the computer. Rogelio was pleased with himself, and I hung up the phone with the information in hand. Mr. Wade Davenport, 1000 Midnight Pass Road, Siesta Key, Florida. I fed more money into the phone and dialed the Florida number. A woman answered in an official tone of voice and informed me that I'd reached Bluewater Development Corporation. I asked if Mr. Davenport was in the office and she said he was on another line, did I want to wait. I told her I'd try back later and hung up.

I deliberated the issue for about a half a minute, then waved good-bye to the cashier and headed south on Interstate 5 toward the Sacramento airport. It was closer than San Francisco, and I was in a hurry.

=27=

I landed at the Sarasota/Bradenton Airport at two the next afternoon. Before leaving Sacramento I had called the Union Street
apartment and left a message for Hank, telling him what I was
up to and that he was going to be responsible for feeding the
pets for a day or two.

A cold winter drizzle had been falling in California when I
took off six hours earlier, but in Sarasota the air was thick and
warm. Too thick and too warm. The elderly woman who sat next
to me for the Tampa-to-Sarasota portion of the trip shook her
head and told me she didn't know what the hell was happening.
She'd lived in Florida all her life, but it never used to be like this.
Used to be you'd get a break from the heat in Florida, but no
more. It was the ozone, she said, pointing up at the roof of the
airplane. The ozone was shot.

I rented a car and took Highway 41 south. It was your basic
four-lane, stop-and-go nightmare, dreadful even by roadside
America standards, littered on either side by Golf Worlds, Hub-
caps USA, Taco Bells, and discount furniture outlets for retirees
starting a new life. Minimum speed limits were posted at regular

intervals so as to remind these same retirees to keep it above twenty m.p.h. There seemed to be funeral homes on almost every corner, built with pressboard but designed to look as stately as Monticello. It was macabre, this block-by-block reminder of your own mortality, but the longer I crawled down Highway 41, the better the mortuaries began to look.

Siesta Key was a pricey little slice of real estate that fronted the Gulf of Mexico. A combination of high-rise condos, opulent private homes, gorgeous beaches, and fancy restaurants. There was something of a town in the middle of the Key, a funky five- or six-block pastiche of beach-related retail outlets, and that's where Bluewater Development Corporation had its offices.

I pulled in front of 1000 Midnight Pass Road and cut the engine. It was a squat, ugly, three-story affair of concrete and glass and faded gray, looking more like the kind of drab, inner-city building where you'd have to go to pick up your unemployment check.

I locked up the car and went in. Three dentists occupied the bottom floor, a law firm and accounting office had the second, and Bluewater Development Corporation had the third floor all to themselves. I rode the elevator up.

The reception area was surprisingly nice—wide, bright, and spacious. Floor-to-ceiling windows looked out over a cluster of housetops to the turquoise Gulf a few hundred yards away. The walls were decorated with pastel seascapes and framed photos of various Bluewater Development Corporation projects. Beachfront time-shares, with retired couples sitting poolside, sipping drinks, tennis rackets propped against their chairs. There were aerial shots from high above so you could clearly see just how much better you had it than the poor, working-class slobs who had to live a few miles inland.

The room was empty, and the receptionist's desk had that organized, wiped-clean look of a desk that had been retired for the day. Behind the desk was a door, and there were voices emanating from behind it. Laughter. The sound of several people talking all at once, then more laughter.

I took a seat and waited and tried to ignore the piped-in

music. WSNY, the Beautiful Music station, with music that makes you feel good. I sat through an instrumental version of "Can't Buy Me Love," then the theme from *Out of Africa,* then regular programming was temporarily interrupted for a test of the Emergency Broadcast System. The easy-listening airwaves were filled with the long, shrill sound of a telephone being melted by nuclear radiation, then it was back to WSNY, the Beautiful Music station. Music that makes you feel good.

After a few minutes the door behind the receptionist's desk opened and a woman peeked out. My presence took her by surprise. She put down her drink, adjusted the areas of her attire that had come loose, and then walked out to meet me with forced casualness.

"I'm *so* sorry," she said. "Have you been waiting long?"

"Just a couple of minutes."

"We're having our office Christmas party," she said, "and the receptionist went home early."

"No problem."

The woman was so heavily perfumed, my initial reaction was to wonder what she really smelled like. She weaved slightly on her three-inch heels, and I thought I caught a whiff of tequila mingled with the eau de whatever. She held out her hand and I shook it. "My name's Nicole."

"Quinn Parker."

"How can I help you, Mr. Parker?"

Nicole's ear-to-ear smile was about as sincere as the instrumental version of "Can't Buy Me Love" I'd just suffered through. The kind of instant, all-inclusive greeting that comes from years and years of looking at everybody as a potential three-percent commission of a fixed asset. She was a fireplug—short and meaty, but not fat. Her breasts were wrecking-ball large, and she had her hair piled and swirled and contoured in waves and ringlets around her smallish head. It was frosted like the stuff you spray on Christmas trees to simulate indoor snowdrifts, and one flamboyant curl bigger than all the others swept across her forehead and preceded her like the hood ornament on a Cadillac.

Nicole was about forty years old. Or thirty. Or fifty. It was hard to tell because her makeup had been applied with a trowel and putty knife. It was anybody's guess what Nicole'd look like if you gave her a good hosing down.

"I'd like to speak to Wade Davenport," I said.

"Regarding?"

"Business."

"I'm a senior sales associate here," Nicole smiled. "Maybe it's something I could help you with."

"Actually, it's *personal* business. I need to see Mr. Davenport himself."

"Personal business?"

"That's right."

Nicole's smile faded about thirty percent. "Like I said, Mr. Parker, we're having our Christmas party right now and this really isn't the best time. Technically the office is closed. But Mr. Davenport will be in tomorrow."

"He's not in now?"

That took care of the rest of Nicole's smile. Her voice went as flat as a two-by-four. "I *said* we're having a party."

"I'll wait."

Nicole planted her hands on her hips. "Suit yourself." Then she turned and huffed away, slamming the party door emphatically behind her.

I hate it when my bluff gets called. Nicole was supposed to waver, see by my stern visage that I meant business, then go mincing off with her tail between her legs to fetch Wade.

I waited five minutes, then walked up and knocked on the door three times, hard. There was an immediate, absolute silence. Guilty silence, like when the police come a-calling. Then the door swung open and I was staring at Nicole's scowling face.

"Party's not over yet," she said.

"Just checking."

We had a stare-off for a few seconds.

"Wade," she said, without turning or opening the door further. "It's that guy."

A voice behind her said, "What guy?"

"The one I told you about."

"Then let him in, for Christ's sake," the voice said. "It's a Christmas party!"

Nicole grudgingly opened the door the rest of the way and I stepped inside. It was a conference room, with your basic round conference table. There were bottles of booze and wine and large serving trays with remnants of crab and shrimp and raw vegetables with dip. A dozen or so people were standing around drinking from Dixie cups and snacking from paper plates. An affable-looking man of fifty-five or sixty in an expensive suit was sitting up on the edge of the table, and as Nicole backed out of the way he pushed himself off and walked toward me. He was a handsome guy, trim and athletic, with silver hair and powdery white eyebrows. His face had a golden tan except where the wrinkling of his brow had formed small arching lines of white.

"I'm Wade Davenport," he said. "How can I help you?"

"Didn't mean to interrupt your party."

"No problem at all," Wade said. "We were just wrapping things up."

The other employees looked at each other. This was the first they'd heard that things were wrapping up, but Wade was the boss and they began tossing down the last of their drinks and gathering up dirty napkins.

"You caught us on kind of a crazy day," Wade said. "Your name again was ...?"

"Quinn Parker."

"What can I do for you, Quinn?" Wade said.

"It's kind of involved," I said.

Wade looked at me curiously. "Okay. Let's go in my office, then."

Wade led me back out through the reception area and through another door to the left. It was a simple, sunlit office. Desk with pictures of the wife and kids and sailboat. Big window with a view of the Gulf. Wade sat behind his desk and gestured for me to sit on the couch. Nicole slipped through the door and stood by the wall. Apparently she was privy to involved things concerning Wade, though it wasn't her picture hugging the kids on Wade's desk.

"You've got my curiosity, Quinn," Wade said. "What is it you want to talk about?"

"I thought we might talk alone."

"Nicole can hear whatever you have to say to me," he said.

"Sure?"

"Absolutely."

"It concerns Frank Matson," I said.

Wade's confusion was only momentary, then his face began to weaken. A slow implosion of the features: eyes, nose, forehead, one by one, like when the edge of a wave touches the sand castle wall. "Who?"

"Frank Matson," I said. "You *do* remember him, yes?"

Wade struggled to recover his composure. "Well, sure. Naturally I remember Frank."

An awkward silence filled the office. Nicole sensed she was about to get her walking papers and plunked herself down on the edge of the desk.

"Nicole, honey," Wade said.

"What?" There was challenge in her voice.

"I really do need to talk to Mr. Parker in private."

"Wade!" Somehow Nicole managed to wring three syllables out of his name.

"Don't give me a hard time, honey," Wade said. "Please do as you're told."

Nicole's neck went red. "For how long?"

"I don't know."

"You don't *know?* What about our plans?"

"We may have to adjust our plans."

Nicole's eyes turned molten red. I stood and told Wade I'd wait for him in the reception room. He gave me a grateful look and I left the office, shutting the door behind me. I resumed my spot on the couch and flipped through the pages of a magazine.

Wade and Nicole yelled at each other all the way through

"Raindrops Keep Fallin' on My Head," with Nicole doing most of the yelling. The partygoers in the other room had long since cleared out. Then suddenly Wade's door opened and Nicole came out and slammed it behind her. She swept by me as fast as her three-inch heels would take her, and I was left sitting in the swirl of her exhaust, a commingling of perfume and tequila and pissed-off libido.

Wade came slowly out of his office a few seconds later. He was shrugging his arms into a tan jacket and shaking his head. "Sorry about Nicole," he said. "A woman scorned ..."

"I understand."

"You had dinner yet, Quinn?"

"No."

"Hungry?"

"Hungry enough."

"Let's go. We'll take my car."

=28=

We drove in Wade's white Jaguar to the Summerhouse, an expensive restaurant farther down the Key with valet parking and a staff of well-dressed, vaguely aristocratic waiters, all of whom seemed to know Wade Davenport by name. The restaurant was away from the Gulf, hidden in a thick shady grove of banyan and palm trees, with a parking area of crushed seashell and an all-window, atriumlike dining area on the second level up among the tangled branches. There was a fountain as you walked in that tumbled and splashed and kept the air cool and misty. Swiss Family Robinson Goes to the Rain Forest.

Wade and I climbed the steps to the second floor. It was early for the dinner crowd, and we pretty much had the place to ourselves. There was a table all the way in the far corner, so that's where we went.

Wade ordered a dry double martini and I made it a beer, then he took a handful of peanuts from the dish in front of us and settled back in his chair. In the natural light I could see for the first time some resemblance to the man in the Pilkow photograph.

"Okay, Quinn," he said. "I'm not big on the cat-and-mouse stuff, so say what you have to say."

"I only want to ask you a few questions."

"Questions about Frank Matson?"

"That's right."

Wade smoothed out his tie and leaned back in his chair. "You know, I was thinking. For someone who just showed up out of the blue thirty minutes ago, you already know a hell of a lot about me."

"I would have said I don't know a thing about you."

Wade shrugged. "You've seen my office. My coworkers. Been in my car and know what I drink." Wade paused, half smiled. "Saw me knock heads with my mistress. Me, on the other hand, I don't know anything about you. Your name is all, and the fact that you look like you could use a double martini, too, but aren't drinking one because you want to keep your head clear. Before we go any further I'm curious to know some of *your* particulars, Quinn Parker."

"Fair enough," I said. "I'm a friend of Frank Matson's son."

"His son?" Wade thought for a moment. "Wait a second. Is this one of those deals where you're trying to track down his dad?"

"No."

"Because if it is, I can tell you right now I don't have a clue. Last time I saw Frank was twenty years ago. Longer."

"We know where Frank is," I said. "That's not what I want to ask you about."

"Then what?"

"I'm curious to hear your version of what happened on the night of March 21, 1969."

Wade didn't change his expression, but it must have been hard. In the distance the bartender sliced his limes. Wade cleared his throat. "It's well documented what happened that night. Three of us went out on recon in triple canopy jungle and got captured by the North Vietnamese."

"I know what the documents say. What I'd like now is to hear from you what *really* happened."

Wade's face hardened. "You act like you already know the answer, so why don't you tell me."

"All I know are the facts."

"Which are?"

"That you and Frank Matson and another soldier named Paul Wilson went out on patrol and never came back."

"That's what I just told you," Wade said. "We went out on recon and got captured."

"The facts don't say 'captured.' The facts say you never came back."

An unfriendlier Wade Davenport leaned forward in his chair. "I was going to buy you dinner, Quinn, but I don't think I like what you're implying. I don't think you're fit company to eat with. If you've got something to say to me that isn't lies and innuendo, then out with it, or I'm headin' out the door and you can either hike up the beach or flag a goddamn taxi back to your car!"

I reached into my jacket pocket and took out the photograph of Frank, Suzie, and Wade sitting at the outdoor bar in Pilkow, Cambodia. I set it on the table, turned it to face Wade right-side up, and pushed it across to him. He was poised to get up out of his seat, but now he settled back down. Stared at the photo awhile. Then I took out the official letter confirming the executions of Paul Wilson and Nguyen Nyu, unfolded it, and slid it alongside the photo. Wade didn't move a muscle.

"There's more," I said. "But this should at least enable us to start telling each other the truth."

"Where did you get this?" Wade said. His voice had turned into a very small little thing. The fountain in the lobby downstairs almost drowned it out.

"Not important."

"What else do you have?"

"Plenty."

I was stretching the truth. Except for the photograph—which might have been taken anywhere, anytime—there had been nothing in the strongbox to remotely link Wade Davenport with

Frank Matson's activities in Southeast Asia. But Wade didn't know that.

Wade looked at the photo, reread the letter. "Did Frank send you after me?"

"Frank Matson's dead," I said. "He was murdered in California a few days ago."

Wade looked up sharply. "What?"

"Shot in the head and dumped in a steel tank filled with wine."

I gathered up the photograph and letter and put them back in my jacket pocket. Wade watched me. "Are you a cop?" he said.

"No."

"Private investigator?"

"I already told you. I'm a friend of Phillip Chesterton, who is Frank Matson's son."

"Then what's this all about?"

"The authorities back in California think Phillip killed his father, and I'm trying to prove them wrong. My motives aren't complicated here, Mr. Davenport. I don't want money from you. I don't want to ruin your life or wreck your business or cause you to have any more fights with Nicole. All I want is to find out the truth about the night of March 21, 1969. Then you'll never see me again. That's as straight as I can say it."

Wade leaned back in his chair, somewhat dazed. "How did you find me?"

"Frank had your address on file."

"He did?"

I nodded.

"My address here on Siesta Key?"

I nodded again.

Wade considered that for a while. "Then how did you know to look for *my* name?" he said.

"I spoke to Jeff Lowery yesterday," I said. "Do you remember him?"

Wade shut his eyes. Ghosts from the past were springing up faster than he could assimilate them. The waiter appeared with our drinks and Wade leaned forward and took the martini right from the waiter's hand and drank half of it before the glass had a chance to touch the table. Then he exhaled loudly, slumped back in his chair, and gave the alcohol a chance to kick in. When he finally spoke he sounded defeated. Resigned.

"I've been waiting fifteen years for this day," he said. "Fifteen years. Don't think a week's gone by in all that time where I didn't find myself thinking about what this moment would be like. I always figured it'd be Frank himself, knocking on the door. Or somebody from the government." Wade finished off the rest of his martini. "I'm glad it's happening. I really am. I'm glad."

The waiter brought Wade a second martini without him having to ask. Wade took this one more slowly, sipping from it, leaning back in his chair and staring out the window.

"You and Frank and Paul Wilson went AWOL that night, didn't you?" I said. "You planned to disappear."

Wade continued to stare out the window. A squirrel raced along the branches. "What's in it for me if I tell you the truth?"

"Silence," I said. "That's what. Whatever we talk about goes no further than this bowl of peanuts."

"Why should I trust you?"

"You don't have any choice."

"And if I don't feel like talking?"

"Then the scope of my questioning starts to spiral out and I won't be able to guarantee anything."

He concentrated on the tree branches beyond the window and thought about it awhile. Then he exhaled and turned back to face me. "Looks like you got me over a barrel, Quinn. But I'm warning you right now, flat-out straight. If I tell you something and you don't keep quiet about it, don't stick to your word, I'm not a man who'll just sit back and take it. I'll come after you. Got it?"

"Got it."

Wade nodded. He'd countered my threat with one of his own, and now he was ready to talk. "Okay, then. Yes. We planned to disappear that night."

"Why?"

"Money."

"What money?"

Wade sighed. "The money we were going to make selling all the weapons."

"You need to back up."

"It was like this," Wade said. "The army had a large stash of illegal weapons hidden in Laos that nobody knew about. They were either going to sit there and rust, or the enemy was going to find them, or somebody could go get them and sell them. We decided that it made more sense to make some money than let 'em rust."

"You and Frank and Paul Wilson?"

"Right."

"How did you know about the hidden weapons?"

"I was the one who hid them."

"You?"

Wade finished his second martini and ordered another one, this a single. "In the late fifties I was sent over to Laos. This was before Vietnam or Frank Matson or anything. It was up in the Plateau de Bolovens, way the hell out in the middle of the most remote country you've ever seen."

"What were you doing there?"

Wade managed a small, tight smile. "Honest to God truth is I still don't know what we were doing there. Official reason was to help the Royal Laotian Army fight the Pathet Lao."

"Unofficial reason?"

"Stockpile weapons for the bigger conflict to come. Of course, that didn't click with me till later. I was just a young, naive kid back then. I thought we were trying to save the world from communism. Let the locals see that we were the good guys. Our detachment worked with the Kha tribe."

"How long were you there?"

"Two years," Wade said. "Learned their language, helped them build rice mills, gravity-flow water systems, public health facilities."

"Sounds like the Peace Corps," I said.

"That's practically what we were. People have this image of Green Berets as a bunch of shoot-'em-up macho men, but know who inspired the Special Forces?"

"Who?"

"Chairman Mao. God's truth. Him and his little band of revolutionaries went out and won over a country of a billion people. How? Because they were *nice!* Simple as that! If Mao's troops slept in a village, they made the beds before they left the next morning. If they ate the villagers' food, they replaced it or did chores as payment. They never stole, never abused the people they were trying to win over. So that was the strategy behind the Green Berets. We were nice guys. It's your conventional soldier you got to watch out for. The guy who's pumping gas one day and strapping on a rifle the next. He's the one who does the rape, pillage, and plunder stuff. That's where your My Lais come from." Wade paused while his third martini came to the table.

"Maybe you should slow down on the martinis," I said.

"Last one," Wade said. He ate the olive first and twirled the empty toothpick around in front of his face. "We were supposed to teach the Kha how to fight guerrilla warfare, but most of the time it was the other way around. They were fierce fighters. I remember once one of the Kha guerrilla leaders came back from an ambush and he told me he had killed seventeen Pathet Lao. I was sitting having my lunch and I asked him how he could be sure of the exact number, and he opened up this bamboo tube and dumped a pile of dried human ears on the table and said 'Divide by two'! I'm sitting there having my lunch!"

Wade shook his head at the memory. Now that the decision had been made to come clean, all the tension had left his face. Now he looked like he wanted to tell it all: the grisly anecdotes, the sweaty camaraderie, everything that had been bottled up inside for so long. I was the safest audience he could possibly have. Someone who'd said he'd disappear once the story had been told and never show his face again.

"Anyhow," Wade said. "Those were the Kha. I left Laos in 1961, all of us did, but we knew that wasn't going to be the end of it. The region was in for a major shitstorm down the road. I thought that if the Vietcong were half as tough as the Kha, we were in for a serious butt-kicking. The army knew it, and that's why we were *really* in Laos. We built a half-dozen rice mills up and down the Plateau de Bolovens, and under each one was a room, sort of like a bomb shelter. We were told it was going to be a place for the villagers to hide if the Pathet Lao moved through, but by the time we left there every single last goddamn cubic inch was stockpiled with weapons. Grenades, antiaircraft guns, dynamite, bayonets, machine guns, flamethrowers. You name it, it was in there. The operation was so secret only four of us in the detachment even knew about it."

"This was in the late fifties?"

"Right."

"And the weapons just sat there?"

"For a decade," Wade said. "Doing nothin' but gathering dust. Would've sat there for another decade, too. Tell you the truth, I think the army just plain forgot all about them. So much covert shit was going on back in those days, this little Bolovens project probably got lost in the shuffle. Anyway, Frank Matson's eyes lit up when I mentioned it one day in Saigon. We used to call him 'Gunboat' Frank Matson because he had this soldier-of-fortune attitude about the Green Berets, and this Laotian thing was right up his alley. Next day he asked me more about it." Wade took a sip of his drink and shrugged. "The thing kind of snowballed from there. Frank was real ..."

Wade trailed off, didn't finish his thought. The martinis were starting to blur the lines.

"Frank was real what?" I said.

"I don't know ... he almost made our scheme sound patriotic. I'm not just trying to cover my ass, Quinn. Not at all. I did the wrong thing and I know it and there's no halo twirling over my head. But Frank made a real good case for going out there and getting the weapons regardless, even if there wasn't a thin dime to be made on it. He dug out a map and showed how the Ho Chi Minh Trail zigged right past those rice mills and what the hell would happen to our war effort if the enemy discovered them. He said we ought to go out and make sure the weapons would get to the right people in Laos so that the North Vietnamese supply line could be cut or disrupted."

Wade nursed his drink and told me how it was supposed to have gone. The three of them were going to try to link up with the Kha tribe, either detonate the secret weapons or find a way to sell them, then sneak back into Vietnam with some harrowing account of near-capture. A month or two months, total.

The scheme came off better than they could have possibly hoped for. That March night in 1969, Frank, Wade, and Paul Wilson disappeared into the jungle and made their way without incident into Laos. The Kha remembered Wade, the weapons were still intact, and Matson—through some wheeling and dealing of his own—found buyers for the guns and explosives. They split the money three ways.

"That was supposed to be the end of it," Wade said. "Frank and Paul looked at the money and saw the possibilities, and the two of them said they weren't going back. Frank had a Vietnamese woman—or maybe she was Cambodian, I don't know—who joined up with him in Laos."

I paused, tapped my shirt pocket where the Pilkow photo was. "The woman sitting on Frank's lap?"

"Yeah. Nguyen. I don't know who she was or where she came from, but she spoke perfect English and became our translator. She knew the ropes, where to go, all that. I didn't know it, but some of the people Frank sold the weapons to were professional arms dealers. He was connected from somewhere. Maybe through Nguyen. I hung in there for a whole year. We set up headquarters in Cambodia where it wasn't so crazy. The business got bigger, the risks scarier. Matson and Wilson got less and less particular about who they sold to. And then as if things weren't bad enough, they started hiring themselves out."

"As mercenaries?"

"I guess you'd call them that," Wade said. "Not that they actually went out there in the trenches, but Green Berets have a lot of specialized knowledge, and Frank was more than willing shop his services around. That's when I threw in the towel. I told them I wanted out."

"I'm surprised they *let* you out," I said.

Wade shrugged. "The way Frank saw it, the pie was getting bigger and bigger, and if I bailed out there'd be one less slice to share."

"They weren't afraid you'd talk?"

"Who was I going to talk to?" Wade said. "And what was the point in cooking my *own* ass? My money was as dirty as theirs. So one day I wired all my money to a safe place in Singapore and tromped back into Vietnam and told my story."

"That you had been captured, but escaped?"

"That's right."

"Frank made the same claim. The army bought it?"

Wade took a single peanut, put in his mouth, and shook his head. "They knew something was fishy, but they couldn't prove anything. The main stink was that the government didn't want to pay me extra benefits for being a POW. But that was all."

The waiter came by the table and asked if we were interested in seeing a menu. Wade nodded and he set the menus before us, where they sat unread.

"You don't know what happened to Frank and Wilson and the Vietnamese woman after you left?" I said.

"Never saw any of them again. My contacts in the area said later that things fell apart. Matson ratted on Wilson and Nguyen to save his own skin and blew the area with all the money. Heard Wilson and the girl got executed, but never knew if that was true or not until you just showed me that letter. Probably part of the deal Frank struck. If Wilson and Nguyen were cosigners with the Swiss bank, Frank couldn't get his hands on the money until they were confirmed dead."

"And you're sure the woman in the picture I showed you is the woman you've been talking about? Nguyen?"

Wade nodded. "Positive. Tough broad. I think she was a Saigon bar girl. Prostitute. Except she and Frank were hot and heavy so we couldn't joke about it. She scared me worse than Frank, if you want to know the truth."

Wade lifted his menu and scanned it without enthusiasm. "You hungry?" he said.

"Not really."

"Me neither. Lost my appetite."

"Tell me one last thing," I said.

"What?"

"Has anybody else ever asked you about this before?"

"No."

"No letters? Phone calls?"

Wade shook his head. "Nothing."

I took care of the check, and we went back out to the parking lot. I kept quiet as Wade drove with remarkable steadiness back to his office.

We stood together in the parking lot and Wade shook my hand. "Hope you don't take it personal if I say I hope we never see each other again."

"No offense taken."

"Thanks for the drinks."

"Jeff Lowery said something else I wanted to ask you about."

"Shoot," Wade said.

"He said Frank Matson put bombs inside of hogs."

A long, slow grin spread across Wade's face. He shook his head and stared up into the muggy Florida sky.

"That wasn't Frank. That was Wilson. There were wild hogs in the area who'd scavenge the dead bodies from massacres or whatever. Wilson had this idea about surgically implanting heat-activated bombs in wild hogs. Then turn 'em loose back in the jungle and wait for the Vietcong to capture them and start roasting them over an open pit. Boom! Just one of those crazy ideas around the campfire." Wade cleared his throat. "Those were insane years, Quinn. Insane. After Vietnam I never wanted to do another crazy thing the rest of my life, ever. I wanted to come back to Florida and sell time-share condos and join the Rotary Club. Which is what I did. I'm a happy man."

"Thanks for the talk."

We shook hands again and I left Wade standing there in the parking lot, gazing off at the other cars. I couldn't tell if he was thinking of the madness of his past or of Nicole, the mad mistress of his immediate present. Either scenario was harrowing enough to merit a fourth martini, but he'd have to drink it alone. I had an appointment to keep back in California.

29

I spent the night in a small beach motel on Siesta Key and took the first flight to California the next morning. I got into the Sacramento airport just before noon, got my van out of long-term parking, and then drove straight to San Francisco.

A cold wind was blowing off the Pacific, bringing with it gusting layers of thin, icy rain. I found a parking space only three blocks away from my apartment and hurried quickly home, eyes to the pavement, collar turned up.

I heard voices as I reached the top of the stairs. A man's voice and a woman's voice. I went cautiously down the hallway and took a peek in the living room. Gunnhilde von Edlund and Hank were sitting on the couch, in front of a cozy fire. When Hank saw me he sprang to his feet and gave me a look like I'd just caught him with his hand in the petty cash drawer.

"Quinn!" he said. "When did you get in?"

"Just now."

Gunnhilde nodded at me and smiled, and I nodded back.

"Be back in just a second," Hank said, and Gunnhilde nodded

again. He took me by the elbow and led me to the study. "Got some news for you."

"I thought you and Gunnhilde were finished."

"She just showed up on the doorstep," Hank said. "I don't know what's going on. She says she's got feelings about me she doesn't know what to do with."

"Pardon me?"

"That's a direct quote," Hank said, "but forget Gunnhilde for a second. Why didn't you check in from Florida?"

"I was only there overnight. What's the big deal?"

"Phillip Chesterton called last night," he said. "*That's* the big deal!"

We went into the study and Hank closed the door, and for a second we just sort of stood there and looked at each other. "Where is he?" I said at last.

"Mexico. Cabo San Lucas, just like you thought."

"Is he alone?"

"Didn't say. All he said was that he was in Cabo, that he was fine, and that you should tell his mother not to worry."

"Did you get his number?"

"No, but he said he was staying in the same place the two of you stayed before."

"Ventana del Sol?"

"That's it," Hank said.

I thought for a moment. "What was his tone of voice?"

"We didn't talk long enough to pick up a tone of voice, and the connection was lousy anyway." Hank turned and looked back down the hall toward the living room. "I should get back."

I nodded, picked up the phone.

"If you're calling the airport," Hank said, "I already made reservations for you."

I returned the receiver to its cradle. "You did?"

"Last night. You're booked on Mexicana Airlines, nonstop to Cabo San Lucas, leaving seven o'clock tonight. Charged it to your credit card as soon as I hung up with Phillip. With the holiday season, tickets were tight. Figured you could cancel if you wanted."

I was momentarily speechless. "You've never planned ahead like that before in your life."

"My senses are sharpened these days." Hank winked, opened the door, and started down the hall back in the direction of Gunnhilde.

I dug up the number for Ventana del Sol, called, and the clerk confirmed in his broken English that yes, Phillip Chesterton was registered there. He asked if I wanted to leave a message and I said no, it wasn't important. If Suzie Wong were down there with him, she was the last person I wanted alerted to my arrival.

Next I called Jimmy Kamamoto's restaurant. Jimmy was a good guy, reliable and discreet, and I was hoping he could take a reconnaissance trip over to Ventana del Sol. See if Phillip was alone, and if he was, maybe take him back and keep him safely on the boat till I arrived. But the Mexican woman on the other end of the phone said Jimmy wasn't there. He'd gone to La Paz for supplies and wouldn't be back until later in the evening. I hung up and chewed on my knuckle. Damn.

I went back out into the living room. Gunnhilde was strolling the area, looking at the books on the bookshelf. She was lovely and seductive, wearing a short white skirt and lots of polished black jewelry around her wrists and neck. Earrings of Aztec silver. Hair loose and tumbling over her shoulders. White nylons, white high-heels. Salmon-colored blouse with no bra.

Hank was in the kitchen, locked in a life-or-death struggle with a stubborn wine cork.

"I'm going," I said.

"Where?"

"Napa."

"Napa? You've got a plane to catch!"

"The plane doesn't leave for six hours."

Hank handed the bottle to me and I got the cork out. "Can't you stick around for a few more minutes," he said in a semi-whisper. "Please?"

"What's the matter?"

He nodded his chin in the direction of the living room. "This could be *it*," he said. "I'm nervous as hell. Just help get me over the hump."

"Bad choice of words."

The downstairs buzzer buzzed. I handed Hank the uncorked bottle of wine, told him to take a couple of deep breaths, then went down to get the door. It was Carol.

"Hi, Quinn."

"Carol!"

I instinctively closed the door a little. Carol placed her hand on the doorknob and nudged it back open the way it was. Then she turned and looked behind her to see if a three-fanged zombie had trailed her up from the street. "Didn't mean to startle you, Quinn. I'm not selling anything."

"What are you doing here?"

"Good afternoon to you, too," she said. "See if you get any more front-porch kisses." Pause. "Can I come in?"

"Come in?"

"Yes," Carol said. "Come in. A two-word phrase meaning 'to enter.'"

"Of course you can come in," I said. "Or ..."

"Or what?"

"Or we could go out somewhere and have some coffee."

"I need to talk to Hank," Carol said, stepping in and brushing past me. "Is he around?"

"Hank?"

Carol stopped, planted her hands on her hips, and stared at me. "What's with you, Quinn? Yes, Hank. Hank Wilkie. Surely you remember. Five-eight, hundred fifty pounds. Birthmark on his left butt cheek, though I wouldn't expect you to know about that. Is he here?"

"Yes," I said. "But he's not alone."

Carol hesitated only for a moment, then the awareness dawned on her. "A woman?"

I nodded.

Carol thought about it, then shrugged in a way meant to suggest that it was no big deal. "I need to talk to him anyway.

Take me two minutes." She started up the stairs, and I followed after.

We got to the living room just as Hank veered around the corner of the kitchen with two full glasses of wine. When he saw Carol he jerked to a stop as though collared neck-high by an invisible clothesline. Half the wine spilled onto the floor.

"Carol!" he said. "What are you doing here?"

"Sorry," she said. "I should've called, but I need to remind you about something."

Gunnhilde had been at the dining-room window, admiring the view, and now she came over to join us. Smiling, bouncy, her unconfined breasts jouncing beneath the blouse. Carol visibly stiffened.

A round of awkward introductions ensued. Hank was on his knees, cleaning the spilled wine from the floor and trying to buy time. It didn't take long for Gunnhilde to figure out who Carol was, and her strategy was to turn up the sexual heat a couple of degrees. Lips fuller, legs leggier, nipples pressed against the fabric of the sheer blouse in vivid relief, like erasers on a couple of brand-new pencils, just aching to be used for the first time.

From his knees Hank asked if there was a problem and Carol said no, there wasn't any problem. Cort's school Christmas show was the next evening and he was playing a ram whose job it was to batter down a door. It was the most important and challenging role of Cort's grammar school career to date, and Hank ought to be there. That was all.

Hank continued toweling off the floor long after the mess had been cleaned and asked Carol if she could hold on just a moment. He'd be through in a second and then they could talk. Carol said of course, and she and I went back down the hall and closed the door of my study.

Carol looked at the closed door, then at me, then leaned back against the wall and let herself slide down to a crouch. "Know what this reminds me of?" she said.

"What?"

"When we were kids. How we had to wait in the back bedroom so Santa Claus could come and do his cookies-and-milk routine."

"Well … it's almost Christmas."

Carol nodded, took a deep breath. "So that's Gunnhilde."

"That's Gunnhilde."

"Attractive."

I shrugged. "If you like busty, blond, Amazonian types, I suppose."

"She doesn't have kids, does she?"

"No idea."

"Bet she doesn't," Carol said. "I used to be sort of busty myself, you know." She gave me a quick sidelong glance to see if I was going to nitpick. "Not *huge,* of course. But nice. Perky. Nursing two ravenous boys ended that. Now my breasts look like a couple of Playtex gloves turned inside-out."

"I've seen you in a swimsuit, Carol. Your breasts are just fine. And your legs are world-class."

She grunted.

"Besides," I said, "most men like a woman with a defect or two."

"You don't have to throw me crumbs, Quinn."

"I mean it. Ever seen the European editions of *Playboy?*"

"No."

"You should. The women aren't air-brushed-to-perfection teenagers. They're mature women."

"Mature?"

"Absolutely. They've got moles, stretch marks, baby fat, everything. Real women. Women you could share a chili dog with."

"Super," Carol said. "Maybe if *National Geographic* starts a centerfold I'll have a future."

More silence. Lola scratched at the door, and Carol leaned over to open it for her. The cat came slinking in and crawled into Carol's lap. The two ladies commiserated awhile, and I suddenly felt the differentness of my sex. How male I was, and how female they were.

"It bugs the hell out of me that I'm even thinking like this," Carol said. "I'm bright and educated and here I am sitting on the floor comparing body parts with some bimbo. It's demeaning."

"I agree."

"So what if Miss Norway out there has mammary glands two inches bigger than mine?"

"Two?"

"Okay, *three!* Or five or ten or whatever! Is that what it all comes down to? Tape measure shots?"

"You're bitching to the wrong man, Carol."

"She wears too much makeup anyway." Carol fell silent, softly stroked Lola's fur, and stared off into space. "So what've you been up to? Hank called yesterday and said you went to Florida."

I told Carol about my trip. I intended to skim over it—sun, sea, how they have to post minimum speed limits. But as I talked I began sorting things out, and by the time I was done Carol had heard the whole thing. Even the details of Nicole's snit.

"So Frank Matson, Paul Wilson, and Suzie Wong were partners over in Cambodia after the war?" Carol said.

"During *and* after, yes."

"Selling weapons?"

"Weapons. Expertise. Probably other things Wade Davenport decided not to tell me. Once Wade got enough money to begin the model-citizen portion of his life, he split."

"Which means only Suzie is left now?"

"Suzie and Leslie McCall."

Carol looked blank, so I backed up and briefly told her of the strongbox Abigail had brought to the house. It was an increasingly extensive recap, with the minutes ticking away, and in the back of my mind I wondered what was taking Hank so goddamn long.

"I see the problem," Carol said. "How did Leslie McCall get his information except from Suzie?"

"Exactly. Wade said nobody's ever confronted him with this stuff before, so it had to have gone to Leslie directly from one of the concerned parties."

"You think Suzie and Leslie are partners?"

"I don't know what else to think."

"But how did they find each other?" Carol said.

"That's what I'm going to find out." I stood and walked to the door. "Hate to leave you in a spot like this, but I've got to get up to Napa right now."

Carol lifted Lola from her lap and got to her feet. "You won't be leaving me. Let me just tell Hank the rest of what I have to tell him and then I'll be gone."

"When this settles down we'll talk more," I said. "Arrange a babysitter and I'll take you out for a nice dinner."

"You most certainly will," Carol muttered. "You and your defective European playmates ..."

Hank and Gunnhilde were standing in the middle of the living room, talking in an animated fashion as we approached. Hank saw us out of the corner of his eye and tried to break it off, but Gunnhilde took no heed. She was angry, and there was a flush of pink to her Scandinavian neck.

"I was just coming back," Hank said.

"I'm not finished!" Gunnhilde said, and she turned Hank back around so he had to face her.

Carol lifted her arms and let them flap down to her sides. "I'm going," she said. "Call me when you're free, Hank."

"Wait a minute," Gunnhilde said to Carol. "I want you to know I do not approve of what you are doing. Do you hear me? I don't approve at all!"

Carol did a wonderfully slow about-face and stared at Gunnhilde. "Are you speaking to me?"

"Yes," Gunnhilde said. "I am speaking to you!"

"Gunnhilde ..." Hank said.

"What exactly am I doing," Carol said, "that you don't approve of?"

"Don't pretend you don't know," Gunnhilde said with a sarcastic smile. "You just happened to come here ten minutes after I came here?"

"What are you implying?" Carol said.

"You throw this man out of the house months ago and now you won't let him live his life! It's fine when he's unhappy, but when another woman comes into his life you are suddenly standing in front of us, talking about your child's Christmas play!"

Hank tried to jump in and defend himself, but Carol ignored him. She was scarily composed, and focused on Gunnhilde. "I do not have a tent pitched across the street to watch Hank's comings and goings," Carol said. "I have a family to raise and bills to pay, and I have neither the time nor the energy to be devious about who Hank, in his current diminished state, chooses to sip wine with. And you, whoever you are, do *not* have permission to talk to me about my private life."

"Diminished state?" Gunnhilde said.

Carol surveyed Gunnhilde from head to toe, and nodded to herself. I was braced for a torrent of pent-up Neapolitan anger, frustration, and indignation, but Carol only smiled. "*Very* diminished," was all she said.

Then Carol turned and began walking down the hallway. Hank moved quickly and caught up with Carol at the top of the stairs. He put his hand on her shoulder, and she gave him a pitiless look.

"I never told her you weren't letting me live my life," he said. "She just plucked that out of thin air. I hardly even know this woman."

Carol sighed and shook her head wearily. "Fuck off, Hank. Just be at Cort's play tomorrow. Seven o'clock in the school gym."

She went down the stairs without another word. The door opened and closed and that was that. Hank and I looked at each other a moment, then Gunnhilde came marching down the hall and toward Hank, fists clenched, breasts going like water balloons. Okay, she said. Time to talk. Time to lay down some ground rules. Is this the kind of thing she could expect all the time from Carol? Unannounced visits and sentimental references to the children back home? Because if it was, she didn't want to have anything to do with Hank any longer. And she didn't like at all the way Carol implied that Hank was only drawn to her because of her body. She was speaking in a very loud voice, and Oscar the parrot started squawking his protests in the next room.

Hank looked weary. Fed up. He explained that the fact remained that he had a family and from time to time it would complicate his life, but he liked the complications overall and maybe Gunnhilde wasn't being sympathetic to that. He wasn't putting much effort into the soothing process.

"Okay," Gunnhilde said. "Then could I go with you to see this Christmas show tomorrow?"

"No," Hank said.

"Why not?"

"Because it would upset Carol and you'd only be doing it to get back at her."

Gunnhilde's face grew red. She folded her arms across her chest. "Then where are your loyalties?" she demanded. "With me, or with Carol?"

Hank thought about it a second. "My loyalties are with Carol."

The silence was so electric, even Oscar quit screeching and waited to see what would happen next. Gunnhilde was silent a moment. She pursed her lips, nodding her head in short, curt nods. Then she went back out to the living room and came walking past us with her shawl over her shoulder and the glass of wine in her hand. As she passed Hank she tossed the wine in his face and headed down the stairs. Never broke stride, and never said another word.

Hank leaned against the banister and licked the wine as it dripped from his forehead. "You'd think somebody with an abiding love of Norwegian music would be more well-adjusted," he said.

"Must be the long, cold winters."

"Well," he said, looking down the stairwell. "I guess it wasn't meant to be. I was outgunned from the start anyway. What chance does any man have against a hundred gallons of precisely aimed shower water?"

"Good point."

"I'll tell you this, though. I've never had two beautiful women arguing over me before."

I reminded Hank that one of the beautiful women told him to fuck off and the other gave him a faceful of Cabernet Sauvignon, but he didn't care. Bogart took his share of grief from women, too. Came with the turf. Hank went out to the kitchen to get another towel and I took a few minutes to stroke Oscar's feathers and settle him back down.

Then I grabbed my van keys and started down the stairs. Hank's Keystone Kops love life was well and fine, but I had more important things on my mind. If Suzie was in Mexico with Phillip, I needed to have some ammunition of my own. Some leverage. I needed to have a talk with Leslie McCall.

=30=

On the outskirts of Napa I stopped and called the *Napa Observer*, and asked for Leslie. The woman who answered said he wasn't there. She asked if I wanted to leave a message and I said I'd try back later. Then I hung up, got back in the van, and started driving in the direction of Shrader-Cox Vineyards.

The parking lot of the Shrader-Cox tasting room was empty, a "Closed" sign hanging in the window. I drove around back and came to an idling stop at the wooden gate. I got out of the van and swung the gate open and motored through, down the twisting gravel road that led to the ranch-style house.

Geese were running around out front as I drove up. Leslie's BMW was parked outside. I pulled alongside it, cut the engine, and climbed the porch steps to the front door. I knocked three times, each louder than the last, but nobody answered. I tried the doorknob. It opened easily, and I carefully stepped inside.

The living room was gray and quiet. Drapes pulled. Nothing stirring. I checked the kitchen and the dining area and the study.

All empty. I thought he might be sleeping, but the back bedroom was empty, too. Bed made, pillows fluffed just so, everything neat and orderly. To the right the bathroom door was open. I stepped inside, and that's where Leslie McCall was.

He was stretched out nude in the tub. The water came right up to the brim, almost overflowing, and it had a faint red tinge. Leslie's face rippled back at me from where it rested a few inches below the surface of the water. His silver toupee had come loose and floated at an odd angle above his skull. His body looked opaquely blue, eyes open. Serene, and utterly still.

I knelt at the tub, cupped my hands under his armpits, and lifted his head above the water. The toupee flattened against the side of his face like seaweed. Leslie was gone. The water was painfully cold, almost like ice. The veins on both of Leslie's wrists had been sliced lengthwise. I released him and he sank softly back to his original spot.

There was a right way and a wrong way for an upstanding citizen to behave in a situation like this. I needed a minute or two to decide which way I was going to choose. I quickly went through the rest of the house. It was business as usual, except for the suicide note in Leslie's office. It had been typed on an ancient Olivette typewriter. The same ink-smudged type, I noticed, that had characterized some of the blackmail letters I'd found in the strongbox. The note itself was a half-page long. In it Leslie confessed to Frank Matson's murder and apologized to those living who would be hurt by his actions. To Holt, who had trusted and loved and endured his terrible moods. To Abigail for the friendship he had betrayed. To Phillip for having been made to absorb the blame for that which was not his fault.

There were details to substantiate his claim to murder. The weapon, Leslie said, was wrapped in newspaper at the back of the gardener's shed behind the house. The key to the mobile home on Route C was in the top drawer, along with the documentation showing he had registered the home in Frank's name long ago. Then the note ended in typical Leslie McCall fashion, with a quote from Shakespeare. "Golden lads and girls all must/As chimney-sweepers, come to dust." The note wasn't signed.

I wandered the office and looked at the walls. Photos and awards. The framed one-way ticket back to Boston that he'd told me about. A large, rust-red brick sat on the desk, and I supposed it was the brick from Italy, the one Signora Capelli gave him after he took the pitchfork and jumped down into the sea of grapes. Poor Leslie. Funny little birdlike man who wore his ascots and kept the trinkets of his past all in one room, like a girl with her high-school scrapbook.

By the time I finished scanning Leslie's office I'd made my decision regarding good citizen, bad citizen. A good citizen would call the police to report the body and wait patiently until they arrived and be as helpful as possible in answering their questions. There would be hostility and suspicion, and I imagined there was a better-than-average chance my homicide guy would be Detective Davis again. A good citizen would probably be detained for a while. Long enough to miss a flight to Cabo San Lucas and long enough to prevent him from alerting Phillip to the raven-haired danger sharing his bed at night.

I took a napkin from the dining room table and carefully wiped off the few items of furniture I'd touched. Then I went back out onto the porch and got into my van. The geese scattered, and I drove away.

=31=

The plane to Cabo San Lucas was jammed. Every seat filled, a dozen forlorn travelers left waiting in the airport on standby, ticket agents glumly shaking their heads and suggesting alternate airlines. As I passed through the boarding gate I lifted my eyes and silently thanked the nearest available god for having given Hank Wilkie an uncharacteristic spasm of common sense at the right time.

It was an active, festive crowd that soared up out of San Francisco's chill purple twilight. To hell with the subtle mysteries of mist and fog. These people had had enough of that. This group was ready for fresh oysters, sun-baked beaches, and all-night dancing. Mexicana Airlines had made a questionable corporate decision to serve unlimited complimentary margaritas on the flight down, and the stewardesses hadn't quit pouring since the seat-belt light went off. Passengers wandered up and down the aisles in various stages of inebriation, cradling their drinks, kneeling and talking excitedly to seated friends. The young single men had already zeroed in on the young single women, and nobody seemed to mind. Propriety had been left on the ground, and the looser, giddier laws governing vacation behavior had taken over. Me, I was the burnt-out case in 38C, and people steered clear.

The flight—unlike almost everything else in my life during the past week—was mercifully uneventful. We touched down in Cabo, and after clearing customs I went straight outside to wait for a taxi. It was dark, and the stars were out. I took a deep breath of the desert air. It was hot and dry, dense with the rich scent of earth and sea and jet fuel. It smelled good. It smelled like Mexico.

The actual town of Cabo San Lucas is twenty miles from the airport, and since cabs are at a premium on the Baja Peninsula, taxi taking in the area tends to be a communal affair. It is understood that sometimes you must share your ride with others. Sometimes with great quantities of others. Like this time.

Three young women were up front with the driver, three young men scrunched in back with me. The sixsome were thick with getting-to-know-you talk and the residual smell of in-flight margaritas. I didn't exist. They giggled and pointed and wondered how in the world the taxi driver was going to get all their luggage on board. The cabbie outside circled his taxi a couple times, then decided on an angle of attack.

Five minutes of inventive and strenuous wedging did the trick. Assuming, of course, that nobody was packing anything more breakable than damp cardboard. But in spite of all the effort, one large duffel bag remained. The driver stroked his mustache, brooded, then decisively hefted the duffel bag onto the hood with a loud thunk and lashed it down with criss-crossing rope, and off we drove into the night like celebrating hunters parading home an eight-point buck.

Visibility, as one might imagine, was severely impaired. Strictly speaking, visibility ceased to exist. The cabbie adjusted for this inconvenience by driving with his head thrust far out the window. And he drove fast. Very, very, very fast. Years of living in Latin America had conditioned me to this, and I felt no undue alarm. Mexicans believe dangerous roads should be traversed at the greatest possible speed so as to minimize the amount of time spent on such a dangerous road. My fellow passengers didn't follow the logic, and there was no more frivolous laughter. They were intensely focused on the road, silently cursing their decision to save a few hundred bucks and do Baja instead of Hawaii.

I rested my head against the vibrating window and thought of Suzie. Suzie Wong, Suzie Wong. Where have you gone, Suzie Wong? Wade Davenport was right. She was the most dangerous of them all. Leslie McCall had not taken his own life. He was too vain a man to take off his clothes and climb in a tub and let his toupee float around in bloody water and let a gang of cops and photographers cast disparaging glances at his white wrinkled stomach, his shrunken genitals. There were no hesitation marks on his slit wrists. His pants had been hung on a peg in a corner of the bathroom, and the pant legs were inside-out, the way a child would take his pants off. Or the way a second party would pull the pants off a person who was already dead and couldn't undress himself.

On the plane ride down I briefly flirted with the idea that Davis himself might have killed Leslie. Leslie knew Davis was on Matson's secret payroll and had photographic evidence of something illegal stashed away in the strongbox. Leslie and his newspaper were probably going to turn up the heat on the Matson murder case, and the heat was substantial to begin with. Davis needed to have a suspect quick, preferably a suspect who was dead and couldn't speak up. The longer the investigation dragged on, the likelier it would be that someone would start snooping around and discover some discrepancies in how Davis and Matson were linked together.

But the Davis-as-killer theory stalled at that point, weakened, then receded. I had no doubt that the murder weapon and the mobile home key and everything else would check out, and if they did then Davis would have had to have planted them, which then brought him deeper into Frank's murder itself. No. The same person who killed Frank Matson had killed Leslie, and my thoughts returned to Suzie Wong.

The taxi had a couple of close calls, but the kilometers clicked off and we managed to survive. One always survives the incredible in Mexico. It's the commonplace that nails you down here. In thirty minutes the lights of Cabo San Lucas brimmed on the horizon, and I sat up straighter. Land's End. Phillip was close now. At long last he was very close.

I asked the driver to drop the others off first just in case I needed him to wait at Ventana del Sol. He did, and then the two of us wound through town. Christmas decorations everywhere, sidewalks crowded with people, lots of noise and activity and the sound of music spilling from raucous bars.

Ventana del Sol was located a few miles west of town. It consisted of a few dozen moderately priced bungalows, all on the beach and far enough away from one another to give the illusion of a private hideaway.

We pulled up to the front and I slipped the cabbie a ten-dollar bill and asked him to wait a second. He told me ten dollars bought more than a second, and I could take my time.

The office for Ventana del Sol was a small thatched hut with one desk, one phone, one lamp. It doubled as a souvenir shop of tacky native arts and crafts. Brandy bottles made from cowhide, Aztec headdresses, sequined sombreros gaudy enough to have turned Liberace's stomach. A teenage boy sat behind the desk in the dim light of the single lamp, doing nothing, absolutely nothing at all, just staring straight ahead with his hands in his lap like a character from an Edward Hopper painting.

"No room," he said, shifting his eyes to meet mine.

I told the kid in Spanish that I didn't need a room, that I was meeting a friend who was staying at the hotel. The clerk asked what was the name. I told him and he opened an oversized ledger and trailed his finger down a handwritten list. He nodded. Phillip Chesterton was in Bungalow 11. But not anymore.

"Not anymore?"

The kid shook his head. Mr. Chesterton had left. He had checked out earlier in the afternoon.

Did Phillip leave a forwarding address? I asked. A phone number?

The kid said no, he didn't leave anything. Just paid and left.

"Was he alone?" I asked.

"Yes," the clerk answered in Spanish. "He was alone. Except for the woman who came to pick him up."

"What woman?"

The clerk pulled the skin at the edges of his eyes. A Chinese woman, he said. Driving a red Chrysler. They left together, and that was the last he'd seen of them.

The taxi took me back into town and dropped me off at Serendipity, Jimmy Kamamoto's wharfside restaurant in the heart of Cabo. I slipped the cabbie another ten dollars and told him that if he or any of his taxi-driving brethren saw an Asian woman with long hair driving a red car, I'd be interested in having them tag along. See where she went. They could leave the information here at Serendipity, and I'd pay a hundred dollars if the information panned out. The cabbie said he'd put out the word, then drove away.

The restaurant was crowded. People three-deep at the bar, all the tables full, with boisterous, good-natured noise reverberating from one end of the building to the other. I told the hostess who I was and asked if Jimmy was around. She wrote my name down on a piece of paper and said that if I would wait one moment she'd go back to the kitchen and get him.

A minute later Jimmy came striding out through the swinging doors to the kitchen, all decked out in his chef's regalia. Apron, tall hat, the whole thing. He was smiling broadly and gave me a big, robust bear hug.

"Where the hell've you been?" he said.

"It'd be easier to tell you where I *haven't* been."

Jimmy laughed, slapped me on the back, and told me to follow him back to his office where we could talk in peace.

I'd met Jimmy Kamamoto more than fifteen years earlier in Guatemala while we were both doing our Peace Corps stint. In the beginning we didn't have the intrinsic stuff of which great friendships are made. It was mostly hi, how are you, what's up. We chatted at expatriate parties and found ourselves now and then on the opposite sides of a volleyball net. That was it. Under normal circumstances we would have been two people who met in a foreign land and perhaps exchanged addresses and then kept in sporadic touch until one year one of us would realize that he hadn't heard from the other in a while and the address wouldn't make it into the new address book. But Jimmy and I shared an incident that changed all that and made us closer pals than we would have been. It happened on the morning of the catastrophic Guatemalan earthquake of 1976.

At the time we were living at opposite ends of the Indian village of Chimaltenango. When the quake struck in the predawn darkness, one-third of the population died instantly, crushed by heavy tile roofs that collapsed on them in their sleep. I was thrown from bed and was waiting on my front lawn in the smoking dawn when Jimmy roared up on his motorcycle and yelled for me to jump on. There was a Red Cross emergency warehouse on the outskirts of the village, loaded with food and water and medical supplies, but nobody knew what the hell to do. We needed to get down there and set up a distribution network, fast.

So I climbed on back and we rode through the chaos down to the warehouse only to encounter a frightened, heavily armed Guatemalan soldier who wouldn't let us in. He had his orders, and they were firm. Jimmy and I needed a signed release form from either Washington, D.C., or his superior in Guatemala City. He could not release the contents of the warehouse without the demonstration of "extreme need."

Jimmy got in his face and explained that there was all the "extreme need" he'd ever want to see running bloodred through the streets of Chimaltenango. But the soldier wouldn't budge.

Procedure was procedure. So Jimmy turned and calmly told me to wait where I was. He got back on his motorcycle, disappeared over the crest of the hill, and returned a half-hour later with a hunting rifle slung over his shoulder. I'll never forget the image of the motorcycle coming back down the hill, silhouetted against the smoke-blackened sky, its roar competing with the distant screams of the terrified townspeople. Jimmy looked almost biblical. Some avenging, hunched-over-the-handlebars angel on a 500cc Suzuki, bringing word of the apocalypse.

When the soldier saw Jimmy he dropped his weapon, turned, and ran for the hills. In high school you'd vote me the guy least likely to shoot locks off Central American doors, but that's what we did. Jimmy took his rifle and I took the soldier's and we blasted the locks off the warehouse doors and started distributing the food.

Many lives were saved because of Jimmy's action, but it wasn't in the Peace Corps training manual to have their volunteers scaring off members of the Guatemalan army with hunting rifles. So when the dust settled, Jimmy and I were marched before the administrative honchos and informed that our services would no longer be required. We said good-bye to Guatemala and went our separate ways. I found out later that two months after the earthquake the Red Cross bigwigs in Washington officially acknowledged "extreme need" and issued urgent orders for the emergency supplies to be distributed at once.

For me the Guatemala incident was a freakish occurrence, a flamboyant but uncharacteristic story of derring-do that I brushed off now and then to share with dinner guests as exaggerated evidence of a riotous youth. But for Jimmy Kamamoto it was just another day in the life. He had an instinct for that sort of thing, and his wild ways continued in Panama, then South America, then Australia. From time to time word would filter up to me in San Francisco about his latest exploits. The mayor's impregnated daughter. The smalltown jail busted out of. I read the letters and marveled from a distance.

Then five years ago Jimmy decided enough was enough.

He'd grown weary of surface wounds and was going to do what he had always wanted to do. Open his own Japanese restaurant on the Sea of Cortez. Quit dodging bullets and settle down to a life of flip-flops, cold beer, and females on vacation. He named his boat the *Extreme Need,* in honor of the stalwart Guatemalan soldier, but that was about the only link he kept with his woolly past.

We edged past the sea of diners and Jimmy unlocked a door just beyond the bathrooms and flicked on a light. His office looked the way a restaurant office should look. Desk littered with invoices. Calculator with paper spooled down to the floor. Stacked cases of sugar packets shoved in the corner. There was one metal fold-out chair and Jimmy told me to sit in it. I did, and he lifted himself up onto his desk, sitting there smiling at me, both feet dangling.

"When did you get in?" he said.

"Few hours ago."

"Zoo out at the airport?"

"Crowded enough."

"Never seen it so busy here," he said. "Every year it gets more and more."

We shot the bull like that for a few minutes, catching up. I told him San Francisco gets more and more every year, too, and he laughed and said he knew what I was talking about. More and more was becoming a worldwide problem.

"See your friend yet?" he said.

I shook my head. "No. He was staying at the Ventana del Sol but checked out this afternoon. Now I've got to find him all over again."

"Hang around," Jimmy said. "He might be in for dinner."

"Somehow I don't think so."

Jimmy shrugged. "He's been in three nights running. Why should he stop now?"

I paused. "You've seen him?"

"Of course I've seen him," Jimmy said. "Why would I have called you telling you I'd seen him if I hadn't seen him?"

Silence. I sat and stared at Jimmy, and he got a funny look on his face. "You feeling okay, Quinn?"

"Let's back up a second," I said. "We're talking about the same person, right? Phillip Chesterton?"

"Right. Phillip Chesterton. The kid who came down with you this summer and went fishing. The one whose picture you Fed Exed down. I know who you're talking about." Jimmy paused, lost some of his smile. "What the hell's going on, Quinn?"

"And you called me about it?"

"Couple days ago," Jimmy said. "I left a message with your answering service."

"I don't have an answering service, Jimmy."

We were stone silent for a full ten seconds.

"Uh-oh," Jimmy said.

"What number did you call?"

"The number they gave me. I don't know where the hell it is now."

"But *I* gave you my home phone."

"It was like this," Jimmy said. "The day after you called about Phillip, I got another call down here from your answering service. Or whatever it was. The guy told me you had to go to New York on business and I was to use this other number temporarily until you got back. The answering service number."

"Do you remember the area code?"

"Same as yours. Four-one-five." Jimmy's tone grew serious. "What's going on, Quinn? Are you in some kind of trouble?"

I briefly told Jimmy what was going on. At the end of it he whistled, long and low. "This Suzie Wong sounds like a nasty woman. What does she look like?"

"Petite, with long, long hair. About thirty-five, forty years old."

Jimmy shook his head. "Nope. Haven't seen her."

"Sure?"

"Positive. I realize that all us Asians look the same, but I would have remembered a woman like that."

I rubbed my eyes. "They're probably long gone by now."

"Maybe not," Jimmy said. "This is one tough little nub of earth to run away from, especially this time of year when all the flights are booked and the ferries are sold out. Even bus tickets are hard to come by. She'd have to get real, real lucky standing around at the airport, or hop in a car and try to drive out. Maybe in La Paz she could find something, but even then … it's a big, lonely desert for someone trying to hide."

"I hope you're right." I exhaled. "Any chance I can sleep on your boat tonight?"

"You're forbidden to sleep anywhere else," Jimmy said. "She's all locked up, but the key's in the usual spot. Remember where?"

"I remember."

"You've got the boat to yourself. I'm staying with a ladyfriend in town these days."

"Thanks."

"So what's your plan of attack tomorrow?" Jimmy said.

"Roam around and see what I find. Check the usual places."

"Got a car?"

"I'll rent one."

Jimmy smiled, dug into his pockets. "You're not getting it through your head what I've been saying, Quinn. This time of year *nothing's* available in Cabo San Lucas at the drop of a hat. I can't even get a reservation at my own goddamn restaurant. Here." He tossed me a set of keys. "Use my Land Rover."

"You sure?"

"No problem. I'm not going anywhere. Besides, I got the old Renault out back anyway. Come on, I'll show you where it's parked."

Jimmy ducked into the kitchen to check on something, then we left the restaurant and walked along the wharf in the crisp, warm night. There was a guarded parking area just behind the small marina where Jimmy kept his boat, and that's where the Land Rover was. He opened it up, sat in the driver's seat, and pointed out, one by one, the vehicle's small idiosyncrasies. What needed jiggling and what needed jangling to make it purr at maximum efficiency. I nodded that I got it, and Jimmy relocked the car and handed me the keys.

"Got time for a nightcap?" he said. "Dinner crowd's winding down."

"Not tonight. I'm beat, and tomorrow's going to be a long day. But if Phillip shows, come and get me, okay?"

Jimmy said that he would, gave me another bear hug, and said there was plenty of cold beer in the boat if I got thirsty in the middle of the night. I thanked Jimmy again and headed toward the dock.

The stars were out. Millions of them. They lit the desert hills behind, illuminated the flat dark ocean beyond. There were thirty or forty slips in Jimmy's marina, and it had a cozy, occupied feel, the way boat communities often have. Lights burned behind curtained cabins. Small groups of people sat on their decks, talking softly in the dark night. The orange glow of cigarettes, soft laughter, the murmur of *buenos noches* as I walked by.

The *Extreme Need* was docked almost all the way at the end of the wooden walkway. I took the key from its hiding place and went below. I slapped some water on my face, dug around in the refrigerator for a beer, and climbed up on deck. Then I stretched out flat on my back on the cushioned seats and slowly drank the beer. The sea was calm. A very soft breeze was blowing from the north, and it brought with it the smell of the desert.

If nothing else, my apartment break-in had been cleared up. I had been so busy trying to find out what was missing that it never occurred to me that the intruder hadn't come to *take* anything at all. My apartment had been broken into so that something could be *added*. Like a phone tap. If Suzie had tapped my phone, she would have heard my initial call to Jimmy in Cabo, as well as the three calls to the hotels in California. Then she could have called all four of them back with the phony answering service business, and from that point on any Phillip sightings would have been diverted to her number first.

I finished the beer, thought about having a second one, but suddenly the exhaustion I'd been ignoring for many, many hours overwhelmed me. I went below and fell into the bunk and slept a deep, dreamless sleep.

=32=

spent the next morning vigorously checking out leads I knew were hopeless. Car rental agencies, major hotels, the airport and the ferry and the bus station. I found out which grocery stores in town made home deliveries and asked the owners if an Asian woman or a young redheaded gringo had been stocking provisions. I snooped around the boat charter people and even went so far as to check the Chrysler dealership in town. Suzie had a history of slapping down large chunks of money at once. Maybe she'd done it again.

But it was all a washout. Except for the blank-faced clerk at Ventana del Sol, nobody in Cabo San Lucas had seen an Asian woman with long hair driving a red anything. It was suddenly one in the afternoon, and I was running out of places to exercise my futility. I was also running out of gas, so I pulled into the crowded Pemex gas station on the outskirts of town and got in line.

I sat and wiped the sweat from my brow and thought about

what I was going to do next. Get gas. Swing by Jimmy's restaurant to see if any taxi drivers had left a message for me. Have lunch. After that I wasn't sure. Maybe just plod it out. Start at one end of Cabo San Lucas and cruise up the first street and down the second street and up the third street and down the fourth street and keep on doing that till I'd cruised *every* street, hoping to miraculously see a red Chrysler parked alongside one of the curbs. Not a thrilling prospect, but I didn't know what else to do.

If things get bad enough you'll draw inspiration from any source, and mine was currently coming from the strangest source of all. Leslie McCall's bathwater. I couldn't get it out of my head how cold it was. Painfully cold. Hypothermia cold. The kind of cold only a great quantity of ice would bring.

I waited in the Pemex line and thought about it. Suppose it went like this. Leslie'd been killed and packed up to his bluish earlobes in convenience store ice and put on slow, slow thaw. Why? What motive could there possibly have been to put Leslie in a temporary deep-freeze but to confuse the authorities when they tried to determine time of death? The killer could then have the chance to fly far away and establish a solid alibi in another place. A place like Mexico. Following that train of logic, Suzie's ability to lay low would then be compromised by her equally critical need to leave verifiable evidence that she was elsewhere at the time of Leslie's "suicide." She would have to be visible to save her own skin, and that's what I was counting on.

It was finally my turn at the pumps and I told the kid to fill it up. While he leaned to the task I asked him if he had seen an Asian woman driving a red Chrysler. Cabo San Lucas, like most smallish towns in Mexico, only had one gas station, and this was it. If Suzie needed fuel, she would have had to have come here.

The kid shook his head. He hadn't seen anybody like that. He topped off the tank and I gave him some money and he wandered off to get change. There were a dozen or so other men working the station, and when the kid came back I handed him a twenty-dollar bill and asked him if he could ask his coworkers if *they'd* seen an Asian woman in a red Chrysler. The money heightened his interest in locating Suzie Wong, and he hurried off to huddle with the other workers.

They talked for a while, then one of the men separated himself from the group and came up to me. He was about fifty. Skid-row beard, bloodshot eyes, and a little trickle of fresh blood behind his right ear. He had a nice smile. The smile of a man who'd spend his last dollar on earth to buy something nice for his grandkids.

He nodded at me and said yes, that he'd seen just such a woman. Oriental. In a red Chrysler. He looked down at the pocket where I would most likely be carrying cash, but so far he hadn't told me a thing the other kid hadn't told him.

"What did she look like?" I said.

He shrugged helplessly. She looked Oriental.

"How old?"

Forty, he said. But *guapa*. Pretty.

"Short hair, yes?" I said, chopping off a spot at the base of my neck.

The man pondered for a second. Twenty dollars hinged on his answer, and he was trying to decide whether to tell me what he'd really seen, or what I wanted him to have seen.

"*No, señor,*" he said at last. His voice was laden with sorrow. Honesty was always an expensive proposition. "*Ella tenia una montaña de pelo,*" he said. She had a mountain of hair.

I gave him the twenty dollars, and his eyes lit up. I pressed for details. She was in yesterday, he said, talking quickly. Twice. Once with a young gringo, the other time alone. One time she had the backseat filled with groceries, but he couldn't remember if that was the first or second time. I thanked the man and asked that he not say anything to the woman should she come in again. He smiled a mostly toothless smile and said he wouldn't. The man assumed I was trying to track down a wayward wife, and men understood men. I told him I appreciated his discretion and pulled away.

There were no taxi messages waiting for me at Jimmy's

restaurant. Jimmy was in the kitchen, chopping whitefish into small chunks.

"Hey!" he said as I came in. "How did you sleep?"

"Can't remember."

Jimmy smiled. He scooped up the handful of fish and dumped it into a large, cast-iron kettle.

"What's that?" I said.

"Ceviche Acapulco. Any luck with Phillip?"

I told him how my day had gone. My futile traipsing about town until the connection with the Pemex man.

"Think he was telling the truth?" Jimmy said.

"He described her hair pretty well."

Jimmy shrugged. "Well, that's the only gas station in town. Be logical he might remember."

"The guy said she'd been in twice the same day."

"Sounds like she's putting some miles on the Chrysler," Jimmy said.

"My thoughts exactly. Any ideas?"

Jimmy didn't answer for a while. He finished with the fish he'd been chopping and removed his rubber gloves and looked off at a corner of the kitchen. "Think I know where you should check first. Just clicked."

"Where?"

"Gringo Hill."

"What's that?"

"Just what the name implies," Jimmy said. "A hill full of gringos. Off the beaten path between here and San Jose del Cabo. Ten, twelve miles. It's mostly surfer shacks and funky beach huts. Phillip and Suzie wouldn't stand out much if they went there, and Phillip knows about the place."

"How?"

"First night he was in for dinner a bunch of us were talking about Gringo Hill. That's what just clicked a minute ago. Phillip perked up. Said he was looking for a place to spend his honeymoon and we laughed. Told him he'd probably want to upgrade accommodations for his honeymoon. He laughed along with us, but you could see it in his eyes. He was curious. He wanted to check it out."

Jimmy's map was drawn with extreme care because the dirt road leading off the main highway to Gringo Hill was unmarked and eminently missable. He said I'd know I'd taken the correct road if I ran into a strange, Swiss-like, A-frame chalet about a half-mile in.

I chose the likeliest dirt road and started up. It veered left, away from the pounding Pacific, and meandered to the base of a sizable hill. I passed the A-frame and knew I was on the right track.

Except for a couple of decent homes right at the top where the view was maximized, Gringo Hill was not so different from Route C in Napa. It had the same shantytown feel. Kitchen appliances in the yard. Old cars up on blocks or down on flattened tires.

I went up the south face of the hill. Several vehicles passed me going the opposite way. Baja buggies, filled with shirtless young people. They didn't pay any attention to me at all.

The dirt road was the *only* road on Gringo Hill, and it dipped and curved, angled and switchbacked up and down the slope of the hill, touching the various houses along the way like a connect-the-dots drawing. I crested the summit and was on my way down the north face when I saw it. A red Chrysler parked in the driveway of a ramshackle house. I kept my speed and waited till I'd gone down the road another fifty yards before pulling off to the side and cutting the engine.

I sat for a moment and thought in terms of a weapon. I rummaged through the Land Rover, and the best I could do was a tire iron that was lodged next to the spare tire in back. It wouldn't help me much if Suzie had a gun, but it was better than nothing. I gripped the heavy metal rod firmly in my right hand and then headed back up toward the house on foot.

If the car *did* belong to Suzie, she had chosen the hideaway well. The house was in the least populated section of Gringo Hill, and there were no other structures in sight. The place looked abandoned. Three twisted strands of barbed wire formed the boundaries of what must have once been a yard, but now the grounds were tangled and overgrown. A television antenna attached to the roof had toppled over long ago and now lay crumpled and useless on its side. The house itself was a dull, yellowish-white. It was made of adobe, but the earthen walls had started to come apart in chunks. Two windows faced the street. Empty black holes, glassless, screenless, like eye sockets in a vacant skull.

I approached the house from the east, sliding around the edge of the wall and keeping myself low. At the first window I stopped and listened. Somebody was whistling inside, light-hearted and casual. I chanced a quick look and brought my head down quick. There was no mistaking the silhouette of the woman sitting in the chair at the far end of the room. The small features, the billowing black hair. I'd found Suzie Wong.

I didn't see Phillip, but the whistling was coming from another section of the house, so I guessed he was there. I flexed the fingers of my right hand, regripped the tire iron. There was nothing to do but confront the situation head on. Suzie wasn't going to blow me away with Phillip right there in the next room. I told myself that twice, then I moved silently through the doorway and into the house.

Suzie sat in her chair, in semi-darkness, looking straight at me. It was impossible to take this woman by surprise. A lamp table was to her right, and a gun was sitting on it, within easy reach. She was prepared, and she was waiting.

"I'm unarmed, Suzie."

She didn't answer. Phillip continued to whistle somewhere off to the right. A tune by Gershwin. Suzie just sat in the dark and watched me. Her hands were in her lap, and I wondered what they concealed. I moved closer, and as my eyes adjusted to the darkness, I could see she was smiling.

"Suzie?"

I moved closer still. There were two smiles on Suzie's face. One on her lips, the other a crimson, coagulated grin that had been sliced into her neck from one earlobe to the other.

My field of vision narrowed. A great, roaring stillness in the room, the sensation of sliding backward, of telescoping back away from the bloodied chair.

The whistling in the next room grew louder, footsteps, the sharp rustle of gathered sheets of plastic, and then Holt Riolo stepped into the room.

33

Holt was closer to the gun than I was. For a second neither of us moved, then Holt dropped the plastic sheet and lunged for the weapon. I let loose with the tire iron, throwing it sidearm like you'd skip a stone across water. It caught Holt squarely in the neck and he stumbled, smashing headfirst into the table and scattering the gun along the stone floor.

I went for the pistol, but Holt shook off the blow with astonishing speed and tackled me at the ankles when I tried to hurdle over him. I went down hard, and he threw a wild punch in the direction of my face. I moved to shield myself, expecting a barrage of lefts and rights, but Holt wasn't interested in a fistfight. He was clamoring over me, scrambling across my chest on all fours, going for the gun.

Holt reached the weapon the same moment I grabbed the tire iron, and I was able to pull the trigger first. I threw from a sitting position, and the tire iron bounced right in front of him and came up in his face, clipping him across the forehead. Holt fell backward, but didn't let go of the gun. He pulled himself up to a sitting position and blinked away the cobwebs. He had the gun, and his head was clearing. And I was all out of tire irons.

I got to my feet and ran. At the door there was a loud explosion, and a piece of the adobe wall blew out above me, stinging my face with a spray of hardened earth. Then I was in bright sunshine and running faster. Through the yard, over the barbed-wire fence, down the hill toward the Land Rover.

I looked back and saw Holt racing out into the yard after me. He stopped, crouched, leveled the gun, but didn't take the shot. I was too far away and moving too fast. Instead he pulled the gun down and took off in the opposite direction, up the hill. I stopped and watched Holt thrash and claw his way into thick underbrush till he disappeared. For a moment I stood there in the hot sun, out of breath, wondering why an armed man runs away from an unarmed man. I didn't have long to wonder about it. The underbrush suddenly came alive with sound and movement, and a second later a brown Volkswagen Rabbit plowed out from behind the tree cover and rocketed down the hill toward me.

I dived into the Land Rover, threw it into gear, and made a swerving, gravel-spewing descent down Gringo Hill. The Volkswagen was maybe ten seconds behind me and closing fast.

I reached the base of the hill going a good fifty miles per hour, the Land Rover bucking violently on the rutted dirt road. I didn't have a plan except to drive as hard as I could. The road flattened out and began a long, slow circumnavigation of the hill, winding back toward the sea. The Volkswagen did not have the suspension to take the road at a high speed, so I had a temporary advantage. But I knew as soon as we got back out onto the paved road, the advantage would shift. A strategy was forming instinctively. Stay in rough terrain. The roughest terrain possible. I had to use the four-wheel drive to my advantage and not get trapped.

I was up to sixty-five miles per hour and fighting to keep control of the Land Rover when I saw the distant figure strolling alongside the road, coming up from the direction of the beach. A young man. He wore a bathing suit and had a towel slung over his shoulder, and as I bore down on him he looked up at the sudden commotion and stepped aside to let the maniac in the speeding vehicle go by. The man in the bathing suit was Phillip Chesterton.

I slammed on the brakes and went into a controlled skid and came to a stop pointed sideways in the road. Phillip slowly recognized me, and his mouth fell open.

"Quinn?"

"Get in!" I shouted.

Phillip stood there, trying to assimilate. "What ...?"

I jumped out and grabbed him by the arm and all but tossed him into the Land Rover. Holt was making up lost ground in a hurry. I jammed on the accelerator, almost lost the rear end of the vehicle, then straightened it out and roared off.

I drove fast and kept my eyes on the rearview mirror. Holt was right up on my bumper. Phillip wrenched around in his seat and stared back wildly in the direction of the Volkswagen. Then he turned to me. His eyes were everywhere, trying to find something somewhere that made sense.

"What are you doing here, Quinn?" he said. "Where's Suzie?"

I shook my head. "Suzie's gone, Phillip."

"What are you talking about, gone?"

"I'm sorry. There's nothing we can do now."

Phillip's eyes lost their wildness. He grew very still and gently repositioned himself in the seat and faced out the front.

"Are you with me?" I said.

He didn't react.

"Phillip, goddamn it! Are you with me?"

He vaguely nodded.

"We've got to concentrate on *this*, now. Do you understand me? *This!*"

The paved highway was just ahead, and I thought of something that might work. If I could hold Holt off for a handful of miles I'd take the rugged desert road that led up into the desolate mountains beyond San Jose del Cabo. There was a ghost town up there called Los Pozos—The Wells—an abandoned mining town that I'd explored a couple years ago on a trip with Hank and Carol. I remembered little of it now except that it was a tortuous road up and we had to leave the kids with a babysitter at the hotel because of the many open mine shafts still up there. The road was brutal, all but impassable at places, but Jimmy's Land Rover could handle it, and I had a full tank of gas. The Volkswagen Rabbit was going to have a lot tougher time. It might not even be able to make it at all. It was my only chance.

Out on the smooth highway Holt's Volkswagen reeled me in, as I was afraid it would. Twice he swerved out as if to pass, and twice I leaned the Land Rover into him so he'd back off. Then he tucked up right behind me and his hand came out the window, and in the next instant the back window of the Land Rover shattered in an iced spiderweb of fractured glass. Phillip cringed and clamped his eyes shut.

"Get your head down!" I yelled.

Phillip didn't react.

"I said *down!*"

I reached over and pushed Phillip's head down, and he let himself sink into the seat. The Land Rover swerved wildly from one lane to the next. Cars wailed by, horns shrieking and tires squealing. Immediately up ahead was the exit to Los Pozos. I waited till the last possible second, then braked hard and wrenched the steering wheel, and Holt was taken completely by surprise. He skidded along the highway and overshot the dirt road, and I was able to open up my advantage again while he recovered.

The road was as bad as I remembered it. Maybe worse. Phillip held on to the door for support as the vehicle bounced and jolted. He looked sick. Physically sick.

"Suzie told me to go to the beach," he said.

"What?"

"I shouldn't have left her." Phillip shook his head. His eyes were red. "I should have known she was trying to protect me.

She knew he was coming. She knew he was coming to kill her."

I reached over and put my hand on his shoulder. "You've got to pull yourself together now, Phillip."

"I shouldn't have gone," Phillip repeated. "She was protecting me. I should have seen that. She wanted me away from the danger."

My desert strategy was working. The road was littered with boulders and cactus, and the Volkswagen slipped farther and farther back until all I could see was its distant trail of kicked-up dust. But Holt wasn't quitting. I thought he might pull up, head back, and lay in wait for us when we returned, but no. He kept after us. Even slipping farther and farther back, he kept after us. The dogged pursuit bothered me. Perseverance like that stems from either utter desperation or supreme confidence. Holt was coming on like a man who had no backup plans, or a man who knew exactly what he was doing.

My forearms were aching by the time Los Pozos came into view. Holt was at least five minutes behind me now, his dust trail a faint white haze in the distance.

I'd made it but so had Holt, and now I had to think what to do next. Los Pozos was a desolate landscape of broken-down buildings, long-rusted machinery, and abandoned mine shafts that filled the bottom of a bowllike valley out in the middle of the starkest desert imaginable. It was mentioned in most of the tour guides, but I had never seen another living thing within twenty miles of the place. Not with Hank and Carol two years ago. Not now.

I drove down the slope of the bowl and motored slowly along the perimeter of the ghost town, scanning the horizon north, east, and west for another way out. I was sure there had to be one. Place always leads to place in Mexico, no matter how remote or unlikely it would seem. But from Los Pozos there wasn't another road. There wasn't another path. As far as I could see there wasn't even a goddamn animal trail. Nothing. I could feel the panic crawling up my spine. I was up against a solid wall of chalk-white mountains. There was only one way out of Los Pozos. The way we'd come in.

"He's going to kill us, too," Phillip said. Except for his mantra of regret at having left Suzie alone in the house on Gringo Hill, it was the first time he'd spoken in twenty minutes.

"He's not killing anybody," I said.

"How can we stop him?" Phillip's voice was high-pitched. The fear was surging back. "He's got a gun! He's got a gun and there's nowhere else to go! He killed Suzie and now he's going to kill us!"

"We'll lead him down here and then go back the way we came."

"Then what?"

"We have plenty of gas. A five-minute head start back in town and we can lose him easily."

Phillip pointed to the southern rim of the bowl. "There he is!"

Holt had crested the hill and come to a stop. He was waiting, idling, the Volkswagen Rabbit pointed in our direction.

"Put your seat belt on," I said.

I slipped the Land Rover into gear and drifted eastward at about ten miles per hour. I watched the Volkswagen on the rim of the hill, half-expecting it to turn its nose slowly to follow our progress. Like something alive. Like a patient, predatory animal.

Holt was still a half-mile to a mile away. If he knew he had sealed off the only escape from Pozos he'd camp there forever. I had to make him think that I'd found another way out. I coasted for about a hundred yards, then slammed on the accelerator and roared off in my dead-end direction as though the jaws of freedom had just unexpectedly opened before me.

Holt went for it. The Volkswagen spun its wheels and sped down the rim of the hill at an angle that would cut me off from my imaginary escape route. Our dust trails converged.

I watched where Holt would have to go if he were to intercept me. It was clear and smooth terrain, but there was a spot where his descent would steepen momentarily. When he committed to it he would be in a severe downslope for thirty or forty yards till the land leveled out again. That was where I was going to have to make my move.

We angled closer to each other, close enough that I could see the driver's window, and Holt's head turned sideways, watching me. He was closing in on the steep hill. Thirty yards. Twenty. Ten. I made myself wait until I saw the nose of his Volkswagen make the plunge and then I braked hard, fought my way out of a skid, and made a violent right and sped back toward the Cabo road, full throttle.

I took one quick look back and my stomach rolled over. I'd miscalculated. I'd made my move too early, and Holt had adjusted. He'd read my fake and somehow pulled the Volkswagen back from the steep incline and was now slanting back straight at us.

There was no point racing for the Cabo road. He had the angle on us and would cut us off easily. Instead I braked again, turned in a choking cloud of dust and sand, and headed back toward Los Pozos. Except this time Holt didn't continue on to resume his waiting position at the narrow exit point. This time he veered to the right, following my lead, and was right on top of me like a heat-seeking missile. This was it. He was going to finish things here. Now.

A shot rang out, and I heard a small metallic thunk somewhere on the Land Rover. Then another. I shoved Phillip down and sped between two dilapidated structures, across a mound of sand that almost launched me airborne, then narrowly missed driving over the boarded-up edge of a room-size mine shaft.

Holt stayed with me. I saw him lean out his window and point the gun, and I tried to weave. He fired three times in rapid succession, and my outside mirror exploded and for a moment I lost control of the steering wheel. When I got it back I was going too fast for the terrain, and immediately in front of me was the yawning black hole of an exposed mine shaft.

This one I wasn't going to miss. I could turn neither left nor right without rolling the Land Rover. If I hit the brakes I'd skid directly over the edge. There was nothing to do but tromp down on the accelerator, hang onto the wheel, and pray.

I heard Phillip yell, and then there was a hard jolt of the front wheels hitting the ridged edge of the mine shaft, and then we were up in the air. Time seemed to slow. I remember silence, looking once out the window at the bottomless pit beneath me, then realizing with sickening finality that the Land Rover wasn't going to make it.

But there was no time for me to formulate the thought that I was about to die. I closed my eyes and felt the shoulder harness of my seat belt yank painfully against my chest. The left front tire slammed hard into the far wall of the pit, and I felt the Land Rover go straight up in the air, nose to the ground, and roll once, twice, and again, seat belts cutting sharply into my chest and shoulders. The engine screamed at a terrific r.p.m. and then died. When the vehicle came to a stop we were sitting upright, facing straight back at the shaft we'd barely cleared.

Holt had been following us tire track for tire track, and now he saw the mine shaft, too. He slammed on the brakes and went into a dead skid, wheels locked, the Volkswagen fishtailing wildly, straight at the mine shaft.

He didn't make it. The Volkswagen Rabbit soared over the mine shaft, dead center, and slammed into the far end very hard. The car did a three-quarter handstand, then the bottom came back down, scraping the inner wall of the mine shaft, and wedged there. Steam poured from the hood. Part of the front fender gave way and the Volkswagen lurched six inches deeper into the thousand-foot hole. It was holding on by a thread.

I could see Holt's head slumped forward on the steering wheel. Then he lifted himself up, looked out the cracked windshield, and saw us watching him. In the next instant he realized where he was, and his eyes went wide. The simple movement of his body made the car lose another six inches. I saw the driver's door slowly open, and Holt shifted carefully in his seat. The car gave some more, slipped a few more inches deeper into the mine shaft. Holt was looking at the edge of the pit. It would be a three-foot leap.

Holt didn't hesitate. In a single movement he kicked the car door all the way open and launched himself at the edge of the mine shaft. The force of his push-away rocked the car loose. A groan of metal, a fender snapping loose, then the automobile slowly pitched over sideways, like the collapse of an immense dying animal, and fell from sight in a turbulence of dust and smoke and screaming metal.

But Holt hadn't gone down with it. He clung to the edge of the mine shaft, fingers clawing, trying to pull himself out. He had a grip on the piece of wood that rimmed the pit, but the rotted timber wasn't strong enough for him to use as leverage. He grasped desperately at the loose sand beyond, hands blindly searching the ground for something, anything.

I jumped out of the Land Rover and ran toward the edge of the mine shaft. I didn't know why I was running. What was I going to do when I got there? Save him? Grab one of Holt's arms and haul him back up onto solid ground and watch him breathe a sigh of relief? Or would I pull up short, look down into the eyes of the man who had done so much damage, and cold-bloodedly wait for him to drop?

It was a question that would remain unanswered. When I was halfway to the mine shaft, the wood Holt was clinging to gave way. It peeled out from the earth like a narrow strip of solidified adhesive tape and swung back out over the center of the gaping hole, taking Holt Riolo with it. He let go, bicycled both arms as if trying to regain his balance, then fell backward into the deep black.

Holt Riolo did not go gently into the good night. He screamed at the top of his lungs all the way down. A thousand feet is as deep as the Sears Tower is high, and the screaming lasted for a very, very long time. Then it abruptly stopped. A needle snatched from the grooves of a record, and the world was silent again.

I walked to the edge of the mine shaft, stood there for a moment, and looked down into the final resting place of Holt Riolo. Or, rather, of Paul Wilson. I'd known from the instant Holt had come out of the side room, whistling his Gershwin ditty, that he was the third member of the unholy trio who'd made their illicit fortune in the jungles of Southeast Asia. Frank, Suzie, and

Holt. Now dead. All of them. I turned from the yawning shaft and headed back to the Land Rover.

Phillip had his face cradled in his hands. The right front wheel was shredded, so I slowly and methodically changed the tire without the benefit of a tire iron, prying at it with a large flat rock. It took me twenty minutes, scraping my knuckles and sweating in the harsh desert sun. Then I climbed in and limped the Land Rover slowly back in the direction of Cabo San Lucas.

34

I t is a sad but basic truth that if you have the resources to spend twice what something's worth, you are not going to be inconvenienced much in this life. So when I was told at the Cabo San Lucas airport that all flights to San Francisco were full, with absolutely no possibility of getting on standby, I decided to stroll the waiting area until I found a passenger who was willing to sell me his ticket for double the money. It was a short stroll.

Transaction completed, I gave Phillip his newfound ticket and sat with him on the hard plastic bench till it was time to board. He was out of his bathing suit and wearing the clothes I'd hastily bought for him an hour earlier in Cabo San Lucas. It was risky but necessary, and I kept the Land Rover parked under the deep shade of a palm tree at the end of a scrubby side road. No sense giving the local constables a bullet-riddled vehicle to contemplate.

Phillip pulled on his shirt, pants, and socks with a blank-faced, catatonic obedience. He'd been utterly silent on the way down from Los Pozos, and utterly silent while I bought his clothes. It wasn't until we passed the dirt road leading up to Gringo Hill that he began to talk. He talked the rest of the way to the airport, he talked while we sat waiting in the lobby, and when it was all talked out he lapsed back into his automaton silence.

Technical problems delayed the flight to San Francisco for half an hour and I began to get nervous, listening for the police siren's inevitable wail, scanning the area for the commotion of onrushing authorities, badges displayed high above their heads, yelling for the pilot to stop the plane. But nothing happened. The ticket agent at last got on the microphone and apologized for the delay, and I gave Phillip a hug and watched him walk down the boarding ramp. I'd already called and arranged for Molly to meet him at the other end, and all I hoped now was that Phillip could hold it together for just a few more hours. Just three or four hours.

But there was no point dwelling on the things that can go wrong at thirty thousand feet. Instead I stood at the lobby window until the plane taxied to the end of the runway, picked up speed, and banked north with a great roar of the engines. Then I turned and headed back into the airport parking lot. There was unfinished business awaiting me back on Gringo Hill.

I stepped through the doorway and paused a moment to let my eyes adjust to the dark. The flies had gotten very bad. Suzie sat in the chair, and she watched through glassy eyes as I methodically removed everything from the house that would indicate anybody had been there recently. I put the tire iron and two large suitcases into the Land Rover, then wrapped Suzie in the plastic sheet Holt had prepared and put her in next to the suitcases. I went back into the house and surveyed all three rooms again, forcing myself to take my time about it. Nothing could be overlooked. There was blood on the floor near the chair, but nothing could be done about that. I scuffed some sand and dirt on it, then left it alone.

The red Chrysler in the driveway was unlocked, no keys in the ignition, glove compartment empty. I pried open the trunk with the tire iron from the Land Rover, but it was empty, too. There were no stickers to indicate a rental car. Suzie'd either stolen it or bought the automobile outright. Not important, and there was no sense trying to be fancy about getting rid of it. I put the car in neutral and pushed it forward, steering the vehicle toward a twenty-foot-deep barranca that sloped away from the driveway on the right. The car crested the edge and rolled at an angle down the side of the ravine, tipping over halfway and rolling to a window-breaking stop, upside-down, in a tangle of brambles and overgrown weeds. I waited for the dust to settle and peered over the edge. The car was camouflaged beautifully. From above it looked like nothing more than usual Gringo Hill discard. Someone would stumble on it eventually, of course, but that could be weeks. Months. Even years.

I went back to the Land Rover, climbed behind the wheel, and started up the engine, glancing at the lump of plastic in my rearview mirror. Suzie Wong had one more trip to make in her much-traveled life. Not hauled out to sea, because corpses wash back. Not buried in the hills, because animals dig up bodies. On this trip Suzie needed to disappear. Removed from the face of the earth. I needed to make one last trip up the lonely desert road to Los Pozos.

My initial fear of passing another car along the way was a foolish one. The Los Pozos road was empty and desolate. The solitary miles slipped by, and I thought about what Phillip had told me on the way to the airport. Tried to untangle the lies from the truth the way I tried to untangle the lines of the plastic parachute man back in the Wilkie house.

Suzie had been surprisingly candid with him. Maybe she figured she had no choice. With all hell breaking loose back in Napa, the unpleasant details were bound to come out sooner or later, and she might have thought it would go better for her if she gave Phillip her version first, with the hard spots softened, the soft spots exaggerated.

The Southeast Asia part of the story was very much as Wade Davenport had described it. The weapons, the danger, the eventual betrayal at the hands of Frank Matson. Suzie and Paul Wilson languished in a Cambodian prison for three years, then escaped. Details of the breakout weren't gone into, but the mechanics didn't matter—money exchanged, a deal cut. What *did* matter was that Nguyen Nyu had dodged disaster the way she'd dodged it her entire life, reinvented herself as Suzie Wong, and then came back to the United States with Paul Wilson to find the man who'd sold them out.

According to Suzie, she only wanted her share of the fortune, nothing more. But Paul Wilson's thirst for vengeance went deeper. Three years of solitude and beatings and fighting off rats in a sweatbox prison cell had, in his case, given birth to a more urgent need: the need to make Frank Matson suffer as he had. From what Paul Wilson could see, only two things ever really mattered to Frank Matson. Money, and the unmet son he'd fathered many years ago in Boston.

So when Paul Wilson finally tracked Frank down, living the good life in the Napa wine country, it could not be a simple case of strolling up to the R. K. Chesterton door to settle accounts. Howdy Frank, no hard feelings, but you owe us some money. Unh-uuh. The money would be forthcoming, but in the meantime fragile, gentle Phillip Chesterton was going to be messed with a little. Tainted. Defiled. He was going to be lured between the legs of his father's ex-lover, the former Saigon bar-whore Nguyen Nyu. And before the final curtain fell Frank Matson was going to learn all about it, in glorious, vivid detail.

So Suzie took an apartment in San Francisco, near Phillip, and Paul Wilson rented a home in Willits, near Matson. Close enough to monitor comings and goings, yet far enough away to make an accidental face-to-face meeting very unlikely.

It was not a difficult task for the provocative and well-armed Suzie Wong to swoop down and snare Phillip Chesterton. He was starving to love, starving to be loved, and Suzie reeled him in with a minimum of effort. Paul Wilson, in the meantime, had changed his name to Holt Riolo and had taken a gay lover in Napa. It was perfect. Leslie McCall was a Chesterton insider who had his own personal ax to grind with Matson. Leslie was also in dire financial straits and ripe to align himself with a lucrative blackmail scheme. Holt innocuously fed Leslie the documentation necessary to begin blackmailing Matson, all the while making it seem the result of Leslie's journalistic muckraking know-how. Holt wasn't homosexual or bisexual or heterosexual. After Cambodia he was an engine of revenge, nothing more, and he would do whatever it took to extract that revenge.

Suzie didn't like it at all. She didn't like what she was being asked to do with Phillip, and she didn't like the risks Holt was taking with his new proximity to Frank Matson and the added blackmail wrinkle. Frank Matson was sharp, and Suzie was afraid he would figure things out and come looking for them. Besides, something else was taking place that Suzie could never have anticipated. She was falling in love with Phillip—truly, genuinely, deeply in love.

When Phillip spontaneously decided to tell his mother and stepfather about this new woman in his life, the game was over. Combined with the Southeast Asia blackmail he'd been silently going through, Frank knew immediately who this mysterious older Asian woman with the obviously phony name had to be. Matson went berserk, and Phillip rushed off to Suzie's apartment in San Francisco. When Suzie heard what had happened, she immediately called Holt to warn him and tell him that she wanted out. Frank Matson had suffered enough. Now was the time for them to take the money owed and leave the thing alone.

Holt called Frank Matson late that same night, mentioning Pilkow Street, and revealed himself. The midnight meeting was arranged at the mobile home on Route C, but Frank Matson had gone storming in, drunk and desperate, ready to shoot it out rather than negotiate. Holt shot first, then drove the body to the Chesterton winery and, using Leslie's code key, let himself in and disposed of the body in the wine vat. Early the next morning Holt called Suzie, told her what he'd done, and outlined what would happen next. Holt was going to frame Leslie for the murder, and see to it that Leslie committed safe, certifiable, no-doubt-about-it suicide from grief at what he'd done. Once the mourning period was over Suzie could marry Phillip. Presto. The two Cambodian cellmates were going to end up sharing much, much more than the piddling million or so Frank had absconded with. They were going to divvy up the entire Chesterton fortune.

Suzie'd hung up the phone in her Hill Street apartment and sat there a minute. She knew then that Holt had gone off the deep end. Blackmail, murder, sexual tainting, and then murder again, dressed up like suicide. The grisly stuffing of Matson's corpse into the wine vat. No. Suzie suddenly knew with a lethal clarity that she was now the only person who stood between Holt Riolo and freedom from his past. She and Phillip had to run. Hide. Get away until they could think of what to do next.

Suzie sat down on the couch and carefully told Phillip everything that had happened. Cambodia, the revenge, her own complicity in bedding him as an act of vengeance. She told him of her unexpected love for him. Phillip listened, half in shock, and Suzie asked him if there was a place he could run to. Someplace far away, where she could join him in a day or two. Phillip had nodded. Yes, he knew a place. Cabo San Lucas, at the very tip of the Baja Peninsula.

Suzie then parked his car in the Fuentes's garage and drove him to the airport in hers. She wrapped up her own affairs the same day in San Francisco and drove her car all night to Tijuana, taking the morning flight to join Phillip in Cabo. And there they sat to await the inevitable.

Holt was then left up in Napa with nothing but the wine-soaked corpse of Frank Matson to console himself with. No money, no wine cellar, no permanent visitor's pass to the Chesterton estate. He'd been betrayed once by Frank Matson, and now he'd been double-crossed by Suzie. When he found out via the phone tap where Phillip had gone, he killed Leslie and put

him on ice to make the time of death coincide with Holt's con-
spicuous and well-documented presence thousands of miles
away.

Suzie had a premonition she was about to die, Phillip had
told me. When she found out Phillip had called me in San Francisco, they quickly moved out of Ventana del Sol and over to
Gringo Hill, but she knew Holt was close. The circle was tighten-
ing. A taxi had followed them out earlier in the day, the driver
going slow and looking closely. That was why she had sent
Phillip to the beach, to keep him out of danger. That was the
kind of woman Suzie was, Phillip said. She loved him.

It was almost sunset when I reached Los Pozos. My eyes
burned and my body ached. I drove to the mine shaft Holt had
gone down, parked, and took the suitcases from the Land Rover
and tossed them down the pit. Then I took the plastic-wrapped
inert lump of tissue and hair and bone that used to be Suzie
Wong and dumped it over the side. I did it quickly, automatically,
so I wouldn't have a chance to think about it and lose my nerve.

The body fell for a very long time, hitting the sides of the
mine shaft several times before the distant, final thud reverber-
ated back up to me.

There was a crumbling adobe building a few feet away from
the open shaft, so I went there and sat on the steps for a minute
and squinted at the setting sun.

There were blanks in Suzie's version of events that I refrained
from mentioning to Phillip. I suspected the bulk of her love still
had more to do with the Chesterton fortune than Phillip's soul.
You could hold a mirror up to her suspicions of Holt and, with
only an amendment here and an amendment there, apply them
to Suzie. With Holt out of the way there was no living link to *her*
illicit past, and I hadn't forgotten the weapon tucked away in
Phillip's glove compartment or the busted-out window of Holt's
car that he'd tried to pass off as the work of queer-haters back
home in Willits. Speculation, but speculation was all I had. The
only two people who knew for sure were stretched out next to
each other a thousand feet below the hot desert surface.

The bottom of the sun touched the white mountains in the distance and turned them purple. I thought of Leslie. Poor Leslie. The little man with his toupee and wine bricks and framed airline ticket hung on the wall. Except for trying to skim some money from Frank Matson in the blackmail scheme, he was completely unaware of his role in the larger revenge setup. Leslie knew nothing of the Suzie-Frank-Holt connection. Perhaps that was why, after the funeral, he'd looked at me so strangely when I told him that Frank Matson's midnight caller had mentioned Pilkow Street. Maybe the gears began to turn, and Holt had to kill Leslie quickly.

The sun was down. The desert was lined with shadows and growing cold already. I needed to nurse the Land Rover home one final time, so I stood, brushed the sand from my knees and hands, and wandered over to it. The silence of the desert was huge. A silence like this made you grateful for distraction. Blessed be the honking horns, the weekend power mowers, the blabbermouth ahead of you in the supermarket line. Without that, you had this. An emptiness so profound that one could not help but be painfully attentive to the fragile sounds of the body: the barely beating heart, the inhale and exhale, the soft, quiet engine that keeps everything running but carries no guarantee.

I drove back up the rim of the valley and paused at the top. I thought of Holt, and of *Moby-Dick*. How one man's crazed obsession finally killed all those around him. All except one, that is. One survived to tell the story.

I looked down at Pozos one last time, at the shadows deeper than the wells themselves, then drove off south against the rapid sweep of night.

35

On Christmas Eve I made myself drive over to Marin to buy a Christmas tree. I decided on the runt of an already pathetic litter, a scrawny little thing about five feet high with a definite sway to the left, but that was okay. There weren't many good trees left the day before Christmas, and living fifty-four steps up in the sky had given me an appreciation of purchases that lacked weight and bulk.

I cleared a spot next to the living-room fireplace and set the tree there. It looked pretty good, and assuming the branches didn't break under the strain of tinsel, I sensed it was going to be a winner. Hank was in his room, and when he heard me banging around he came out to investigate.

"What's that?" he said.

"Our Christmas tree."

He looked at the tree from top to bottom, letting his eyes trace the curve of the skeletal sway. "You went all the way to Chernobyl to buy a Christmas tree?"

"Very funny," I said. "Grab a box of tinsel and help me."

He did, grudgingly.

"What you do is start at the bottom," I said, "and work up."

"I had a mother once, too."

Hank took his box of tinsel and I took mine, and we fell into a comfortable, tree-decorating silence.

There had been a good amount of silence at 1464A Union Street in the past week. No more surprise pop-ins from Gunnhilde. Carol called once and we chatted for a minute, and I told her about Hank taking the wine in the face. But nobody came to visit. Maybe friends and family were seeing a pattern of what happened to the people Quinn Parker hung out with. They ended up shot or packed in ice or submerged in wine vats or lay broken and bleeding at the bottom of abandoned mine shafts. I didn't take the neglect personally. If I'd been someone other than me, I would have avoided me, too.

I did have one visitor. Molly. She'd come by the first evening I was back to tell me how the meeting with Phillip at the airport had gone, but things were awkward between us. I asked her if she wanted to stay over and she said no, she didn't think so. She swallowed, cleared her throat, and suggested instead that maybe we'd be wise to take a time-out and "reframe" our relationship and I nodded while she spoke as though I agreed with her, all the while feeling something die inside. Then she stood and gave me a kiss and went quickly down the stairs before I could see the pain in her eyes.

The Frank Matson murder got another shot in the arm in the wake of Leslie's death and Phillip's dramatic return. An anonymous caller had tipped the *Napa Observer* about some of the discrepancies surrounding Leslie's "suicide," and there was a minor hue and cry surrounding the slipshod manner of Leslie's autopsy. Closer inspection revealed that the water found in Leslie's lungs had not come out of the bathtub faucet. It was purified water. Like bottled drinking water. Or, I thought to myself, like melted ice water.

Detective Davis was back on the hot seat again, and there were clips on the Ten o'Clock News of him coming down the steps of various buildings, cameras jostling for position, microphones shoved in his face. Davis gravely intoned that Holt Riolo, Leslie's "mystery lover," was now the number one suspect. There was solid evidence that Mr. Riolo had flown to Cabo San Lucas, Mexico. Of course there was evidence, I thought. The paper trail to Mexico was to have been Holt Riolo's alibi for the Leslie McCall murder. Detective Davis puffed out his chest and expressed utmost confidence that the suspect would be apprehended. The Mexican authorities had pledged to cooperate, and Davis vowed not to rest until Mr. Riolo was apprehended and brought to justice.

I spent an anxious day or two myself when I first got back, waiting for the dreaded phone call, with hard official voices on the other end asking hard official questions about my own questionable activities. My first few nights were spent staring at the dark ceiling and rehearsing how I was going to explain my presence at Leslie McCall's bloody bathtub, or what I was doing bumping around Gringo Hill, or what exactly was the long-distance business that required my overnight attention on the Gulf Coast of Florida.

But the general silence of my apartment extended to the forces of law and order as well. I'd covered my tracks well, particularly where Leslie was concerned, and nobody seemed to be looking all that hard at me anyway. I was perceived as the schmuck phobia therapist who was protecting his client, and now Phillip was known to be innocent. The manhunt was focused on Holt Riolo, the enigmatic character with the false name who'd fled the scene for the safety of another country.

Jimmy Kamamoto chanced a call a few days after my return, just to get a feel on what was happening. Before flying out I'd returned the Land Rover to him, bullet holes, crumpled roof, bent axle, and all. I told Jimmy to get a damage estimate and I'd take care of the repairs, but he didn't seem terribly concerned. Jimmy understood. Hell, he was almost impressed. He stood back and surveyed the damage and nodded his head. It was the way he might have returned a car himself after a spin in the country.

The first morning back I called Abigail and asked if she could have a messenger send down an extra set of keys to Phillip's white Mazda and I'd drive the car up. She said I didn't need to bother, that she could send her own driver down, but I told her it would be better if I handled it personally. Abigail asked if I was sure, and I said I was sure. I was positive. Abigail didn't press the issue.

When the keys arrived I went out to Hill Street and sweet-talked my way one last time into Mr. and Mrs. Fuentes's garage. They were glad to see me and glad to be rid of the strange vehicle and didn't inquire at all about Suzie Wong.

I left my van across the street from Suzie's old apartment and drove the Mazda up to Napa, stopping along the way to thin out the glove compartment. There's a small bridge on Blackburn Point Road that crosses over one of the many northern fingers of San Francisco Bay, and I pulled off to the side there. I went to the guardrail and took a deep breath of air, admiring the view, and when no cars were coming in either direction I quietly dropped Suzie's pistol into the bay, thirty feet below. It splashed harmlessly and sank silently, and I continued on to Napa.

Phillip and Abigail asked me to stay for lunch, so the three of us sat out on the terrace and ate and talked. Nothing was said about Mexico or Suzie or recent events. The fact of Phillip's return had just been announced, and they were bracing for the inevitable media onslaught. From time to time, while Abigail was talking, Phillip's eyes would rise to meet mine. There was empti-ness and pain in his expression, but also a kind of strength. An emotional and spiritual resilience that made me think—in a small, greedy way—that all the time we'd spent together had made a difference.

At the end of lunch Phillip excused himself and went outside toward the pool, and Abigail gestured for me to come with her. She wanted to show me something. I followed as she went upstairs and down the hallway to Phillip's room. It looked the same as it had the day Hank and I had taken the tour, with one exception. A painting had been hung on one of the wide, empty walls. A small reproduction of a Vermeer, with mother and infant child bent over a smooth porcelain jug, the child lost in the mysteries of the jug, the mother lost in the mysteries of her child. The addition of the small painting on the flat expanse of empty wall only served to make the room look emptier, but that would change. This was a start. Abigail knew it, and I knew it. This was a start.

"Whoever thought up tinsel anyway?" Hank said.

I fought my way out of memory. "What?"

"Tinsel. I don't get it. Stringing popcorn makes a lot more sense. Smells good. You can eat it."

"Then make some popcorn."

The doorbell rang. Hank kept working while I went down the stairs. I opened the door and Carol was standing there.

"Merry Christmas Eve," she said. "And welcome home."

"It's good to see you."

"Is Hank here?"

"Up in the living room."

Carol glanced upwards. "Alone, this time?"

"Very."

She stepped in, kissed me on the cheek, and the two of us went up the stairs together. When Hank saw us he stood awkwardly, brushing stray tinsel from his pants. The tinsel wouldn't brush. It stuck there and he kept swatting at it.

"Carol," he said. "What are you doing here?"

Carol turned and looked at me. "Hank and I need to talk for a second, Quinn. Is that okay?"

"Sure thing."

I gave them their privacy and went back into my office and closed the door. The files were still a mess. Maybe tonight would be the night. I sat at my desk and looked at the photos on the wall. Hank and Carol and family at the zoo. Molly on Angel

Island. A gag photo of me in the ring at Newman's Gym, gloved hands held aloft over a sprawled and defeated Roscoe Laughinghouse. There was an eight-by-ten black-and-white of Phillip standing on the wharf in Cabo San Lucas next to the marlin he'd landed during our first trip there. He was beaming, and a lot of the Mexican fishermen in the area were crowding into the picture, too. I sat and stared at the photo, then there was a knock on my office door and Hank and Carol came in.

"Hank's coming home," Carol said.

I looked up at Hank. He was smiling the first genuine smile I'd seen on his face in months. "No kidding?"

"I'm going to pack a few things," he said, and headed in the direction of the guest bedroom.

"This is good, Carol," I said.

"I can't play it tough," she said, sitting on the edge of the desk. "Not anymore. I'm like the kid with her nose against the candy store window. I love him, Quinn. For every dozen reasons I come up with to keep him thrown out of the house, I'm still up against the fact that I love him. Besides that, the next woman he meets might throw something harder in his face than red wine, and the kids need their daddy."

Hank came around the corner clutching a small travel bag. "I'll get the rest of my stuff later."

Carol blew me a kiss. "Talk to you soon, Quinn." She turned and left, but Hank lingered. He watched her go, then turned to me. "Well," he said. "It's been interesting."

"That it has."

"Thanks for tolerating me."

"No problem."

"Seriously, Quinn," Hank said. "You're a hell of a friend. I mean that. And I don't intend to be sincere like this again with you for a while, so savor my words."

"Consider them savored."

Hank nodded, smiled, took a look at his ring. "Think I'm going to go ahead and take your advice."

"What advice was that?"

"To have some of that sand flown in from Hawaii and put it in the backyard."

"Expensive," I said.

"Damn the expense," Hank said.

And he went down the stairs, down to where Carol was waiting for him.

I spent Christmas morning with the Wilkies. Watched their boys fill the air with torn wrapping paper and then thunder off down the hallway to try out the new toys. It was nice, and I appreciated the invitation, but soon it became family time and I begged off, feeling oddly out of place.

I drove home through the empty streets. Everybody had gone to visit somebody else, and I had my choice of parking places. I cut the engine and sat there a minute, looking up at the third-floor windows of my apartment. Nobody had their noses pressed against the glass for me. I wondered if anybody ever would.

That evening I wandered over to the only open market on Polk Street and bought a rib-eye steak and one baked potato and one ear of corn and a bottle of red wine. A parody of a bachelor dinner, and the woman at the checkout counter joked with me about it.

Back at the apartment I popped the wine, dragged a chair up to the rooftop deck, and fired up the barbecue. The fog was rolling in and it was cold. I went below, pulled on a sweater, then went back to the roof and stretched out in the chair and watched the coals burn and turn gray.

I thought of Suzie. As the days had passed I'd grown more and more convinced she was the cold-blooded opportunist she'd always been. She didn't love Phillip. I doubted she'd ever loved anybody. After Frank Matson was dead, she and Holt were liabilities to each other. She probably took the first shot, missed, and then Holt eventually tracked her down and took care of business.

At least that's how I felt at the start of my bottle of wine. But I drank and watched the lights of the city and the fog rolling in, and toward the bottom of the bottle my attitude softened. I allowed myself to think that maybe some tenderness *had* crept into her cold and criminal heart. The one variable that Holt and Suzie couldn't have anticipated was that she might actually fall in love with Phillip. Perhaps up on Gringo Hill she *had* sent Phillip away from the danger when she sensed Holt closing in. Who knows? I finished the last of the wine, looked up at the remains of the stars, and thought of what Leslie had told me about the ancient Persian leaders. How they discussed all issues twice. Once sober and once while drinking. There was some wisdom in that.

I ate my dinner and then built a fire in the living-room fire-place and went back to my office wall safe to get the strongbox Abigail had given me. I sat cross-legged next to my Chernobyl Christmas tree, opened it up, and fed the incriminating papers to the flames, one by one. It was over. The blackmail and the weapons and the twisted revenge. Phillip and Abigail needed to get on with their lives, and I didn't want any loose paper floating around that might interfere with that.

I paused when I came to the Pilkow photo. Held it to the light of the fireplace and studied it. The youthful, exuberant Suzie on the lap of a laughing Frank Matson, Wade Davenport sitting to the side enjoying the moment. I wondered what had been said to have caused such laughter. Had Paul Wilson himself taken the picture, and were they reacting to him? I looked at the photo a final time, then put it in the fire and watched the images curl and blacken.

The only tidbit from the box I didn't destroy was the curious photo of Detective Davis and the unidentified stranger. I had no idea what it was about, but I was sure it was nothing good and that was reason enough to put it in an envelope and mail it anonymously to the *Napa Observer*. Davis was puffing his chest too much for the camera crews. He needed polishing off. I walked down to the streetcorner and smiled as I dropped the envelope in the slot. The good detective had given me an early birthday present once, and it was the least I could do to return the favor. Ah, the Christmas spirit!

I was giving thought to bed when the doorbell rang. I thought it might be a group of urban carolers, and I wasn't in the mood for "Rudolph the Red-Nosed Reindeer," so I went to my bedroom window and peered down at the street below. It was Molly. She saw me looking down at her and held up a package. Gift-wrapped, with a small red ribbon tied in the corner.

I headed down the stairs and she stepped into the entryway. "Merry Christmas," she said. "I know what we agreed on, but it's nothing much. Just a little something I couldn't resist."

Last month Molly and I had decided that our Christmas present to each other this year was going to be a weekend in Big Sur with all the trimmings. But those plans were made before our current troubles, and I didn't know where we stood.

"Come on up," I said.

We went into the living room and I opened the package. It was a hard-bound copy of *The Great Gatsby*.

"You were asking about it the other day," she said, "so ..."

I got up and walked over to where she was sitting and leaned down to kiss her on the lips. She held my face to keep me there awhile.

"That story you told me up in Napa," she said, releasing me. "Was it true?"

"Which story?"

"About the town in Mexico where the people dump water into the ground?"

"Yes," I said. "It's true."

"I've thought about that story a lot in the last couple of days. How Noel *has* been making my life scarce."

"And ...?"

"And I still don't know exactly what I'm going to do about it."

We were silent a very long time. The fire popped and sent embers swirling up the flue. Molly sighed, got to her feet, and walked over to sit right next to me. Shoulder to shoulder, thigh to thigh, like she did on the bench at the museum. She looked at me in a way she hadn't looked at me in a while. "Those people in Mexico, they only did that once a year, right? Pouring the water into the ground?"

"That's right."

Molly looked at the Christmas tree and smiled. "December 25," she said. "This date would certainly be an easy enough one for us to remember."

"The First Annual?" I said.

Molly put her arms around my neck, and kissed me softly on the lips. "The First Annual."

"Unlikely we'll be waiting till next Christmas for a Second Annual," I said.

Molly continued to kiss me. Little kisses. Soft kisses. "A virtual impossibility."

"Which could start things up all over again."

"A risk we'll have to run."

We stopping talking. Molly stood and led me by the hand back down the hallway to the bedroom, to soft sheets and warm possibilities. If you were looking for a place to make your life less scarce, you could do far worse.

So that's where we went.